SECRETS IN BLOOD

A Wild Fens Murder Mystery

JACK CARTWRIGHT

CHESTNUT PRESS

SECRETS IN BLOOD

JACK CARTWRIGHT

PROLOGUE

THE SANDBANK WAS HER FAVOURITE PLACE. A SINGLE MAN-MADE dune that stretched the length of Moggs Eye Beach on the hardy yet beautiful Lincolnshire coast. Protecting the fertile land from crashing waves and the harsh North Sea winds, it was a landmark and a shield to most. But in one particular spot, hidden from view, Jessica Hudson felt safe.

The hollow in the sand was her favourite place to sit. Wild, tall grass provided shelter from the wind making the spot feel a few degrees warmer than its surroundings.

As a child, she had hidden there spying on her parents, her aunt, and her uncle through the thick and thorny bushes. As an immature teenager, Jessica and her cousin had stolen a bottle of wine from her parents, and had chosen that place for their first foray into that world where nothing is as it seems.

Now, as a young adult, it was only right that she should select that sacred spot to experience love for the very first time, though not without trepidation.

Her body shook with the extreme cold at first, even in the hollow. But warmed by love and body heat, she found a new cause for her trembling. Soft fingers grazed her skin and her own dug deep into foreign flesh. Pleading for the sensation never to end, she rode that wave of ecstasy to new heights, screaming out, savouring the sweet release with all the careless freedom their solitude afforded.

She had been told it would be over too soon. That the first time rarely met expectations, and that it wasn't like the movies. But for Jessica, it had been sweet, and as her adrenaline waned post-climax, a chill fell across her body. They dressed while lying down, giggling at the awkwardness, then held one another tightly using her favourite sweater as a blanket.

"Do you think it'll always be like that?" she asked. "Every time?"

"I hope so."

Few things induce such a satisfied sleep as contentment, hope, and mutual love. And though deep down she knew *they* would never understand, and that they could never be together, she slept in her lover's spoon and dreamed of another life where they could walk an unfamiliar path and answer to nobody.

But the hope that had fuelled those lustful dreams faded to black, as if a shadow passed over her. Faceless against the dark sky, only the glint of moist eyes shone. Was it the devil, come to escort her from mortality for her sins, for their love?

But the devil wouldn't pin her shoulders to the freezing sand. The devil wouldn't shed tears as his hands gripped her throat. And the devil wouldn't whisper into her ear, as Jessica breathed her last mortal breath, "I'm so sorry."

CHAPTER ONE

The North Sea was in a state of post-storm calm, flat and sober. The tide was out, and water pooled in the sand, shimmering in the afternoon sun. A breeze blew in from the east and the stretch of beach was dotted with slow-moving dog walkers enjoying the crisp winter's day.

Freya Bloom leaned against her motor home with a shawl wrapped around her shoulders. She wore jeans with knee-high boots, a thick sweater, and her long, woollen coat. Her face and hands were cold, but after the long drive, she welcomed the touch of winter on her skin as she surveyed her new home.

She had parked her motor home at the dead end of a small access road beside the sand. Further along was a gap for emergency vehicles to enter the beach. The cars of a few dog walkers were parked nearby, but there were no other campers at this time of year, and for that, she was grateful.

It was an ideal place to stop. A large sandbank ran parallel to the coast, which, she presumed, was to prevent a rogue wave from flooding the land. Not that there was much to flood. Miles of boggy grassland with the occasional caravan park was all that hugged the coastline.

It was beautiful, and exactly what she needed after a brutal decade in London, and an even more brutal marriage. The kettle on her small gas stove began its early whistle and rattled on the burner.

She used to loathe making dinner and tea in the small space, while Greg did what he called blue jobs – banging in the wind breaker with his wooden mallet, or tying the awning. Blue jobs and pink jobs, boy jobs and girl jobs. There would be no more pink jobs or blue jobs. From this moment on, every job was pink.

She tipped the contents of a sachet of ready-made, three-in-one coffee into a mug and poured in the water, fighting that more refined part of her that longed for a Peruvian blend of the finest beans. Then, like it or not, the seasoned camper in her showed its face. She tipped the remaining hot water into a flask to save boiling the kettle again next time she wanted a drink.

The motor home was nothing special, not compared to what some of their friends had. But she was glad they had bought it. She hadn't felt it before, the freedom. Not when they had gone away for long weekends as a family, or when they had joined the convoy of London suburbans heading south in search of peace.

But she felt it then. Alone for the first time with space to breathe, to contemplate her misgivings. The cold would be a battle she would have to endure, but to wake up each morning with the sea on her doorstep was priceless.

A new start.

Pulling the collapsible chairs from the locker at the side of the camper had always been deemed a blue job. But that was before. That was a time when making tea had been a pink job.

There were three collapsible chairs, one for each of them. She pulled the red one free, slipped it from its bag, and plonked it down beside the camper door. There was also a little fold-away table, but the wind was gusting and it was a pain to set up. Greg had stored two hessian sandbags in the exterior locker. He used to fill them with sand from whichever beach they happened to stop on and use them to weigh the table legs down. The task seemed like a lot of effort. She could do that another time.

From where she was standing, Freya had a view through the open door – which she had tied back to prevent it from blowing in the wind – and along the length of the camper's bleak interior. The furnishing was drab, but the facilities were modern. It was as if the camper had been designed in the seventies and built in the twenty-first century. The curtains were dull. She had always meant to change them, but had never gotten around to it. The bench seat with the little dining table had been upholstered in a brown and orange floral pattern. The few areas of wall that weren't occupied by storage bore a similar design to the seats, only lighter in colour. But it was the grim sight of the lounge area at the rear of the camper that crushed Freya's remaining enthusiasm. Three couches formed a U-shape for socialising or relaxing in front of the TV that was mounted to the wall. With a few adjustments, the couches transformed into a large double bed, which, as she wasn't expecting company anytime soon, was how Freya had left them.

She had hauled her case onto the bed when she had left Greg and Billy, and there it had stayed for the journey to Lincolnshire. The camper had initially been bought to keep up with the Joneses. A few other couples in their social circles had bought one, and the camper gave them an opportunity to build a little network of friends. Had she known at the time that the network of friends would mean the end of everything Freya had, she may have put up more of a fight. But they had taken to camper holidays, attracted by the simplicity of the life and the ability to get away for a few days at the drop of a hat.

But the ability for Greg to get away had been the beginning of the end, and as hard as she tried, she couldn't blame him. A six-month sabbatical from her job for stress hadn't provided the rest and recuperation she had needed. If anything, although she would never admit it, she found herself losing long periods of time, during which she couldn't account for her actions. Talking to therapists hadn't helped. There was so little to say. A single traumatic event had caused a paralysis of her mind. Three full days had been removed from her memory. Three full days during which neither she nor anybody else could tell what had happened to her. She recalled a hypnotist that she had seen during her tour of London's top therapists. Regression techniques, she had called it. Freya had her own name for it – dragging up the past – which the hypnotist had taken offence to, even after Freya had explained that she didn't want to regress. She didn't want the three days back.

The Freya Bloom that had once been standing in a forest in the dead of night. A small house or a hut was silhouetted against the sky, and a lake shone in the moonlight beyond. That was her last memory of her old self.

Then there was darkness. A three-day period of nothing. No sounds. No smells. No images. Just black.

Then chaos.

A gust of wind blew through the open doorway, and Freya's newfound freedom quenched the bitterness that was rising like bile in her throat.

She smiled at the promise of adventure.

CHAPTER TWO

Christine Barnes braced against the cold wind that seemed to burn her exposed cheeks.

A weak sun shone someplace far away, offering only ambient light to the far reaches of Lincolnshire. Dressed in three layers beneath her fleece and with her husband's heavy parka on top of that, she hugged herself as she made her way along the shoreline, telling herself she must do it, if not for her own sanity, then for her family. Or at least, what remained of it.

Memories of the previous night played out like an old movie in her mind. Piper had been barking – he always barked – and Charlie had yelled, threatening to run away. All of her children had yelled at some point, but never before had Christine struck any of them, and she had regretted it immediately. The sting of the slap was still alive in the palm of her hand.

The barking and yelling were all normal. The din was so regular that it formed the ambient noise in their house. But the slap of that bitter, ungrateful face and the accompanying sting were a step beyond. They were new. But at that moment, when Charlie had looked up into her eyes with bitter hatred, Christine had known everything would be different from then on.

Finding Charlie's bedroom empty, the bed in the same state as it had been the previous night, and the wardrobe devoid of clothes, Christine had known where to look. Charlie's favourite spot. Out of the wind. Out of sight.

Christine had set out to make amends. With Derek working away and her eldest two away, Charlie was her only hope. Even her youngest, Justin, had already displayed the tell-tale signs of a Barnes.

She was on a mission to make amends.

Besides, she thought, the walk might tire Piper out for the day and with any luck, he'd sleep on the rug in front of the fire.

But Piper, her seven-year-old golden retriever was showing no signs of lagging, now barking at the gulls and entering into a chase with a wild bird that Christine had seen before, but she still didn't know the species. He sprinted across the sand leaving a meandering trail of footprints that a drunk man would be proud of. Bored of teasing him, the bird took off, but the ever-distracted dog caught sight of a group of gulls that were squabbling and squawking high up on the dune. He tore after them.

Having learnt long ago not to waste energy by chasing him, Christine continued her walk with one eye on the melee of activity and her stupid dog. He would catch her up when he realised he was on his own.

At seven years old, there was no hope. For years, she had been telling herself that they had just picked a stupid dog. His recall with Christine was appalling. He never sat for her, refused to lie down, and with each refusal of a given command, he offered her a contemptuous glare.

It was a different situation for Derek, who only needed to lower the tone of his voice for Piper to obey his every instruction. He even gave a little tail wag as he sat, or lay down, or went to his bed.

But Derek wasn't always there. He spent as much time away as he did at home. It wasn't uncommon for him to arrive home from a ten-day shift to find the house in disarray and Christine nestled into her armchair nursing a smoke and a glass of wine in an effort to blur reality.

Discipline was not Christine's strongest point. That much was apparent. A series of phone calls from the headmaster at school was a clear indication that Justin, her thirteen-year-old, was on a slippery slope. It was the same slippery slope her older children had struggled with. During her first pregnancy, she and Derek had often engaged in long conversations about what they would and wouldn't let their child do, reminiscing on their own childhoods in the hope of shaping something better for their baby. Now they had four children, each with wayward minds of their own, and the boundaries they had tried to implement were stretched so thin they barely existed.

Reality had struck her hard when Derek had started working away. The job was a means for him to go straight, to leave behind petty crime and provide stability. But each time he went, Christine found herself sinking deeper into herself. Venturing out of the house to walk the dog had become her limit, and even that was often fraught with the tuts, sneers, and snide remarks of indignant passers-by as Piper barked at other dogs, stole food from picnics, or even did his business on the pavement.

Lost in her thoughts, and hopeful she would find Charlie, Christine walked with her head bowed. The tide was coming in, leaving a froth on the sand with every encroaching pass. With each footstep, she had to move further up the beach until she had passed the line of flotsam and walked on the harder, still frosty sand that crunched beneath her weight.

The previous night's storm was evident in the sand – tiny pock marks from the rain and debris littering the beach. Charlie would have had an awful night.

Behind her, Piper continued to irritate the swirling birds, his bark carried by the wind. Turning, she found the flurry of flapping wings on the dune. But there were more birds than before. In fact, there were so many birds in a frantic squabble that Piper could only be seen when the birds chased him away. He returned, of course, tail wagging, and the fight began all over.

"Is that your dog?" said a voice, male and light in tone. An elderly man approached from the little access road further ahead, smiling at the chaos a few hundred metres behind them. A fat Labrador idled by his side, far more reluctant to be out walking than its ageing owner. "*She* used to be like that. It gets better with age, don't worry. What is he? Two? Three?"

"Nearly two," Christine lied, but couldn't think of much else to add.

"Give him time. Bramble here used to be a right mistress," he said, and bent to stroke the Lab behind her ear. "Didn't you? It was treats that done it for you though, wasn't it?"

"Treats?" said Christine.

"Lots of them. My wife jokes that her training hasn't improved, but she's got so fat and lazy that she can't run around and cause trouble anymore. There's always that. If you can't train him, make him fat."

There was a joke in there somewhere, but it was lost on Christine. She stared after the diving birds, avoiding eye contact with the man whose smile faded, and he moved on, calling over his shoulder for her to enjoy her day.

"I might if I can get my bloody dog back," she muttered, too quiet for the man to hear. "I'm not going after him," she told herself. "I'll stand here all day if I have to. I'm not chasing that dog around the beach."

Inquisitive as to why the birds were causing such a commotion, the man and his overweight Labrador took a path that ran along the foot of the dune. But even the sight of the man's dog wasn't enough to distract Piper from his raucous behaviour. The birds scattered as the man approached; only a few lingered long enough for him to get within a few feet, then they took flight and circled above.

With a clear view of Piper now that the birds had taken flight, Christine sensed something wasn't quite right. And when the man turned and called out for her from atop the dune, a familiar sense of dread washed over her.

His voice was urgent but distant, and the wind masked any clarity his words may have had. Reluctantly, she walked closer, expecting him to begin a torrent of abuse about her unruly dog.

He met her halfway, breathless with the effort, and she prepared to receive the backlash.

But there was no backlash and no torrent of abuse about Piper's behaviour. What he said was, somehow, far worse than she could possibly have imagined.

CHAPTER THREE

It was early enough in the morning for Detective Chief Inspector Will Granger to have opened his first report, and for his coffee to still be giving off steam. He removed his glasses, pinched at the bridge of his nose, then sat back in his chair.

The incident room door further along the corridor opened with a squeal like a wounded beast, then slammed closed.

"A word, Ben," he called, as Detective Sergeant Ben Savage passed the open door. Ben paused in the doorway, his eyebrows raised waiting for Will to issue a command. "Come in. Close the door."

He did as he was instructed, then sat, resting his hands on his knees.

"Guv?" he said.

"How do you feel about attending a course? It's a three-day program."

"What course is it?" He looked bemused, almost defensive, as if the very mention of self-improvement highlighted a flaw in his abilities.

"It's a transformational leadership course. There's a space available, and Arthur..." He paused to correct himself. "Detective

Superintendent Harper wants me to put somebody forward. He says we should make it known that we're self-sufficient. We don't want the powers that be to think we're sitting idle out here. Not since..."

He paused, and held Ben's stare. Both men knew how the sentence ended.

Arthur was the friendly nickname the team had given Detective Superintendent Harper. For all his knowledge and experience, the man only seemed capable of starting a job then handing it over to a lower rank to complete. Thus, the nickname half-a-job Harper had been introduced, which was a bit harsh, considering he was an okay bloke. Arthur was the shortened and friendlier term. And it had stuck.

"If you think I need it, guv–"

"You need it."

"Thanks for the vote of confidence," said Ben, failing to mask his feelings at the comment.

"You'll need it if I'm going to put you forward for detective inspector. You'll need all the help you can get."

"Detective inspector? Me?"

"You've been standing in for DI Foster for six months. I think you've earned it. Unless you'd rather stay a DS?"

"No. No, it's what I want. I just didn't think–"

"You didn't think I'd be looking to fill the gap so soon?"

"No, sir. The thought crossed my mind, but I thought it too soon to ask, and, well, I figured David's team would be folded into DI Standing's."

"If there's one thing I've learnt over the years, Ben, it's that if there's a budget, spend it before it gets taken away. Besides, Detective Inspector Standing has a full complement that already do very little. If it takes some healthy competition to get Standing and his team off their backsides, then I'm all for it."

Ben nodded, clearly picturing the incident room in a new light.

"When is the course?" he asked.

"Next week. It's in Lincoln HQ, so you'll be home by dinner time each night."

"You don't think the others will think any less of me for–"

"For filling a space?" finished Granger. "If they do, send them my way. David Foster was one of the best DIs I had the privilege to work with. He was also a good friend. He would have wanted his place filled by you. Of that I can be sure."

DS Ben Savage stood and made for the door, his chest swollen with pride. Granger opened his desk drawer in search of his mobile phone. It never seemed to be where he left it.

"Thank you, guv."

"No need to thank me, Ben. It's the natural course of things." He slammed the drawer, felt his jacket pockets for his pen, and sensed Ben still loitering at the doorway. He met his stare to offer him some reassurance. "We don't mess with the natural course of things, Ben."

"Yes, guv."

"Do me a favour. Close the door on the way out. I'm going to write a letter to David's wife."

"Of course."

———

The incident room felt different when Ben returned to his desk. It wasn't a large office to begin with, but after his conversation with Will, it felt smaller. The people he'd always regarded as colleagues – and most of them as friends – stared.

But he wouldn't let it spoil his high.

The room was long and divided into two areas, each with a whiteboard to visualise investigations, wall space on which they pinned pretty much every document in an investigation, and desks for the teams to collaborate.

The area closest to the door was where Ben and his team

worked. Now that David Foster was gone, it was just him, DC Gold, and DC Chapman. The space at the far end was where DI Standing and his much larger team worked. According to Standing, he enjoyed not having any Tom, Dick, or Harry looking at his screen as they walked past. The space was shared, but there was a clear delineation, and Standing defended his space vehemently.

He moved his mouse, and his computer awoke. The screen turned from black to the image of him and his father. It had been taken so long ago that he barely recognised himself.

"Ben?" said a voice from behind him. He knew the voice, and he prepared to be taunted. Taunting was better than being ignored, so he turned to face her. "Good for you," said Jackie, and she winked.

Of all the people that should have been mad, angered, or embittered by the decision to push Ben forward, it should have been her. She had been close to David, a good friend. To have her support meant the world to him.

"What do you mean?"

She smiled sheepishly, the way she often did. "I was on my way to the loo. I heard."

"You were listening?" Ben whispered.

"No. I overheard. There's a difference."

There was no arguing with her. Ben was still too overwhelmed to care.

"Thanks, Jackie. There's a long way to go. It's not in the bag yet."

"We're behind you," she said, dismissing his attempt at modesty.

"Feels weird, doesn't it?" he said. "Not having David around. I still can't believe he's gone."

"Same," she said, shaking her head. "His poor wife, and that baby boy. I wonder if he'll remember his father when he's older. You know, like an image. Something."

"The guv is pretty shaken up. Not his usual self, that's for sure."

"They were good friends, him and David. I think they saw each other out of work as often as they did in work. I know David was younger, but he was kind of old for his age. Mature, wouldn't you say?"

"Either that or the guv is young for his age," countered Ben, and the two of them shared a smile, both leaning towards the former of the two options. "Are you going to the funeral?"

Jackie nodded. "Yes. I wouldn't miss it. I don't think we ever had cause to fall out, David and I. That's a rare thing."

"You and *I* have never fallen out."

"Except for when you ate my lunch."

"Ah come on, that was a mistake. We both wrap our sandwiches in foil."

"And the time you walked into the ladies."

"I was new here. How was I to know? There wasn't even a sign on the door."

"Never with David though," she said wistfully. "Not that I recall."

"Can I tell you something?" Ben lowered his voice so DC Chapman couldn't hear, turned his chair to face Jackie, and leaned into the space beside her computer monitor. "I feel a bit guilty."

"Guilty? Whatever for?"

"For the position. For what Will said. He hasn't even been buried yet, and here's me getting excited about replacing him."

"You won't replace him, and besides, you've been acting DI for months. David was David, and you are you."

She was good like that, thought Ben. She knew how to say the right thing. "The guv won't fill that space with just anybody. He thinks a lot of you. You don't need to feel guilty."

"Yeah. He said something similar. But still. It doesn't feel right."

The incident room door burst open, and in a heartbeat, the

atmosphere changed. DI Steve Standing entered, his puffy eyes a sign of a heavy night. He grumbled a greeting. At least Ben thought he did. He could just as easily have offered an insult. Whatever it was, it was unintelligible.

Behind him came the first of his team, DS Gillespie. He was a large man, only a fraction shorter than Ben's six foot two, with a thick Glaswegian accent and a tendency to say things how he saw them.

"Morning, losers," he said, and though neither Gold nor Chapman looked up, they both smiled at the greeting. Gillespie was a decent detective. He was the same rank as Ben but was held back only by his immaturity and inability to keep his mouth shut. He called out as he worked his way to his desk at the far end of the room, "Have you used the ladies this morning, Jackie?"

"Excuse me?" she said, startled by the question.

"Stinks to high heaven out there. Thought maybe you'd been and–"

"What?"

"You know?" he said, and he hung his coat on the back of his chair. "Been and read the paper. Dropped the kids off."

"Read the paper? No, I have not," she said, defensively. "Why me? Why not accuse Steve? We all know how long he takes to..."

She paused, and Gillespie smiled, waiting for her description.

Seeing the teasing smile, Jackie laughed, realising he'd goaded her into a toilet conversation, and she shook her head.

"Speaking of which," Standing said. He worked his way back through the office carrying a file. "I'd better go and read this."

He drummed a beat with the file against his free hand and hummed a tune that Ben didn't recognise.

"You're not taking that to..." Jackie began.

"Multi-tasking, Gold," Standing replied. "That's why I get paid the big bucks."

Both Gold and Chapman wore horrified expressions and the

room silenced. Standing's team had arrived and set the tone for the day, and the tune Standing whistled as he pulled open the door and disappeared from sight was a sign he was pleased with the result.

But the door did not slam shut, and a new figure appeared in the doorway.

"Morning, Michael," Ben said, mildly amused at how Gold and Chapman were still reeling.

Sergeant Michael Priest was a man who, by his own reckoning, had worn the police uniform longer than anybody in Lincolnshire but had never ventured further than sergeant. A fact that, when asked, he put down to being *so damn good at it.*

"Is Will about?" he grumbled in his thick Yorkshire accent.

"He is, but he did ask not to be disturbed."

"It's urgent."

"Okay," said Ben, and took reassurance from Jackie's approving nod. "We can help."

"We just had a call from a man down at Moggs Eye. Said there's a girl down there on the sandbank."

"Dead?" said Ben, not wanting to state the obvious but seeking clarity.

"As they come, apparently," replied Priest. "I'm heading down there now if you care to join."

———

In all her thirty-nine years, Freya had never fallen in love with somebody so readily and easily as she had with Billy. He had just been a toddler then, and she had felt like an intruder. Their relationship was akin to that of one of those soppy movies, where the new parent is introduced and, over time, as they help the child deal with issue after issue, they become trusted.

But Freya Bloom's life was far from Hollywood, and as sad as it was, her love for Billy was just not enough for her to endure a poisonous relationship with his father. It would have been good for nobody in the end.

Staring at the camper in the beachside car park she had chosen to be her temporary home, she was reminded of the boy during previous family holidays. Billy had loved the camper and the freedom.

The emotions that had flooded her that morning had drained her of any energy, and she felt the cold bite of the North Sea wind on the side of her face. A gust blew her collapsible chair over, so she folded it away and stowed it in the locker, then climbed inside the camper. Her new life would start in just a few hours, and aside from hanging her clothes on hangers in the hope that the creases would fall out, she had done little to prepare.

She sighed an involuntary sigh of relief when she sat on the bunk. The wind howled at the camper in fitful bursts, and the vehicle rocked enough to trigger the doubts that had been loitering at the back of her mind.

Was it all just a flight of fancy? Had their relationship really been as bad as they had thought?

Despite the doubt, the idea of freedom was alluring. To be able to go where she wanted and when she wanted had seemed so far away.

The interior of the camper was drab and dull. She had a single bunk that doubled as a couch, with a small pop-up table that would give her somewhere to eat. The small kitchenette had a double hob, a tiny fridge, and a hand basin that was smaller than her only saucepan. A small washroom was adequate for a single person. The shower rained down on the toilet. But she'd get by. At the far end of the camper was the seating area that would stay converted into its alter-ego – a huge double bed.

She had dumped her bags on the bed before her escape. She would deal with them later. With the prospect of adventure before her, she figured on a walk to clear her mind and help her get to know her surroundings a little better. She pulled her coat around her, and in one of the cupboards above the bed, she found her woolly deerstalker among a pile of winter weather gear. That would be enough to keep her ears warm at least.

When she had pulled on her hat and fastened the buttons on her coat, she looked around at all she had left. She sighed, then promised herself to put one foot in front of the other. That was, after all, the only way to get to reach your destination. All she needed to do was to picture that destination, which was easier said than done.

She locked the camper door, looked left and right, then settled on walking left, north along the beach. She would save a southward adventure for another day, such was the joy of a single life in a new place.

The wind carried a fine spray of rain with it. It wasn't hard enough to call rain, not like the previous night's storm, but within five minutes, a drip had formed at the end of her nose. The sand wasn't golden like the beaches in Cornwall had been. It was darker, but it still felt good beneath her boots. The going was hard, and although she exercised regularly, walking in the sand used muscles she hadn't used for some time. So much so that after less than a mile, she climbed the top of the sandbank to take a rest and enjoy the view. But as she climbed the ten-foot-high dune, momentarily leaving her memories behind, she caught sight of a commotion further ahead.

The sight was familiar. Gulls circled overhead, and in the distance, two police cars had parked with their blue lights lighting the scene like a beacon. And she knew at that moment the new start she had been looking for had begun.

———

Ben knew Moggs Eye Beach like he knew the fields his family had farmed for decades. A few miles from tourist-heavy beaches, Moggs Eye was a local hangout that, although busier during holidays and summertime, offered little in the way of shops and attractions. During the winter months, the place was barren, save for dog walkers and the odd horse owner trotting through the surf. Recalling many a misspent day, Ben had a nostalgia about the place. But he now looked upon it with an altogether different view.

"Let's have a unit at the top of this access road. Priest, nobody gets through without reason. And have a cordon put up a hundred yards either side of the scene. If the FME confirms murder, you never know, we may get lucky and find some prints in the sand."

"I'll get the boys on it now," replied Priest, and he strode towards the two liveried police cars, clapping his hands to get his team's attention.

"Jackie, any news from CSI?"

"I spoke to Michaela. They're two minutes away," she called, pulling on her boots at the rear of the car. She stomped her feet into a comfortable position, then fastened the collar of her heavy anorak. "They're coming all the way from Lincoln, but they'll be here soon."

"I'll go and have a look at what we're dealing with then. While I have a chance." Peering along the length of the dune, it was clear where the body was. One hundred metres away, thirty or more gulls fought over a prize. "That's if there's anything left of her."

Ben made his way along the top of the dune, mindful to use a path which was less obvious, and therefore disturbing only the squabbling gulls and not the scene. The birds circled above for a while, then disbanded to loiter elsewhere until the opportunity arose for them to return.

But Ben wasn't concerned with the gulls. He approached the scene, flashes of colour showing through the tall grass, and felt that tightness in his chest. Anticipation. Or maybe it was just dread.

And there she was. To the inexperienced eye, she may have

been sleeping. But if the pale complexion and bruising on her neck didn't tell him otherwise, the stillness did. It was hard to describe, he thought. The peace and emptiness of death.

He wondered who she was, as anybody might, and what a girl so young could possibly have done to deserve it. There were marks in the sand that he was sure would tell part of a story, but it wasn't a story he could read without a translation from CSI.

Uniform had cordoned off the beach as Ben had requested. In the car park, Jackie was briefing CSI and Doctor Saint, the local forensics medical examiner, who nodded a greeting to Ben. Just ten feet from the girl's body, seeking a place that was both out of the wind and with a decent phone signal, Ben settled for a spot in the lee of the sandbank that gave him two bars of signal. It was only when he was out of the wind that he realised how loud and constant the racket had been.

He took a breath and dialled the number. He'd gathered all the information he could and had the right people doing the right things.

"Granger," came the voice on the other end of the line.

"Guv, it's Ben. We took the call for Anderby. We're at Moggs Eye now."

"I heard about it from uniform."

"You said you weren't to be disturbed. I hope that's okay?"

"That's fine. I don't need to be in on everything that comes our way. What was it anyway?"

"A body, guv."

The slightest of silences ensued as Ben imagined Will shifting in his seat.

"A body?"

"At Moggs Eye Beach. A girl. Seventeen or eighteen maybe. She was found by a local man walking his dog."

"Okay, make sure you talk to him," Granger said. "How about CSI?"

"Jackie is briefing them now, and the FME has just arrived too."

"Is it Doctor Saint?"

"Yes, guv."

"Good. He's a decent man."

"I know. He was close to David too."

Will's silence, Ben presumed, was due to him swallowing his emotions at David's name.

"Any idea what happened?"

"None yet. There's some bruising around her neck, but we won't know for sure until Saint takes a look."

"What does your gut say?"

"Hard to tell. If it's murder, it's going to hit the local community pretty hard. Local girl is murdered off-season. The likelihood is that her killer is local too."

"What makes you so sure it's murder?"

Glancing back up the dune to where the body was hidden in the thorny grass, Ben caught sight of a woman wearing a woolly hat. She was standing fifteen to twenty feet from the young girl's body.

"Just a feeling, guv," said Ben, catching the attention of the strange woman.

"What do you need from me?" said Granger on the other end of the line.

"Nothing yet. Listen, I have to go. I'll keep you updated."

"Whatever you need," said Granger. He sounded genuine, almost enthused.

"Thanks, guv."

Disconnecting the call, Ben stood. One hundred yards away, he could see Jackie helping CSI unload their van with the folded, white tent and their toolboxes. Nobody else had seen the woman slip around the cordon.

"Hello," the woman called out before Ben could ask her to leave.

She wore a long, woollen coat, the type that city girls wear that was useless against the open landscape of the fens, and a knitted deerstalker which was a little more appropriate, but still a fashion statement. She stood with her feet planted to brace against the wind up there. "What's happening?"

"It's police business. You'll have to move on, I'm afraid. You shouldn't be here."

She didn't reply. She just stared at the tall grass in which the girl's body lay concealed in the hollow. Judging her distance, Ben estimated that if she took just a few more steps, she would see the body. It was as if she was reading the situation.

"I'm staying in a motor home back there. Should I be worried?"

"No. There's nothing to concern yourself with. Don't come any closer. I need to ask you to leave, please."

Beneath her collars and hat, she seemed to smile at him as if she wasn't used to being told what to do.

"Now, please," he reiterated, and reluctantly, she took a few steps backwards, then disappeared down the far side of the sandbank.

"Ben?"

It was Priest, calling out to be heard above the wind. He was standing beside one of the liveried cars with a mature gentleman and his Labrador. The man's face was the only part of him that was exposed, and he wore a shocked expression.

"This is Albert Stow. He's the gentleman who discovered her."

Ben retraced his steps back to the car park, with a few furtive glances behind him to make sure the strange woman hadn't tried to get closer.

"Jackie, grab your notebook," said Ben, and after closing his car door, he approached the man. "Mr Stow? How are you feeling?"

"Well, I..."

"Can we get this man something to sit on?" Ben called out,

and Priest opened the boot of the police Astra, gesturing for Mr Stow to sit on the bumper. "You've had a bit of a shock, Mr Stow. Is there anybody I can call?"

"I'm fine—"

"I'm sure you are, but we wouldn't really be doing our job if we didn't have someone come and be with you. Do you have a wife or...?" Leaving the question open-ended, Ben made it clear that he wasn't going to give up on getting the man the care he needed.

"My wife," he said, then recited a phone number to Priest. "We live nearby."

"I'll see she's contacted. We'll ask her to come and get you."

"Oh, she doesn't drive. No. Never has."

"Well, then I'm sure we can have you taken home," Ben said.

The dog must have sensed her owner would be there for a while and resigned to curl into a ball beside his feet.

"Can you tell me what happened?" asked Ben, and glanced at Jackie to make sure she was ready to take notes.

"Nothing much happened," Mr Stow began. "Except for the bloody dog chasing after the birds. I thought something was up. Greedy blighters, them gulls." He glanced across to the scene along the dune, and the colour drained from his face.

"It's okay, Mr Stow."

Leaning forward, the elderly gentleman braced to vomit. But nothing came, and he spat on the ground.

"The closer I got, the more I knew what it was. I should have just called you lot. I didn't need to see it."

"We all do things we don't expect to."

"Most of the birds flew off. But a few stayed and pecked at her." Pausing to remember the chain of events, his voice softened. "Her skin was still soft beneath their beaks. I think that's what did it for me."

"Did you or your dog touch her at all? We just need to identify any third parties. Dog saliva and such."

"Bramble? No. She wouldn't leave my side. Only climbed the dune because I did, lazy bugger."

"But you said a dog was—"

"Not Bramble. There was another one. A golden retriever. Its owner was way over there. A woman. I didn't get her name."

Scanning the beach but seeing nobody else around, Ben looked back to Albert Stow.

"Where is she now?"

"She left when I called you lot. I saw the girl and didn't know what to do. So I went to her. I told her what I'd seen and asked her to call the police. But she said she couldn't. Strange girl, she was. Like the weight of the world was on her shoulders."

"And her dog? You said her dog was beside the body."

"It was. I was standing over there with her," said Albert, pointing to an empty space on the beach some three hundred metres from the crime scene. "I asked her to call, and she refused. Said she couldn't get involved or something. So I had to phone you. Lucky I had my phone with me. Not often I do. My wife always moans when I leave it at home. Says anything could happen and nobody could reach me. I keep it turned off, mind you. Saves the battery."

"Did you see which way she went?"

"Back that way towards the road. She screamed at her dog and it ran after her. Odd woman, she was."

"Did you say the dog was a golden retriever?" asked Jackie.

"That's right. Nearly two, she said it was. A puppy. Big for a puppy, mind you. Needs some training too. Piper, its name was, or Pepper, or something."

"Can you describe the woman?"

"Late thirties, early forties. Hard to say really. It's so bloody cold, I only saw her face. Couldn't even tell what colour her hair was. At a guess, I'd say she was a redhead. You know, blonde eyebrows and freckles and whatnot. But I couldn't really say."

"Mr Stow, you've been a great help," said Ben. Then he called out to Jackie, "Jackie, please don't let Mr Stow leave without FC taking his boot print." Turning back to the elderly man, who appeared panicked, Ben added, "It's okay, Mr Stow. It's just so that we can eliminate your prints from the crime scene. Hopefully we won't need to contact you again, but if we do–"

"If I can help in any way. Poor girl deserved better than that. Her parents will be devastated."

"I'm sorry, did you know her?"

"Of course. Everyone knew Jessica. Well, if they don't know her, they'll know her father at least."

"Jessica?" said Ben, waiting for a surname.

"Jessica Hudson," said Albert. "The family lives in Chapel St Leonards now. Moved there a few years ago. They used to live here, though. Had a little cottage up the road. Lovely girl, she was."

CHAPTER FOUR

"DS Savage?" said Doctor Saint as Ben approached Jessica's body, reminding Ben that in the not-too-distant future, people would refer to him as DI Savage. "We met before. The body that washed up on the beach a few miles north, if I recollect."

"That's right. How are you, Doctor?"

"Call me, Peter, please. As for how I am, I'm doing better than her, I think."

Running a hand through his unnaturally dark hair, he glanced over to the sandbank, then back at Ben. For a man in his fifties, Ben would have expected to see a few grey hairs at least. Peter Saint didn't appear to be the type of man who would dye the grey hairs out. He recalled the time they had met before, but couldn't remember noticing them back then either. Deducing that he was one of the lucky ones, Ben stepped back to let him do his work.

Donning a pair of latex gloves from his inside pocket, Peter prepared to examine the girl, showing no sign of distress at the sight. It always amazed Ben how steeled these professionals were.

"Are you leading this one?" he asked, and Ben replied with a nod. "He was a good man, was David. A solid pair of hands."

"Yes," Ben said. "Yes, he was."

"And his family?" asked Peter. "He had a wife and child, if I recall."

"He did. Will takes care of them as best he can."

"Terrible news. Well, you have big shoes to fill."

"Thanks, Peter. Will you attend the funeral? It's in a few days," said Ben. "The entire station will make sure he has a good send-off."

"That's good to hear. I'll be there."

"It's in Nocton. There's a church there by the forest. It's a small village. You can't miss it. I'll ask DCI Granger to send you the details if you like."

"Thank you, Ben," he said sincerely. "Right then, let's see what Jessica has to say."

The morbidity of the man's statement was a testament to his comfort with death. He bore the bedside manner of a GP, but Ben guessed a career as an FME had nurtured a humour that bordered tastelessness.

While Peter Saint examined Jessica's body, Ben scanned the horizon to the south, searching for the strange woman in the woolly deerstalker. She was nowhere to be seen. Looking back toward the car park, he found the two crime scene investigators waiting for Saint to finish his appraisal, while further on, Jackie was helping Albert Stow into a liveried car.

"Bruising around the neck and her swollen tongue suggests she's been strangled," said Saint, as he stood and came to stand beside Ben. "There's nothing to indicate otherwise. Given the onset of rigor mortis, I estimate that Jessica Hudson breathed her last breath late last night. The pathologist will be able to be a bit more accurate. Lastly, I can't see any sign of sexual interference. She's clothed, but that's not to rule it out. We need to get her to the lab, ideally. Nearest one is in Lincoln City Hospital. There's not much else I can do, I'm afraid."

He was right. The girl was clothed in jeans, trainers, and a t-shirt, but that was hardly sufficient for a winter night on a Lincolnshire beach.

"I think we're missing a few items. A jacket or something," the doctor said.

"I was thinking the same. Nobody in their right mind would come out here without a jumper at least... Maybe she wasn't in her right mind? Maybe she didn't intend on coming here?"

"That's for you to work out, Ben. For what it's worth, I hope you catch them. Nobody should go like that."

"You've been a great help, Doctor."

Seeing the CSI itching to get involved, Saint moved away and headed back to the cars. They nodded their thanks as they passed him at the top of the dune and Saint looked back at Ben.

"One last thing," Saint called, and Ben waited for him to continue. "Do you want to talk about the elephant in the room?"

"What did you have in mind?" Ben asked.

"Why do you think she's laid out like that? She looks peaceful. It's like she was arranged. Somebody took the time to fold her hands and cross her feet like that, and might I add, while her blood was still warm."

"Maybe her killer wanted her to be found that way?" replied Ben, glancing back at the scene for a moment's contemplation. He turned back to Saint. "Maybe they loved her?"

CHAPTER FIVE

Heavy boots kicked against the wooden door, the noise dragging her forward from a place darker than dark. Where her own foul breath beneath her hood cast images of a forest. Not the glorious ranks of trees through which sunlight shines in narrow beams, where snowdrops and wild garlic litters the ground and bird song choruses and echoes throughout. This was a far darker forest. Too dense even for the brightest of sunlight to coax life from the earth, and where the carcasses of rodents lie undisturbed. For it was a place where few ventured, and a place where the darkness of night was perpetual.

The door gave way to the heavy boots, crashing against the wall, and the image of that foul forest was gone, leaving her blinded by her hood, bound by rope, and vulnerable to her assailants.

Men shouted, and a bright torchlight washed over her veil, inducing a momentary glimmer of hope then realised devastation as the light faded to dark once more. Radios crackled, and the cacophony drowned her screams, until all the sounds were muted, discordant, and singular, dizzying Freya's mind beneath the hood.

"Guv," a girl called out, their voice cutting through the din as a butcher's blade slices raw and tender flesh. Then she was not a girl but a woman,

whose voice bore the rich confidence of authority. A tone Freya knew well and had once enjoyed. "We've got someone."

And then there was light, brighter than anything Freya had ever seen. Breath as warm and sweet as the juice of a ripe plum, and the touch of a soul, a tender hand on her shoulder as vivid as life itself.

"Freya?" she said, her face silhouetted against the torches that stilled behind her. "Freya Bloom. Is that your name?"

No words could describe that moment, none that Freya could summon as the emotions tore through her with all the momentum of a runaway train.

The warmth of a single tear tracked its way across her skin, rising on her upper lip where it threatened to give way, like the held breaths in the room surrounding her.

"You're safe now," the woman said, and she held her.

———

The wind caught the door and it slammed against the side of the motor home, rousing Freya from another of her spells. She glanced around, recognising her surroundings at once, but couldn't recall how she had got there.

"I was on the dune," she said to herself, scrambling back until she pressed against the makeshift bed, remembering the man, the detective, and the words he had said.

Glancing down, she saw that she was still wearing her boots, and two sandy boot prints marked the patterned carpet.

She stepped outside for some air and doubled over to spit the bile from her throat. Crouching to sit on the step, the wind caught the door again, slamming it onto her leg. But she felt little, and held it at bay while she gathered her thoughts.

Looking north along the beach, she saw very little. There were no dog walkers, just empty space. The dune to her left showed dull sand and the cold North Sea breaking every few seconds. But further up the beach, lives were being altered.

"What the bloody hell am I doing here?" she muttered to herself, then baulked at hearing herself talk to nobody but her own fragile mind. "Oh God."

The thought of meeting new people that day brought with it a tightening of her chest. Pulling her phone from her pocket, she found no missed calls from Greg. No messages and not even a voicemail. Not that people left voicemails anymore. She found his name in her contacts and recalled that on his phone, Greg had put a little heart icon next to her name. He had told her it was so that when she rang, he was reminded that he loved her. His details in her phone just said his name. Greg. No icon. No heart. She wondered if that was because she didn't need reminding, or if her subconscious refused to admit that she had a weakness.

Glancing down at her watch, she wiped her eye to focus on the tiny dial. It was another reminder of Greg. He had bought it for her thirty-fifth birthday. There was an inscription on the back. But that little treasure of a moment was of little consequence when she saw the time.

It was nine forty-five. She had just forty-five minutes to get ready and find a taxi in a place she could only describe as the edge of nowhere. After only a few moments of deliberation did her tenacity rouse itself and rise above her self-pity enough for Freya to adjust her mindset and regard the place as, instead, the beginning of something new.

CHAPTER SIX

Ben had dragged a small table beside the whiteboard, on which he placed his coffee. He stood, waiting patiently as Will Granger entered the room and took a seat beside Jackie. Although Ben's direct audience consisted only of Jackie Gold, Denise Chapman, Michael Priest, and Will Granger, DI Standing and his team were noticeably quieter, preparing to listen in and no doubt offer unhelpful comments. But it was Ben's time to shine. It was his time to step up, and Standing's unruly mob weren't going to ruin it for him.

He cleared his throat, allowing Will time to set his drink down and make himself comfortable.

It was just as he was about to speak that the door squealed open and Arthur walked in, a rare occurrence in the incident room. All heads turned to face him, and when they saw who it was, the team all stood from their chairs.

"Sit. Please," said Arthur, holding the door open, beckoning somebody outside to enter.

It was her. The woman from the sandbank. She wasn't wearing the woolly deerstalker, but it was the same long coat, and those same grey eyes, and even from across the long room, Ben's taste buds caught the scent of expensive perfume.

"Carry on, Detective Sergeant Savage," said Arthur, using Ben's full title by way of a distant yet informal introduction.

The two of them edged closer, coming to a stop behind Ben's seated team.

He had the story mapped out in his mind, the findings, and his plan of action. But all he could think of was the woman.

"The body of a teenage girl was found on Moggs Eye Beach this morning. She is believed to be Jessica Hudson from Anderby. We won't know for sure until we get a positive ID, but the man who found her, a Mr Stow, recognised her as a local."

"You told me earlier he was walking his dog," said Will. "Does he usually walk his dog there?"

"Apparently so. We'll be investigating that route, but right now we have no reason to believe otherwise. Moments before he discovered the body, he encountered a woman on the beach who was acting strangely."

"Describe strangely," said Will, again pushing Ben into providing a clearer picture.

"Before he found Jessica, he tried to talk to the woman, just as one dog owner might approach another. But she was loath to talk, like she had the weight of the world on her shoulders. Then, when he discovered Jessica's body, he went after her for help. She refused to call the police and by the time the old man had turned his phone on and dialled nine nine nine, she had gone. All we know is that she has a golden retriever named Piper and she headed in the direction of Anderby."

"So, what next?" asked Arthur. It was usual for him to voice an easy question.

Surmising that it made the old man still feel part of the team, Ben continued, "Chapman, we'll need Jessica's background and anything you can find about her parents."

"I've put the address on your desk," she said, as reliable as ever. "I'll see what else I can find."

"Thank you," said Ben, happy that Chapman and her research skills were on the team. "Doctor Saint attended the site. His initial examination suggests that Jessica was strangled. Bruising around her neck corroborates the analysis. There was no sign of the attack being of a sexual nature. The pathologist will confirm all this for certain, but at least we have something to go on for the time being. We'll develop a list of close family and friends, and we'll begin our initial enquiries, starting with a visit to Mr and Mrs Hudson."

"And what is your plan?" asked Arthur.

Finding his throat dry, Ben had to swallow to stop himself from breaking under Arthur's scrutinous glare, and as if Jackie felt it too, she squeezed her eyes closed in preparation.

"My plan, sir, is to go to speak to the parents and get a positive ID. We can't do much before then."

"And then?" Will asked.

It was as if he was being tested, with questions coming from both Will and Arthur.

But before Ben could launch into his well-rehearsed plan of attack, detailing the resources he would need, and the process of building Jessica Hudson's network, Arthur spoke again.

"Before we make any plans, DCI Granger, perhaps we might have a quick discussion in my office?"

CHAPTER SEVEN

The incident room door slammed closed, leaving behind what felt like a vacuum. Only Jackie, Chapman, and Michael Priest remained with Ben, while Standing called out from the far end of the room.

"You handled it well, Ben," he said, in a rare moment of praise.

"Aye, keep them on the line," Gillespie added. "Don't play your cards too soon. That's what I say."

"Thanks for your advice, Gillespie. The next time you're being interrogated during a briefing, I'll be sure to remind you."

"No bother," he replied, clearly not catching Ben's sarcasm. "Who was that with him, anyway? I can smell her all the way up here."

Standing and the rest of his team were all listening in. They waited for Ben to answer as if he might know who she was.

"I have no idea, Jim."

"Looks like the love child of Princess Di and that actress from the X-Files."

"Gillian Anderson?" Chapman said, her face clearly showing that she didn't agree or approve of him making a comment about Princess Di.

"Aye, that's the one," he replied. "If you have any trouble with that one, and you will, send me in. I'll be more than happy to deal with her."

"You're such a bloke, Gillespie," Jackie called, then turned to Ben. "You handled that well."

"Yep, no doubt you did good," said Priest, as he stood and carried his chair back to the desk from which it came. "If you can manage Harper, you'll manage anyone, I don't doubt. I'll be at the desk if you need me. Sounds to me like there's a plan brewing, so call me when I'm needed and I'll rally the troops."

"Thanks, Michael," Ben called across the room.

Jackie stood and joined Ben at the whiteboard, and he held out a marker, inviting her to demonstrate where she would begin the investigation. She wrote Jessica's name and circled it, then drew two lines from the name at opposing forty-five-degree angles.

"Her parents?" asked Ben.

"Yes," she replied, writing the words mother and father above the lines.

But then she stopped.

"We don't have much to go on."

"How about the dog owners?" suggested Ben, encouraging her to broaden her perspective. To one side of the tree she had formed, she wrote *Albert Stow*, and then alongside it, a third tree began with the name *Piper*.

"I guess we have to find Piper," she said.

"I guess we do," replied Ben. "How do you propose we do that?"

"Go to the beach and call out his name every time we see a golden retriever?"

It was more of a joke than a genuine suggestion, but Ben's appetite for jokes had waned.

"Chapman, see if there's any record of a golden retriever named Piper registered to any of the local vets," said Ben, and

Jackie cursed herself out loud for not thinking of it. "Jackie, can you lean on CSI and the pathologist? I don't want any heels dragged on this one."

"Will do. Aren't you going to the parents' house?" she replied.

"Arthur said we should wait before making a plan," Ben replied. "Besides, I want to see who the woman is. I'm not getting a good feeling if I'm honest."

"I told you," Gillespie called out. "I'll take care of her for you."

"Shut up," Jackie replied, her tone not as harsh as the words. She switched on the small radio on the windowsill beside her desk. It wasn't loud, but it took the edge off the room while the team worked.

Curious, Ben opened the door and peered into the corridor in time to find Will emerging from Arthur's office.

"Ah, Ben," he said, wearing a grave expression, his shoulders slumped in defeat. "I was just coming to find you. I think there's something you need to hear."

Glancing back into the incident room, Ben's chest swelled with pride at the sight of Jackie and Chapman carrying out his wishes. But an ill feeling stirred in his stomach.

In Arthur's office, Ben was offered a seat beside the woman whose perfume seemed to fill the space – a thick, masculine scent that reminded Ben of an aftershave he had been given one Christmas. The office was as sparse as Will's. It seemed that, regardless of their position, everyone whose rank allowed for an office received the same budget allocation – a cheap L-shaped desk, a matching bookshelf, and terrible paint.

Will closed the door behind him and stood to one side.

"Well done, Ben. I thought your initial briefing was..." Harper paused, searching for the right word. Not too complimentary but suggesting room for improvement. "Informative."

Informative? Ben thought. *I didn't have the bloody chance to be informative.*

"Thank you, sir," said Ben, hearing his voice crack.

"I'd like to introduce you to Freya Bloom," Harper said, and presented the mystery woman with an open palm. "Detective Inspector Bloom will be leading the Jessica Hudson investigation. I thought it would be a good chance for you to develop your skills. To see how it's done, as it were."

Arthur leaned on his desk with his fingers interlocked. The language he had used left little room for interjection, and any angles to manoeuvre the decision were duly taken care of by his rank. Never would a lowly detective sergeant question a detective superintendent.

"Any questions?" he asked the room.

"Any point?" Will countered, clearly as unimpressed as Ben.

"None at all," Arthur stated without pausing for breath. "Thank you, everybody. That'll be all."

CHAPTER EIGHT

In true Arthur form, when Ben and DI Bloom had left the office, he called Will back, gesturing for him to close the door.

"Sir?" said Will, watching through the office window as Ben and DI Bloom went their separate ways without exchanging a word. Bloom's perfume still lingered in the air, a reminder that the team Will was reforming was in for a rocky ride.

"They might need a little help getting along. Have them work closely for me, will you?"

"With respect, since when do you tell me how to manage my team, sir?"

"Since now."

Living up to his name, Arthur had excelled at doing half a job of knocking Ben to his knees, then expected Will to pick up the pieces.

"Who is she? I wasn't made aware David was being replaced so soon."

"She's not a replacement," he said in that tone that seemed to make everything Will said sound melodramatic. "She's on secondment from London. Needs some fresh air. We might not have the volume of crime they have down there, but what we do have is fresh air and a hole in the squad, Will."

"A hole I'm filling from the team."

"Savage is not a replacement for DI Foster. You know that as well as I do."

"Not yet he's not. But that's my job to get him there. It's *my* call to make."

"Well, now you've got Bloom to help you."

"I don't even know her background, Dennis. Help me out here."

A lengthy working relationship allowed the two men the freedom to interchange between formal titles and first name terms with neither man taking offence. Arthur's tendency to reserve Will's first name for manipulative purposes was acknowledged by Will, whereas Will would use his first name only in anger, resorting to sir in all other instances.

"She comes highly recommended, and from what I hear, she's a mover and a shaker," said Arthur, as he selected a file from a pile of three on his desk. Will would have killed to have just three files on his desk instead of the stack that had set up camp there. Opening the file, Arthur perused her details. "She's up from London. Been in the force for more than a decade and was involved in the successful resolution of more than a dozen murder investigations." He closed the file and shoved it towards Will. "We don't have that experience between us all, Will. Not now that DI Foster is no longer with us."

"You bastard–"

"Now, now. I miss him as much as anyone," said Arthur, holding his hands up. "But the fact remains that for the past decade, anything more serious than a road traffic accident has been dealt with by DI Foster. The team haven't the experience."

Will nodded. There was no denying it.

"Like it or not, he's no longer with us, and it's left quite a hole in your team. It seems to me that DS Savage has stumbled on what could be a complex murder enquiry and–"

"He can handle it, Dennis–"

"Try as he might, he hasn't got the experience to deal with it. DI Bloom *has*. Now we can either argue about this, or we can use it as an opportunity to bring Savage up to speed. Bloom won't be here for long. Let Savage know he has some work to do. Make him fight for it."

"He *was* fighting for it."

"Not hard enough. By the time Bloom heads back to London, I want to see a whole new Savage. I want to see him leading the briefing, pushing back when he gets interrupted, and I want to see him fired up. You mark my words, Will, DI Bloom will have a positive impact on your team, and you'll have me to thank for it."

Snatching open the door, Will turned at the threshold to face his old friend. He tapped Bloom's file on his leg, refraining from voicing what he truly wanted to say, finding a compromise in his argument.

"No doubt the same can be said for the negative."

Looking up from his desk, where he was squaring away the two remaining files, Arthur raised his eyebrows, inviting Will to explain.

"If she makes a mess of my team and I end up with more holes, I'll be coming to you for thanks, Dennis. You mark my words."

Through the window in the incident room door, Will watched Ben carry on with his work. He was too professional to just quit the battle, but from where Will was standing, Ben appeared to have lost the spark he had been carrying.

"Ben?" he called, leaning into the incident room. "My office, please."

Ben peered up from his meticulous arrangement of paperwork.

"Guv."

"Take your time."

Back in his own office, Will slung the file onto his desk and flipped the front cover open.

He scanned for a summary of who Ben was up against. Detective Inspector Freya Bloom. Married. No children of her own. She had been a DI for three years, and had turned all the right heads during that time.

"Sir?" said Savage from the open doorway.

The interruption roused Will from his reading.

"Come in, Ben. Close the door," said Will, as he closed DI Bloom's file.

Trying to gauge Ben's mood, Will offered him a chance to summarise the investigation and the progress that had been made. He began much in the same way that he had with David, even in the latter stages of their working relationship. He tapped the file on his desk.

"I've just been reading all about our new DI."

"I'm sure I'll catch up to Arthur's expectations," said Ben. He hid his disappointment well, but not quite well enough. Sensing the need for a confidence boost, Will moved the discussion forward.

"I see you already set the team to work. What's the plan?"

"Like I said, guv, we can't do a lot until—"

"I know, I know. But we all know you've got some gears moving. You're not going to sit back and let her walk all over you, are you?"

Ben stared at him from over the desk; the very idea that he would be so weak clearly appalled him.

"I've asked Chapman to research local veterinary clinics for a goldie named Piper. Jackie is putting some pressure on CSI and the pathology results. We also have uniform conducting a detailed search of the area. I don't want to wait on this, guv. We need to act fast."

"Is that your thoughts, or David's?"

"Both," said Ben, sharp but honest. "It's what he would have done."

"And what about DI Bloom? How do you feel about that?"

"I feel like I waited the entire game to score a goal, and just as I got the ball, the whistle was blown."

Will smiled at the analogy. He wasn't a football fan, but he understood.

"Do you feel ready for the role?"

"Of course, guv. I would have said something otherwise. I'm not perfect. I'm not David–"

"Nobody is suggesting you need to be–"

"But I've been doing the role for six months already. This was my chance to prove myself. I've had what, two hours? And let's face it, you've been doing Arthur's job for as long as I've known you. I imagine you feel the same, guv. When you get promoted–"

"When I retire?" he said with a smile, and was pleased to see a genuine grin creep onto Ben's face. "Look. Let's ride it out. These are the cards we've been given. There's no point upsetting the applecart. If we make life hard for DI Bloom, neither of us will be in new roles for a long time. But, if it's any consolation, it sounds like she's good at what she does. Her record is outstanding. She'll make a good mentor for you."

"David was a good mentor, guv."

"Well, sadly, David isn't here. So use her experience to your advantage. Lean on her. The whistle hasn't blown yet and *you* still have the ball. She's going to need you as much as you're going to need her. It'll work out, I promise."

"Did you know, guv?"

"That she was coming? No. If I had, I would never have brought you onto the pitch, Ben. Harper is keen for you both to work together, and if I'm honest, that's the only way I can see this working. So go find her and make it work. She might have the experience, but you're the glue that holds all this together. She doesn't know the locals like you do."

"Yes, guv."

Ben was just closing the door behind him when Will remembered something.

"Oh, Ben..."

"Guv?"

"Gold and Chapman are behind you, as am I. You'll do well to remember that. Use them to your advantage."

"Yes, guv," said Ben, then loitered in the doorway. "Can I ask *why* she's here? I mean, if she's so good at what she does, why has she come here? Where nothing ever happens?"

Will leaned back in his chair and dropped his pen onto his desk. "She's on secondment. Needs some fresh air. Why don't you show her what us Lincolnshire boys are all about, eh?"

CHAPTER NINE

Finding DI Freya Bloom in the incident room cleaning the whiteboard, Ben approached, not even trying to hide his confusion.

"DS Savage," she began without looking up. "I'm just piecing all the facts together. We need some lines of enquiry."

"We had already done that."

"I need to make a plan," she said, seemingly oblivious to the work they had already done.

"We have one of those too."

Peering up at him through her over-sized eyelashes, she bit her lower lip as if she was refraining from saying what she thought.

"Why don't we go through it?" she offered, and removed the pen lid. "Start from scratch, as they say."

"From scratch?"

"As I understand it, we have a dead teenage girl. Nothing more."

"We have a dead and strangled teenage girl."

"You're not looking at the wider picture," she said, as she began to rewrite Jackie's work almost identically.

"We're investigating the dog," said Ben.

"Oh. That's a good start," she replied, not even trying to hide her sarcasm. "You're hoping to find out who the woman on the beach was."

"The way I see it, there were two women on the beach."

"Two?" she said, and silently invited him to explain.

"The one with the dog named Piper, and the one with the silly hat. Didn't you tell me you were in a motor home further along the beach?"

"I can assure you, DS Savage, that the one with the silly hat didn't arrive until the early hours of the morning, and she's happy to provide all the DNA and evidence you need to remove her from the investigation. What else do you have?"

"The one with the dog?" said Ben, growing more disheartened by the second.

"So we're looking for a woman with a dog in a county where it seems everyone has a dog?"

"It's a lead," Ben said. "If you pardon the pun."

"It's a lead to a woman who was made aware of a murder and ran away through fright. By all means use valuable resources to track her down, but don't expect her to drop to her knees and confess to the crime."

"I don't expect that at all. I'm just being vigilant."

"What time is it, DS Savage?"

"Eleven a.m."

"And how old was Jessica Hudson?"

"She was a teenager. Seventeen or eighteen."

"Has anybody reported her missing? I mean, we can make a reasonable assumption that she wasn't living alone. She probably still lived with her parents."

"The odds are pretty strong."

"I don't work with odds, DS Savage. I stick to the facts." She paused, as if she had heard the tone of her own voice, and like a switch had been flipped, her persona shifted. "Can I call you Ben?"

He shrugged. "If that's what makes you happy."

"Look, I haven't come here to make waves, Ben."

Over her shoulder, a wide-eyed Jackie looked up from her computer at the remark.

"You're the DI," he said. "Let's do things your way."

She eyed him with a measure of distrust, then nodded.

The phone on Ben's desk rang, and he glanced across at it. Seeing the position he was in, Jackie leaned over and answered it, leaving Ben to continue with DI Bloom.

"Dead and strangled girl," Freya said, as if she was voicing an understanding by reiterating the facts. A line in the sand had been drawn. "Yet nobody reports her missing."

"Seems to me we should pay her parents a visit," Ben said, alluding to the plan he had mentioned earlier.

"I'd agree with that. We need to build a list of everyone who was close to her."

Behind Bloom's back, Jackie shook her head again.

"Exactly what I was thinking," Ben said, unable to hide the sarcasm in his voice. It was as if he had dreamed the briefing he had given only thirty minutes ago.

"You'll have to drive," she said, pulling her long coat on and grabbing her bag. "I'm picking up my rental this afternoon."

She flicked her hair from her collar. If Ben had been asked what colour it was, he would have said auburn at first, but now she was closer to the window, he saw a variety of tones.

She was beautiful, of that there was no doubt, but the air of authority she carried, along with her hoity-toity, public schoolgirl accent, made her as appealing as standing outside on that cold November morning in the nude.

As Ben made his way to the incident room door, he glanced up at Standing's team. Standing made a gesture that suggested Ben should give her backside a slap, silent of course, while Gillespie winked at him then pointed to himself.

As if he stood a chance. The man may have been the same rank as Ben, but it wasn't just his Glaswegian that was thick.

The rest of Standing's team, DCs Moray, Vaughan, and Nillson, did what they did best – smile and laugh at the two senior officers' jokes.

He had to walk fast, but he caught her on the fire escape stairwell. It had taken her just half a morning to work out that the lift was terrible and unreliable and the actual staircase they were meant to use on a day to day basis was so far away, it served little purpose for a team who needed to access the ground floor cells, interview rooms, and the car park.

She waited by the rear doors, eyebrows raised as if she had been waiting for an hour.

"What?" Ben said, and she seemed to appraise him with a glance from his feet to his crop of messy hair.

"How tall are you, DS Savage?"

"Six two, six three, something like that," he replied, defensive, checking his collar and shirt tails were tucked in. He held out his hand, inviting her to exit first. "Why?"

She smiled at him approvingly. "No reason," she said, and shoved open the door.

———

The cold wind snatched the station's rear door from Freya's hand, nearly jerking her from her feet. A strong hand grabbed her arm, stopping her from falling down the few concrete steps, and the door slammed.

She eyed Ben's hand on her arm.

"Thank you, Detective Sergeant Savage."

"Ma'am," he replied.

"Freya," she replied. "Call me Freya, unless, of course, you're in a position where you can't, in which case boss will do fine. Is that okay?"

"Fine by me, boss," he said, and let go of her arm.

Her ears were hit almost instantly by the weather, like somebody held two bags of frozen peas to them. The indicators on a Ford flashed once, and DS Savage made his way across the station car park, the wind having almost no effect on him, except for his coat tails that flapped wildly.

Freya climbed into the passenger seat, doing her best to bring her hair back into order.

She found Savage looking at her with a wry grin raising his cheeks.

"It gets a little windy up here."

"Really?" she said, and she lowered the visor to check her reflection.

He drove well, not too fast, not too slow. They left the town and, with no reason to complain, Freya settled into her seat, keeping an eye on the speedometer. The fifty miles per hour limit on the A-road seemed a bit restricting, but that was okay. She needed time to make an appraisal of her new DS. But to do that effectively, she would need to wait for him to speak first.

That was okay. She was good at waiting.

"What's your story?" he asked her eventually, while she gazed out the window at the landscape. Lincolnshire wasn't as flat as she had heard. It wasn't the Alps, but it certainly wasn't Holland either. From the confines of the car with the heater on her feet, it was, on the surface at least, remarkably beautiful.

She checked her watch. It had taken nearly thirty minutes for him to start the conversation. At least twenty-nine more than she had been expecting.

"Secondment," she said, and in her mind, she pieced together the story she had prepared. "I've had a few tough cases in the last few years. I needed some air."

"So why here? I mean, surely you had the pick and choose of where to go?"

"Not really. You can only really go where there's space, unless, of course, you opt for another city unit. But like I said, I needed air. What about you? I guess if we're going to work together, I should know a little about you. All I know so far is that your name is Ben Savage and you want my job. That's not much to go on."

"Who said I want your job?" he said defensively.

"And that you're emotionally unintelligent."

"E...what?"

"Try to hold your tongue. Think before you speak. You'll give a better impression of yourself," she said, and then struggled to refrain from smiling at his reaction. "Don't react."

He glanced out of the driver's side window, visibly agitated.

"I should also add that you're thorough, and you take pride in your work. If ever there was a foundation for excellence, that's it."

As expected, Savage was showing signs of confliction. Freya's initial statement had jarred him and triggered an emotion. The follow-up comment was designed to soften those emotions and put him off guard long enough for Freya to continue.

"Listen," she said. "Despite what you might think, I'm actually looking forward to working with you. But you'll have to get used to my ways."

"Is that right? What makes you think I'm emotional?" he said, as he turned off the main road.

"Because nearly every single response you've given me since I saw you at the crime scene has been a display of your emotions. You might not realise it, but your voice rises in pitch. On the sandbank, in Harper's office, in the incident room, and now."

He didn't reply. Not because he was doing as she had asked, she guessed. It was more likely that he was speechless. But she let him have that moment as a win.

"See," she said. "No emotional response. Far better."

He stopped the car, still shaking his head in disbelief at what she had just said.

Releasing her seat belt, Freya reached for her bag.

"Right then, Detective Sergeant Savage," she said with as friendly a smile as she could muster. "Which house is it?"

"The middle one," he said, still digesting what she had said. He nodded at centre house in the row of three large, detached properties. A paved driveway ran alongside a neat lawn and two pillars at the entrance gave the house a sense of grandeur. "Number three. The one with the red door and climbers around the windows."

"Good. I shall lead," she said, and climbed from the car leaving him no opportunity to argue.

CHAPTER TEN

The coastal town of Chapel St Leonards enjoyed the ebb and flow of holidaymakers during summertime and braced itself for the peace and quiet of often harsh winters. With nearly as many caravans in the surrounding holiday parks as there were houses on the streets, one might be forgiven for believing it was the type of place where a person might come to lose themselves.

"Mrs Hudson?" said Bloom to the wide-eyed and timid looking lady who held the door open a few inches and peered through the gap. Bloom held her ID up, gripping it tight against the fierce wind. "Might we have a few minutes?"

It was the worst part of the job, and even to that day, Ben had never had to say the words himself, being always in the shadow of David, and now Bloom. But witnessing the heartache was just as hard as delivering the news.

"What's this about?" she asked.

"It's probably best that we speak inside," Freya urged, having to shout over the noise of the gusting wind. "Is your husband home?"

Stepping aside, she relaxed her hold on the door, then pushed it closed when Freya and Ben were inside. He offered a tight-lipped smile that was more of a condolence.

Despite being ravaged by the wind outside, Bloom's brown hair settled onto her shoulders like she'd just stepped from a hair salon. With a few, deft sweeps of her hand, she looked as good as she had in the car, and in a few short seconds, the Hudsons' hallway was filled with her perfume.

A large hallway with a moulded ceiling welcomed them. Overhead, a chandelier rocked from the breeze, and sparse, expensive looking furniture filled the gaps providing an almost perfect balance of space.

Presenting a set of double doors with a sweep of her hand, Mrs Hudson coaxed them inside. "Please," she said, with a soft tone that reminded Ben of his grandmother, "take a seat. I'll fetch my husband." She, loitered for a moment, doing her best to keep a level head, but even the hardiest of people baulked at the sight of two police officers at their door. Following Bloom into the open-plan living room, Ben was taking in the sense of open space, the rich woods and attention to detail, when Mrs Hudson spoke again. She inhaled loud and sharp as though she was going to ask a question, but hesitated. "I'll just give him a call."

"That would be great, Mrs Hudson, thank you," Bloom added, reassuring the lady.

Bright, white walls and rich, warm, timber floors were accented by a stylish Chesterfield lounge set, vases of fresh flowers, and just enough soft furnishings for it not to feel like a museum. An armchair sat beside the bay window flanked by a side table with leather inlay. To one side was a matching Queen Anne wingback with a footstool, and a dog-eared romance novel was open and lying face down on the seat.

At the far end of the room, a baby grand took pride of place beside the glazed rear doors. In stylish, white frames, a series of family photos hung on the walls at equidistant intervals and identical heights. The images looked professionally taken and were monochrome. The family were lying on their fronts with a plain, white background, and in the centre of Mr and Mrs Hudson were two girls who could have been twins, were it not for a clear difference in size.

Although she was younger when the photo was taken, Ben recognised Jessica immediately. In the photo, she wore her blonde hair down with a neat fringe that accentuated her blue eyes. She was smiling for the camera, but there was something about her smile that made Ben think that it was a permanent fixture. There was a happiness about her, a beautiful glow.

While they were alone, Ben took the opportunity to give Bloom the nod. "It's her," he whispered, to which she took a deep breath.

"My husband is just coming," Mrs Hudson said as she came in from the kitchen, then she stopped, as if she was afraid to get close. "It's brutal out there today."

Ben nodded a silent response, and for the first time noticed how pristine her skin was. If she wore makeup, it was disguised well. He saw no cracks or wrinkles, and her wide, blue eyes sparkled between long lashes.

"Will he be long?" Bloom added. "I'm afraid it's rather urgent."

"He's in the middle of something," said Mrs Hudson, and if it wasn't for her husband entering the room, she might have embellished a little. "Here he is now. Tim, this is erm…"

The man filled the doorway. He wore a stylish, tweed waistcoat, grey, woollen suit trousers and jacket, and a plain, white shirt. Should he have arrived with a shotgun breached over his arm, Ben might have thought he was modelling for Country Life magazine.

"Detective Inspector Bloom," Freya said, showing her warrant card. "This is Detective Sergeant Savage."

"What's this about?" was his opening statement. His voice was gruff with a heavy local accent and his brow was furrowed. Mr Hudson was what Ben's father might have called 'well turned out'.

He turned to his wife. "You have told them we're going out, haven't you? We don't have time to—"

"Perhaps you'd both like to take a seat?" Bloom began. If ever there was a well-matched adversary for Mr Hudson, it was Bloom. "Please," she added, softening her tone.

He did as he was asked with reluctance, a move that Ben put down to his placid wife's pleading eyes.

"I'm sorry to say, there's been a recent discovery," Bloom began. "The body of a young woman has been found not far from here at Moggs Eye. We have reason to believe it's your daughter Jessica. I'm sorry."

A silence ensued, as vicious and bitter as any scream.

"Is that so?" whispered Mr Hudson, breaking the silence as his wife squeezed her eyes closed and leaned onto his shoulder. "You're positive?"

"We'll need one of you to formally identify her, but yes. My colleague here has seen her. I realise this must be a terrible shock."

"I'm afraid you're wrong," he replied. "See, our Jess is away for a spell. It can't possibly be her."

"Away?" Ben said. "I'm sorry, Mr Hudson, but is that Jessica in the photo there?" Ben pointed to the photo on the wall.

"It is, yeah. That's Jessica."

"I attended the scene myself," Ben replied, shaking his head with regret. "It's her."

"Is that right?" he said, his gruff tone softening as he suddenly seemed to believe the news.

"You said she was away. When did she leave?" Freya asked.

"Day before yesterday. My wife took her," he said, then turned to Mrs Hudson who had buried her face in her hands. "You took her. You took her, didn't you?"

Slowly, she raised her head, her eyes red raw, and in place of that perfect complexion that Ben had admired just a few minutes ago, a red and blotchy complexion was forming.

"I...I dropped her into town," she stammered.

"You dropped her into town?" Mr Hudson exclaimed.

"She wanted to go alone. She's old enough–"

"I told you to take her to Skegness. I remember saying it. I said take her to Skegness, see she gets the train okay."

"She didn't want me to take her," the mother replied softly.

"Patricia–"

"That was the day before yesterday, was it?" Ben said, sensing an eruption developing. "Can you tell me what she was wearing?"

Mrs Hudson nodded, seemingly grateful for the interjection. She sniffed loudly and wiped at her nose with a tissue she had produced from her sleeve. "At around three. Her train was leaving at five-thirty. She wanted to grab a coffee. She should have had plenty of time."

"And her clothes?" asked Ben.

"A yellow sweater. One of those hooded ones kids wear. You know? She wore it everywhere, and with anything. Jeans, skirts, over the top of dresses. She loved it."

"Have you spoken to her since?"

"She called when she got there, and again yesterday."

"When she got where? Where was she heading?"

"To London. She was going to stay with her sister for a few days," said Mrs Hudson, then she broke. "I'm sorry. This is all a bit too much to–"

"I understand, Mrs Hudson," Freya said, and the strength in her voice softened to provide a comforting warmth that Ben hadn't expected.

"Can we see her?" her husband asked. In contrast to Bloom's softening tones, Mr Hudson's gruff growl had returned.

"As soon as we finish the examinations," said Ben, and he sensed the elephant in the room was about to make an entrance.

"Examinations?" Mr Hudson said. "What are you doing with her? What exactly happened?"

"We're looking into the cause of death," said Ben, easing them into what was perhaps going to be the bitter cherry on an already sour cake. "Who was she close to? Did she have any friends?"

"Only Beth," said Patricia, her words entwined with a high-pitched whine. She cleared her throat. "Beth Fraser. They were best friends, but I think since we moved here, Jessica made new friends. A different circle of friends. You know how kids are."

"Why would you need to know this?" said Tim, doing little to hide his suspicion. "How exactly did she..." His voice trailed off.

"Your daughter was the victim of an attack," said Bloom, pulling the proverbial plaster off the wound in one painful stroke. "I'm sorry, I know that's not easy to hear–"

"An attack?" Mr Hudson's face flushed red, and his voice dropped to a baritone boom as his wife gave off a whine. She reached for a box of tissues from the coffee table.

"I'm afraid so," said Ben, seeking some kind of damage repair. "As soon as we can, we'll be in touch to arrange a visit for you. But in the meantime, we need to know who she was meeting, and perhaps we can have a look at her room?"

"Her room? For God's sake."

"Oh, stop it, Tim. Just stop." The outburst from Patricia Hudson came out of the blue, and waned back into tears just as fast. Realising his abrupt manner was causing his wife more distress, Mr Hudson placed his hand on her shoulder.

"I'm sorry," he said, then looked at Freya and Ben in turn. "This is all a shock. Of course. Do what you need to do. My wife will show you Jessica's room. I need some fresh air. Is that allowed?"

"Of course," said Bloom. "We all need fresh air from time to time."

———

Following Tim Hudson into the kitchen and through a set of French doors, Ben made his presence known with a gentle cough.

The patio featured a two-foot-high, cherub-style bird bath at its centre, and ornamental palms provided shadow in the borders. Seated on an old garden bench, Jessica's father stared up at him, red-eyed. Glancing back to make sure they were alone, Ben made the most of the man-to-man moment.

"It's never easy," he said, and his comment fell by the wayside.

"Do you have children, Detective?" Tim asked, revealing a new and compassionate tone.

"No," Ben replied. "Not yet, at any rate."

"Well, if you get the chance, don't hesitate. Best thing you'll ever do."

"I'm glad I caught you alone, Mr Hudson—"

"Tim. Call me Tim, please."

"Do you have any idea why somebody might have attacked Jessica? Is there someone who might want to hurt her?"

Staring at a spot at the far end of the two-hundred-foot lawn, Tim Hudson seemed to reflect on the question with the beginnings of a sad smile.

"Tell me, Detective..." He waited for Ben to provide his name.

"Savage. Ben Savage."

"Tell me, Ben," Tim began, and glanced into the house to make sure his wife wasn't listening, "did you find her?"

"A dog walker found her."

"But you saw her. You attended the scene."

"I did," said Ben. He was about to announce that he was leading the investigation when he remembered that, in fact, he wasn't. "I looked after the crime scene."

"Beautiful, wasn't she?"

There was no easy way of telling the man that Ben had seen his teenage daughter presented as no young girl ever should be. But he was right. Jessica had been beautiful. Death had paled her skin and a sheen had formed over her like a glossy varnish. But her beauty was preserved for eternity in Ben's memory.

"Yes," he said.

"Was she..." Tim's question stalled, and Ben knew in an instant where he was heading.

"No. Early reports suggest not," said Ben, saving the man from having to verbalise the question. "When something like this happens, we have what's called an FME attend the scene."

"An FME?"

"Forensic medical examiner. He or she will give an appraisal of the cause of death, estimated time, and suggest any possible leads that might give us a head start. The FME that attended the beach today was a man I've worked with before. He was quite sure that the attack was not of a sexual nature."

The news seemed to provide some relief. Tim sighed audibly, then leaned to one side of the bench to spit into the flower bed where a tall palm was suffering the harsh winter. He stayed that way for a while, presumably controlling the rising bile in his throat.

"I'm sorry to ask again. But do you have any idea why somebody might have—"

"No," he said, breathless and urgent. Then he softened. "No. She was an angel."

––––––

The staircase was wide enough for three people to walk side-by-side, with thick, cream carpet underfoot and a handrail that appeared to have been carved from a single piece of oak. In such a place, there was always the temptation to break the silence by acknowledging the decor. But in Freya's experience, women with a weak disposition such as Patricia Hudson required a firmer approach. The reality was harsh, but a softly-softly approach would only prolong the inevitable. The landing at the top of the stairs split left and right and wound around the staircase, so that all the upstairs doors opened onto the view of the hallway downstairs and were at eye level with the hideous chandelier. There was no denying it, the house was impressive – gaudy, yet impressive.

"It's this one," Patricia said, as Freya peered into what appeared to be the master suite. Turning to find her at a closed door with her hand on the door handle, Freya offered a compassionate smile.

"Perhaps it's best if I go in alone," said Freya.

"Is that necessary? I thought–"

"If there is any evidence, we need to preserve it. Have you been in here at all since you dropped Jessica off?"

Glancing at the chandelier to think, Patricia mumbled something inaudible, then shook her head.

"I don't think so."

"Not to collect laundry or–"

"I haven't been inside. Nor has my husband, come to think of it. He never goes in the girls' rooms."

"Ah, that's right. You have another daughter. Do you mind if I ask where she is?"

"She's away at university. The Royal College of London."

"Very nice."

"She's training to be a chef, of all things."

"That's a good career. What about Jessica? Did she have any ambitions?"

"Jessica wants to be happy," she said, then corrected herself. "Wanted. She had the intelligence to do anything. She was a grade-A student for the most part. I think she would have travelled. She had an affinity for music and art. She was always good at both, but I think she would happily go wherever her violin takes her." Focusing back on Freya, there was a despondence in Patricia's eyes as they both silently acknowledged Patricia's use of present tense. "Of course, none of that matters now, does it?"

"I can arrange for a family liaison officer to sit with you."

"It's okay. I don't need to talk."

"See how you feel in a while. These things have a habit of creeping up on you."

Staring at the chandelier, Patricia Hudson leaned on the bedroom door, then lay her hand flat against the wood. It was her last connection to her daughter, a boundary she could not cross, as if the doorway was the threshold of life and death, and that somehow she might reach through and touch Jessica.

"Do you have children?" she asked, her voice thick with grief.

"No," Freya replied, but said no more. This was not her time. It wasn't about her. Besides, Billy wasn't her son. He was Greg's. That claim belonged to him. Making an obvious reach for the door handle, Freya found Patricia's stare. "I'll just be five minutes. Why don't you wait downstairs?"

Entering the room, Freya found thick carpet once more. The walls were plain white, or brilliant white, as she had seen it called. A silk finish gave the walls a slight shimmer, but not a shine like gloss. There were no posters on the walls, only sketches of the human body and dramatic landscapes. Above the small, neat desk was a graphite sketch of a man's shoulder. It showed the definition in his arm, and his fingers were splayed across his chest. Other sketches showed a tensed fist, a toned buttock, and a head turned so that the muscles of the neck were taut. They were studies in muscle definition, and they were quite exquisite in detail.

Above the bed was a painting. Not being arty in any way, shape, or form, Freya's appraisal was immature. It was an acrylic painting, of that she was sure. But the subject was an eerie reflection of the beach where Freya's camper van was parked, and where Jessica had breathed her last breath. With the waves crashing onto the beach on the right of the scene and the tall grass atop the sandbank on the left, it could almost have been the very spot where Freya had been standing when she had encountered Ben Savage for the first time.

A sense of voyeurism crept over Freya's skin as she opened the top drawer of a tallboy, Jessica's underwear drawer. Experience had taught her to be thorough and fast. She found nothing and moved on through the drawers, surprised at how neat they had all been kept. The wardrobe was also neat and tidy. It was almost impossible not to notice that the clothes all faced the same direction and each of the hangers were identical. The dresses were all together, as were the jumpers, hoodies, and blouses.

Wondering if the fastidious attention to detail was Patricia's or her daughter's, Freya moved on. The bedside table bore little that was out of place, so Freya sat on the bed and looked about the room. It wasn't like other teenage girls' rooms. There were soft toys, but they were few in number and sat on top of the wardrobe peering down at the bed. As a last resort, she removed the bottom drawer of the bedside table, then dropped to her hands and knees to search beneath, but the space was empty.

She dropped to a seated position, sitting back so that she leaned against the bed, and imagined Jessica in the space. Letting her eyes wander, they settled on a painting beside the bedroom light switch. The canvas was black, and portrayed by vertical strokes of white paints was a forest of silver birch trees.

The painting was quite stunning. Just enough light and shade in just the right places had created the effect of a moonlit forest that invoked the beginnings of a memory that therapists had been trying to find for months.

————

"You're safe now," the woman said.

It was cherries that Freya could smell. A boiled sweet maybe? The type her grandmother might have carried in her handbag.

"Freya, can you hear me?" she said, then turned away to the team standing behind her. "Bring a car up as close as you can."

"We have an ambulance on its way."

"*She doesn't need an ambulance. She needs to be away from here. Do as I bloody say and bring a car up.*"

"*Ma'am,*" the man replied, and he retreated to the tune of a crackled radio.

"*Freya, we're going to get you to a hospital. I'm going to help you stand, okay?*"

Her words came in time with the movement of her jaw, her silhouette offering only a hint of expression, just enough for Freya to know she was real. But however real she was, however warm her touch and sweet her breath, there seemed to be a disconnect between Freya's mind and mouth. She wanted to speak. She wanted to cry. But it was all she could do to fix her stare on those two shiny glints that were the woman's eyes.

A single word formed on Freya's lips, though she knew not if she had spoken it. It was a name. A girl's name. The girl's name. And the answer came through the wooden walls like an echo from a wild mountain valley.

"*We've got another one,*" a man's voice cried out, and Freya's heart skipped as hot bile rose in her throat. "*She's alive.*"

"*Freya?*"

The voice was different from the woman's; it was male, and distant like a dream.

"*Freya, are you okay?*"

"*Should I call an ambulance?*" another voice said. It was a woman's voice, clear but distant like the man's.

The hood had been removed from Freya's head, but the room was still dark. The owner of the man's voice leaned over her. He smelled clean, like the soap her father would have used.

She recoiled as he drew closer, as he reached out a hand and touched her.

"*No,*" Freya shrieked, and pulled her knees close to her chest, burying her face. "*Get away.*"

"*Freya? It's Ben. Ben Savage. Are you okay?*"

———

"I'm fine," she said, her vision refocusing on the painting of the forest on the wall. She found herself sitting on the floor of Jessica Hudson's bedroom with her arms wrapped around her legs.

The darkness cleared, and not for the first time, Freya was left wondering what was real.

"Can we get some water, please?" asked Ben, and Patricia, who had retreated to the doorway, left the room in a hurry. He crouched beside Freya and touched her shoulder again. Not hard, just enough to show he cared. "What happened?"

"Nothing happened. What do you mean?"

"You were gone. I don't know, you were staring at the wall. It was like you were somewhere else."

"I was thinking," she replied, and she held his stare, noticing the compassion in those big eyes of his. "That's what we do. We empathise. We think. We deduce."

The look on Ben's face indicated her explanation wasn't as compelling as she had hoped.

"I'll see you downstairs in a minute," she said.

"I can wait, if you—"

"I'm fine, Ben. Stop fussing. I was imagining Jessica. Here in her bedroom. We don't need them to do the same. They have enough on their plates. Now go. Leave me to it," she said. "Oh, and Ben, arrange for a family liaison officer to visit. It hasn't hit her yet."

Once she was alone, Freya stood and straightened her jacket. She walked through to the bathroom, splashed some cool water onto her forehead, being careful not to disrupt her makeup, and stared at the mirror, puffing her cheeks as she sought composure. Losing portions of time had been a regular occurrence. But twice in one day was a first. Using a rolled-up length of toilet paper, she dabbed at her face and gave herself a once-over in the mirror, wondering if what she saw was actually what others did.

Then, flushing the tissue, she took a breath, and mentally planned her next steps as she descended the stairs.

At the foot of the stairs in the hallway was an old-fashioned telephone table with a cordless handset plugged into the charger. Beside it was a small notepad with scribbles and notes in no particular order, along with some doodles that one might draw while listening to somebody talk.

Among the notes, one scrawled line caught her eye.

Jess, call Charlie.

She found Ben in the kitchen with the Hudsons. With Mrs Hudson's hands clasped around a mug of tea and her husband on the opposite side of the breakfast table looking strangely helpless, the two could not have been further apart.

"Mrs Hudson, do you have any idea if Jessica was in any trouble?"

With her back to the entrance, Mrs Hudson hadn't heard Freya approach, and startled at the sound of her voice.

"No, of course not," she said, turning in her seat. "Are you sure you're well, dear? You look a little peaky."

"I must confess, this isn't the highlight of my job. It never gets any easier. Apologies if I alarmed you, I was lost in thought," said Freya, then turned the attention back to the parents. "You said that her friend Beth isn't involved in this new circle of friends."

"That's right," said Tim. "Beth and Jessica grew up together. They're cousins."

"Cousins? From which side of the family?"

"Does it matter?" Tim Hudson spat, rolling his eyes at Freya's surprised expression.

"Everything matters, Mr Hudson. Every single detail."

"My sister is Beth's mother, Hetty," Patricia said.

"And these other friends?" asked Ben, clearly aiming to bring the emotionally volatile father back into the conversation.

"Locals. I said they were trouble."

"Oh, Tim, just stop it," his wife said, her frustration clearly growing.

"I told you they were no good. I told you we should have stopped her going out."

"So, it's my fault, is it?" Patricia said, on the verge of a breakdown.

"And what made you think they're no good, Mr Hudson?" asked Freya, keen not to witness a domestic between them.

"Nothing they did. I've never even seen them, but since she started hanging around with them, she changed. Staying up late, talking online, and telling little lies."

"Lies?"

"Lies. Like saying she's going down to her sister's, which she clearly didn't do."

"That's just part of growing up," his wife exclaimed. "She's seventeen years old."

"She wasn't like it before. That's all I'm saying. I put it down to them. She never stayed up late, she never slept in, and she never told lies."

"Where do I find these friends? Do you have their names?" said Freya, seeing her attempts at avoiding an emotional disaster failing.

Sheepishly, Tim deferred to his wife.

"Does the name Charlie sound familiar?" Freya asked.

"That's it. Charlie," Patricia said, giving her husband a look as if to say, 'See, I'm not such a bad parent. At least I know her friend's name.' Then she added, "I'm not sure of a last name."

"Have you met Charlie?"

"Well, no. But they're always talking."

"I see. Did Jessica have a mobile phone?"

"No," said Patricia sadly, and she offered her husband a grim stare.

"We didn't think she needed one," Tim explained. "Not at her age. Who does she want to talk to?"

"She was seventeen, Tim," Patricia said, and he turned away to avoid what Freya thought might be a recurring argument. But the tears came before the argument ensued, and Patricia buried her face in her hands.

Allowing the distraught mother some time to gain control over her emotions, Freya eyed Ben to see if he was paying attention. The toughest question of them all still had to be asked, and she wondered if he had the gumption to ask it. But he glanced at her, seemingly missing the cue.

"I'm sorry to ask this at such a time," she began. "But, in order to build a picture of the events that took place last night, I'm going to have to ask you where you were."

"You what?" Tim said, his emotions lost to a thickening growl. "How dare you–"

"I need to eliminate all parties, Mr Hudson. I can assure you it is not an accusation."

"We've just lost our daughter. Do you have any idea how that feels? Do you have any idea of the pain of that?"

Staring back at him, Freya was experienced enough to know when not to speak.

"I didn't think so," he continued. "You should be out there finding out who did it, instead of in here bloody insulting us with your–"

"Tim." The single word cut through his tirade. Along with her platysmal bands protruding from each side of her neck and her reddening face, her voice dropped into a guttural slur. Her words came staccato. "Just stop. For one second can you just please stop trying to control every single bloody thing."

With her husband silenced and seated, Patricia composed herself and spoke not to Freya, Ben, or to her husband. She stared through the glazed doors into the garden and spoke to whomever cared to listen in a despondent tone, faraway.

"*I* had an early night," she announced softly. "It's always quiet when Jessica is away, especially with her sister at university. I'll need to call her," she said, finding a new trail of thought. Turning in her seat to find Freya's gaze, she voiced her thoughts, "Perhaps

I'll ask her to come home. I shouldn't tell her over the phone, should I?"

Shaking her head softly, Freya agreed, then flicked her eyes toward Jessica's father.

"I stayed up," he said. "Never been one for early nights. I was in my office until late. Unlike my wife, I enjoy the peace and quiet." He nodded towards a door at the end of the kitchen, indicating his office.

"You're a local solicitor. Is that correct?" asked Ben.

"Yes, that's right," he replied, a question that, had it been asked at any other time, may well have swollen his chest.

"What are you working on? Anything that could have any bearing on what happened?"

"Of course not. What the bloody hell do you think I am—"

"Tim," Patricia said, her voice hushed, and she frowned at him like he wasn't being completely honest.

Clearly something had happened that he wasn't particularly proud to speak of. But he resigned to the confession with a sigh.

"I was accused of assault. A few months ago," he said. "Obviously I didn't do it. And obviously there was no evidence. And anyway, that was six months ago. It's in the past."

"Who was it that accused you?"

"Do you really need to drag this up?" he asked, his face reddening.

"I believe we do," Freya said. "At this stage, we need to know everything. The smallest detail, Mr Hudson."

He sighed and looked away, while his wife rested her head in her folded arms.

"Local bloke. Derek Barnes. Said I touched his wife. I did no such thing. We were away. We have proof."

"But why would he make such an allegation against a solicitor?"

"Because I told on him," he said, then met Ben's eye. "He's a drug dealer and I was the only one with the gumption to tell you lot about it. People are afraid of him. He's a nasty piece of work."

"I know Derek Barnes," Ben said, nodding to Freya as if to add substance to Tim Hudson's claims. "And I remember the charges. He got off, didn't he?"

"To this day, I don't know how."

"You informed on him, and he retaliated?"

"Except *my* allegations were based on fact. His were just vindictive."

"I've just lost my bloody daughter," Patricia snapped, bringing the focus back to Jessica and quietening the room. She lowered her voice to an angry hush, bitter yet out of character. "Can we just have some bloody peace and quiet so I can remember her without Derek bloody Barnes being mentioned anymore? He's told you what happened. I'm sure you have records."

"Of course," said Freya, admiring Tim Hudson's bitter expression. "I'm sorry to have had to ask, and I'm sorry to have delivered such terrible news. There's just one thing we'll need for now. Then we'll leave you in peace."

Silent and still, only Patricia's eyebrows moved, a sign she was ready for what Freya had to ask.

"Where would I find Beth? I'm afraid we might need to involve her. She might know more about this Charlie and Jessica's other friends."

CHAPTER ELEVEN

The car ride from the Hudsons' house to Albert Stow's was short enough that Ben kept his jacket on, but long enough for the elephant in the car to announce its presence. For the first time, Ben was experiencing Bloom's brooding – silent and on guard.

"That has to be, without a shadow of doubt, the worst part of the job," he said, as he pulled away from the house.

"It doesn't get any easier," Freya replied, staring out of her window, looking away from Ben.

"Do you want to talk about it?"

"About the murder investigation? Or how Mrs Hudson overreacted?"

"I wouldn't call it an overreaction. We thought you–"

"Well, then you both overreacted," Freya said, raising her voice. "Like I said, I was thinking."

"What about, exactly?"

Sighing, Freya turned to look at him for the first time. "Mum drops daughter off in town to get the bus to the train station. The father wants the mother to hold her hand all the way to the train station."

"That's not unusual. By the time I was seventeen, my parents didn't know what *I* was doing, where I was, or who I was with. I don't suppose it mattered. My dad thought *all* my friends were up to no good."

"You're male."

"So? I thought this was the era of equal rights?"

"I've known you two hours. Are we really going to discuss sexism?"

Ben laughed, if anything, just to lighten the mood.

"It's not about sexism at all. Times have changed. You're from the city. Maybe it's different there. There's more danger. Maybe parents have to be more cautious?"

"Parents need to be cautious wherever they are," Freya said. "But, the point is, Jessica and her mother had secrets. They had a relationship that Jessica did not have with her father. Why is that?"

"Daughters are generally closer to their mother, I suppose. They talk about stuff. Stuff a girl might find difficult to talk to her father about."

"Or she was afraid to talk to her father."

"Why would she be afraid?"

"He's a control freak. You heard her say it."

"That's making a leap, don't you think? The bloke just lost his daughter. I think we need to extend him some kind of tolerance for his behaviour."

"You can extend what you like to him, Ben. But I don't think we should rule out Timothy's run-in with the drug dealer."

"Derek Barnes? He's a small-time pain in the backside."

"That he may be, but it's an indication of Mr Hudson's personality. He's used to getting his own way."

Thinking back to the moment Ben had found Tim Hudson in the garden, Ben mused on what Freya had said.

"He was upset, you know? When you went upstairs with Patricia, I followed him out to the garden. He has a little, quiet spot down the side of his office. He took himself there to have a little cry."

"He didn't want his wife to see."

"That's natural, isn't it? I don't like people to see me when I'm upset either."

"Are you married, Ben?"

"No. No, I'm not."

"When you're married, your spouse is your rock, and you become theirs. It's one of those things that keep you together. They help you through the hard times. Being each other's rocks allows you to fight, to clear the air. You both need each other. If you can't open up and lean on your spouse, you don't have a rock, and if you don't have a rock to lean on, you fall."

"I'm sorry, is this a lesson in marital psychology, or are we investigating a murder here?"

"Don't be petulant, it doesn't suit you, and if I have to explain everything to you, then you're in for a rough ride with me, Ben Savage."

A small B-road led from Chapel St Leonards to Anderby, running adjacent to the beach just five or six hundred yards inland, by Ben's reckoning. Beach access roads were few and far between, with Anderby Creek being the most popular for tourists on account of a small shop that sold ice creams and drinks. But further along, lesser developed access roads provided locals with a little more privacy, less screaming kids, and an all-round nicer experience. Filling the spaces between the access roads, the B-road, and the man-made sandbank at the edge of the beach was a mix of farmland, marshland, and caravan parks.

Passing the access road to the crime scene at Moggs Eye, Ben turned into a lane heading inland. With a watchful eye on the house numbers, he searched for the address Chapman had provided. Stow's property was at the end of a row of detached bungalows. Opposite, fields ran on as far as the eye could see, bordered by an old, dry stone wall.

"Well?" she said, as Ben pulled over to park the car.

"Well, what?" he replied.

"Do I have to explain everything? Or do you think you can work it out?"

The day was getting worse. There had been a glimmer of hope that he might actually get along with Bloom. But that glimmer was fading fast, and her perfume was getting up his nose.

"They have marital problems, Ben. The Hudson house is not a happy place. We need to bear that in mind when we're trying to understand Jessica's actions."

Reaching for the door handle, Ben climbed out, closed the door, and found her peering at him from across the car roof.

"Thank you for your insight, Doctor Bloom," he said, and he walked up the driveway, turning his back on her scathing expression.

CHAPTER TWELVE

"Mr Stow, hi, it's DS Savage. We spoke earlier on the beach," said Ben, fishing his ID from his pocket.

Through the opaque window in the front door, Albert Stow's eye was clear, while his surrounding face appeared monstrous, distorted by the glass. The security chain rattled as he opened the door a fraction and peered out. A dog barked once from further back in the house, but it was half-hearted, almost obligatory.

"Oh, I remember now," said Albert through the small gap. "Hold on one second."

A few seconds passed while Albert fumbled with the chain, and Freya came to stand beside Ben.

"Try not to psychoanalyse this one," Ben muttered to her. "He's on our side."

"That's half your problem, Ben. You think people are on our side," she replied quietly as Albert opened the door and stood back to invite them in. "Mr Stow, I'm Detective Inspector Freya Bloom. It's a pleasure to meet you."

"Oh," said Albert, smiling as Freya entered the house. "Likewise. You're helping him, are you?"

Wiping his shoes on the mat, Ben entered and inhaled the

familiar flavours of a cooked breakfast. Bacon, sausages, black pudding, and fried onion served as a reminder that Ben was yet to eat. Albert Stow dressed exactly as Ben's grandfather might have dressed – smart trousers, neatly pressed, with a collared shirt beneath a V-neck sweater. Over the top of the sweater, he wore a cardigan, and beneath it on his chest was a faint bulge, which Ben assumed to be a tissue or a handkerchief stowed in his breast pocket. Albert was clean-shaven, and his grey hair had been neatly combed into a side-parting.

"I'm his senior officer, Mr Stow. I'm leading the investigation into Jessica Hudson's death."

Seeming a little surprised at Freya's elevated rank, he glanced at Ben. "Well, it takes all sorts, that's what I say," he said, and moved through the hallway into the kitchen. Following closely behind, Freya studied the photos on the walls, while Ben, trying his best to suppress a laugh at the old man's dated attitude, watched her from the hallway. She didn't miss a trick. In the few short seconds it had taken her to enter the kitchen, she had taken in the scene of all three family portraits that hung on the walls and glanced into each of the rooms.

"Is Mrs Stow around?" she asked.

"No, she's out right now. Running errands, I expect. Shall I make some tea?"

"No, there's no need–"

"That sounds lovely, Mr Stow. Thank you," said Ben, cutting Freya off. Waiting for Albert's back to be turned, he leaned in close to Freya. "Leave the locals to me. You don't turn down their hospitality and expect their good graces."

"Sorry?" said Albert, from the far side of the room. "You'll have to speak up. I'm getting a little mutton in my old age." Filling the kettle, he rattled the lid back on, then positioned it on the hob before turning to appraise them.

"I was just telling my colleague that you also have a dog. Where's Bramble?"

"Oh, I see. Bramble will be in the warmest spot in the house," Albert replied, then wrinkled his nose and tilted his head back to peer through his glasses at Ben. "In front of the fire. I'm amazed she hasn't cooked herself she lays so close."

"My colleague tells me you made the discovery this morning. How are you feeling? A little shaken up, I imagine?" Freya asked, offering him a fine sympathetic tone in stark contrast to the bitter glare she had given Ben. "I don't suppose it was a pleasant experience for you. I can arrange for you to talk to somebody, if you'd like?"

"Talk to somebody? What about?"

"The experience. Sometimes talking helps–"

"I don't need to talk to anybody. I'm damn near eighty years old. I've seen a body or two in my time. What help is talking about it going to do? Especially with somebody who is probably too young to have seen anything like that themselves. No. I'm fine. Thank you for the offer, missy, but I'm fine."

"You said you've seen a body or two before, Mr Stow?" said Ben.

"Of course I have. I was with the coast guard in my day. Thirty years, I served. Thirty years of rolling waves, high winds, and salt water in my face. My wife jokes that I'm actually only fifty. I just look this old because of the sea and the weather."

"I imagine that was a wonderful career, Mr Stow," said Freya.

"Wonderful? No. It was bloody freezing. Your hands get so cold and numb you can barely get your wet gear off. No. It was the people I liked," he said. Then he added wistfully, "Friends, good friends. Lost a few too, over the years. It's a shame. We'd pull people out of the sea, alive if we found them in time. Dead if we didn't. A few we found by chance. Bloated and pecked at by the fish and the birds." He pulled a disgusted face, and lowered his voice to a grumble. "Sorry souls they were."

"Well, I'm grateful Jessica was found by someone with your experience," Ben said, moving the conversation on before they were lost to a barrage of anecdotes. "Do you often walk Bramble along the beach?"

"Of course I do. It's a ten-minute walk from here. You can even hear the sea on a quiet day."

"And you always walk the same route?"

"Not always. We go up the lane, see. Then cross over into the access road. Have to keep her on the lead, mind, at least until we cross over. Kids use these lanes like racetracks. They don't know, do they?" he said, tapping his index finger to his temple. "They haven't seen what you and I have seen. They don't understand the consequences. They were at it last night. Tearing up the lane. I'm sure they do something to the cars to make them louder. Cars were never that loud in my day."

"I'd like to talk about Piper, if I may?" said Freya. "The golden retriever you saw at the beach."

"Piper? Oh, yes. He was only a puppy. He didn't know any better. Mind you, judging by the owner, he probably never will. Wasn't even trying to call him back. She was just standing there gawping."

"Had you seen her before?" asked Ben.

"No. No, I told you that at the beach. Must be new around here. Too late in the season for tourists, mind."

"And you can't describe her?"

"She had two eyes, a nose, and a mouth, sonny. Everything else was covered up in scarves, hats, and coats."

"So this lady was already on the beach when you arrived?" Freya asked.

"Yes. I told you. Bramble and I came along the access road and onto the beach. Sometimes we go left. Sometimes we go right. This morning, we turned right. Hadn't gone but a hundred yards when I saw the commotion of the birds and the dog. Then I saw the woman. She was standing so still I didn't see her at first. I went over to her, but she weren't the talking type. You find that with dog walkers. Some don't even say hello or good morning.

Most do. Most people love to talk about their dogs. Usually, the only people who'll listen are dog owners. Crikey, I've met some in my time. Some of them I see often. There's Rosie, she's a Lab like Bramble. Tennyson, he's a little cocker. Too much energy for me, them cockers. And there's a beautiful collie named Buddy. Fast as the wind, he is. Runs rings around Bramble." He gave a little laugh and smiled as he recalled the dogs he'd see on his lonely walks.

"But never before have you seen Piper?"

"Nope. I'd have recognised him. I have an eye for these things, you know. I might be old, but it's all still ticking along nicely," he said, once more tapping his temple with a gnarled index finger.

"I wonder, Mr Stow," Freya said, reaching into her pocket and retrieving a card. Handing it to him face up, so he could see her name and mobile number, she caught his gaze and held it. "If you see her again, would you call me please? We'd like to have a word with her."

"Of course. I'm happy to do my bit. She was killed, wasn't she?"

"We can't really discuss the details, I'm afraid."

"That's okay. I know she was. Saw it with my own two eyes. I've seen enough to know what I've seen." Tutting, he shook his head. "Have you spoken to her parents? Her dad?"

"Yes, we—"

"We have a protocol to follow, Mr Stow," Freya interjected, closing Ben down. "I'm sure a man of your experience will understand."

Nodding, he winked back at her. "Don't you worry. The secret is safe with me. I'll be watching out for her from now on, and anyone suspicious. I'll not have our beach become a hotspot for trouble."

"How do you know Jessica, exactly?" said Freya, referring to the few notes that had been passed on to her. "I see that you recognised her, even though she's from the next town."

"Hard not to know her. She's Tim Hudson's daughter. Or was,

I should say. Anyone who's anyone knows Tim Hudson. He helped us buy this place, back in the day. Course, he's got much bigger now. More people need his services. But when we bought this place, everyone knew everyone. We had a little house in Chapel. Got too much for us in the end. You know? Our kids grew up and moved out and we were left rattling around inside. We wanted somewhere peaceful and without stairs."

"It's a lovely house," said Ben.

Nodding at Ben's remark, the old man continued, "That's how we know Tim Hudson, and that's how we know his daughter. His sister is nearby too. What's her name now? Helen? No…"

"Do you mean his sister-in-law? Hetty?"

"That's it. Do you know her?"

"By name only, I'm afraid," said Freya. "Listen, it's been an absolute pleasure talking to you, Mr Stow."

"I've enjoyed the company. I'm sorry I couldn't be more helpful."

"Where has your wife gone today? Anywhere nice?"

"Oh, she comes and goes. I don't ask anymore," he replied, and gave Ben a sly wink. "Best to let her be, and make the most of her when I can."

"So you'll call us if you see the dog walker again?" asked Freya, smiling at the little man-to-man moment.

"Of course. Right away. I'll keep a keen eye out for her. I've got one of those mobile phones. Take it with me just in case, I do. Don't you worry. Old Albert's on guard," Albert said, proudly, then his eyes widened. "Oh, I haven't finished making tea."

"That's okay, Mr Stow," said Freya, giving Ben a sideways glance. "I think we have all we need for now. We'll leave you to join Bramble by the fireside."

"Well, if you're sure. It's no bother—"

"We have a lot to do, Albert," said Ben, offering the old man a warm smile.

"Is this you and your wife?" asked Freya from the doorway. She pointed at an old, framed photo on the wall in the hallway.

"Whitby, nineteen sixty-three," he replied, proudly recalling the date the photo had been taken. "We ate at the Grand Royal Hotel. I had haddock and Margaret had cod. She's always preferred cod over haddock. She says haddock is too oily. She'll be back soon, if you wanted to talk to her?"

"Another time, Mr Stow," said Freya, and she moved through into the hallway. Stopping at the front door, she turned again and smiled at him. "Just one more question, and I hope this doesn't sound a little too invasive. Did you go anywhere last night? Or were you at home?"

"I was here. Margaret was with me. Why?" the old man asked, his voice rising in defence.

"Oh, no reason. If you had gone out for a walk, I wondered if you might have seen anybody on your travels."

"Last night?"

"Yes. Do you walk Bramble in the evenings?"

"I do. Well, when you have to go, you have to go, don't you? She seems to have to go more than me these days."

"Did you go to the beach?"

"I did. I always go there. I told you. I took her out around ten o'clock. I know it was ten o'clock because that funny fellow was on the TV. You know the one with the big ears?"

"Albert, did you see anybody while you were there?" Freya asked, and she glared at Ben for not asking the question before.

"I didn't see much, I can tell you. It was in the storm. Soaked, we were. All I saw was the car I told you about."

"The car? I'm sorry, which car was this?"

"The one making all that racket. Came hurtling down the lane from the beach. Damn near knocked us over."

"Last night?" Freya said.

"That's what I said, wasn't it?"

"Did you happen to see the driver? Or can you give us a description of the car maybe?"

"No. They came screaming down from the beach. Another few seconds and they would have hit Bramble and me. Going too fast to see anything, what with the storm and all. They ought to put a sign up or something. That'd stop them speeding."

"What time do you think you got home from your walk, Albert? This is all very helpful, thank you."

"Well, we like to have a little cuddle in front of the fire." He smiled fondly at another framed photo on a small table beside a telephone. A man and a woman, who Ben presumed to be Albert and Margaret, were standing beside an old Ford Popular. "I had bubble and squeak, leftovers from the Sunday roast. Winter is for hunkering down and making the most of what you have, you know?"

"I agree, Albert," Ben said, motioning toward the door, and shaking his head at Freya for her to drop the question. "Thank you so much. We'll let you get back to your fire."

CHAPTER THIRTEEN

Closing the front door, Albert Stow re-engaged the security chain and then moved through to the living room where Bramble was lying beside the stone hearth. Using the net curtains as cover, he spied the two detectives leaving the property, and was mildly amused at the body language between them. The woman had made a point about being his superior yet the dynamic between them had shifted during the questioning.

Glancing down at the card she had given Albert, he noticed that the phone number was not a Lincolnshire dial code. It was an 0203 number, which he knew to be London, as his sister-in-law had the same code.

Deducing that she might have been brought up for other reasons, such as training, he admired the way her tight trousers hugged her body as she climbed into the car, and how she waited for her male colleague to start the car. She may not have been a local girl, but she definitely wore the trousers in that relationship.

"They won't work it out, Bramble. No. You mark my words, they'll give up, just like they did before."

With that, he made his way toward the bedroom. The curtains were still drawn as it had still been dark when he had got out of bed to walk Bramble. Opening the door to the wardrobe, he parted the bank of shirts he hadn't worn for several years and reached for an old, wooden box. Dropping it onto the bed, he struggled to kneel on the rug, and then, with the tip of his tongue poking through his dry lips, he gripped the old box, and opened the lid.

Removing a brown envelope from the box, he held it open with two fingers, and was about to delve into a pile of old photographs when the kettle on the stove began to emit a low whistle. Familiar with his kettle, he knew he had around one minute before it began raging, enough time to withdraw the heavy bundle wrapped in cloth from the bottom of the box and then open it up to view the old, but still deadly, contents.

CHAPTER FOURTEEN

About a mile from Albert Stow's house, on a larger than average property, enclosed on all sides by tall trees, was the Fraser house. One day, Freya mused, as she considered the finer details, the house would have been impressive, and the owners proud. But years of neglect had left the place a sorry sight. The narrow driveway was riddled with weeds, and the windows needed replacing with double glazing. A row of outbuildings flanked the side wall, and a small, decaying orchard occupied the far end of the property. But beyond and all around, fields and wild fens gave the place a foreboding sense of solitude. It was true that the nearest houses were less than a mile away, but from nowhere on the plot that Freya could see was any sign of civilisation visible.

Hanging from a tree in the front garden, a rope swing rocked in the breeze. The strength of the rotten plank of wood was questionable, but for a child in the summertime, such a simple toy would have been a joy. Reflecting on her own childhood, her parents' small back garden had boasted a steel-framed swing that had faded with too many seasons, and rusty chains that had pinched and discoloured her hands.

"Have you gone again?" asked Ben, the first words he'd spoken since she'd instructed him to drive to the Fraser house.

Turning to face him, she found him staring at her like she was some kind of patient, and he the expert doctor.

"What is that supposed to mean?" she said, doing her level best to keep her voice calm and low.

"Just checking you're okay? You were quiet."

"I was thinking."

"Just like you were thinking in the Hudson house?"

"Just like that, yes. And if you're forming an opinion of how I operate, then I suggest you communicate that so I can steer you onto a clearer path. I wouldn't want you running away with any ideas of your own."

"Don't worry. I'll tell you what I'm thinking when I'm thinking it," he said, as he opened his car door and climbed out. Leaning down into the car, he stared at her. "But I only tend to give thought to things that are worth my time and energy."

Pushing open the passenger door, Freya too climbed out and closed the door harder than she meant to. Raising a questioning eyebrow, Ben looked displeased.

"And what's that supposed to mean?"

"You know, for someone who is supposed to be a damn fine detective, as Granger put it, you need a lot of things explaining."

He turned to head toward the house, leaving her standing beside the car, but after a short burst, she was by his side, matching his speed despite his longer legs.

"I won't tolerate it," she said, refusing to let him have the last word. Reminded of Greg, and how he would always have to get in a spiteful comment before leaving, she was keen not to fall into the same trap again. "Do I need to remind you of my rank?"

"You don't need to remind me of anything, DI Bloom," he said, holding his hand out toward the front door. "Seeing as you're the superior officer, I'll let you lead with the questioning. I'll just be here to take notes."

"Good," said Freya, straightening her coat and flicking her hair out from her collar. "I'll talk to DSU Harper when we get back."

"About what?"

"About moving you off the investigation. I'm sure there's more fitting work elsewhere."

———

The doorbell didn't work the first time Freya pushed the button, and it didn't work the second or third time she tried either. Leaning forward, Ben rapped on the window then stepped back. But his smugness faded as he inadvertently touched her behind with his free hand as he withdrew.

And if he could have asked the world to swallow him whole right then, he would have, gladly.

"I'm sorry, I–"

The door opened and a middle-aged woman appeared just as Freya turned and glared at him.

"Can I help?" she asked.

"Mrs Fraser?" said Freya, her tone harsher than necessary, and the homeowner's expression hardened.

"Yes."

"I'm sorry, may we come in?" Freya asked, a little flustered from being caught off guard.

"No. Who are you?"

Restraining the smile that threatened to expose Ben's amusement, he reached for his ID, while Freya searched her bag for hers.

"We're from CID, Mrs Fraser," said Ben, flashing his ID, much to Freya's annoyance. "It's a sensitive topic. We wondered if we might have a quick word with your daughter."

"Beth? Why do you need to talk to her?"

Had Freya not been distracted by Ben's accident, Ben was sure she would have handled the situation well. After all, Will had referred to her as a *damn fine detective*. Feeling partly responsible for the frankly shocking introduction, he sought to regain some credibility.

"Mrs Fraser, we're investigating the death of a young woman not far from here. We think Beth might be able to shed some light on a few things for us."

"A death? Who?" she said, clutching the collars of the floral blouse she wore beneath her cardigan and displaying visible signs of abhorrence.

"It's not really a matter for the doorstep, Mrs Fraser," Ben suggested. "We're sorry to intrude. Is Beth home?"

A few seconds passed as Freya showed the ID wallet she had found in her bag, and Hetty Fraser looked them both up and down. She opened the door and stepped back.

"You'll have to be quick."

Moving into the hallway, a silence fell, as the sound of the incessant wind died and the front door closed. The house was hot. Too hot for Ben's comfort. Loosening his tie and jacket, he searched the hallway in case he was standing too close to a radiator. But he wasn't. Perhaps they were overcompensating for the cold that got in through the old, wooden sash windows.

The hallway floor was of black and white checkered tiles, and the ceiling boasted a detailed moulding, much like the rooms of an old Victorian home and, indeed, of the Hudson house. A grandfather clock caught Ben's attention, but the pendulum was stationary and the time was only accurate twice per day.

The stairway had been installed with equal flamboyance to the decor, and an equally long time ago. Since the house had last been decorated, Ben surmised that the fashions had come and gone, and had probably even circulated again. It was as if time stood still on that remote plot of land. A wooden handrail and turned banisters gave the hallway a Gothic appearance, added to by a small stained glass window at the top of the stairs.

To break the silence and recover some credibility, Freya opened her mouth to speak, just as Hetty called up the stairs.

"Beth? Beth, dear? Can you come down?"

"I'm busy," came the reply.

"There's somebody here to see you," the mother said, and she glanced at each of them once more. "It's the police."

It took less than three seconds for Beth to run from her room and lean over the handrail.

"Hi, Beth," Ben said, in as friendly a tone as he could muster. Talking to children and women were not his strong points. Not having any children of his own, and having lost and found his one true love a long time ago, he had always struggled to find the right thing to say or sound natural.

Saying nothing, Beth descended the stairs, barefoot and wearing a pair of jeans with a thick, woollen sweater.

"It's nothing to worry about," said Freya. "We just need to ask you a few questions, that's all."

"We can talk in the parlour," Hetty suggested, and led them through a pair of double doors to another room in need of modernisation. Two low-backed couches had been placed either side of a wide coffee table set before a large, open fireplace. Fresh logs had been stacked up to one side of the hearth and a small basket of kindling rested on top.

Taking a seat beside Freya, Ben faced Hetty and Beth. Grateful that Freya had elected to lead the questioning, Ben waited for her to start by retrieving his notepad from his pocket and clicking the end of his pen.

"I'm afraid our reason for disturbing you is twofold," she began. "Firstly, I have to deliver some bad news to you both, but then, I'll need to ask you some questions, Beth. Is that okay?"

"What are you getting at?" Hetty asked, her tone filled with suspicion.

"I'm afraid we found the body of a young woman at the beach this morning. She's been identified as Jessica Hudson."

Letting her mouth hang open, Beth's eyes widened. Her mother appeared incredulous.

"What?"

"I know it's a lot to take in. Believe me, this is a terrible thing to have to do."

"How?" said Hetty, clutching her daughter and holding her close. "What happened?"

"It's likely she was attacked," said Freya, electing for a direct approach. The damage had been done; there was little need for fluff now. "We are treating the death as suspicious, and she's being examined in the lab. We'll know more when the pathologist gets back to us. But in these circumstances, we have a finite amount of time to gather all the evidence we can. That's why we need your help, Beth."

With her face buried in her hands, Beth Fraser sobbed. "How? What happened to her?"

"I can't go into details right now."

"What about her parents? My sister..." Hetty said, her voice rising with every word.

"We've been to see Tim and Patricia this morning. They suggested we talk to Beth. Is there anything we should know, Beth? Her parents mentioned that you two were close but that she had another circle of friends."

"I don't know. I was never invited. She liked to keep us separate, I think."

"Why would she do that? You were cousins, weren't you?"

Nodding, Beth sniffed and cleared her throat, and her mother took the cue to disappear for some tissues.

"I don't know," Beth continued. "It didn't bother me. She said they got drunk a few times. It's not really my thing."

"They mentioned the name Charlie. Does that ring any bells?"

"Charlie?" she said, shaking her head and turning her nose up at the idea. "Not Charlie Barnes?"

"We don't have a last name."

"There's only one Charlie that I know of. At least around here."

"Barnes?" said Hetty, re-entering the room with a box of tissues. Her face paled a little in complexion at the same time as Ben's stomach tightened.

"Yes," said Beth quietly. "I didn't know they hung out. That's the only Charlie I know, but I can't see why they would even speak."

"Why is that?" asked Freya.

"Jessica is lovely. She would much prefer to play her violin all day long than get into trouble."

"Is that what Charlie does? Get into trouble?"

"I know the Barnes family," said Ben, though Freya didn't look his way. "I'm not aware of a Charlie though. It's worth us paying them a visit."

Unable to go into detail about Derek Barnes and his history with Jessica's father, Ben elected to say nothing more.

"Well, we can't be sure just yet," Freya said, and glanced in Ben's direction for him to make a note. He circled the name from the chat with the Hudsons, marking the note that he would ask Chapman to investigate.

"How's my sister?" asked Hetty, as a man appeared in the doorway behind her, making no effort to hide the fact that he was listening in.

"She's as well as can be expected," said Freya. "Perhaps you could reach out to her? She'll need you right now."

"Perhaps, yes," she muttered, though somehow Ben doubted she would.

With his head cocked to one side, the man at the door entered the room. He wore casual clothes, smart but loose-fitting – a check shirt, dark blue jeans with a brown leather belt, and work boots.

"What's happening?" he asked, and he stared at the foursome as if they were conspiring. It was Hetty who spoke first.

"They're police, Jack. They found a body," she said, and she stared up at her husband vacantly, though her sharp tone belied her expression. "It's Jessica."

CHAPTER FIFTEEN

"What?"

The single most common word used by individuals buying time to think of a suitable response. When the subject was reporting a death, it was, in Freya's experience, usually followed by disbelief or tears, sometimes both.

Reeling from his wife's statement, Jack Fraser had yet to even meet Freya's stare. He was a large man with broad shoulders and a narrow waist, somehow achieving the V that men think all women enjoy. Obviously a man who followed fashion trends, despite him being in his forties, he sported stubble not quite long enough for a beard but trimmed and cared for so that it was clearly not the result of simply having not shaved. It was as he approached that Freya caught his leathery aroma; the masculine aftershave was the polish to his appearance. From where Freya was sitting, he didn't look like an emotional man. Instead, she deduced that he would enter into the realms of disbelief.

"Dead?" he said, allowing his shoulders to sag. "That can't be. Our Jessica? Jessica Hudson? Are you sure you have that right?"

In the short space of time it had taken the man to deliver five concise sentences, the red arteries that spanned the whites of his eyes had emboldened, which, together with the sheen of tears signalled an emotional outburst was imminent.

Accepting that she couldn't be right all the time, Freya altered her opinion of the man.

"I'm afraid it's true, Mr Fraser," Freya said, standing to meet him eye to eye. But still, he refused to look at her. "Her body was found this morning. I'm sorry to have to break the news to you."

"But how?" he whined.

"It's too early to–"

"Who did it?" he asked, his voice rising in pitch.

"Who did what, Mr Fraser?"

"Well surely you're not here just to tell us..." He paused and cleared his throat, unable to complete the sentence. "I'm assuming there's more to it than..."

"That's what we need to establish."

"Oh God," he said, then dropped to one knee before his daughter. He placed his phone and his keys on the coffee table, and cupped her face in his hands. "Are you okay, baby?"

A single nod was all Beth Fraser could do to respond. Blinking away her empty stare, she glanced once at her father, then at the floor. It was during times like this Freya had learnt to look away, offering the family a brief private moment for them to digest the news. She studied the room and its antiquated decor. A restoration would cost thousands, but in Freya's opinion, it would be worth it. Her eyes fell on the man's keys and phone on the coffee table. A yellow, plastic key caught her eye, as it was similar to one Freya had for her motor home which opened the door to the gas bottle. His phone was an old model with a crack across the screen. He was not a rich man, she surmised, but clearly loved his family.

"Hetty?" he said, remaining by their daughter's side but turning his attention to his wife.

"How am I feeling?" she asked him, her reaction colder than expected. "Shocked. Shocked and scared, Jack."

Turning to face Freya, his face was a picture of grief. "Have you spoken to her? Patricia? And Tim? Do they know?"

"They've been there and done that," Hetty answered. "They think Beth might know who Jessica was hanging around with."

"Do you, Beth? Did she tell you anything?"

"No, Dad. Honestly, she hasn't told me anything for ages. We're not close like we used to be."

"Why not?" said Hetty. "Has something happened?"

"No, not that I know of. She used to message me all the time. But she doesn't anymore. She doesn't often reply to my emails either. Ever since they moved."

Turning to Freya and Ben, Hetty began to explain.

"They used to live closer. Near to the beach. But my brother-in-law being my brother-in-law thought he knew better than anyone else. He moved them into Chapel last year sometime. It's still only a ten-minute drive, but I guess Jessica found new friends. You can see for yourself, this place is not exactly overpopulated."

"So you and Jessica must have been quite close," Freya said to the girl, who nodded and sniffed. With her mother's arm around her, and her father resting his head on her knee, Beth appeared well-loved. Though the language and tones shared among the parents were indicative of friction, much like Jessica's parents, and if Freya was honest with herself, it was much as her own marriage had been. Subtle bitter undertones were used as vehicles to deliver spite and revenge. It was the small-arms fire that took place before developing into full-scale war. They were the early tremors and plumes of smoke a volcano might give off, signalling that it could erupt at any moment.

"Where was she found?" Jack asked, raising his head, but still holding onto Beth's hands.

"The beach," said Freya. "A dog walker discovered her this morning."

"And was she..." He paused, realising that his question was not suitable for all ears, given the circumstance. But Freya read enough into his meaning that she was able to deflect the question with experienced precision.

"I'm afraid we're not in a position to provide exact details. Not yet anyway. What I'd like to do is eliminate all known parties from the investigation. At this early stage, it's imperative we understand her close network."

"What do you mean eliminate all known parties?" Jack asked, holding onto his daughter's hands and biting down on his lip.

"I'm sorry, but I have to ask you all where you were last night."

A terrible silence hung in the air, as if time itself had stopped. But it was Hetty who once more fell into line.

"That's perfectly fine," she said. "If it helps you find him."

"Or her," her husband added, offering his wife the briefest of sly glares.

"We were here all evening," Hetty said, holding her husband's stare, then turning to Freya and Ben, and summoning every ounce of authenticity. "All of us were."

CHAPTER SIXTEEN

"What do you think?" asked Ben, as he drew his seat belt across his chest and fought with the socket and his jacket.

Saying nothing, Freya closed her door. The cold air warmed with her perfume, and as Ben's seat belt clicked into place, he stared at her, waiting.

"Is this how it's going to be?"

"I meant what I said, DS Savage. As soon as we're back at the station, I'll be requesting your removal from the investigation. So, in answer to your question, what I think doesn't matter to you. I'd be wasting my breath."

"I thought you might like to go and see Charlie Barnes and his dad."

"I'll go and see Charlie Barnes on my own if necessary. But given the circumstances, I think it's best if we cut it short sooner rather than later."

"Rip the plaster off, you mean?"

"If that's the level of analogy you want to use, then yes."

"What analogy would you use?"

"I wouldn't use an analogy. This is a murder investigation and I'm far too long in the tooth to entertain the idea of working with a colleague who A hasn't got my back, and B can't keep his hands to himself."

"Oh, come on, that was an accident."

"Save it for Harper."

Arguing with her was pointless and reminded him of why he chose to be single. He had nothing against the opposite sex, in fact, he admired them. His problem was with the relationships, not the individuals.

Barring the love of his life, which was a relationship he'd ruined himself, all other relationships he'd experienced had ended poorly, and if he was truthful to himself, he preferred his own company. He could work whenever he wanted to, sit down and eat whenever he wanted to, and if he needed company, his brothers, who both worked for his father on the family farm, lived less than one hundred metres away.

Pulling away from the house, he caught sight of a face in the upstairs window. It was a female with blonde hair, so could have been either Hetty Fraser or her daughter. The sight turned his attention to the trauma the Hudsons must have been going through. They had both held it together during the initial meeting, well enough for him and Freya to gather at least some kind of evidence. But then, as his thoughts meandered, he found himself considering the idea of being pulled off the investigation at the word of a woman who had been in Lincolnshire for less time than the dark clouds on the horizon. There was no way Will Granger would stand for it. He'd sooner see her sent back to London, to whatever hole she been seconded from. But Arthur, on the other hand, saw things differently. Until that morning, Ben would have said that Arthur would have had the same reaction as Will. But after their meeting, it was clear he saw something in Freya Bloom that Ben and Will did not. Either that, or he had far less faith in Ben than Ben had thought. Either way, Freya's arrogance could be the end of what Ben was hoping to be a new start.

They passed Albert Stow's house, and out of interest, Ben

glanced at the little bungalow as he passed, noting the unkempt grass and the small gate that needed mending. It must be tough at that age to get out and keep the house maintained, he thought. Less than a minute later, Ben had to slow to pass a man walking his dog. It was Albert Stow.

"Don't stop," said Freya, who too must have recognised the old man. "I don't have time to enter into a conversation with him. I need to get a car hired and get back out here. I'm going to be busy, it seems."

"You could always take one of the unmarked cars."

Her reply was delayed, as if she was deciding if she wanted to converse with him.

"Are there any free?"

"Usually. You'll have to sign it out."

"I know what the procedure is. I just assumed that out here—"

"What? That we can't afford cars?"

"No, but there's less need for them."

"You're right. There is less need. Sergeant Priest is the man to see. I can put a word in for you if you want?"

"I'm sure I'm capable of arranging a car, thank you," she said, her posh accent becoming stronger as her attitude grew.

At the end of the road, Ben stopped the car. It was a tricky junction. To turn right would lead them back towards Chapel St Leonards. Turning left was the coastal road all the way up to Mablethorpe. And ahead of them was the little beach access road that led to the crime scene. The view to the right was obscured by an overhanging tree, so Ben edged out. A car shot past, and seeing the gap that followed, Ben floored the accelerator.

"Where are we going?" Freya asked, holding onto the door handle to stop the bumpy road from throwing her out of her seat. Easing the car to a slower speed, Ben ignored her, feigning interest in the fields on either side of the track. "I've been in Lincolnshire long enough to know that this is not the way to the station."

Her attitude amused Ben. Perhaps that was the way he should deal with her. Let her arrogance wash over him. Take no notice of her big, fancy words and subtle slants.

"Right, that's it," she said, pulling her phone from her pocket. "I'll call Detective Superintendent Harper and have him send somebody to collect me. You're disobeying a direct instruction."

The slower Ben drove, the more infuriated she seemed to get. Amused, he dropped into first gear and voiced his thoughts.

"There's no way anybody would walk across the fields to get to the beach. Not in the winter. Look at the state of it. It's too boggy. We'd have seen prints."

"Some of us haven't had the chance to see the body."

There we are. Conversation.

"You got close enough. A few more steps forward and you would have seen her," said Ben. "But then, I didn't know who you were at the time, did I? I thought you were the general public, or a reporter or something. The killer would have had to walk this way, or at least drive this way. Albert said he saw a car race away."

"You're not working your way back into this case, DS Savage."

"So how did Jessica get from Chapel to here?"

Making a mental note to make a physical note, to have Jackie or Chapman check the buses, Ben nursed the idea from infancy, but it led nowhere. It was yet another clutch at a hope.

The access road raised in elevation slightly as it cut through the sandbank and into a little car park. Ben knew it well. He and his friends had frequented the beaches in their youth. Ben had spent more time tearing up the sand on his old Yamaha dirt bike than he had on the roads. But that was before he joined the force. When he would have baulked at the idea of working for the police.

Pulling the car into the end parking spot beside an unmarked white van, he noted the police tape cordoning off the area. A white tent had been erected over the spot where Jessica's body had been found. Two uniformed officers were positioned at each end of the site to stop interested or worried neighbours from getting too close, and a team of two or three white-suited investigators were still active on the dune.

He killed the engine and glanced across at her, noting her finger poised over the button to call. The contact on her phone read *Det Supt. Harper*, and she was staring out of the window, unable to look him in the eye.

"I'm going to check in with CSI. I'll give you some privacy for your call, shall I?"

CHAPTER SEVENTEEN

Flashing his ID at the uniform, who Ben recognised as Griffiths, he ducked beneath the cordon and stood at the foot of the dune. Steel steps had been placed in the sand by forensics to form a wayward path to the tent at the top. The path meandered through the tall grass and sharp thorns, taking a route that had been identified as clean and free of prints. Taking the path, he worked his way toward the tent, doing his best not to glance in Freya's direction.

"How's it looking, Michaela?" he asked, holding back one of the tent flaps and peering inside.

Jessica's body had been removed, and two white-suited individuals turned to face him, their tired eyes showing through their thick protective goggles.

"Oh hello, Ben. I've been better," she said. "But we're nearly done."

"What do we have?" Ben asked.

"One clean print. Size eleven. Looks like a work boot. We checked it against the man who found her–"

"Albert Stow."

"It's not his." Michaela, an attractive, blonde woman who

seemed to live for her work, shifted her position, and moved to another of the steel stepping stones where, with the end of her trowel, she made a circle in the air above a faint boot print. "Stow's print is smaller and simpler."

"He was wearing wellies when I spoke to him."

She pointed at where her colleague was working. "Whoever that print belongs to has much larger feet. I'd hazard a guess at it being a boot, but don't quote me on that yet."

"Size elevens are pretty common. I'm an eleven."

"You were wearing shoes this morning. Your prints are flat, as are Doctor's Saint's," she replied and leaned over to where Ben had been standing that morning. He had tried to keep a distance and had only got close to Jessica's body once, to look for an early clue.

"So that's all we have? A boot print?" he asked.

"We're doing what we can. But with the storm, it's a pretty tall order. There's a sign of a scuffle, but there's nothing of any use. What I can say is that more than one person was lying here. The way the sand is distributed, there was activity of some description."

"There was no sign of intercourse."

"A struggle maybe. It's hard to say, but she wasn't alone here. Doctor Bell will tell you more."

"Doctor Bell?"

"The pathologist. Haven't you met her before?"

"The Welsh girl?" Ben asked, picturing her clearly.

"She's a hard one to forget, Ben. But she's good at what she does. I suggest you talk to her with regards to the body."

"Anything else you can find will be appreciated." Catching sight of movement over by the parking lot, Ben glanced across and saw Freya climbing from the car. He turned his attention back to Michaela. "When can we expect your report?"

"I'll prepare it as soon as we finish up here and I'll send it through to you."

"Don't send it to me," he said, and the girl appeared bemused. Pulling one of his cards from his pocket, Ben wrote Jackie's email address on the back and handed it to her. "Send it here. I'm being moved off the case."

"That's a shame," she said. "I thought you were giving me your number."

"I, erm..." Ben began, and she smiled at his awkwardness. He opened the tent flap and paused at the threshold. "I'd better go."

"One of these days I'll get you, DS Ben Savage."

He turned to her as she raised her goggles. She was attractive. Stunning, in fact. But he didn't feel the attraction. He couldn't put his finger on why. Instead, he returned the smile and left the tent, tripping over the flap on his way out.

He stumbled across the dune to the car park, tightening his jacket and raising his collar again. To his left, a car door closed. Leaning on the roof, Freya watched him; for the first time, she wasn't hiding her stare. Or was it a glare? It was hard to tell the difference from so far away. Either way, she was watching his every move. Folding her arms, she braced against the wind, as if she was appraising Ben's actions.

There was something about her that he enjoyed. She didn't have youth on her side, not like Michaela, but there was something about her. Something that Gillespie at least had recognised. It was like a schoolboy's crush on a girl in the year above. To add to the complexity, there was something about her he loathed, and he tried to work it out as he drew close. He nearly had it. The idea was close in his mind. But then it vanished when she offered her finest reproachful stare.

But by God did she smell good.

CHAPTER EIGHTEEN

"One size eleven boot print," Ben said. "A work boot, possibly. The storm has damn near washed everything else away."

Impressed at how he was handling himself, Freya leaned on the car, quizzing him to see if he would keep any information back.

"Are they sending a report?"

"I gave them Jackie's email."

"Jackie?" she said.

"DC Gold. Jackie Gold."

"Ah yes, the pretty one who likes you."

"I don't mix my personal and work lives."

"Good to hear. Anything else?"

"Jessica wasn't alone. Now her body has been removed, you can see where two people were lying."

"A lover?" Freya said, and the name Charlie Barnes sprang to mind.

"Perhaps. But there was a struggle there. You can go and see it for yourself."

"Do you think he tried to rape her?" she said, going straight in for the worst-case scenario to see how he handled a potentially awkward conversation.

"Does my opinion count for anything?" he said, kicking the car wheel to shake the loose sand from his shoes.

Ignoring his comment, Freya let her jumbled thoughts loose. "There's something bothering me. What was she doing here in a storm? Was she meeting somebody? Was that person her attacker?"

"She was laid out with love and care," said Ben, and Freya smiled inwardly. He was more intuitive than she had given him credit for. "And she was strangled–"

"That hasn't been confirmed yet."

"It's likely she was strangled."

"So what does that mean?"

"The attacker was close to her."

"There are examples of serial killers strangling their victims."

"And dumping them in rivers, yes, or hiding the bodies. But leaving her laid out like that? No. Somebody loved that girl. They wanted her to be found, and they wanted her to be found presented like that."

"Like what? Like a trophy?"

"No," Ben said, shaking his head. "With dignity."

"They loved her?"

"You asked for my input," he replied, opening the car door. "But it's your investigation. You do as you see fit."

Closing the driver's door, Ben started the car and Freya felt his impatience as she took a last look at the scene. Opening the passenger door, she climbed in, pulled her seat belt across her, and waited for the right moment. With one hand on the steering wheel and the other on the gear stick, Ben gazed at the crashing waves a few hundred feet away. It was as if he was about to say something but couldn't find the words.

"I think she was waiting for him," Freya said, breaking the silence.

"For her killer?"

"For somebody, at least," she replied, happy to have him engage with her again. "Do you want to hear my theory?"

"Do I have a choice?" he asked, then retracted his arrogance. "Go on."

"She arranged to meet somebody. He wanted more than she was willing to give. They struggled. He killed her. He panicked and ran."

"Are you suggesting the marks in the sand are from them struggling?"

"I am, yes. Our man may even have scratches on his face or arms."

"The lab guys are running tests now. So I guess we'll find out soon enough."

"Okay," she said, enjoying his arguments more than she had previously. "How about this? If there are signs that she struggled and fought back, skin beneath her nails, perhaps, or somebody's hair, then we do things my way. But if she didn't struggle, then we do things your way."

"You didn't call Harper, did you?"

Staring at the perpetual breaking waves, she inhaled, long and deep.

"Listen, this whole move to Lincolnshire is about me having a second chance. It's only fair I give others that luxury. Perhaps I was too harsh before."

"I'm still on the case?"

"You have until the end of the day to prove me wrong," said Freya, and a glimmer of a smile formed on her lips. In her heart, she knew that Harper would never take Ben off the case at her say so. After all, he had only known Freya for a morning, even if she did come with a glowing reference. But there was no harm in adding a little competition into the mix. Put the younger detective under some pressure. Had the roles been reversed, Freya would have been delighted at the chance to prove a senior officer wrong. She might not have had the authority to ditch him and cause a stir, but a demonstration of his determination would be helpful, and, Freya thought, it would be a hell of a lot of fun to watch.

"Challenge accepted," he said, and even without looking at him, she knew he was wearing that boyish smile. "Shall we pay Charlie a visit? I imagine by then we can drop the pathologist a visit too."

"That's pretty much what I was thinking, yes," she said, using the mirror in the sun visor to check her appearance.

"And just for the record, I did not touch your backside on purpose."

She smiled inwardly.

"Do you always have to have the last word, DS Savage?"

CHAPTER NINETEEN

During the day, they had travelled from the highest peaks of Chapel St Leonards society at the Hudsons' home, to rural Anderby, and as their last port of call before heading to the hospital, a far less affluent end of Chapel. The streets were quiet and they passed few people. Parked outside the homes, a variety of very average looking vehicles occupied the drives and roadside so that Ben had to squeeze between two other cars to park.

Freya was torn. There were moments when she thought they could really get on and work well together. But there were times when she just wanted to tell him to stop the car so she could get out and be alone. Ben was a large man, handsome in a rugged and natural way. He clearly paid little attention to his hair, he wore no aftershave, yet he was clean and his clothes were pressed. In her past career Freya probably wouldn't have noticed him. But the more she pressed him, the more he displayed strength. And that, she thought, was attractive.

They had said very little during the short journey; perhaps he was sensing Freya's contemplation and not wanting to upset her. Another positive sign.

"Mrs Barnes?" Freya said, when the front door had opened to

reveal a middle-aged woman wearing a man's long vest adorned with an image of a surfer riding a wave on the front. Despite the freezing temperature, her legs and feet were bare and the lacy hem of her underwear peeked from beneath the vest. Designed to fit a man, the armholes hung low, revealing more than an ample amount of her feminine charm. Had the woman been twenty years younger, Freya may have admired her brazen appearance. But the dark rings around her eyes, her poor complexion, and gaunt appearance were less than appealing, reminding Freya of the Brixton crack dens she had raided in her twenties. Although a familiar pungent aroma wafted from inside, possession of cannabis was not the reason for their call. "We're looking for your son Charlie."

Slowly, a smile crept over the woman's face, and as if in collusion with the woman, her dog barked from somewhere at the back of the house.

"Is that right?" she said, her voice throaty. A lifelong smoker, perhaps?

"We'd just like to ask him a few questions. Is he home?"

"You're not from round here, are you?" she asked, and she leaned against the door frame, folding her arms in defiance. "I don't recognise you. Him, I recognise, but not you."

"We're not here to talk about me, Mrs Barnes."

"No, you want to talk to my Charlie. Been up to no good again? Or have you just got a crime to solve and you thought you'd come and knock on the Barnes' door?" Pushing off the door frame, she leaned into the living room and issued the age-old command aimed at poorly trained dogs, "Shut up!"

The dog continued to bark, as had every dog ever issued the command before it. Even Freya knew that calling 'shut up' was not an effective way to silence an ill-behaved pet.

"We have reason to believe your son is linked to the death of a young woman, Mrs Barnes. So if you don't mind, I'd appreciate it if you could give him a call. Does he have a mobile phone?"

With tobacco-stained fingers, she wiped her lank hair from her forehead. The mention of death had rattled the woman, and although she did well to hide her reaction, Freya was far too experienced to miss her unease. Fumbling, Mrs Barnes turned to her right to check her reflection in a small mirror. She pulled her hair back into a ponytail using a frayed band that had been on her wrist. The movement raised her over-sized vest, providing Ben, Freya, and the rest of the street a full view of her chest in profile. Whether through embarrassment or good manners, Ben turned away, feigning interest in the alleyway down the side of the old council house.

From the weathered doorway, Barnes smiled at him, her stained teeth like ancient tombstones. From her expression, it was clear she thought Ben was embarrassed, but she said nothing and returned to her spot leaning against the door frame.

"Charlie doesn't have a phone. Have you tried the park?" she said, turning her attention to Freya, fixing her with dark eyes. "Charlie likes the park. All the *girls* hang out in the park. And Charlie likes the girls."

An old caravan had been dumped, rather than parked, on the unkempt lawn, its sides covered in green mildew. Its tyres had been flat for so long that they were rotting in situ. Ben walked over to it and opened the door, producing a loud creak that caught the attention of both Freya and Mrs Barnes.

"You can't go in there," she said from the front door. "Not without a warrant."

"I wouldn't go in there with a hazard suit," he replied, his face showing his disgust at the smell of rot. Turning away, he approached the doorway of the house again. "Where's your husband, Mrs Barnes?"

"He works away. Won't be back for nine days. It's just me, I'm afraid."

"So Derek has a job now, does he? He must be moving up in the world."

"He works off-shore. On the rigs. He left the day before yesterday." She flicked her eyes towards the coast, then back at Ben, who said nothing, waiting for her to embellish her statement. She sighed. "He's a cleaner. It's agency work. Cleans the mess room, corridors, that kind of thing. Someone has to do it, I suppose."

Handing her a contact card, Ben held her stare. "Have Charlie call me, Mrs Barnes. This is not the petty crime your husband gets involved with, this is serious."

The woman seemed to pay heed to Ben's statement but was defiant in her response.

"I'll try."

"Do we need to issue a warrant for his arrest? Because if so, harbouring him will make you an accomplice."

"Like I said, I'll try," she replied.

"And get dressed, Mrs Barnes," said Ben, gesturing at the rest of the street with a flick of his head. "Nobody needs to see you half-naked. Least of all us."

CHAPTER TWENTY

In the kitchen, the dog barked continuously like he hadn't even taken a breath. In the living room, where a fog of weed hung in the air, silvery grey against the flock wallpaper she had always hated, Christine watched the two police officers leave. She despised them for reasons she knew to be invalid. Had it been one of her own children found dead, she would have expected them to knock on every door in Chapel.

But it hadn't been her child, and they *had* knocked on her door. And if her experience with the law had taught her anything, then they would be back. They would find Charlie, and Her Majesty might end up hosting two Barnes children at her royal pleasure.

Finding the remains of her joint in an overflowing ashtray, she sparked her lighter and took a long drag. For years, she had told herself that it calmed her nerves. But she would need something a lot stronger than a joint to get her through the next period of her life. But before that, she would need to hear Charlie's side of the story. She would defend her children using whatever means necessary, regardless of their alleged crimes. That was who she was. That was her mothering instinct.

The detectives pulled away. It was the man who was driving. Christine couldn't remember his name but she recognised him as one of the ones that tried to put Derek away. The woman, Bloom, a name she would never forget, was sitting in the passenger seat enjoying having her subject drive her from place to place.

"Bloom," she said aloud. It wasn't a name she recognised. Perhaps she had been sent in from Lincoln HQ?

Slipping her phone from her pocket, she checked her text messages and emails, hoping to see something from Charlie, or even Derek. But a hope was all it had been. With limited access to a connection, Derek could almost be excused. But Charlie? No. Protective mother or not, there would be hell to pay if Charlie had anything to do with it.

Stoned and lost in her own imagination, she stared at the road outside where the car had been parked. A crash from the kitchen broke her train of thought. The dog's barking grew even louder and more frantic.

Christine took a deep breath and closed her eyes.

"Enough," she called, using the growling tone that every family member recognised as her breaking point. Everyone, that was, except for the wretched dog, who continued to bark regardless. Marching toward the kitchen door, she snatched up a newspaper from the settee, rolling it into a tight tube as she walked. "This'll shut you up for a while," she muttered as she snatched open the kitchen door.

But words failed her when her eyes fell upon a sight that no mother should ever have to see. Standing before the sink, with dishevelled hair and a face scratched from yesterday's slap, was Charlie, who stared up at Christine, wide-eyed, pale, and feeble with fatigue.

"What have you done, child?" she asked, hearing the fear in her own voice. The back door was wide open, and the dog barked at the pigeons that lined the outside wall.

"I'm in a lot of trouble."

CHAPTER TWENTY-ONE

The hospital was an hour's drive from the coast. They had spoken intermittently, and since their little altercation, Ben had become far more reserved, forcing Freya to either compose questions to drag some conversation out of him or choose to let her thoughts overwhelm her.

But that was the trouble. Her idle thoughts often took her to that forest, that cabin, and the unknown.

It was a place she dared not venture, and during those moments, she relied on Ben to keep her mind occupied.

He parked, and said nothing until he climbed from the car, where he leaned on the roof and waited for her to do the same.

"This isn't easy for me, you know?" he said.

"I don't recall saying that it was."

"If we're going to work together, I need to know who you are."

"Ah," she said, and turned to appraise the hospital car park. "You might not like what you hear."

"Try me."

"Here's where I am. I've been seconded to Lincolnshire, and I've been given a team I know nothing about and who, by all accounts, are all still grieving for my predecessor."

"Shall we leave David out of this?"

"My point is," she said, checking her watch, "in the few hours I've been working with you, you've insulted me, and my methods, and you've clearly made an assumption that I'm here to rock the boat. Which, I'm afraid to say, couldn't be further from the truth."

"Why come here?" he asked.

"I told you, there was a gap."

"That's bull and you know it."

"Well, again, I needed fresh air," she said. "Shall we walk while we talk? I'd like to at least have all the basics covered before the end of the day. Seeing the body being one of those basics."

He locked the car and they walked fast. He was two or three inches over six foot in height, and Freya found herself taking three strides for his every two.

"Have you ever worked away from Lincolnshire?" she asked.

"Never had the need to. I've spent some time at Lincoln HQ when resources were sparse."

"How did you find it?"

"Busy," he said. "Not unfriendly, but not like—"

"Anybody knew you?" she said, purposefully interrupting him.

"Yeah. It wasn't close, like—"

"Like the environment you're used to? That's fine. So, you felt alienated. Alone, perhaps?"

"It was different, that's all," he replied as he held the door for her, and they entered a long corridor in the hospital building. It wasn't the main entrance, but she trusted him to take them by the shortest route.

"Understand this, and this is by no means meant as a slant on this place, but working in the city, in London, you really are alone. You can trust everyone as far as your life is concerned, but your career? That's your lookout. I made DI by the skin of my teeth and had to fight for it. Hard. I was up against men who had more than double my experience, played golf with the senior officers, and who would happily have trodden on me to get me out of the picture. It's brutal, Ben. Performing is measured on a daily basis, and if you don't fit the template, you either rot or you sink. Nobody will remember your name."

"So why stay there?" he asked.

It was a good question, and one Freya had considered many times.

"Because of those reasons," she said. "Because I was surrounded by fighters. Because there was opportunity. Because of the buzz. If you don't work your backside off, you get nowhere. And when you do start getting somewhere, you cannot let off. You work harder. I loathed the people I worked with, and no doubt they loathed me. But we had a respect for each other. We all recognised how hard we worked."

"We work hard," he said, not defensively but to make a point.

"You wouldn't know hard work if it slapped you in the face," she said. "And I don't mean that to sound–"

"I know how it sounds," he snapped. He didn't need to be spoon-fed. It was fair; she had goaded him into it. "You came to Lincolnshire for a rest."

"Kind of," she agreed. "It's a slower pace. Simpler crimes."

"Simpler people?"

"I didn't say that."

"You didn't have to. We're not all simple, you know."

"Look at the team. There's no drive. There's no finesse. There's no class–"

"No class?" he said, and this time, he was insulted.

"There's no sense of class, because there's no need for it," she said. "It doesn't matter where you lunch because the best restaurants are all twenty miles away. It doesn't matter what you wear because staying warm is more important than wearing Jimmy Choos."

"Jimmy who?"

"Exactly. It doesn't matter," she said, as they approached a pair of double doors with a little buzzer to one side. Faintly, Freya heard a familiar tune coming from inside. "I'm here because none of those things matter. I'm here because there's no fight to get to the top, because it doesn't matter what you wear, because the pace is slower. It's not better or worse than where I'm from. It's just different. It's what I need. People don't wear some kind of facade here. I like that."

"Do you think you're better than us because you wear Jimmy shoes?"

"Choos," she corrected him. "And no. Not better. That's a surface thing. That type of thing matters in some parts of London, but not here. But what does matter, no matter where you are, to me, at least, is culture. Refinement. The finest things in life don't always have a price tag."

"You live in a motor home."

"For the time being," she agreed. "But don't you see? That's me shedding my image. But listen..." She held up a finger, savouring the perfect harmony of notes that emanated from the door.

"It's a piano," Ben said. "She always listens to music. It's her thing."

"This is class. This does not have a price tag. This, I cannot live without," she said, as they heard somebody on the far side of the doors. "This is Chopin, one of the greatest composers that ever lived, in my opinion. And it gives me hope."

The door opened, and a girl in her mid to late twenties filled the space. She had bright orange hair, piercings in her eyebrows, nose, and even her lower lip, and aside from the smock she was wearing, she wore a pair of bright red Crocs on her feet, with multi-coloured, fluffy socks beneath them.

"Help you?" she said in a thick Welsh accent. Then she

seemed to recognise Ben but was clearly disgruntled at being interrupted. "Well? Will you stand there letting the heat out or will you come in? Haven't got time to watch you stand there gawping at me now, have I?"

CHAPTER TWENTY-TWO

"Now then," Doctor Bell said. She gave Ben a smile, then appraised DI Bloom. And in that moment, when only moments before, Freya had been talking about refinement and class, Doctor Bell reached behind herself, pulled her underwear away from her backside, and sighed with relief as she let the elastic snap back into place. "Who do we have here then? New, are you? Taken you under his wing, has he?"

She turned back to Ben, leaving Freya slightly dumbstruck.

"Heard about David. Terrible thing. I suppose I'll have to get to know you a bit more, won't I?"

"I suppose you will," Ben replied.

"Are there any masks and gowns?" Freya asked, clearly keen to get on. "And where should I hang my coat?"

"You can hang your coat over there. Masks, gowns, and hats in the cupboard," she replied, pointing with a chubby, little, tattooed forefinger. Then she turned it toward the doors. "When you're done, I'll be through here."

Recalling Michaela's comment about how Doctor Bell was memorable, Ben suddenly understood. He'd only met her once or twice, and even then David had usually done most of the talking.

Chopin blasted out when the doors opened, then quietened as they closed with the soft hiss of the brushes that retained the cool air inside.

"How do you like her?" Ben asked. "Lincoln's finest."

"Not what I had in mind," Freya said, clearly a little bemused by Bell's unorthodox manners. She pulled on her gown, tying it around her noticeably slender waist. "But she has good taste in music, so she still has a chance yet."

Surprised at how the gown showed Freya's figure, he caught himself staring at her. But not before she too had caught him, although she said nothing of it, and pulled her mask on as she brushed past him.

"Let's try to focus, shall we?" she muttered.

He followed her through and found Bell standing beside one of six stainless steel benches.

"Here we are then," she called above the music, and laid her hands on the bench beside Jessica Hudson's body, which was covered in a blue sheet. "Haven't had long, so I'll just give you a rundown of where we're at. Toxicology will take a few days, but my guess is you don't want to wait that long. Right, am I?"

"A preliminary report will suffice for the time being," Freya said, which Ben guessed was mostly a guess at whether or not Bell had actually asked a question.

"Right," Bell said, and she studied Freya unabashed. "Not from round here, are you?"

"I'm sorry, I can't hear you. Do you think you could turn Chopin down a little?"

"Show who?" Bell replied.

"Chopin. Do you think you can turn it down?"

"Show pan? Do you mean the music?"

"Yes. I can hardly hear myself think."

"Hey Siri, turn it down, will you?" Bell called out, looking up as if she was talking to the gods. She waited for the music to drop to a more reasonable level, then smiled and praised the powers that be. "God bless Siri. Don't know what I'd do without him, I don't."

"Thank you," Freya said quietly.

"Not a fan of classical music, are you?" Bell said, and Freya appeared perplexed at the phrasing.

"I love classical music," she replied. "But I do enjoy being able to hear what's being said."

"I'm not a fan, if I'm honest. I just listen to it because it doesn't have any words," she explained, leaning forward to each of them in turn. "Stops me singing along, you see?"

"How about that preliminary report, Doctor Bell?" Ben said, seeing that she could clearly venture into a rabbit hole about the music she enjoyed.

"Ah, yes. Ms Hudson. Terrible thing."

"So she was murdered then?" Ben asked. "You can confirm that much?"

"Oh yes. Without a doubt," she said, and then pulled the sheet back to the girl's shoulders. Whipping a pen from her breast pocket, she pointed out the bruising on the side of the neck. "Fingers here, and thumbs here on her windpipe fracturing her hyoid."

"Her killer was on top of her?" Freya asked, and the doctor nodded. She pulled the sheet further down, exposing Jessica's chest, shoulder, and arm.

"The bruising here indicates she was knelt on. It would have been slow. A minute or two."

"A minute or two?" Ben said.

"It's not like the movies, DS Savage. This is real life. It would have been a terrifying experience."

"She was dressed..." Ben said, then paused, hoping that one of the two women would be able to pick up on where he was going and finish the sentence for him.

Neither did.

They stared at him, eyebrows raised, and silent.

"Was there..." he continued.

Again, they waited for him to finish the sentence.

"What I'm trying to ascertain, Doctor Bell, is whether or not her killer took advantage of her beforehand. Or afterwards, for that matter."

"Sex?" she said, matter of fact, as openly as if she had said the word *banana*.

"Well, yes."

"You want to know if the killer had sex with her?"

He rolled his eyes. "Yes."

"How would I know that?"

Seeming to enjoy the awkward position Ben found himself in, Freya folded her arms and, oddly, seemed to side with the pathologist, equally as keen to hear Ben dig himself a deep hole.

"Well, you're the pathologist. If anybody can tell, it's you."

"You're right. I'm a forensic pathologist. A physician. I study death. One thing I'm not, however," she said, her voice deepening as that authoritarian affliction rang out, "is a bloody mind reader. I might look like Mystic Meg, but I can assure you, I'm not."

"You don't look anything like—"

"Your question, DS Savage, was did the killer have sex with her, either before or after he killed her? Am I right?"

"That was my question, yes," Ben said, already tiring of the doctor, and people in general. In the past five hours, he had met, fallen out with, and possibly restored a working relationship with Freya Bloom, delivered the worst possible news to the parents of Jessica Hudson, been insulted and flashed at by Christine Barnes, and now he was being made to feel about two inches tall by Doctor Bell.

"No," she said finally.

"No?" he replied. "As in, no her killer did *not* have sex with her?"

"Neither before nor after he killed her."

"Right."

"Somebody did. But we don't know who, see?"

"What?"

"Sex, DS Savage. Sex." That word again; it seemed to echo around the sterile room.

"I think what Doctor Bell is trying to say," Freya added, "is that Jessica did in fact engage in sexual activities with somebody, but as yet we don't know if that somebody was the same somebody who was responsible for her death. Am I right, Doctor Bell?"

The doctor squinted, rocking her head from side to side as she played Freya's comment over in her mind; the rocking of her head formed an affirmative nod as she came to her conclusion. "Yes."

"Right," Ben said, exhaling long and loud. Then he replied with a single word of his own for her to ponder. "Fingernails."

"Fingernails?"

"Did she put up a fight or a struggle in any way?" Ben asked. "I presume you scraped her fingernails?"

"Of course I did," Doctor Bell replied.

"So?"

"So we'll know when we get the lab results back."

"Right. How long, please?"

"Two to three days. But I must say, Benjamin, you're a little twitchy today. Not how I remember you at all. Something on your mind?"

"No," he said, a little too snappy. "I'm fine. It's just been one of those days."

"He met me," Freya said, and it was clear the two women would be getting on just fine and that Ben would, from that moment, be the butt of their jokes. "I don't think he's used to being bossed around by a woman."

"Oh," Bell said. "So you're the boss?"

Freya nodded slowly.

"Oh, now I see." It was as if the doctor had just discovered the cure for some incurable disease. She pointed between them and let her mouth hang open revealing her pierced tongue. But she said nothing more, just nodded her head enthusiastically.

"My first day today," Freya added.

"Well, Benjamin," Bell began, and Ben sensed a mini-lecture coming on how he'd have to toe the line, "looks like you've got your work cut out, eh? A new boss to impress?" She turned to Freya. "How does he measure up? Is he the strong, silent type he looks like?"

"I am here," Ben announced, but they both ignored him.

"Well, if I'm honest, he's already made one sexist comment, groped my backside, and a few minutes ago, I caught him staring at my..." She cast her eyes down to her chest, then back to Bell.

"No?"

Freya nodded.

"More importantly," Ben said, seeing no way of defending himself in this particular battle, "we have a murder investigation on our hands, and as much as I'd love to stand around here, Doctor Bell, we really should be going."

"I don't suppose you could get those lab results on fast track could you, Doctor Bell?" Freya asked.

"Of course. I'll put a good word in for you. Lovely meeting you, it was," Bell replied, as she held out a hand for Freya to shake. "I didn't get your name. Too busy admiring you."

"Bloom," Freya said, clearly loving the feminine bond she had formed with the doctor. "DI Freya Bloom."

"There's a name I won't forget. As for you, big boy..." the doctor said, eyeing Ben up and down like he was a piece of meat. Freya was already halfway toward the doors, and after a quick check to make sure she was out of earshot, Bell tapped a forefinger against her temple. "Sex."

"What?"

"Sex. Get it off your mind. Focus. You're in there, but you can't let what's in your pants rule your head. Play it cool. If you find your eyes wandering, just think of me. Remember what I said."

Unable to think of anything else to say that wouldn't invoke another conversation, Ben simply shook his head. "Thank you, Doctor Bell. You've been a great help."

He ditched his gown, hat, and mask in a pedal bin, joined Freya in the corridor, and walked out of the hospital, surprised that the temperature was higher outside the building than inside.

"Happy now?" he asked. "At least you can go home knowing you made one friend today."

She didn't rise to his backhanded insult. Instead, she put her hands in her pockets and pulled her coat in tight around her. "Thank you, DS Savage," she said. "That was the most fun I've had since I arrived here."

———

Settling into a seat in the incident room, Ben paid close attention to Freya's expressions as she prepared to brief the team. Feeling somebody looking at him, Ben glanced up to find Jackie offering a sympathetic stare. It was either sympathy or disappointment. Ben was unsure which, and the sound of Freya's voice took priority.

"Jessica Hudson was found dead at a beach in Anderby this morning," Freya began. Watching her from his seat at the end of the little semicircle, Ben had to admire her confidence. Clearly, this was not the first time she had stood in front of a group of relative strangers to give a briefing. Her pig-headed nature, however, was far from admirable. If the two were to get along, each of them would have to put some work in. "The pathology report indicates that it is highly likely that Jessica Hudson was strangled to death. Chapman, what does this tell you?"

"Me?" Chapman said, wide-eyed.

"You're Chapman, aren't you?"

"Intimacy," said Chapman. "I've read about this. Either the

killer knew her, or..." She paused, clearly trying to recall what she had read.

"Or what?"

"Or they knew nobody. A loner. The close proximity of strangulation gives the killer a chance to be intimate for a brief period, but then return to the safety of their seclusion. They would be introverted, socially awkward, perhaps as a result of a perceived deformity."

"Extremely good," said Freya, genuine in delivering her praise. "So, where does that leave us?"

"You're looking for a socially awkward individual with size eleven boots?" DI Standing called out from the far end of the room, and all eyes turned on him. "He's sitting right in front of you. Goes by the name of Ben Savage."

A few of his team laughed, including the youngest and smallest, DC Gabriel Cruz, who then reddened and turned away when Will Granger cleared his throat and glared at them all.

"DI Standing, I presume I'll have your report by the end of the day."

"Report, guv?" he replied.

"Yes, you know, the report on your team's performance. How long they spend sitting on their backsides and how many investigations they've actually closed that have resulted in a successful prosecution."

"You haven't asked for a report, guv," Standing replied, and he looked to each of his team in turn, as if they might have failed to pass on a message. But then he fell in with what Granger was saying.

"Oh dear," Granger said, in a mock sympathetic tone. Then he hardened. "My desk. By close of play tonight."

Granger stepped back out of view, content he had dealt with any further interruptions, and Standing, now out of Granger's sight, tossed his pen at Cruz in anger.

"What?" Cruz said defensively. "It weren't just me."

"Ben?" Freya said, inviting him to answer her earlier question.

"One step forward, two steps back," said Ben. "We now have two lines of enquiry. Those who knew and loved her, and given the tourist nature of Anderby, those who might be simply passing through."

"Agreed. Chapman, task number one for you. Contact every hotel, bed and breakfast, and caravan site, and cross-check the names of every guest with police records. It's off-season so it shouldn't be too hard. Start with males anywhere between twenty-five and forty-five first."

"Why is that, ma'am?" she asked. "Why that age group? And why not include women as well?"

"CSI found a size eleven boot print at the scene. By all means, check women and anybody that falls outside of our target IC, but if you start there, you'll get results faster."

"Ma'am," Chapman confirmed, scribbling notes in her notebook.

"We also need mobile phone records checked of every individual we speak to."

"I can do that," Chapman said, raising the end of her pen, as if she was still at school. "I have a contact at Lincoln HQ. It won't take me long."

"Good, thank you for volunteering," said Freya, and she stared at the rest of the group, which comprised of DC Jackie Gold, Sergeant Priest, and Ben, although Will observed from a distance. Seemingly happy that all eyes were on her, Freya continued, "Right then, let's pull this together."

Turning her back on the team, she pulled the lid from a whiteboard marker and wrote the names of the mother, aunt, uncle, and cousin, Beth. "Family," she said, then moved on without stopping.

Below Jessica's name, Freya drew another branch and wrote a single name.

"The Barnes family?" Jackie Gold asked. "Not Derek Barnes, surely? How is he involved?"

"Are you familiar with the Barnes family?" asked Freya, turning her head to peer at Jackie over her shoulder.

"I think everyone in this room has had some kind of dealing with the Barnes family, if you don't mind me saying, ma'am. They're just one of those families that attracts trouble."

"I only know the father Derek," Ben added. "He has a history of petty crime. Jackie, wasn't it you who led the drug dealing investigation against him?"

"Not that it did much good," she replied.

"Why?" Freya asked.

"He got away with it, ma'am. CPS said we didn't have enough to go on. We had to let him go, much to the annoyance of the town."

"It's funny you mention that," Chapman said, snapping her laptop closed. "I ran a search for Jessica Hudson's father on the database."

"Her dad? Why?" Freya asked. "I didn't ask you to do that."

"I thought you might, so I wanted to be ready," she said. "I found it immediately. Which led me to wonder why we had his DNA on file in the first place. It turns out he was accused of sexual assault a few months ago."

"Go on," said Ben, keen to find out if Chapman's research lined up with what he and Freya had learnt.

"More interestingly, the person who reported it was Derek Barnes," she said. For a timid, young officer, Chapman seemed to thrive in her research, retelling the accounts with deliberation. "So, I did some more digging. Have a guess who reported the drug dealing offence we nicked Barnes for?"

"Timothy Hudson," said Freya, offering Ben a sideways glance. "So we do indeed have a grievance. We need Derek Barnes checked out. Jackie, you might just get your chance at him again."

"She did nail his son," Ben said, hoping to remind Jackie of her success with one of the Barnes family.

Nodding, Jackie blushed. "TDA."

"Taking and driving away. That won't be his last offence. Mark my words," Priest added. "He'll be back at it when he's out. The only one who's got any sense is the eldest. The one who joined the army."

"When we spoke to Beth Fraser, Jessica's cousin, she mentioned Charlie Barnes. She said that Jessica had new friends, and that Beth had been left out of the group but didn't know why."

"Charlie?" said Jackie, pulling a face. "I don't know him. He must be one of the younger ones entering the family business. They've got about six kids."

"We need that like a hole in the head, another Barnes to watch out for," said Priest.

While Jackie and Priest verbalised their opinions of the Barnes family, Freya removed the lid of a red pen and drew a vertical line through the entire board, including Jessica's name. Turning, she waited for the gossip to fade.

"On this side of the board, we have close family, friends, and acquaintances." She tapped the board with the end of the pen, and then moved to the blank side. "On this side of the board, Chapman is going to write the names of the individuals she finds in her research."

"Ma'am," Chapman said, not in the slightest bit fazed by what Ben knew to be a monumental task.

Using the end of the pen, Freya tapped on the names of Jessica's parents, aunts, and uncles. "Gold?"

"Ma'am?"

"Jessica's family all have alibis. DS Savage has the details. I want every alibi confirmed and I want you to do some digging on them all. See if you find anything interesting. We know that the father had a grievance with Derek Barnes. See what else you can find. We need the full story."

"Yes, ma'am."

"In the meantime, Sergeant Priest, can we have uniform on the lookout for Charlie Barnes? I'm sure he's around somewhere, and I'm sure he has something to say."

"Do we have a description, ma'am?"

She glanced in Ben's direction, and he shrugged. "I didn't even know he existed until this morning."

"Gold," Freya said, making a decision on the fly, "check the local schools, and check the births, deaths, and marriages registers. Inform Sergeant Priest when you have a description for him to go on."

"No problem," replied Jackie.

"In the meantime, Michael, if you can find anything on him, do let us know."

"Will do, ma'am," he replied, his dulcet tones and thick Yorkshire accent providing the cello-like bass to a quartet of tenors and baritones. "The Barnes family is well-known though, like Jackie said. I can't say I know a Charlie. Been a while, mind, since I had the pleasure of dealing with them. Since Jason was put away, at any rate. But we'll find him."

"Thank you, Michael."

A silence fell over the room, just as the sun had slipped behind the horizon. The long nights and short days of winter were always the most challenging, offering just seven daylight hours in which to operate effectively.

"We'll meet tomorrow at the same time. By that point, I'd like to be in a position to focus our attention on just one or two of these names. Let's get these alibis checked out and we'll start closing in. That's it for today."

"Hold on, hold on," said Will, who until now had been a silent bystander. "I'm not convinced this is the right approach."

Of all the people Freya thought might have made life difficult for her, she knew it would be Granger. He was far too chummy with Ben and, by implication, protective of him. He clearly had his eye on Harper's position, and given Harper's age, it was his for the taking. All he had to do was bide his time.

"Walk me through the Hudsons' stories," he said. He had been engaged from the start, a silent spectator. It was almost as if he had been looking for a weakness in Freya's delivery. "You said they had alibis. Give me an objective overview."

"Mrs Hudson dropped her daughter off in town at three p.m. to catch a bus to Skegness and then the five-thirty train."

"To where?"

"She was heading to London to stay with her sister. Timothy Hudson didn't approve. Said she should be dropped at the train station. Her father seemed out of the loop. Kind of kept at arm's length. Mrs Hudson had an early night. She watched Netflix in bed while her husband worked late in his home office."

Nodding, Granger glanced at Jackie. "Get a report on when the Netflix account was accessed," he said, then turned to Freya. "And circle the father's name. We need a means to understanding if Timothy Hudson left the family home that evening."

"I could try the 4G service, sir," Chapman said. "If he used his phone, we may get something from the mobile towers."

"Good," said Freya, regaining control of what was essentially her briefing. She wasn't about to let a man take her investigation from her, especially one that hadn't left the station all day. "Chapman, work with Gold on that, will you?"

"What about the aunts and uncles?" said Granger. "You mentioned some other family."

"Jessica's best friend was Beth Fraser. She's also her cousin. Beth's mum is Patricia Hudson's sister," Freya said, drawing a link between them on the board. "As I understand it, they all lived in

Anderby at one point. The girls grew up to be close. But Timothy Hudson's business, for one reason or another, took off. The Hudsons moved into Chapel."

"And that's why Jessica had a group of new friends?"

"Precisely, sir. I imagine Beth felt quite left out."

"And where was young Beth last night?"

"At home. With her parents. Hetty Fraser, the mother, made it quite clear they were all at home."

"But you don't believe her?" Granger added.

"There was something off, guv," said Ben, speaking up from the end of the little semicircle. "I don't know about you, Freya, but I had the feeling the parents weren't entirely forthcoming."

"Agreed," said Freya, and she only had to glance in Chapman's direction for the detective constable to pick up on the cue.

"Jackie and I will add them to the list. We'll get the PUC codes from the mobile providers and see if our contact in Lincoln HQ can hook us up with the 4G network. As long as the phones were actually used, any changes in proximity or location can be identified."

"While you're at it, have Derek Barnes' phone looked into. We might as well build a picture of them all while we're talking to the 4G provider," said Freya.

"Ma'am," Chapman said. "What about Jessica's phone? Do we have her number? We might be able to find it if it gets turned on."

"She didn't have a phone," Ben said. "Wasn't allowed one. Didn't need one. Was too young for one. Her father's words, not mine."

"Brutal," said Jackie. "Poor kid."

"I agree with DCI Granger," said Freya. "Let's prioritise these phones. It might be the quickest way to see who was where, to confirm these stories."

"Will do, ma'am," said Chapman, and she peered at Gold who nodded, the two of them apparently quite happy to be working together.

"That leaves one more item to be put on the board," said Freya, turning to create a new branch from Jessica's name. With the whiteboard marker poised to write, she waited for somebody to call out. It was a little test to see who, if anyone, was switched on.

"Piper," said Ben, and Freya smiled inwardly.

"Piper, indeed."

Writing the dog's name, she turned back to the team.

"I contacted every veterinary clinic in the district, ma'am," said Gold. "There are a few Pipers, but none are golden retrievers."

"Anything close?"

Referring to her notes, Jackie flipped a page or two in her notebook. "A collie, a beagle, and a Weimaraner. Nothing that even resembles a goldie."

"Right, tomorrow, we need to find that dog. That's an open end."

"Yes, ma'am."

"Good, thank you. DCI Granger, how does this approach work for you?"

"The phones are our best bet."

"Agreed," she said, then moved on before he had an opportunity to dwell on the matter. "Right. We all have jobs to do. Gold, Chapman, strike through the names as you get confirmation of their whereabouts and make a list of any tourists of interest. Tomorrow is going to be a busy day," said Freya, and she stared at them all individually to look each of them in the eye. After lingering for longer than expected on Granger's scrutinous gaze, she finished, "Bring your A-game. One or more of these people isn't being honest."

CHAPTER TWENTY-THREE

The house was cold when Ben returned home. Closing the front door silenced the wind and the hallway lights lit the empty space, but a chill hung in the air like he shared the space with the dead.

It wasn't a soulless place, not by a long shot. But it was moments like this, when, in the dead of winter, Ben noticed more than usual the lack of children's feet and voices. In contrast to the hum of activity in the station, the house was, at times, like a crypt.

His was one of three houses that formed a U-shape around a central courtyard. His father, like many other Savages before him, lived in the centre house, the family home. The third house, directly opposite Ben's, belonged to his brothers, who had followed in their father's footsteps stumbling blindly to an uncertain future in farming.

Fearful that he might be outcast when he delivered the news that he had been accepted into the police force, Ben had waited patiently for his father to be in the right mood, and for his brothers to be elsewhere. As the eldest son, it was tradition that he should don his overalls and take on more of the farm. But farming wasn't what it used to be. Supermarkets created pricing wars and had driven down the revenue, despite his father owning most of the land as far as the eye could see. The result was that Ben's father had actually welcomed his decision to join the force. The future of farming was uncertain. The family needed to diversify; it needed an alternate source of income. And if Ben was totally honest with himself, the family name needed dragging out of the mud.

The gift, for his twenty-first birthday, had been the house, although Ben didn't actually own it. The farm owned the house, so it was in Ben's interest to help where he could. It had been a smart move of his father's to do so, and Ben had never once argued against it. Instead, during harvest, he would stand alongside his brothers in the long evenings and bring in labour as and when it was needed. It was work he enjoyed, and perhaps in another life, the Savage heritage would have continued. But after a decade in the force, Ben Savage the third was a policeman through and through.

The lack of children's voices and toys on the living room floor was perhaps an early indication that a new line of Savages, a line that might develop a constabulary tradition, might not be forthcoming.

A pack of cold ham and a block of cheese was all that greeted Ben inside the fridge. The freezer offered an equally uninspiring menu. With a three-mile drive to the shop, Ben considered his options. Never one to be without meat and produce, his father's pantry would be stocked well. But independence was independence. In his father's own words, it was not a selective state of mind.

Leaning on the kitchen counter, Ben stared through the window into the garden. A row of hawthorn and ash trees both formed the half-acre garden border and acted as a defence against the fierce, south-easterly, prevailing winds that tore across the open fens. Ben's little pocket of peace and quiet was a sanctuary in the midst of wild nature, which, in the moonlight at least, appeared calm. It had been Ben who had made his father aware of the scheme where landowners surrendered space for wildflowers to grow naturally in return for government funds. The funds were minimal, but when collated with other environmental schemes, such as the ponds and orchards, the pay-outs that landed every three years added up to a nice sum. The advantage was that the dead space that was deemed inefficient to farm, as well as the strip of land surrounding the three houses, was alive with nature. Entire ecosystems had developed in those spaces.

Often, Ben wondered if the look of the property would be to the taste of the three Savage men that had first cultivated the land in the early 1800s. Rumour had it that the father, a convicted livestock thief, who would have been Ben's great grandfather three times over, along with his two boys, had invested the remains of some funds of doubtful origin into the original plot. Over the years, through callous and less-than-moral means, they had increased the plot, encroaching on the surrounding farms and, by crook or foul play, had grown their wealth year on year. Two centuries had passed since those days of unscrupulous means, but to some of the locals, the Savage name still invoked them to hack and spit into the fertile soil.

Each time he considered those three Savage men, and what they might think of the wildflowers, natural ponds, and orchards, he could only see them smiling to themselves, deeming the effort a pitiful waste of time and energy.

It had fallen to Ben to educate his father, to whom every inch of soil bore an associated pound sign, that allowing nature to claw back some space, for the wildlife to breathe, was of value to all of their futures, which had been more than a challenge. But over time, by developing those inefficient spaces, by digging ponds in the flood spots besides the overflowing dykes, and by establishing fruit trees alongside existing forestry, they could diversify so that, should a crop fail, as is the luck of the farmer, they would have some source of income.

He saw the same challenge with Will and Arthur, with Freya as a metaphor for the wildflowers, insects, and fruit. For her to succeed, and for the stability of the team, a new means of existence had to be developed in David's wake. It wasn't diversification exactly, not as Ben understood it, but the analogy worked. But there was something he needed to know. For him to educate his seniors, much as he had educated his father, he would have to understand exactly what DI Freya Bloom was all about.

Behind the kitchen door was a small pantry. With a modern fridge taking pride of place in the kitchen, Ben rarely used the pantry for anything other than over-sized items. Often, this was in the form of alcohol. As uncultured as Ben was, he knew a good wine by the label. He selected a two-year-old red with a picture of a sailing boat on the label and a screw-top lid, and dropped it into his deep inside pocket. Then, closing the front door behind him, he walked to his car.

The keys were kept in the ignition where he had left them, so he started the engine, strapped in, and smiled to himself as he planned the route in his head. It was pitch black in the dead of winter, a balmy one degree Celsius outside, and he was heading for the beach to begin another journey of diversification. To understand the woman who, by his own admission and that little schoolboy grip that warmed his loins, had fascinated him for the past twelve hours.

———

The beach, in all its wild glory, offered little protection from the wind. The old motor home rocked on its springs, making pouring a drink perilous and cooking on the little gas stove out of the question. With winds so loud Freya could barely hear herself think, and nothing to entertain her mind save for memories of a time she would rather forget, the space between the memories seemed to grow larger.

But still, she savoured every moment of that time to herself. Her newfound freedom was never going to be an easy ride, and every challenge she came across was met with her tenacity. The challenge she faced now was understanding what the bloody hell she was doing there.

It was while she was pondering her decision that a pair of headlights, the only form of light in the two-mile stretch of visible beach, pulled into the beachside car park and stopped a hundred feet away.

Instinctively, she killed the little lamp, and from the cabin bed above the driver's seat, she withdrew a child-sized cricket bat. It was of hard enough wood to put even a large man on his backside yet small enough to manoeuvre within the confines of the camper. Even so, fumbling for her jacket, she slipped from the door, locked it, and then crept to the back of the vehicle to watch. As safe as Lincolnshire was, being inside the motor home offered little means of escape. And besides, she thought, a young girl had been murdered just a kilometre up the beach less than forty-eight hours earlier.

Detective or no detective, Freya Bloom would never willingly put herself into a situation with no means of escape again.

A man emerged from the darkness. Lincolnshire, with its sparse population, was perhaps one of the darkest areas Freya had ever stayed, even darker than Cornwall and Devon had been, although she couldn't be sure. But it was dark. A pale moon loitered behind a bank of silver clouds, so that it appeared as a great torch in the densest of fogs, casting light enough only for Freya to identify the outline of the figure as he approached the motor home. She stepped backwards into the darkness as he grew closer, walking casually, as one might saunter along the aisle of a supermarket. Reaching the dark shadows of the sandbank, Freya stopped, crouched, and watched the man's every move.

Performing a complete circle of the motor home, knocking once, and then trying the door, which thankfully, Freya had locked on her exit, he then peered in through the near side window, striving to see along the length of the camper.

That was when Freya decided that being a victim was not part of the new self she was trying to create. Her new start would not involve living in fear. Confident that the man was alone, she made her move, creeping up to the van and working her way around to the front.

With his face pressed up against the glass, the man didn't see her, and with the howling wind covering her steps, she was able to get within a swing of the cricket bat before she announced her presence.

"Looking for something?" she said. In her mind, the pervert would turn to look at her, surprised and horrified to be caught, leaving her enough time to deliver a blow and cuff him. She swung the bat at him.

But things had a habit of playing out differently to how she expected them to. On hearing her, he instinctively ducked as the bat hit the side of her camper, and he jumped back out of reach.

"Freya," he said, and for a moment, she couldn't place the voice. It was familiar, but the circumstance, the darkness, and the disorienting wind masked his identity. "I was just–"

Misguided and misjudged, the second swing hit the side of the motor home with another great bang, and the man scrambled away to safety by the rear wheel.

"Freya, it's me, you lunatic."

She stopped, the bat poised ready to defend herself.

"Ben?"

"Who else would it bloody be?"

"What are you doing here?"

"I bought you a present. I thought you might like some company."

"You were staring through my window."

"I was looking for you. I knocked but you didn't answer."

"I could have caved your head in."

"I know you bloody could. I was just trying to be nice."

It took a few seconds for her to process what he said. Then she lowered the bat.

"I'm not used to that," she called out above the wind. "I'm sorry, I just..."

"It's okay," he replied, opening his jacket and reaching into his pocket. He pulled out a bottle and edged closer, handing it to her. "I didn't mean to scare you."

"Why?" she asked. "Why, after how I treated you?"

He responded with a smile as natural as the wind and the sea and the sand. "I thought you might like some company."

———

"I see you started without me," he said, as he followed her into the motor home. Too busy glancing around to make sure her smalls were not lying about, Freya had passed her glass of red wine that she had left on the little fold-out table.

"It's okay. It's the end of the bottle. I'm ready for something new."

"Is that right?" he said, and he raised the glass to his nose. "Smells nice."

Without being judgemental, she assumed his palette to be of limited experience. The phrase 'smells nice' confirmed her thoughts.

"It's a Chianti," she said, waiting to read his expression.

His expression did not falter, thereby confirming her thoughts.

"Mine is a little sailing boat," he said, holding the screw-lid bottle up. "Where do you keep the glasses? In here?"

He reached across to open a small cupboard above the sink where a few cans of food were stored, just as Freya leaned over to the cupboard beside him. They froze, intimately close yet equally awkward.

"Apologies," he said and, being the gentleman that he was, backed up against the door.

"It's nice with a family in here," she offered, forcing a smile. "But it is a little tight with guests."

"Seems cosy to me," he replied, as she checked the wine glass and gave it a wipe with a clean towel.

Handing him the glass along with a bottle opener, she held his gaze. "You didn't come here because I'm alone, did you?"

"You got me. I drove all the way out here because I was too warm in my house."

"Well, don't let my hospitality keep you."

"Have you always been this bitter?"

"You're insensitive," she replied, and felt her throat dry at the sight of him.

Ignoring the offer of a bottle opener and unscrewing the lid, Ben poured himself a drink, and then nodded at her appraisal, a childish smile curling the ends of his mouth.

"So we both have our flaws," she said.

"And we both have our secrets."

"Indeed," she replied, watching a sheen of moisture spread over his eye.

"I'll drink to that," said Ben, and he raised his glass toward hers.

Holding his stare, she raised her glass, then took a polite sip before their glasses could connect.

"One doesn't clink glasses," she said, hearing her own middle-class father in her tone. It was a tone she despised. In an effort to recover, she moved away, and set her glass down on the table again, while she pulled the blanket over the bed as a distraction. "It's poor etiquette. Did you know that?"

Turning to face him, she found him looking bemused yet quite clearly amused.

"I'm just a country boy," he said, and unbuttoned his coat with his free hand. "Remember?"

"It doesn't matter where we're from. What matters is that we know how to engage with our peers," she said, then fluffed her pillows, setting them down in an effort to at least make a show of trying to be tidy. "At least, that's what my head mistress taught us. One must always demonstrate an understanding of one's environment."

"When in Rome?"

"Something like that," she said, surprised he was even listening.

"Let me tell you something–"

"If I refuse, will you tell me anyway?"

"Probably."

"Well, go on then. Educate me."

Collecting her glass from the table, he moved toward her. He seemed to fill the narrow corridor and the glass looked insignificant in his huge hand as he passed it to her, which she accepted.

"Around here. We always clink glasses. One must always demonstrate an understanding of one's environment."

"I'll educate you yet, DS Savage," she said, using his formal title in a playful manner as a means to re-establish the boundaries. "I intend to bring a little culture to the station."

"Culture is fine, if that's your thing," he said. "But round here, we know what we like, and we like what we know."

He clinked her glass while she was lost in his eyes.

"To being alone," he said.

CHAPTER TWENTY-FOUR

"Do you still claim that Jessica died without a fight?" she asked, and Ben sensed the distraction.

That moment of electricity between them had passed, and in its wake was a void, a chasm that Ben could not cross. Instead, he found himself blocking her escape, as a predator might trap its prey. Her distraction had worked. Talking of Jessica being attacked was akin to throwing a bucket of cold water over a horny dog. As such, he turned and moved back to the spot behind the driver's seat. A safe place, out of the way, offering Freya a clear path to the door.

"You didn't come here to talk to me about the case either, did you?" she asked.

"Not really," he said.

Her probing question unsettled him. Perhaps it was the way she seemed to stare through his skin, reaching all the corners of his mind he preferred to keep hidden away.

"You came to investigate *me*. Tell me, Ben, are you trying to gain my trust, to know more about me and my past?"

"I came because you need a friend."

"And who said I need a friend?"

"Why do you always do this? Why do you always turn things on their head and make assumptions about my motives?" he said, and for a fleeting moment, a flicker of doubt passed over her eyes. Fleeting as it had been, he'd seen it, and like the loose edge of flaking paint, he caught his nail beneath it. "Do you want to know what happened?"

"I suppose you'll tell me regardless."

"I got home tonight, opened my uninspiring fridge door, peered into my empty living room, and stared out at my empty garden. It's not often I do that. It's not often I consider my own circumstances. I'm a happy bloke. Yes, I'm single. I don't have a family, but that doesn't bother me. If it happens one day, then great. But tonight, and I don't know why, tonight I got home and I thought of you. I thought of you being alone out here."

"How did you know I was here?"

"You told me at the crime scene. You said you were camped further down the beach." His response seemed to appease her, but the question had been yet another of her distractions. Which meant his speech had hit home. She was reacting. "So I picked a bottle from the pantry–"

"A fine choice. Little sailing boat, wasn't it?"

"And I came to be a friend. Nobody knows you. Will Granger doesn't know you. Arthur doesn't know you, and even if you do come with high recommendations, he won't trust you yet. I'm all you've bloody well got, so when I'm being nice, accept it. Maybe you could even try to show a little gratitude as well. We're not all trying to get into your head, Freya, and believe me, if I was to dig for answers, the first thing I'd ask is why the hell you're living in a motor home in the middle of winter. The second thing I'd ask is if you're okay. So stop pushing me away."

While he had been talking, he had heard his tone rising in pitch, so that what might have been construed as a motivational speech had morphed into more of a defensive rant. But he had found a flow, and now there were no more words that could convey what he felt, thought, or cared for.

"There's those emotions again," she said, yet her face belied the conviction with which she spoke.

Downing the remainder of his drink, he set the glass down on the little stainless steel draining board and turned to the door, where he stopped, and glanced her way once more.

"Don't say I didn't try to help. I'll see you tomorrow."

Opening the side door of the motor home to be greeted by a fierce gust of wind felt like he had opened a stage door to a death metal concert. It was a sensory overload. Blinded by the dark night yet deafened by the incessant wind, he stepped down to the ground, closing the door behind him.

This time, he did not peer through the window and he did not saunter across the car park with all the time in the world. Instead, he took long strides, getting away from her poisonous tongue as fast as he could. But there was a magnetism about her. He was sure he had felt it. They had been close. Close enough that should she have tilted her head back and closed her eyes he would have kissed her.

That hungry schoolboy charm swelled at the thought of her.

Embittered by the conflicting thoughts, his emotions settled on anger, as they always did in times of confusion, or denial, or whatever it was. How could he even try to understand her when he didn't understand himself?

The car was unlocked. It wasn't worth stealing anyway. The door creaked open, and he had one foot in when he thought he heard something. He glanced back at the motor home, only to find it still. The lights were on inside, and he could see no movement. Starting the engine, he flicked the heater on to full. He could suffer a few minutes of a cold blast before the heat came. Reverse was always a tricky gear to find. Double-pumping the clutch, he winced at the sound of the old gearbox, and then sighed as he found the gear.

He reversed from the spot, using his mirror for one last glance at the motor home, where it glowed in the darkness like a single flame burning in hell. He flicked on the headlights and was about to floor the accelerator when he stopped. There, in the middle of the empty access road, was Freya Bloom, blocking his way.

Lowering the window, he reduced the intensity of the blower to hear what she had to say as she sidled up beside his Ford.

Staring down at him, she wrapped her long, woollen coat around her, holding the collars together at her neck, as a child might, or as a mother might when she received the news every mother dreads. Even in the pale moonlight, her eyes shone with tears that had either been and gone, or were yet to come.

"I didn't want to be found," she began. "That's why I brought the camper. Something terrible happened to me that I don't remember, and what I do remember, I'm ashamed of."

Ben said nothing. He swallowed, slightly ashamed of his actions.

"But more importantly," she continued, "you're right. I do need a friend."

CHAPTER TWENTY-FIVE

"They call it dissociative amnesia," she heard herself say, as if she was a third person in the small motor home, voyeuristic and helpless to stop. "Personally, I call it denial."

He poured the wine from the little sailing boat bottle, and right then, Freya couldn't have cared less if it were a cheap Merlot from the bargain bin of a corner shop or a 1787 Chateau Lafitte from the cellar of the Mandarin Oriental, Paris.

"What *do* you know?" he asked, his voice soft, and that subtle Lincolnshire accent of his was alluring. Of all the British accents, Freya enjoyed the rhythm of the Midlands. Her own middle-class accent was flat. She couldn't even claim the personality of the east and south London dialects. She was well-spoken, but even she tired of hearing her voice. Every T, S, and P was pronounced well, every syllable articulated and delivered with equal clarity. But still, it was bland. Flavourless like a shrink-wrapped supermarket steak and as dull as old boots. The Lincolnshire accent, however, was that same supermarket steak, but it had been seasoned and grilled at just the right heat for just the right amount of time, so that one might savour every morsel.

"I know that the Freya Bloom who started that journey is not the woman who sits before you," she said, and gazed at him. There was an honesty about Ben. Not a naivety, no; she wouldn't respect that. An honesty. A carefree manner that stirred her own truth enough to raise its weary head, restless from its dormancy. A hatchling. "I know that whatever happened to her was the beginning of the end. This new girl, the Freya you see, is not nice. I drive people away, you see. I'm not sure why. I know I do it. I see it. I hear myself. I even tell myself to stop, but I'm not terribly convincing, even to myself. You might as well know that I drove my husband so far away that he sought the arms of another lover. Somebody warm, perhaps. Somebody who knows how to treat a man with neglected needs. In contrast to an old has-been, who would sooner curl beneath a blanket on the floor than share a bed with a man again. Who baulks at the idea of just being held, let alone feel a warm, hard erection being pressed against her. Do you understand, Ben? Do you see who I really am?"

"I don't see that," he said, sipping at his wine. "I see a woman who has been through the seven layers of hell, been stripped of all the things she once held dear, and is fighting for a new life. Born again, like a phoenix."

"A phoenix?"

"So the phoenix signifies, fresh in the fold, the might of the God-child, when he rises once more from the ashes into the life of lives, equipped with his limbs."

"What's that?"

"It's a line from a poem I read once. It's ancient."

"You read it once and can recite it?"

"Only that line, and I've read it a few times. It resonates with me somehow. I hadn't thought about it for years until today. You're not a bad person, Freya. You're on to a fresh start. Rising from the ashes, as it were."

"You've only just met me."

"I'm a good judge of character. I have to be."

"Why are you being nice? As I understand it, you were all set for a promotion, then I came along and accused you of touching me up and peeping through my window."

"You're certainly not dull, I'll give you that. You know full well I didn't mean to touch you, and you know that I wasn't looking through your window for a cheap thrill. I was looking for you. You were simply looking for a crack to exploit. It's a defence mechanism, isn't it?"

"I'll tell you what. You stop making assumptions about me, and I'll stop analysing you. How does that sound?"

"The station needs someone like you, Freya," he said, nodding his agreement. "The team needs a leader. Someone to challenge Will and Arthur. I think there's a place for us both."

"I can challenge them alright."

"But you're going to need someone to help you convince them you're a good fit."

"And that person is you, is it?" she asked.

"As it happens, it is. But I need to know why you're here. No lies."

She lay back on the bed and stared at the ceiling, aware of him watching her from the far end of the camper. She closed her eyes, and for a moment, she glimpsed something. Her past. A piece of her memory that was missing.

"Freya," he said, softly.

"I'll tell you," she whispered. "When I know what happened myself."

CHAPTER TWENTY-SIX

"My name is Detective Sergeant Savage," Ben called into the speaker phone, as he leaned forward in his seat. It was seven a.m., and as usual, he was the first of his team in. "I work for the East Midlands Special Operations Unit, and I'd like to speak to somebody who can verify a passenger."

"The police?" the woman asked.

"Yes, the police," Ben said.

The woman who had answered the phone seemed to hesitate.

"Is there a problem?" Ben asked.

"Sorry, I was erm... Well, I was wondering if this was a scam or something."

"A scam?" Ben said, exasperated. "It's seven o'clock in the morning. I'm investigating a serious crime, and I need to know if somebody was actually on a flight from your airport."

"Right, yeah. Sorry. You never know though. They ask all sorts these days, don't they? Had one tell me my national insurance number was going to be cancelled unless I paid a fine the other week. I mean, you can't even cancel a national insurance number, can you?"

"No, you're right to be cautious. If it makes you feel better, you can call me back. Just go to the East Midlands Special Operations Unit website, ask to speak to Detective Sergeant Ben Savage, and you'll be put through to me."

"Right," she said, clearly not the sharpest tool in the box. "And what is it you need?"

"I'm looking for a passenger that supposedly came through your airport three days ago. He would have gone through the heliport. Domestic flight to an off-shore rig. I don't know which one. Are you actually able to help me with this, or should I be speaking to somebody else?"

The incident room door opened behind Ben, squealing loudly, and then slammed closed.

"Alright, Ben," a familiar voice said in a heavy Glaswegian accent. "Where is everyone?"

Checking his watch, Ben noted that Gillespie usually arrived ten minutes after everybody else. He reached forward and hit mute on the phone.

"It's seven a.m., Jim. You're over an hour early."

"Aye, Steve put the fear of God into us last night. That report he had to do highlighted a few discrepancies in the team. And if someone has to go, I'm going to make damn sure it isn't me."

"Hello?" the woman said on the line. "Are you still there?"

"I'll leave you to it," Gillespie said. "I'll open a few files and whatnot."

Ben nodded to him, unmuting the call.

"Hi, yes, still here. So what do you want to do? Do you want to be routed through to me?" Ben said, watching Gillespie work his way through the desks to the far end of the room.

"It's just a passenger check you want, is it?" the woman asked.

"That's right. Just a passenger check. That's all I need."

"You want a coffee, Ben?" Gillespie asked, winding his way back through the desks. He had removed his jacket and Ben noted his untucked shirt and that his tie was just hanging around his collar, yet to be tied.

"And can I take the name please?" the woman asked.

"Derek Barnes," Ben said, giving Gillespie the thumbs up, and the door squealed open and slammed shut.

"And you said two nights ago. Is that right?"

"No, three nights ago. Not last night or the night before. The night before that. Three nights."

"And the passenger's name was Derek Barnes?" she asked, as the door squealed open again.

"You want sugar, Ben?" Gillespie asked.

"Yes," he said, to both, then held a single finger up to indicate one sugar.

"And is this the right number to call you on?" the woman asked, then read Ben's number out loud.

"Yes. This is my desk phone."

"Right. The boss said it's fine to share those details with you. I'll check our records and call you back. Is there anything else I can help you with today?"

"Not for the time being. I just need confirmation that Derek Barnes flew from Humberside Airport three nights ago," Ben said. "And I appreciate your help."

"No problem at all," she replied. "Enjoy your day."

Ben hit the button to end the call. "Enjoy my day?" He groaned and rested his head in his hands as the door squealed open yet again.

"Here we go, Ben," Gillespie said, placing a cup on Ben's desk and inadvertently spilling a little. "What's up? You seem a little stressed."

"Honestly?" he replied. "I don't know. Do you know when you speak to someone and you can just hear it in their voice that they don't get what you're saying? Like they're thick."

"Aye, all the time. You should try working with DC Cruz. I have no idea how he made the team. He can barely tie his shoelaces. Is this the dead girl thing?"

"The dead girl thing?" Ben repeated, amazed at how a murder

investigation could be referred to as *the dead girl thing.*

"Aye, the murder down at Anderby. Heard you say the name Barnes. Not Derek Barnes, surely?"

"The very man," Ben said.

"He's no murderer," Gillespie said, sitting back on the edge of a nearby desk. "The man's the worst criminal I've ever met. He's been arrested more times than anyone I know. In fact, we should ask Jacob on the front desk to laminate a wanted poster with Barnes' mugshot on it. It'll save us a fortune in printing."

"Jacob?" Ben asked, not really listening to Gillespie; he'd been planning on asking Chapman, who had far more patience than Ben, to contact Humberside Airport.

"Yeah, you know the fella. Big eyes that bulge from his face. Looks like he has breakfast in the class-A section of the evidence room."

Ben laughed at the poor description, yet somehow knew who Gillespie was referring to.

"Anyway, do you really think Barnes is capable of murder?" Gillespie asked. "The family is scum, aye, but they're too bloody thick to get away with something like that."

"Well, somehow his name has come up, and we have to investigate," Ben said, taking a sip of his coffee. He dragged a tissue from the box on Jackie's desk and mopped up Gillespie's spill. The coffee was awful, but it wasn't his fault. The coffee was notoriously awful.

"How about the lass?" Gillespie asked, raising his eyebrows a couple of times, as if the very thought of Freya excited him.

"You mean DI Bloom?"

"Aye. What's she like then?" he said. "Bet she's a right hard one. The type that'll cuff you to the bed and make you beg for mercy, if you know what I mean?"

"Honestly, I don't see it," Ben replied. "I think you have mother issues."

"Mother issues? Ah, come on. I mean, aye, she's no spring chicken, but you can tell, right?"

The truth was that Ben could see it. His imagination wasn't depraved enough to imagine any scenario involving the handcuffs that Gillespie had spoken of, but he had admired her, and he could see the appeal. And it was something he was trying to get out of his mind.

"She's good," he said.

"Aye, I bet she is."

"She's a good detective," Ben added, and he shook his head trying to dismiss the idea Gillespie was forcing into his head. "She's actually okay to work with. She'll be good for the team."

"I thought she was temporary. You know? I thought you were going for DI?"

"I am, or was at least."

"Ben, man," Gillespie said, sliding from the desk, "this was your chance."

"Why are you bothered by it? You're not in her team."

"Aye, I know. But if you get promoted, then that makes me next in line. I can't work for Steve all my life."

"Right, I see," Ben said, seeing the ulterior motive. "I think she'll be good for us. I think the shakeup is good for the team."

"Ah, Ben, you disappoint me. I thought you had more balls than that. I thought you'd at least put up a fight. You know what happens when someone new comes in. Everything changes. New rules. New ways of doing stuff. I'm happy, Ben. We're all happy. Don't ruin it. Fight for us."

"I don't think I can be bothered to fight, Jim," Ben said, as his desk phone began to ring.

He glanced at the phone then at Gillespie, then hit the button to answer the call.

"Is that Detective Sergeant Savage?" a voice said. It was female and familiar.

"Yes," Ben said, as Gillespie backed away towards his end of the room.

"I have some news regarding the passenger you were asking after. A Derek Barnes?"

He looked up to find Gillespie motioning a boxer with his one free hand. "Fight for it, Ben," he said. "For all of us."

CHAPTER TWENTY-SEVEN

In Freya's past life, where giant buildings blocked the sun and the wind, where the fertile soil lay beneath a synthetic crust, and where trees were planted to add a splash of green, a flock of taxis would have drawn up beside her outstretched arm. In Lincolnshire, however, where wild fens and fields remained as they had for all of time, where the unfettered wind tore across the landscape, and both sun and rain gave life to the fertile soil, there was no such demand. There wasn't a taxi for miles.

Hiding behind the raised collar of her heavy coat, Freya made her way along the beach, passing the access road from which she had arrived only days before, choosing instead to venture further along the beach to the crime scene. Today would be pivotal, she knew in her experienced heart. The broad list of names to investigate would be whittled down to a few, or even one. The hunt would be on to find evidence or gain a confession, whatever it would take for Crown Prosecution to approve the charges. Finding the perpetrator was often the easy part. Proving it was where the challenge lay.

Hugging the foot of the sandbank soon led her to the area where Jessica Hudson had been killed. The strong winds had wiped the beach clear of any sign that police and forensics teams had spent the day on the beach. A single piece of police tape fluttered in the wind, still tied to one of the steel posts uniform had hammered into the sand. But there was nothing more.

Treading carefully to avoid disturbing any sign that may remain, she studied the area from beach level. Although she doubted there would be any remaining evidence, being mindful was a good habit to maintain. With her hands deep in her jacket pockets, she surveyed the beach and the dune. In her mind, the scene played out like an early home movie, in high contrast and saturation. Jessica Hudson idled along the beach in the dark. The image of the girl as an unhappy soul was a result, Freya thought, of meeting the girl's parents. Her father in particular had been a cold and bitter man; though, having only just learnt of the news when Freya had met him, that opinion was unreliable. Even so, it was during those times that true emotions were displayed. The real person behind the charade is shown. If Jessica was indeed looking for an escape, it was down to his overprotective and controlling nature, of that Freya had no doubt.

Jessica hadn't known she was walking into a trap. She hadn't been aware of her killer's intentions.

Conjecture, that's all the scene that played out in Freya's mind was. A theory. Walking hand in hand, Jessica and her lover had perhaps stopped to enjoy a kiss. With the sandbank shielding them from the wind, they lay beneath the stars, using each other's body heat to keep warm. He wanted more, and she didn't. Sometimes it was that simple.

And so he turned on her. He had held her throat. Straddled her. His face close to hers, watching the life ebb from her body.

"Why on top of the dune?" she asked herself, gazing up the ridge line at the thick and thorny tall grass.

To sound her thoughts, she pulled her phone from her pocket. Just two bars of signal showed, so she remained stationary for fear of losing the weak signal, and dialled Ben. The call rang on for what seemed like an eternity, and when the voicemail message played, Freya spoke just a handful of words, enough for him to get the gist.

"Ben. Yellow sweater. Where is it? And where's her bag?"

She disconnected, grateful that the signal had held out long enough for the call.

That was when she saw them. Two eyes, dark and scared, and shielded behind a crop of hair so tangled, it almost blended with the surrounding grass. It was a girl. Sitting in that spot. By chance?

Surely not.

Keeping eye contact, Freya moved forward, climbing the dune, slowly so as not to scare the girl, who was sitting like a wild thing among the thorns.

Stopping at a point where Freya was eye level with the girl, two-thirds of the way up the dune, she checked around her to make sure they were alone.

"Hello," Freya said, as friendly as she could.

Noting the sand in the girl's hair and embedded onto the side of her face, Freya took a step further up the dune. The girl gave no response; she only stared with cautious, distrusting eyes.

"I'm Freya Bloom. Who are you?"

Wearing only a small, red anorak, a black, hooded sweat-shirt, and pair of tight jeans, the poor thing must have been freezing, despite Jessica's final resting place being almost out of the wind.

"Did you know her?" Freya asked, being careful not to reveal too much.

The ensuing nod was so faint that Freya nearly doubted she had seen it, but was reluctant to press for confirmation.

"Do you know what happened here? Do you know who did this?" Freya asked, seeking a way to break the girl's silence.

But again, she received no response. Those big, dark eyes and boyish lips drew a blank expression.

"Are you local?" she asked, edging closer. "Is your house nearby? Your mum maybe?"

The girl's eyes widened at Freya's less than tactile approach, and when the sand gave way beneath Freya's boot, causing her to stumble, the girl took her chance. Leaping from the hollow, her white trainers finding soft sand, she disappeared down the far side of the sandbank. Scrambling up the dune, Freya could only look on in dismay. By the time she reached the top, the girl was down the far side, sprinting along the edge of the water-logged field.

CHAPTER TWENTY-EIGHT

By the time Ben had debriefed Will Granger, the teams had arrived. An excited hum marked the various conversations, topped with Gillespie's loud and gruff voice.

The incident room was buzzing with activity. Ben hadn't seen so much activity in there since David was alive. He was always able to draw the team together, get things moving. Momentum, he had called it. Even if the leads are cold and suspects aren't talking, the game is to keep things moving. Keep the team busy.

Pushing open the squealing door, he felt grit underfoot – a small pile of sand, not large enough to notice with the eye but enough to stick to the sole of his Oxfords. At the whiteboard, Freya was busy making updates gained from Chapman. From where he was standing, he could see the sand marks on the back of her boots and the trail she had walked.

"I would have thought the crime scene would have been shut down by now?" he called out, and Freya turned in the middle of her writing, followed Ben's eyes to the old, tatty, blue carpet, and then looked back at him.

"You could always run the vacuum around," she said, her smile belying any malicious undertones.

"Jackie, how did you get on with the Netflix thing?" he asked, assuming that would be the greatest challenge she faced following the previous day's briefing.

"She did just fine," said Freya, then added, "everybody is doing just fine. But we still have a long way to go." She stepped back to examine the new detail she had added to the board, then replaced the lid on the pen.

"Jackie, Ben, come in close please," she said, then waited for Jackie to come to Ben's side before continuing. "Here's where we are. It's eleven a.m. and we've made good progress. However, don't get complacent. We need to push this hard." Tapping her pen on the board, she began. "Jackie has confirmed that the family Netflix account was being accessed all evening and well into the night. That supports Patricia Hudson's story about her going to bed early. Not conclusive, but sufficient for now. Tim Hudson's phone was also stationary all evening. DC Chapman here has been onto the 4G network and..." She moved to an A3-printed map that had been crudely taped to one side of the board. The Anderby and Chapel coastline was instantly recognisable to Ben, and he took a guess at the four circles that had been drawn on, which Freya confirmed as she continued. "These circles indicate the four 4G masts in the area and their approximate ranges. What's interesting to see is the overlap."

"Why do they overlap?" asked Jackie. "Surely it makes sense to spread them out more?"

"Locations aren't always easy for 4G providers to procure. Local residents always put up a fight when a mast is proposed, arguing anything from health reasons to aesthetics. Secondly, the ranges vary slightly due to atmospheric conditions, weather, and power. The overlap is based on worst possible conditions, whereby the lowest signal would be achieved."

Seeming content with the response, Jackie nodded, although Ben wasn't entirely sure she understood. Knowing her well, Ben guessed that Jackie had more questions but was keeping quiet for fear of embarrassment.

"The overlap serves us well, though," Freya continued. "Imagine you're driving along a motorway and you're on the phone—"

"Hands-free, of course," Ben added.

"Of course," Freya said, suffering his childish comment with a roll of those tired eyes as he would expect.

"As you move through areas, you pass through the ranges of the masts along the way. The network is intelligent enough to know and deal with this. If it didn't, your phone call would drop when you left the range of one mast, and you'd have to redial when you joined another. Nobody would ever finish a call if that was the case. But, as it happens, the network software ensures our calls are uninterrupted. They call it *handing off*. One mast hands the call off to the next, and so on. This is done during the time we spend in the overlap. Where does this help us?"

Glancing at the three of them like a schoolteacher, Ben was mildly amused to watch the responses. Jackie, the shy but intelligent girl, pursed her lips as a sign she was trying to work it out, while Chapman voiced her opinion.

"The overlap helps us identify a person's location," she said. "Instead of us searching the entire range of a single mast, we only have to search the overlap."

"Exactly, Denise," said Freya, and she stabbed the pen in Chapman's direction to accentuate her point. "We know that the Hudson house falls in the overlap between mast one and mast two." She turned to the board to indicate the area in question, then looked back over her shoulder to Ben. "Before you say it, Ben, the masts do have more technical unique identifiers, but for the purposes of our conversation, I'm keeping it simple."

"Simple is my middle name," said Ben, amused that she felt the need to make the point, and also warmed by the fact that she was already on first name terms with Jackie and Chapman. He and Jackie had been friends for years, so first names were used every day. But despite working with Chapman for over a year, even he still used her last name. Until then, he'd never even questioned it, and she had never asked him to call her Denise.

"However," said Freya, and she paused for sufficient time to build suspense, "all that tells us is that Tim Hudson's phone was in his home for the duration of the evening. He's a solicitor. One might expect him to know about 4G networks."

"What about the aunt and uncle?" asked Ben.

"Ah, I'm glad you asked," said Freya and once more she used the map, this time to identify the Fraser house. "You can see that the Fraser house falls under mast three. The overlap between mast two and three covers the Anderby area, including the crime scene. According to Mrs Fraser, the whole family were home on the night in question."

"But one of them was out?" suggested Ben, his mind racing to guess which one of the odd couple were not where they said they had been.

"Wrong," said Freya with a knowing smile. "They were both out."

CHAPTER TWENTY-NINE

"Both of them?" said Ben. "Why would they lie?"

Although mildly amused at Ben's outburst, Freya was also quite impressed with his question. It showed experience. He hadn't asked where the Frasers had been. He had asked why they had lied. Asking why somebody made a particular decision was a far more appropriate question. Where they had been was secondary.

"To protect their daughter from something, perhaps?" said Freya. "To keep something secret from her. Or perhaps to hide something from us?"

"That's more likely. Did they stay local?"

"They did, but what's intriguing is that they weren't together." Turning to face the map again, she moved to one side so everyone could see where she was pointing. "Mrs Fraser passed through the overlap between masts two and three, then through the field of mast two, and into the range of mast one."

"Chapel?" said Ben. "What time was this?"

"Around eight p.m."

"And the dad?"

"Thirty minutes later," she replied, admiring the way he processed the information.

"Where did he go?"

"Straight to mast four. No passing go. No collecting two hundred pound."

"What's in the area?" he asked, and leaned in to study the map.

"Residential. You should know. We were there yesterday."

"We were there? The Barnes house? No, surely not?"

"Maybe he didn't go to the Barnes house, but he did go to the area. We need to know two things – where he went, and why he lied about it."

"He didn't lie," said Ben, and he stared down at her, standing tall above all three of his female colleagues. "She lied. Mrs Fraser said it. When you asked where they were, it was *her* that said they were all home."

"You're right. Do you remember the way she looked at him when she said it? I thought it was odd." She then turned to the board and circled Mr and Mrs Fraser. "Denise?"

"Ma'am?"

"You know what to do. These two are your focus for the day. I want to know exactly where they went and why they lied," she said, then returned her attention to Ben. "And what about you?"

"I found something interesting. Barnes didn't fly out three days ago. He flew out two days ago. Which means he was still on the mainland when Jessica was killed. I've asked Humberside to send us the footage to make sure it's actually him."

"Why would his wife lie unless he was hiding something?" Freya asked.

"I don't know. I do know, however, that Derek Barnes is a pain in the backside. He's a petty thief, and a bad one at that. But he's no more a murderer than I am."

"How do we know you're not a murderer?" she asked, amused at his response.

"You'll have to take my word that I haven't killed anybody," he replied, his face lighting up with the banter. "At least not today."

"I want Derek Barnes either struck off that list," she said with another of those alluring eye rolls. "Or I want him circled. Which is it?"

"Circled," Ben said without hesitation. "For now."

Uncapping the pen, Freya circled Derek Barnes, and perhaps purposefully, she turned her attention away from Ben to Jackie.

"Jackie, where are we with the dog?"

"Piper? Denise and I have contacted every vet in the area. He isn't registered anywhere."

"What does that tell you?"

"That either his owners just moved here, or they never bothered to register him."

"Do you have dogs, Jackie?"

"No, ma'am."

"I do. At least, I did. And let me tell you something. It's not uncommon for dog owners to care more about their dogs than their families. Albert Stow said he hadn't seen the woman or her dog before."

"Tourists?" said Ben. "It's winter. The tourist trade isn't exactly thriving."

"Jackie, Ben, work together. I want every bed and breakfast contacted. We're looking for a family with a dog, specifically a golden retriever named Piper. When you're done there, find me Charlie Barnes. See if uniform have picked him up yet. If they haven't, then get out there and find him. He has to be somewhere. Denise, you said you would research him."

"Sorry, ma'am," she replied, wide-eyed with guilt. "I'm just snowed under right now. I'll get to it today."

"Make sure you do. Our list is still too big. We need to know where the Frasers went. We need that damned dog. We need Derek Barnes struck off. And we need his son, Charlie, in a cell with a cup of warm water in his hand mulling over a charge sheet. Get to it."

Jackie and Chapman made their way to their desks while Ben loitered. Freya made a show of tidying up the board, aware of his presence, but not giving him the satisfaction of being first to engage.

"What about you?" he asked.

"I have a lead of my own to follow up on," she said. Then she turned and leaned into him, whispering into his ear, "I may have sand on my boots when I return, so be a good boy and fetch the vacuum cleaner."

"You're not going out alone, are you? Round here, we call that glory hunting."

"I call it getting my hands dirty," she replied, and backed off, aware that they were standing far too close. Had he been a few years older, in another town, in another life, she might have been tempted to see what was underneath those tight, white shirts he wore. From the look on his face, Freya guessed he was wondering if he could handle her.

It was Denise Chapman who broke the tension.

"Ben, Humberside called. Your CCTV footage has been uploaded," she called from across the room.

Lingering for a few moments longer, he raised a hand to acknowledge Chapman, but never once removed his eyes from Freya's.

"Chop chop, Ben," she said softly. "Focus, remember?"

CHAPTER THIRTY

"I've emailed you a link to the files," said Chapman, as Ben sat down at his desk. He rattled the mouse to wake the screen then logged in, and had just clicked on Chapman's email when his laptop did what it did best. It froze. A spinning wheel appeared on his screen, and he sat back in dismay.

The door to the incident room opened with a squeal, then slammed shut in the wake of Freya's heavy perfume.

Less than a minute later, the laptop fan kicked in, whirring loudly for no apparent reason. Then the screen went black.

"Ah for Christ's sake," he said, and looked around, as the rest of the team's laptops all seemed to be working just fine. "I've just had this replaced."

"Must be all those important emails you get," said Chapman.

"Yeah right," he said, just as the screen flicked back on and Chapman's email opened as if nothing had happened. "Here we go. And so begins the long and arduous task of watching dull and boring footage," he announced to no-one in particular. "In this episode, people we don't know walk through an airport terminal doing nothing out of the ordinary."

"I don't know why you didn't just get the flight manifest," Jackie said, grinning at his dejection.

"Barnes wasn't on the passenger list for the twelfth, but he was on the thirteenth, I need to make sure it's him before I dig any deeper. Can you get me an up-to-date photo of Derek Barnes please?"

"Sure, I'll see what we have on file."

Skipping through the footage of the thirteenth, Ben found the spot when passengers were let through into the holding gate. Slowing the footage to quarter speed allowed him to check the faces of each individual, and he was thankful it was the helicopter terminal where the number of passengers was limited to just a dozen per flight.

"Coming through to you now," said Jackie, and in the bottom right corner of his screen, an inbound email flashed up, which he clicked on and dragged to his second screen for reference. Being a new terminal, the quality of the security footage was good. Unlike so many other grainy and out-of-focus recordings Ben had endured in the past, he found he could pause the video and zoom into each face and still retain a quality high enough for facial features to be recognised. Good enough for a jury anyway. "Found him."

"Who? Barnes?" said Jackie, coming around to join him at his desk.

"Take a look for yourself," he said, as Jackie leaned in. She rested her hand on his shoulder, and in contrast to Freya's expensive scent that probably cost one hundred pounds for a bottle, Jackie smelled of soap. It was nice soap, with a feminine, floral touch. It was light and pleasant.

"That's him," said Jackie, leaning in closer, holding onto Ben for balance. "Look, you can even see his earring."

"So Derek Barnes definitely did not fly on the twelfth, he flew on the thirteenth."

"So where was he on the night of the twelfth? And why did his wife say he was working?"

Instinctively, they both looked across to Chapman, who had the relationship with the 4G network and who was dialling a number on her desk phone. Hitting the loudspeaker button, she carried on typing until the call was answered, then requested to be put through to her contact – a man by the name of Chesney Barker.

Surprised at the name, Ben listened in, trying to put a face to the voice. The only Chesney he had ever heard of before sang a record that he couldn't quite remember, and acted in a film Ben had seen when he was a boy.

"Chesney, it's DC Chapman again. I'm sorry to bother you," she said, while both Ben and Jackie looked on. She signalled for Jackie to come to her desk and, pointing at the screen, asked her to confirm the phone number on record for Derek Barnes.

"What can I do for you, Denise?" the man replied, and she glanced up at Ben and Jackie, embarrassed that the man had used her first name.

He sounded young, mid-twenties maybe, but with the confidence of someone who knew their stuff. Ben imagined the tech guy to be wearing faded jeans, scuffed trainers, and a t-shirt with some kind of corny slogan on it.

After a few frantic seconds of Jackie cross-checking the phone number, she gave Chapman the nod.

"I have another number for you. I'm sorry to be a pain."

"Ah, you're not a pain at all. Let's have it then."

Chapman read out the number for Chesney, and Ben watched Chapman's facial expressions. She bit her lower lip and looked wistfully at the phone, enough for Ben to get the impression that there was a little more than a professional interest going on.

"You're going to hate me," Chesney announced after a small delay.

"You can't help me, can you?" she said flatly.

"I can help you, but..." He paused, as if he was shifting in his seat and preparing to make a statement. "Listen, do you have a smart phone?"

"I do, I—"

"On your smart phone, you have apps. Like messaging apps, music apps, maps, and stuff, right?"

"Well, yeah," Chapman said, not sure of where Chesney was leading her.

"Good. Well, some of the apps, like maps and cloud services, are in constant communication with the cloud."

"Right. That make sense," she said.

"That means, when you give me a number to track, I can see which masts the smart phone has been in contact with to establish that connection to the cloud. I can give you a minute by minute account in some instances."

"I'm sensing a *but* coming," she said.

"Standard mobile phones don't allow me to give you that. They don't have apps that are in constant communications with the cloud like a smart phone."

"When you say standard phones, you mean like an old Nokia?" she asked.

"Exactly like an old Nokia."

"And this number is one of those?"

"It looks to be. The phone has to be in use for a mast to register it. Failing that, the phone offers something out to the masts called a keepalive. It's the technology's way of maintaining a connection when it's needed. You may have heard it being referred to as a ping."

"I've heard of that, how often—"

"Every thirty minutes."

"So every thirty minutes, this phone will talk to the nearest mast to establish a connection?"

"That's right. What do you need? I can give you the last three days' activity again if you want?"

Glancing up at Jackie and Ben with disappointment, Chapman silently asked for their input.

"Three days is fine," said Ben quietly.

"Can you send it through?" Chapman asked.

"Chesney?" called Ben.

"Hello?" the man said, a little confused at hearing another voice.

"Chesney, this is DS Savage, thanks for your help on this. Can you send the data through to DC Chapman?" He pulled the map from the whiteboard and returned to his desk. "But can you answer me this? I'm sure you can read the data far easier than we can."

"I'll do my best."

"I need to know if that number was in a particular area on a particular day."

"Sure," he replied.

"The twelfth. In the evening."

A few keystrokes could be heard through the loudspeaker.

"Was that phone in Humberside, by any chance?" asked Ben.

"Humberside? No," Chesney replied. "That phone was static. Looks like a little coastal town. Hang on, let me zoom in."

Jackie, Chapman, and Ben exchanged intrigued glances, each of them tuned into Chesney's voice.

"Chapel St Leonard."

"Chapel?" said Ben. "Are you sure?"

"Positive. The data doesn't lie."

Searching Freya's map for the identifier for the mast closest to the Barnes house, Ben read it out.

"Is that mast identifier Papa Echo six two six?" he asked.

"No, that's the next one inland. The last mast that PUC registered with was via a keepalive to mast Papa Echo five nine four. It's a little closer to the coast."

"I see it," said Ben, finding PE594 on the map. He glanced at Jackie and lowered his voice. "That's mast one."

"Is that okay?" Chesney asked.

Nodding at Chapman for her to continue the conversation, Ben sat back down at his desk and pondered the crude map.

"That's great, thanks, Chesney. Send that data through in case we need to track it further," said Chapman. "You've been so helpful."

"Sure, no problem. I'll break the movements down into days again to make the data easier to read. Anything else I can help you with today, Denise?"

Sensing that Chapman did indeed have something that Chesney could help with, but not something she was likely to discuss with him and Jackie listening in, Ben turned his back on Chapman to relieve her embarrassment.

"Update that board, Jackie," he said, nodding at Freya's list of suspects. "Underline Derek Barnes. Then we can hit the bed and breakfasts. Another joyous task."

"So, Derek Barnes wasn't where he was supposed to be either?" said Chapman, as she ended the call.

"Looks like a lot of people have a lot to hide," said Ben. Then he couldn't help but toy with her. "Chesney seems nice."

"Oh, leave it," she said, blushing. "He's the only one with clearance to give us that information. There's some kind of agreement between the force and the network."

"So, Chesney is the one and only," Ben mused, smiling to himself. But the joke was lost on his colleagues, who were both on the wrong side of thirty to understand, and they exchanged bemused expressions.

"Aha," Jackie said suddenly, looking from her notes to her screen to double check something. She looked up to find both Ben and Chapman staring at her. "Jack Fraser. I know where he went."

CHAPTER THIRTY-ONE

Ben winced at the sound the door made as he stepped from the incident room, leaving Jackie and Chapman to their phone calls.

Fifteen feet away, standing outside Arthur's office, Freya was leaning against the closed door, staring at the ceiling.

The door slammed behind him, and she must have sensed his presence, because slowly, she emerged from that place that she seemed to slip into, and she stared at him.

"You okay?" he asked.

A nod was the only reply he received, although her eyes were glazed just as they had been before.

"We've hit gold," he said, hoping a little good news would bring her around.

"Describe gold," she said, her voice far less enthusiastic than he had hoped.

"Gold as in Jack Fraser not being where he said he was two nights ago. As in his workplace being in area one. If we can prove he went to work that evening, for whatever reason, then we can strike him off the list."

"If he wasn't there, where else would he have gone?"

"That's what I'm going to find out."

Raising her eyebrows in a way that conveyed disappointment, she carried her gaze back to the ceiling briefly. "Bronze at best," she said. "Gold would be a signed confession. Gold would be Charlie bloody Barnes walking into the station. Gold would be Piper the golden retriever bringing me my slippers and telling me who his owner is. Striking Jack Fraser off the list is not gold, Ben."

"I still need to go and check it out," he replied, undeterred by her play on his words.

"Then I'll come with you. I could do with the air."

"I thought you had your own lead to pursue?" Ben said, and she flicked her eyes to the room behind her, then back to Ben.

"I'm pursuing it now. Please don't question me."

Remembering the conversation from the previous night, Ben nodded, and gestured for her to follow him to the stairwell. Checking below to make sure they were alone, Ben looked her in the eye to judge her sincerity.

"What's happened? Are you okay?"

"What makes you think something has happened? And what makes it any of your business?"

Dropping a few steps down, he leaned on the banister and stared up at her. "I don't get you. I can't do this on and off thing you do. You told me you have a problem. Let me help you deal with it. You're not going to win any friends by shutting me out."

"Is that how you used to talk to DI Foster?"

"In here, yes. There's no rank in the stairwell. We're equal in here. Do you remember I said you needed a friend?"

She nodded.

"Well, this is where friends come to give advice. If you want to pull rank, then do so in the incident room. Not here. This place is off-limits."

"Passionate, aren't you?" she said, and the tension that had been building broke as the corners of her mouth curled into the beginnings of a smile.

Shaking his head at letting himself get worked up on her behalf, Ben turned and descended.

"Don't push me away," he called back to her. "That's all I'm saying."

Reaching the ground floor, he stopped at the exit door with his hand on the long brass handle, then looked up at her.

She was casually leaning on the handrail, her fingers splayed and her arm extended. She bit down on her lower lip in a way that, had she been wearing a little black number instead of a trouser suit, he might have thought was suggestive.

"If you have another episode, you tell me."

"Is that the deal?"

"If you can't do that, then you're on your own."

The beginnings of that smile bloomed and altered the shape of her face the way a wildlife documentary might show a time-lapse video of a flower opening.

"Do we have a deal?"

She stared at him, trying to read something else in the offer he had made. But he was offering nothing else. A simple deal. Be honest, or be alone.

"Okay," she said playfully, and she sauntered down the remaining stairs wearing a gleeful expression that roused caution in Ben's gut, and once more stirred his childish fancy. "But the deal works both ways. You need to be honest with me as well. I need to know who you are, why you're single, and why you joined the force."

"That's a big conversation for a stairwell chat," he said.

"So tell me later," she said, as she brushed past him. "Over dinner."

CHAPTER THIRTY-TWO

As a city girl, Freya was amazed by how vast and open the county of Lincolnshire was. Small pockets of developments could be found dotted about the landscape, presumably close together for electricity and other services. They pulled into a lane on the outskirts of Chapel St Leonards and drove past the entrance to a caravan site that offered a lake, electricity hook-ups, and clean facilities.

Finding Big Barn Timber at the end of the narrow lane, Freya checked her makeup in the passenger mirror while Ben parked beside the other customers' cars. A forklift rattled past, unladen, and men browsed stacks of wood, presumably sizing them up for various projects. One man, wearing smart jeans, a bright, white shirt, and a long coat that would not have looked out of place in a London bar was raising the ends of some – peering down the length, seeing how straight the lengths were, Freya guessed.

"What is it with men and these places?" she said, suddenly aware that her leaning forward into the little mirror in the sun visor was blocking Ben's view of the side mirror. She sat back and closed the visor. "You always have to be ripping something down or putting something up, painting or fixing."

"Is that a dig at men in general, or is it aimed at me in particular?"

"It's an observation, Ben. That's all," she said, amused that she had once again riled him.

"Wow, we're already getting to the battle of the sexes," he replied, checking his watch. "That took about forty-eight hours. A new record."

"There's those emotions again, Ben," she said, opening the door and climbing out as the forklift rattled past once again, returning in the direction from where it had come the first time around. She called out to the driver, "Excuse me?"

Coming to an abrupt stop, the forklift driver looked back over his shoulder, his gloved hand still resting on the wheel and his woolly hat half-covering his eyes. He waited for Freya to speak.

"I'm looking for the manager," she said, holding up her ID for him to see.

When an individual sees an ID being produced, in Freya's experience, they act in one of two ways. A strong emotional reaction, be it panic or over helpfulness, or no emotional reaction at all. Both could be used as indicators of guilt, but it was an observation Freya found interesting.

His face was stoic, his eyes glancing from the card that he wouldn't have been able to read from that distance to her eyes, as he carried out a split second assessment.

"Yellow jacket," he said, and Freya followed his outstretched arm to find a man on a mobile phone leaning on a wide-fronted barn.

"His name?"

"Keith," said the forklift driver, as he released the brake and rolled on.

"Thank you," Freya muttered to herself, as Ben joined her, adjusting the collar of his jacket.

"So if Jack Fraser came here that night, we need to know why."

"But if he didn't come here, then we need to know where else he might have gone," she said, retrieving her ID once more. "Excuse me, sir, are you Keith?"

"That I am," the man replied, and he shoved off the barn door he was leaning on, just as a loud saw fired up and the metallic screech of hard wood became unbearable.

"I was wondering if you could help us with an investigation," she called out above the din. "We just have a few questions."

Offering a look that told Freya he would have rejected her cause if he could, he glanced around the yard, then once over his shoulder, before sizing up Ben, then settling on Freya's unrelenting stare. "Walk with me."

A wide dyke separated the yard from the neighbouring fields. It was so wide and deep that neither the farmer nor the owner of the wood yard had seen fit to erect a partitioning fence. In two rows alongside the dyke on the side of the wood yard were pallets and pallets of timber. There were no prices on show, which meant that customers would have to ask the price, which, in Freya's opinion, was a practice of inconvenience. But it was into the corridor between the piles that Keith led them, presumably not wanting to be seen talking to the police, although one could argue that it was the best place for a discussion – out of the wind and away from the banshee-like wails of the saw.

"What can you tell us about Jack Fraser?" asked Freya, walking side by side with Keith, while Ben walked behind a few steps, close enough to hear but far away enough not to crowd the man.

"Jack?" he replied, a little surprised. "He's a decent enough bloke. Family guy. Why?"

"And he works here?"

"Yeah, he's been here years. Never let us down."

"Us?"

"This is a family business. My dad started it, and the lad on the forklift is my eldest."

"How nice that you can provide employment for your son."

"I'd rather he had passed his exams and become a lawyer or something," he said, and smiled for the first time, as people often do when they speak of their children. "But he's okay here. He's taking us digital. We're online now apparently. He takes photos, puts them on an internet marketplace, and sells it that way. People come for miles away. He's the next generation of Hammersleys. He'll do well."

"And was it you who hired Jack?" asked Freya, aware that they had deviated from her line of questioning.

"It was, yeah. What's this about? Is it his niece? If he needs a character reference, I'd be happy to—"

"It's okay, thank you. You're right, we're investigating an attack on his niece. I didn't know it was common knowledge if I'm honest. The first stage of any investigation is to eliminate the people that knew the victim. Sadly, this means having these conversations. I can assure you, he's not in any kind of trouble. We're just looking into his whereabouts, that's all. Just to confirm his movements."

"His whereabouts?"

"Yes, on the evening of the twelfth. Would he have had any reason to come here?" Freya asked, as they reached the end of the corridor. "I doubt you work evenings here, do you?"

"We shut the shop at six p.m. Monday to Saturday."

"This would have been after that. More like nine or ten."

Shaking his head, Keith pulled a negative expression. "No. He wouldn't have even got in."

"Does he have keys?"

"Only three people have keys to this place," Keith said. "My father, me, and my son."

"What about security cameras?" Ben asked from behind. "I see there's a camera fixed to the main barn."

"It's a dud. It used to work, for about a year. We had a series of break-ins about ten years ago. I had it installed. It was more of a deterrent really. Anyway, we caught the lad. Haven't really had any need for it since."

"A lad?" said Freya, glancing around the yard. "What was he after with this place?"

Her question could have been taken as offensive, but Keith Hammersley was made of stronger stuff, it seemed. He nodded at a series of smaller sheds.

"See that old building? That's the old slaughterhouse. Can't use it for that now, but it was operational when my dad worked the farm."

"Sheep?" asked Ben.

The man nodded. "There's all kinds of restrictions on livestock now."

"So you re-purposed the building?"

"What else was we supposed to do?" he said. "We use it as a workshop. We build benches and tables. Garden furniture, you know?"

"Decent money," said Ben. "I'd have done something similar."

"It's a slow burner. We don't earn much from it, but it all helps. Anyway, the roof kept leaking. Destroyed a bunch of orders. That's when we realised half the lead was gone. The next day, more went missing. So I had the camera installed. That's the only spot where you can see the whole yard."

"And what did you see?"

"Young lad on a bike. He was coming here in the dead of night, climbing up the drainpipe and stripping off as much lead as he could fit in his rucksack, then he was off."

"A boy?" said Freya.

Keith shrugged. "Thirteen or fourteen. Local family. Trouble, if you ask me."

"What kind of boy knows how to do all that?" Freya asked.

"A Barnes," said Ben, and Freya was intrigued to see the two men exchange nods. Turning to Freya, Ben offered an explanation.

"Will Granger handled that one. I was still in uniform, and David must have still been a DC or DS."

"That's him," said Keith. "Barnes. Should have known it would be one of them lot."

"Have you had much dealing with them in the past?"

"Of course. We gave Derek Barnes a chance once, before we knew what he was about. Had him shifting timber, loading lorries and whatnot."

"When was this?"

"About a month before we caught his boy stealing lead," said Keith. "Bad blood, that family. Everyone knows it."

"Mr Hammersley, is there any reason at all that Jack Fraser would have come here on the evening of the twelfth?" asked Freya, steering the two men back onto the line of questioning.

"None at all," Keith replied. "Gates would have been locked, and like I said–"

"Only the three family men have keys, yes, I remember," said Freya, pondering the result. She stared past the car park, along the long driveway, and past the gates. "Thank you, Mr Hammersley. You've been a great help."

Waiting for Keith Hammersley to be out of earshot, Ben voiced his thoughts.

"You're right," he said. "Bronze, at best."

"Not necessarily," said Freya, her keen eye fixed on the little sign at the far end of the lane. It was too far away to read, but she remembered what she had read when they had passed it, and she remembered something she had seen in the Fraser house. "It's a long shot, Ben, but you just may be onto something."

––––––––

The sign at the end of the lane read *Chapel Brightwater Holiday Park*. Despite the narrow lane, the entrance had been made wide enough for cars to turn into the park towing a caravan and for long motor homes to make the turn too. With his limited knowledge of holiday parks, Ben thought the site appeared clean and family-friendly, even in the dead of winter when very few tourists used such places.

There were, of course, the people for whom the park offered more than a holiday home for two weeks of the year. The retired community often used holiday parks as a second home, and spent as much time in their static or touring caravans as they did their permanent residences. But in such close proximity to the fens, with the vicious winds tearing through the landscape, November would be a quiet month for the owners of the Chapel Brightwater Holiday Park.

A pretty, little bungalow overlooked the entrance, presumably the owner's dwelling, so they could see the comings and goings of holidaymakers.

Two cars were parked side by side in the car park. One, a Volvo estate, the other, a small, blue hatchback. Both were just a short walk from a single-storey building that, according to the various signs, offered ice creams, teas, and coffees. Hanging in the window was an assortment of inflatable toys, balls, and animals that had taken on a deflated and sad demeanour. The shop was, of course, closed. But a sign above a side entrance marked the way to the office.

"What on earth makes you think Fraser has a place here?" Ben asked, as he buttoned his coat and raised his collar against the wind, understanding why Keith Hammersley had taken them into the corridor between the wood piles to talk.

"Just a hunch," Freya replied, holding her hair from her face with little fuss. He had to admit, even in the hardest of environments, she carried herself with a ladylike grace.

"A hunch?"

"Did you ever get that feeling in your gut? Like when you know somebody is hiding something, but you can't prove it?"

He stared at her, incredulous. "Every time I look at you."

"I'm following my instincts," she said.

"Oh, why didn't you say? I mean there's nothing like a hunch to follow when we have a murderer on the loose."

"And if I'm right?" she said.

She was toying with him. Shaking his head in disappointment that he had fallen for her dry wit once more, he held his hands up in defeat. "If you're right, I'll never question a decision of yours again."

"That's good enough for me," she said.

"But if you're wrong," he called, stopping her in her tracks and offering a smile to say the game was on, "if I'm right and this place is a dead end, you cook dinner."

"Loser cooks dinner?" she said, clearly happy with the odds. "So first of all, you wanted to bet on whether or not Jessica fought back, and now you want to gamble on my hunch being wrong. Sounds to me like you've lost faith in your original theory."

"I haven't lost faith. The stakes are higher, that's all. Mark my words. I'll tell you what's going to happen. We'll go inside here and hit a dead end. Then, when we get the lab results, we'll see that there's no sign that Jessica fought her attacker. After, we'll be doing things my way, and I can sit back eating my dinner trying not to be too smug."

"Is that so?" she said, and right then he knew he had her. She was tenacious. She couldn't resist a challenge. It was probably why she was so successful as a detective. But her tenacity and desire to win would be her undoing. That's how he would get the upper hand with her.

"Do you still have faith in your hunch?" he asked. "Do you honestly believe in a gut feeling more than facts and science?"

Glancing once at the building, then back to Ben, she looked doubtful, then, as a gambler on a downward spiral might do, she put all her chips in.

They met across the roof of the car, and for a moment, it was as if nothing else existed, only them and the incessant wind.

Never before had he been toyed with so much. Nor had he ever encountered a senior officer who seemed to toy with the standards of police work, as if none of it really mattered at all. Sure, professional bets and banter were all part of everyday life, if you were a brick layer or in an office. But they were investigating a murder, and the seriousness of the situation seemed to be lost on her quest to save her ego. It was enlightening.

"A deal is a deal," she said. "And by the way, when you're cooking my dinner later on, I like my steak medium rare."

CHAPTER THIRTY-THREE

"Hello," Ben called out, as Freya peered through an open doorway following the scent of two-stroke oil.

Inside, the building seemed silent compared to the raging winds outside, and Freya's cheeks burned from the change in temperature.

There were two doors off the little hallway. The first led into the camp shop, which they could see through the small glass window in the locked door. The second seemed to be some kind of stock room combined with a place to store maintenance equipment. A ride-on mower was parked to one side, along with various other landscaping tools, the source of the two-stroke engine smell.

"I hate that smell," Freya said, almost to herself, as she thought of her father's tool shed.

"I love it," Ben said. "It reminds me of my father's barn."

Along the far wall, a shelving unit held boxes of toilet rolls, cleaning equipment, and other consumables the park might use, as well as boxes that had been marked with tea bags, coffee, crisps, and other snacks. Presumably, Freya thought, they were left over from the previous season, and wouldn't be restocked until after Christmas.

"Hello?" Ben called out again, and this time he was heard. From the other end of the long room, a figure appeared in the doorway.

"Now then. What can I do for you?" the man said, his tone suspicious. The overalls he wore had once been a dark blue but had adopted the shades and hues of several layers of oil. Using a rag to clean what appeared to be a piece of an engine, he sized up Freya and Ben, not afraid to show his displeasure.

"Are you the manager?" Freya asked, doubting he was anything but the maintenance man; but, knowing little of the workings of a holiday park, let alone the hierarchy, she left the question open.

"That's me," he replied. "Groundsman, cleaner, receptionist, security, and manager. And you're trespassing."

"Detective Inspector Bloom," she said, and let her ID fall open for him to see her warrant card. "This is Detective Sergeant Savage."

"Savage, eh?" the man said, and then eyed Ben as he stepped closer, as if the name rang a bell. "The girl on the beach?"

"That's right," Freya said, luring his attention back to her. "We're eliminating suspects. We thought you might be able to offer some insights into a member of the girl's family."

"Go on," the man said, encouraging her to say more.

"I assume you maintain a list of caravan owners? I'd like to see them if I may, Mr..."

"Chalk. Barney Chalk," he said. "And yes, I have a site register."

"May we see it?"

"It'll be quicker if you just tell me the name of who you're looking for," he said, reaching for a clipboard that was hanging on the wall. He handed it to Ben.

"There must be four hundred caravans out there," said Ben,

jamming his thumb in the direction of the park. "You can't know them all."

"Try me," he said playfully.

"Jack Fraser," Freya said, getting in there fast in case Ben made a comment about divulging sensitive information. Turning to him, she saw his mouth was part open and his eyes were narrowed, questioning her comment. Clearly, she had been right.

"Back row. West field. Next to the forest," said Barney.

"You've seen him here recently, have you?" Freya asked, restraining the smug grin that was emerging on her face.

"It's wintertime. You tend to see more when there's less to see, if you get my meaning."

"I do," said Freya. "When was he here last?"

"I watched him through my living room window. That's my bungalow at the gates, see?"

"When was this, Barney?"

"Yesterday, the day before that, and every day for a week or more. Comes and goes like a lady of the night," he said. "If you pardon the expression."

"Could he just be getting his caravan ready for winter?" asked Ben. "Battening down the hatches, as it were, ready for when his family returns next season?"

"He might have been. Who knows? None of my business what people do in their caravans."

"That's a healthy approach."

"I've seen some sights in my time, I can tell you. All sorts of goings-on."

"I'm sure—"

"Most people are respectful, mind. You know, the families and whatnot. I tend to keep them on the north field, next to the lake."

"So why is Jack Fraser's plot in the west field?"

"That's where he wanted it. I keep myself to myself. I don't ask no questions if I can help it."

"It says here he rents the caravan. He doesn't own it."

"S'right."

"It says you own it. He rents it from you?"

"Right again. Not everyone owns their own."

"And he's only been renting it for a few months. That's why you knew his name," Ben said.

"He's sharp, this one," Barney said to Freya with a smile.

"Do you mind if we take a look?" she asked.

"Be my guest," he replied. "You can drive down there. Keep to the track, mind you, or you'll get stuck in the mud, and I'm about to go for lunch, see."

"We will. Thank you, Mr Chalk."

"Barney," he corrected her. Then he paused to ask a final question. "So is he involved then? Is that what all this is about? I don't want no bad publicity."

"No. No, I don't think so. He was her uncle after all. We just have to check where everybody was, that's all. It's a process of elimination."

"Oh, he was here alright. Back and forth for most of the evening, he was. Not sure what he was doing, mind."

"Did you happen to see him with anyone?" asked Ben.

"No," he said, shaking his head. "No, sorry. It was pitch dark, but I recognised the headlights and the sound of the engine. It gets pretty quiet out here at night time. Be surprised what you hear and see."

"You've been a great help, Barney. Thank you," said Freya, encouraging the man to leave them to discuss what they had found out.

"Well, mind how you go then," he said, and he turned toward the door through which he had entered.

"Strike one," said Freya, under her breath but loud enough for Ben to hear.

"How did you know that?"

"I'm observant," she replied. "But as much as I'd love to spend hours gloating, I have a few concerns that need addressing."

"What concerns me is why Jack Fraser was here when his wife said they were all at home," said Ben.

"Oh really?" Freya said. "I'm a little more concerned that the man pays for a caravan plot less than three miles from his house."

CHAPTER THIRTY-FOUR

Exactly as Barney Chalk had said, Jack Fraser's caravan was positioned on a hard-standing at the edge of the forest that marked the boundary to the property. A wooden stile had been built into the fence to allow pedestrian access to a public footpath denoted by a small sign beside it.

With a raised, wooden platform running around three sides, the caravan was what Ben knew to be semi-permanent. The electric hook up, a small box on a wooden post, was disguised by long grass that hadn't been touched for months, and a blue plastic pipe provided mains water via an exposed valve.

"Decent setup," commented Ben, but Freya offered little evidence of being impressed.

While Ben climbed the few steps to the raised porch to try the doors, Freya walked to the front of the caravan.

"It's locked," he said, then felt stupid for saying so. Of course it would be locked. "You don't suppose Barney would have a key?"

"Try this," Freya called out, and she emerged around the corner of the caravan and tossed him a key on a ring.

"Where did you–"

"Just try it," she said, and the beginnings of that smug grin began to emerge. "It was in the gas bottle locker. I'm a camping pro, remember?"

The key worked, as Ben knew it would, and he fished a pair of disposable latex gloves from his inside pocket before pushing the handle.

"Jack Fraser placed two items on the coffee table yesterday. What were they?" she asked, as she too climbed the steps and took the proffered gloves from Ben.

"His phone," Ben said. "I remember the cracked screen. It reminded me of my brother. He's always dropping his phone."

"And?"

"His keys?" said Ben, unable to recall the scene in its entirety.

"That's a guess. What was on the keys?"

"Look, if you're going to gloat, at least have the decency to—"

"A key to the gas locker," said Freya, and she held up her own keys, showing him the yellow, plastic triangle key. "Not all motor homes have them. But mine does. I recognised it immediately."

"Of course," he said, remembering that she was living in a motor home and would be familiar with the ways of life. "Are we scoring points on observation now? Or is this just a test of transiency?"

"No points needed. You're losing. We've established that."

Pushing past him, she stepped into the static home, seeming to glance at everything in one sweep, then returned to each item for a more detailed inspection.

"Definitely not a family caravan," she said, eyeing a few empty beer cans that had been left on the table and the pack of tobacco with its accompanying ashtray. She sniffed at the air, but all Ben could smell was her perfume. "It could do with a clean."

"It's not exactly a hovel, though, is it?" remarked Ben. "Everything is put away. I wonder what the bedroom is like."

Leaving Freya to inspect the main living space, Ben moved through into the narrow hallway, poking his head into the little bathroom.

"No toothbrush or soap," he called out, then moved on, not expecting a response.

There were three bedrooms, which, if Ben's guesses were accurate, were designed for six people. The first was for children, due to there being two small beds side by side and a single wardrobe. The second and third bedrooms were each doubles, with one being only marginally larger than the other.

Each of the rooms were immaculate, none of the beds had sheets, and the curtains had been pulled back to let the light in.

"He doesn't use the bedrooms, that's for sure," he called out, again expecting no response. But the flowery charm of Freya's scent grew nearer, and Ben turned just as she squeezed past him. For a split second they were face to face, closer than they had been the previous night, and touching.

"Excuse me," she said, meeting him eye to eye, and the moment passed as she stepped into what Ben had assumed to be the master bedroom. She opened the wardrobe, and Ben kicked himself for not doing so. Then she reached down and dragged a sleeping bag out, holding it by two fingers. "*Somebody* sleeps here."

"Do you think it's his getaway?" said Ben.

"We can make a reasonable assumption, and we can strike him off our list," she said, and opened the palm of her hand inviting him to lead the way back into the larger space. "After you."

On the dining table, beside the smokes and the empty beer cans, Freya had placed a small device, about the size of a CD case, only fatter, and beside that was an old newspaper that had been folded open on the sports page.

"What's that?" he asked.

"That's a 4G router," she replied. "And that's the betting pages. I found them in the kitchen cupboard."

The two items needed very little connecting, and Fraser's reason for being there became a little clearer.

"He comes here to get away from his wife," said Ben.

"I agree," Freya added. "He comes here to do what men like doing."

"We don't all enjoy drinking beer, smoking, and gambling," said Ben, ready to defend the male species following her earlier comment on man's desire for home improvement.

"I mean, it's an escape for him," she said, rolling her eyes at his defensive tone. Turning away from him, she wiped her finger along the surface of a shelf and shook the curtain to watch the dust collect in the air. Then she stopped, and bent to peer closer. "Damn it."

"What is it?" Ben asked, assuming the tone of her voice was the result of more than her hatred of anything dirty. He stooped beside her and followed her gaze through the window, where he caught sight of a red blur disappearing behind the next caravan. "Who was that?"

Running to the door faster than he thought she could manage in her boots, Freya called back to him, "It's her. It's the girl from the beach."

Then she too disappeared from view.

CHAPTER THIRTY-FIVE

Against the green foliage, the red anorak was the moving target. Younger and fitter, and with a clear head start, only the girl's footsteps could be heard as Freya launched herself over the stile and landed with both feet on the muddy footpath. Stopping for a few seconds to gauge distance and direction, Freya tuned into both, then ran as fast as her boots would allow.

Not being familiar with the track's twists and turns, and with an eye on the muddy terrain, Freya moved slower than the girl. But the one thing on Freya's side was that unstoppable tenacity.

The footpath rounded bend after bend, low hanging branches whipped at her face, and puddles of brown, muddy water had formed on the bends, forcing Freya to either go wide and trample down the foliage, or cut the corner, risking a slip and a fall at speed.

It wasn't long, though, before the footpath straightened, and opened up into a beautiful forest. Slowing to a stop, Freya searched every direction. The pathway through the centre of the forest was clear, but the girl had deviated. She must have, or else Freya would have seen her. She must have run into the forest.

Above, high in the sparse winter canopy, birds chatted amongst themselves. At least two squirrels were darting about the forest floor, late in the season, but gathering some last-minute supplies maybe.

With no sign at all of the red waterproof jacket, Freya moved forward on the path, keeping her breathing light and controlled, and listening for a sign. Any sign.

It came in the form of birds taking flight, spooked by something unseen. Something way off among the trees. Her fingers grazed the rough bark of each tree she passed, as if touching them might keep her from slipping into that place in her mind.

But the similarities were all too clear, and as she delved deeper into the trees, lured by a glimpse of what might be, a dark vignette enclosed her mind, suffocating her vision until reality faded away.

————

She stared into the space between the trees, enticed by the dark shape of the old, wooden house on the lake, and lured by the opiate of saving a girl's life.

No birds sang in the canopy above, and no rodents scurried in the dry leaves on the forest floor.

She was alone.

Four girls had fallen so far, and their pained faces flashed through Freya's mind like an old movie. Images held in her file that she had forced herself to study, to understand and to empathise. Where others turned away in disgust or horror, Freya had endured the grim reality.

She wouldn't turn her back. Not ever. And now she was close. Now she had him. But something held her there, to that spot. Marley's fifth girl was inside, while her distraught parents lay awake far away.

And all Freya had to do was enter the house.

The darkness had never been a problem before, yet now it seemed to close in on her. The air, clean and fresh, had turned stale.

Reaching for a tree, she caught a breath and swallowed against the rising bile, while the quickening beat of her heart pounded like some kind of distant tribal drum.

It was fear. She knew it was fear and she loathed the iron-like taste in her mouth, she despised the cool layer of sweat that was forming at the small of her back, and she blinked at the darkness that was closing in on her vision.

Maybe it was her body's way of telling her to stop, to turn away, to get help.

But there was no time. Tonight, he would end it. Tonight, another family would lose their child, and tonight, Marley would return to the hunt.

Maybe he'd even drop Freya a note, just as he had done before. Maybe he would tease her with his sordid dreams, savouring the thought of the lab technicians telling her that, once again, the note bore no clues.

Steeled by the thought of him winning once more, Freya braced her primal instinct. Wiping her eyes and taking a deep breath, she spat her fear to the ground and took the first step.

But something held her there. Something indescribable that crushed her resolve.

A presence.

She felt him, and froze in fear.

She was not alone.

And his warm breath licked at her nape, as a flame might gently seduce the grain of a log before devouring it, smothering it, and changing its form forever.

CHAPTER THIRTY-SIX

With barely an hour of remaining daylight, and too far behind Freya and the girl in red to be of any use giving chase, Ben opted for the car. At the gates, he didn't stop.

Beyond the holiday park, the road was lined with the same thick forest that stretched to Jack Fraser's caravan and beyond. Keeping one eye out for a flash of red and the other on the road, Ben gauged the distance from the caravan, through the forest, and to the main road, estimating that even at a sprint, it would take at least five minutes to run through.

A flash of red ran across the road ahead, then stopped. Braking hard, he slewed the car to one side to avoid the girl who was frozen in the centre of the road, wide-eyed. He nosed the car into a clearing in the forest, and came to a hard stop. In seconds, his seat belt was off and he was out giving chase to the youngster.

But she was nowhere to be seen. The forest was vast and old and offered refuge in almost every direction, save for that from which she had run.

Returning to his car, he expected to meet Freya along the way. She would be breathless and likely irritated at herself, and so he prepared for her change of mood and mentally readied the phrasing of the questions he would ask as to who she thought the girl might be.

She had said something about the girl from the beach. There hadn't been any girls on the two occasions Ben had been to the crime scene, yet there had been sand on Freya's boots earlier that day. She had been there alone, that morning. Perhaps that was when she had first seen the girl.

Ben did not find Freya standing beside the car. Crossing the road, he ventured into the forest from where the girl had run.

"Freya?" he called out, taking a slow walk and being sure to keep to the path. For a moment, he contemplated driving back the way he had come in case she had returned to the caravan. A few minutes more, he told himself, and his instinct proved to be correct.

At the far end of the open spaces, where hawthorn and brambles formed a wall, a flash of colour caught his eye. It wasn't bright red, like the girl's coat had been. It was muted, grey, and natural, had he seen it in any other surroundings.

He found her on her hands and knees, eyes closed and head hanging, so that her hair brushed the carpet of dead leaves.

"Freya," he said softly, and he crouched beside her to touch her shoulder, and to offer her comfort. "Freya, it's me."

Startling at his touch, she reeled and scrambled away, before conscious thought returned to her, visibly altering her expression, and then recognition followed, the precursor to her embarrassment and shame.

Having seen her fall prey to an episode before, he knew to say nothing. Instead, he chose to wait for her to settle, offering her his hand and his warmth without judgement.

With her eyes downcast, it was clear that some kind of mental battle was taking place inside her mind. Perhaps she was seeking an excuse? Or maybe she was preparing to open up to him. His eyes wandered, allowing her space to recover and perhaps say something. Glancing around, he found a small game trail, a cut through the dense brambles made by something large, probably a deer.

But for the third time that day, he was steered by a flash of colour. The first had been the red-coated girl, the second, the dull, muted colours of Freya's woollen overcoat glimpsed between the trees. But the third was in front of him, in the midst of the game trail. Stuffed into a place where nobody would ever willingly venture was a bright yellow sweater. He edged closer, peering beneath the tangle of thorns, and he stepped into the thicket with a single large stride so that he could reach the garment.

That was when he knew. That was when his mind made a leap. He turned to Freya, and in that moment, he too had that feeling in his gut that she had described earlier.

"It's Jessica's," he mumbled.

"I know," she whispered.

———

Nothing was said of Freya's momentary lapse of reality. Either Ben was being respectful, given their conversation that had followed the moment she had in Jessica Hudson's bedroom, or he had actually forgotten. Finding Jessica's belongings had overshadowed everything that had followed. In the space of ten minutes, Will Granger had been contacted, a warrant for Jack Fraser's arrest had been issued, along with a search warrant, and a squad of uniforms were gearing up ready for the operation.

"He'll come quietly," Ben said, as they sat in the car less than a mile from the Fraser house, each of them monitoring their respective side mirrors for the transport van to arrive.

"He won't even be there," Freya replied, hoping that Jack Fraser would indeed be home, but seeing the opportunity to enter into another playful bet with who was shaping up to be a good detective.

"Is everything a game to you? Why can't you just—"

Laughing, and letting her head fall back onto the head rest, she eyeballed the mirror, waiting for him to fall in.

"Oh, bloody hell," he said, and that short burst of incredulity faded to his mild amusement and annoyance. "One of these days, your little wind-ups are going to land you in a lot of trouble."

"My little *wind ups*, as you call them, have been landing me in trouble for the past forty years, Ben," she said, and she rolled her head across the headrest so that she could study his profile. "Something about old dogs and new tricks."

"He's not at his caravan and he's not at work, so if he's not home, he can't be far."

"Don't you want to talk about the elephant in the room?" she asked, and watched him process the question.

A few moments passed like a thousand as he considered what he might say, and when he said it, Freya sighed with relief, inwardly, for demonstrating that relief would highlight that there were in fact two elephants in the room. Two elephants made for a crowded car.

"Who was she?" he asked.

"Just a girl I saw at the beach," she replied, knowing that if he had chosen that particular elephant to talk about then he was unsure about the other.

Turning to face her, he studied her eyes for signs of deceit.

"Just a girl?"

"She was sitting at the crime scene when I paid a visit this morning."

"The sand on your boots," he said.

"I had to walk to the main road to call a taxi anyway. I figured I'd swing by and take a look without the forensics team and uniforms around. They did a good job. Clean and fast."

"You're avoiding the subject."

"I'm avoiding nothing. She's just a girl I saw at the crime scene right now. But I'd like to know more about her."

"Why didn't you mention it this morning?"

"I did. I told you I had a lead to follow up on."

"It's hardly a lead. Not even bronze, if you want to continue using this morning's terminology."

"Not yet. But she has a part to play, of that I'm certain."

"Tell me what happened at the beach. Did she approach you?"

"No. I didn't even know she was there at first. It was only when I was climbing up the sand dune that I saw her. She was sitting in the exact spot."

A slightly disgusted expression formed on Ben's face. "Where she was killed?"

"The exact spot. Bearing in mind that all signs of the crime had been removed, either by the wind or the forensics processes. She could have chosen to sit in any spot along that entire sandbank."

"It's over a mile long."

"But she sat there. A little odd, don't you think? She wasn't sitting to one side. She wasn't standing over it, staring down at where Jessica had been lying. She was in the very hollow. Out of the wind."

"Did you say anything?"

Hoping that her eye roll would answer his question, she watched as he imagined the scene, glancing at the mirror once more. Then he turned back to face her.

"And then she ran? Without saying a single word?"

"Yep."

"Did she leave anything behind?"

"A size five footprint."

"So what do you think she was doing at the caravan park?"

"I think she overheard me on the phone to you. I think she overheard me leaving you a message."

"The yellow sweater message?" he said, and an idea struck him with obvious effect. "I want to suggest that Jack Fraser killed Jessica Hudson, then stored her belongings at the caravan. But I can't find a why. There's no reason to it all. Maybe the girl knew about it and was helping him?" But the confidence in his tone waned with every word he spoke, to the point that, by the time he had reached the end of his sentence, he was questioning his own thoughts. "That doesn't make sense."

"No, it doesn't. None of it does," she said. "First of all, if it was Jack, why take her belongings?"

"To remove any evidence."

"Doubtful," she said. "But let's go with that for a second. Let's say it *was* Jack Fraser. He was her uncle, so he would have been close enough for our theory on asphyxiation, but..." She pulled a face at the idea.

"You don't believe it was him, do you?"

"I can't seem to find a motivation that fits the crime."

"So why are we here waiting to nick him?"

"Because he knows something. Because we found Jessica's sweater a short walk from his caravan. Because the fact that he even *has* a caravan where he goes to be away from his family. And because of the girl in the red coat."

"You just want to find out who she is."

It was as the transport van pulled around the corner in a small convoy of liveried police cars that Freya showed her hand in its entirety. She pulled her seat belt across, as Ben too caught sight of the van in his mirror.

"I think Jack Fraser knows who she is," she said. "And arresting him for the suspected murder of his niece should be enough to make him tell us."

———

A momentary respite in the wind allowed Ben time to gather his thoughts, while Freya knocked, ignoring the dormant doorbell this time.

For an innocent party, to open the front door and find two detectives backed by a handful of uniformed officers was often enough to create hysteria. If not hysteria, then at least questions, denial, or proclaimed innocence would be offered.

But Hetty Fraser offered none of the above.

A quick glance at the piece of paper that Ben held was enough for her to step to one side, and she let the door swing open, expressionless, as if it were her they were looking for and the game was up.

The search warrant was folded in Ben's hand as he handed it to her, and it remained folded as he, Freya, and the handful of officers entered the house.

The squad had been briefed. A detailed search plan had been developed and would continue while Ben and Freya escorted Jack Fraser to the station.

But Hetty Fraser said nothing. She offered not a single outburst, nor did she utter a breath of innocence.

She just stared, her mouth parted as if a question or protest clung to her lips. But she said nothing.

The first raised voice was Jack's. It came from upstairs. It seemed that despite his wife's inability to argue a cause, he had no issue in doing so. Handcuffed and raging, he was guided to the top of the stairs and led down to the hallway, where Freya and Ben waited.

"What the bloody hell do you think you're playing at?" he snarled, when the two uniforms presented him.

"Has he been read his rights?" asked Freya to the uniforms, who confirmed he had, and then she nodded toward the driveway. "Good. Take him away."

The house fell into relative silence when Jack had been removed. The sound of drawers being opened and cupboard doors being closed was all that could be heard.

"Is Beth home?" Freya asked, and Hetty, who now appeared stunned and almost relieved, shook her head. "Is there something you want to tell us, Mrs Fraser?"

The pause indicated there might have been something on her

mind. But the temptation to voice it passed, and once more, she shook her head.

"I suggest you make yourself comfortable," Freya advised. "Your husband has been arrested on suspicion of murder. This search could take some time. I'll ask an officer to sit with you–"

"That won't be necessary," she said, the first words she had uttered, and they were dry like leaves crunching underfoot. "Let them do what they need to do. If they find anything, well..." She hung on those words and swallowed, as if preparing to finish the sentence. But she never did.

"You have my number if you want to talk," Freya told her, then gestured for Ben to lead the way outside.

"I do love him," Hetty said.

Such a random thing to say stopped both Ben and Freya in their tracks. Ben turned in the front door, feeling the wind outside tug at his trouser legs.

"I don't doubt that," said Freya. "But if you do have something to say, now really is the time to say it, Hetty."

"Things haven't been great between us," Hetty continued, and Ben closed the front door, catching sight of Jack Fraser peering up at him through the rear window of the waiting marked car. "They haven't been great for a while."

"Why don't we go through to the kitchen?" Freya suggested, and before Hetty could protest, she encouraged her with a gentle hand on her arm.

The kitchen was as traditional as country kitchens come. A terracotta, tiled floor, an AGA large enough to heat the old house and cook dinner for a large family, and a range of copper pans that hung above an eight foot long kitchen island.

Opening a dialogue with Hetty required sensitivity. Moving to the stove, Ben gave them both a little space, at least until Freya had established a flow. The kettle, a large, black, old-fashioned looking implement, had already been filled. He placed it on a burner and used the dial to raise the temperature, then sought the tea making facilities.

"Hetty, I know this is a difficult time. But you should know that during our investigation, we have to eliminate close family and friends from our enquiries."

Hetty stared at her. The statement had been cleverly delivered, leaving enough of an invitation for Hetty to freely communicate any alterations to her previous statement.

But the opportunity came and went, as if the howling wind had carried it away.

"We know that neither you nor your husband were home on the night of the twelfth, Hetty. Would you like to revise what you told us?"

Finding some cups in a cupboard and the tea bags in a small pot, Ben continued making the tea as quietly as he could, listening in for subtle clues in the dialogue.

"Jack is an unhappy man," Hetty said, the statement lacking emotion. It was spoken as a child might recite *the cat sat on the mat*. But the lack of emotion ended there. The intonations that Ben had been listening for, with his back to the two women, came thick and fast. "I don't know where he goes, and the truth is, I don't care."

"I'm sorry to ask this, but is there another woman?"

A single stab of laughter emerged as a breath from the pit of Hetty's stomach.

"We stay together for Beth. Everything you see is a show. On the surface, we're this happy couple with a beautiful daughter. But Jack doesn't love us. We share a bed still, if only to keep Beth's suspicions at bay. But he's cold. There's no love. I like to think that he has another life. Another woman. That when he's there, he becomes the man I used to know. Fun-loving. Caring." She paused for a moment, as Ben placed two teas on the table, then returned for his own. "Sexual."

"But you don't know if there's somebody else?"

"I don't know anything about him. He goes to work an eight-hour shift at the wood yard and comes home twelve hours later. I gave up questioning him a long time ago."

Dragging one of the teas toward her, she then placed her hands around it, linking her fingers.

"Hetty, I'm going to ask you a question, and it's going to be hard to hear, but understand, we're just doing our jobs."

"Could he have killed Jessica?" Hetty said, and she looked at Ben, then at Freya. "A decade ago, I might have laughed at the question."

"But now?"

"I don't know. He's just a man that shares my bed and pays the bills, who cares for Beth more through obligation than genuine love."

"Would he have any reason to have hurt Jessica, or her parents maybe?"

"No. He hasn't said a word to Patricia or Tim for years."

"Did they fall out? Did Jack argue with Tim at all?"

"Not that I know of, no. When they first bought the house nearby, it was exciting. We were close. We had family dinners and barbecues, you know? It was nice. We lost our parents quite young, Patricia and I, so to be close was special. Then the kids came along, but instead of us becoming closer, we kind of drifted apart. It was just Jack at first. He saw them less and less. I think that kind of drove a divide. I still visited, and they came here, but Jack would saunter off somewhere. He wasn't interested. The girls were close though. That pleased me and I feel guilty for letting our relationship affect them. It got to the point where I felt awkward seeing them. She's my sister. I shouldn't feel awkward. But I did, and I think I felt ashamed."

"Ashamed?"

"Of Jack. Of his behaviour. I always said he was the way he was because of Tim's success, but whenever we spoke about it, Jack always brushed it off. By the time they bought the new house, the house they're in now, in Chapel, they were moving in different circles. Tim knows everyone, and everyone knows Tim. We were kind of left behind a little, and to be honest, I don't blame them. Nowadays, it's about keeping up appearances with them. They have to be seen to be the best. Tim's ego is nearly as big as his reputation."

"Do you think Jack is jealous of Tim's success? Or perhaps he feels like a failure?"

"Not jealous. He's never been driven by money. That's what attracted me to him."

"Where did you meet him? Do you mind if I ask?" said Freya, just as a uniform stepped into the kitchen and caught Ben's attention.

"You might want to see this," the officer said, and Hetty squeezed her eyes closed.

"I'll be there in a moment," said Ben, not wanting to disturb the flow of Hetty's account.

"I've lived here all my life," Hetty said, her voice sounding older than her years. "Here in Anderby. Patricia and I were always close. Tim lived in the village too. We all walked to school together, played together. Not just us. There were a few others, but Tim was the nicest. He was the one our mother approved of. She used to say that it was obvious that one of us would end up with him. And she was right. That left me on my own, while my sister, my best friend, began a new life with Tim. There were a few local boys, but nothing serious. Not what my mother would call suitable, if you know what I mean? What was a girl like me to do in a town that for half the year is hit by thousands of tourists?"

"Jack was a tourist?" asked Freya, reading between the lines.

Taking a sip of her tea, Hetty nodded, and she bore a shameless expression. "His parents had a place in one of the holiday parks on the coast. Down by the beach. It was one of our favourite places to go when we were young. The booze in the clubhouse was cheaper and somebody always had a party afterwards. He was nice. Different somehow. We went for a walk along the beach and we chatted. We shared a bottle of something and the rest is history. We consummated our relationship right there and then, and suddenly I was back. Suddenly I had what Patricia had. Suddenly people took me seriously, instead of treating me like a little girl. Above all, Jack took me seriously. He didn't have much money, and he had even less ambition, but what he did have, he spent on travelling here every weekend. My dad managed to find him a job locally so he could move here. I think he always felt like an outsider though. Everybody made him feel welcome, but I don't think he ever truly felt like part of us. He was..."

She paused for thought, and Ben felt rather than saw Freya's fleeting sideways glance.

"He was different," she finished.

CHAPTER THIRTY-SEVEN

"In here, Ben," the uniform who had interrupted them called out when he heard Freya and Ben ascending the stairs. His voice came from the master bedroom at the front of the house, and when Freya entered the room, he reddened a little. "Sorry, ma'am."

Moving from the far side of the bed, where the contents of the wardrobe had been stripped out, he stepped over an evidence box, which Freya noticed was empty, and brought her attention to the tall boy.

"It's these, ma'am," he said, and seemed to be a little more at ease with Ben in the room. He handed her an envelope. "Photographs, ma'am. I thought they might be of use."

"Where did you find them?" Ben asked.

"Bedside table. The gentleman's side. They were hidden beneath a few old books."

"What's your name?" asked Freya, carefully peeking inside the envelope at the images.

"Dicks, ma'am."

"Good work, Dicks," she replied, and handed the envelope to Ben. "Out of interest, where are the books?"

"I put them back in the drawer. I didn't really see the significance," he said, and stepped back over the empty box to retrieve them.

Taking three books from him, Freya studied the titles, then passed them to Ben.

"A Guide to the Odds," he said. "Beat the Odds."

"We already know he's a gambler," said Freya. "Have Chapman check his bank accounts. He might be in financial difficulty."

Dropping the books onto the bed, Ben nodded to Dicks – a silent yet friendly instruction for the books to be bagged and tagged. They left the room as silently as they had entered. Stopping at the top of the stairs, Freya eyed Ben.

"Want to stay and see what else they find?"

"Not really. I want to go and see what Jack has to say," replied Ben, as he too peeked inside the envelope. He was about to open his mouth to speak, when Freya placed her forefinger on his lips, mouthing for him to hush. "Damn it, Freya. These are exactly–"

"What will cause a lot of trouble if they get into the wrong hands," she finished, then gestured for them to leave.

On the way out of the house, they met a uniform at the door, stationed to prevent unauthorised access or departure. The protocol was designed to prevent evidence contamination should anything be found that may later be relied on in court.

"See to it that somebody sits with Mrs Fraser, will you?" Freya said. "She may need some support."

"Will do, ma'am," the uniform replied.

The vehicle with Jack Fraser had already left to begin the custody processing, which left just a handful of police vehicles – the transporter in which the uniforms had arrived, a single liveried car, and Ben's car. The driveway was large enough for Ben to manoeuvre out of the spot and then out onto the lane. But he stopped in the same place they had waited earlier, applied the handbrake, and retrieved the envelope from his pocket.

"So impatient," Freya said.

"This is important. I can't stop thinking about it."

Pulling on a pair of latex gloves, the last in the small supply he kept in his pocket, he withdrew the photos. There were just five images, and they appeared to have been taken at different times, as the people in the images were the same but they wore a variety of clothes.

Holding the first image up for them both to see, Ben provided the narrative, as if it was a test in which he must identify all the clues.

"Jessica Hudson. Yellow sweater. Jack Fraser. Caravan," he said.

"That doesn't prove anything."

"There's a bag of weed on the table."

"It's not illegal after the fact. I didn't find any at the caravan."

Moving to the next photo, Ben issued a hissing sound in lieu of anything of worth. Then again, he gave his narrative, "Bloody hell, Freya."

"I know. She was closer to Jack than we imagined."

"It's not just me, is it?" he said. "He's closer than any uncle should be. He's touching her."

"Nope, not just you, Ben."

"I mean, look at him sitting there with his arm around her, and his hand on her thigh, like she's some kind of possession."

Waiting for him to fall in with the key element that was on Freya's mind, she said nothing, allowing him to peruse the rest of the images. He went to flick to the next image, but Freya placed her hand on his.

"Before you go any further," she said. "Tell me exactly what you're thinking."

Pondering the question for a while, he stared out of the window for long enough that Freya could withdraw her hand from his without breaking his concentration.

"Who took the photos?" he said, as if what the images had shown had blinded him from seeing the obvious.

"Bingo," she replied. "Now turn the photo over."

He did, and his reaction was exactly as Freya had expected.

"Bloody hell."

———

The incident room door swung open so fast there was little time for it to squeal, but it slammed closed behind Ben with more than its usual ferocity. Two heads peered above their computer monitors, glanced at each other, then tentatively voiced their concerns.

"Are you okay, Ben? How did it go?" Jackie said.

"I saw Jack Fraser downstairs," Chapman added. "What can we do?"

"Everything," said Ben, as he rifled through his paperwork, searching for the notes he had made when he and Freya had first visited the Frasers. "Get me anything and everything you can on him. Bank accounts, criminal records, DVLA records, anything. We've got twenty-four hours, thirty-six at a push, to get this over the line. How are we doing with the lab results?"

"Still not arrived," Chapman said. "I've asked Doctor Bell to have them couriered rather than posted."

"Good, thank you," he said, as he found the page in his notebook and searched through his terrible handwriting for anything worthwhile.

"Ben?" Jackie said, sounding timid.

Realising he may have come across as bad-tempered or unapproachable, he softened his response, although the interruption had left him irritated.

"What is it, Jackie?"

"I found an Airbnb in Chapel that might be of interest."

"Go on," he said, still scanning his own notes. Then he stopped and looked up at her. "Dog?"

"No dog. Just a man and a woman."

"So? What's the relevance?"

"They arrived in separate cars. Apparently that's not unusual, according to the host anyway. A lot of their off-season traffic is for one-night stands, affairs and whatnot."

Unable to see the relevance, and with his patience running thin, he coaxed her on as softly as he could. "What does it have to do with Jessica? She didn't drive."

"Not Jessica. It was Derek Barnes, Ben. That's why he wasn't on the flight on the twelfth. I checked with the contractor firm he works for. He wasn't due until the thirteenth."

The combination of his scrawled notes and Jackie's verbal report was beginning to jumble. Rubbing the back of his neck, he tried to make sense of it, and how it was relevant to Jack Fraser. Seeing his reaction, Jackie continued to explain.

"He told his wife he was going out on the twelfth but stayed in an Airbnb with another woman, Ben. He's having an affair. That's all."

"Who with?"

"We don't know that much. But if she drives, it couldn't have been Jessica."

That terrible squeal of the incident room door interrupted Ben's thoughts, but a charming voice steered his concentration.

"Ben?" said Freya from the doorway. "Are you planning on joining this interview anytime today?"

"Good work, Jackie," he said, and snapped his notebook shut before heading out of the room, catching the door before it slammed.

Already in the stairwell, Freya's heels echoed loudly as she descended the steps, urging him on.

"Ah, Ben," said Arthur, as he passed his office.

The heels of Freya's boots on the concrete stairs faded as the fire exit door closed with a click.

"Sir?" he said, taking one step back and peering into the office.

"I was hoping to catch you. How are you getting on with DI Bloom?"

"Very good, sir," he replied, very aware that her mood would be altering with every second he delayed.

"Very good?" Arthur replied.

"She's a good detective, sir. A good fit for the team too."

"Is that so?" He spoke, Ben imagined, as any man of his position might, with all the time in the world to appease his wonderings. "I told you she comes highly recommended."

"You did, sir. DCI Granger also reiterated that. From what I've seen, I can understand why."

"How's her mood?"

Slipping into the realms of darkness right now. By the time I get down there, she'll be a seething demon waiting to banish me to hell.

"Her mood, sir? I haven't noticed anything unusual."

"Keep an eye on her for me, will you? Between you and I, as much as we need someone like her, she also needs a little support. She's been through a lot."

"Will do, sir," Ben said, seeing an opportunity to end the conversation. "Will that be all?"

"Just that..." he began, then seemed to search for the right words. "If she seems a little odd sometimes. Tell me. I need to know."

"You want me to spy on her for you?"

"No, don't sound so dramatic. I'm trying to look out for the woman. Just give me an idea of where she is..." he said, gesticulating with his hands. "Mentally."

She's the most messed up woman I've ever met, is what he should have said. But what he actually said was, "Will that be all, sir?"

"Yes, yes. I don't want to keep you," the old man finished. But then he added the caveat, "Oh, Ben?"

"Sir?" Ben said, stepping back into the doorway. He could almost hear Freya's blood boiling from downstairs.

"Just between you, me, and the gatepost. Okay?"

"Sir."

Ben entered the fire escape and leaned on the handrail, peering downstairs. Whichever way he turned, he would betray somebody he respected. The feeling sat uneasy on his mind as he considered how he might relieve himself of the responsibilities.

CHAPTER THIRTY-EIGHT

"Detective Sergeant Ben Savage has finally entered the room," Freya said, for the purpose of the recording, which she had clearly initiated already.

Ignoring the underhand dig, Ben took the seat beside Freya, noting the red, flashing light on the digital recording device, then the empty chair beside Fraser.

Freya watched him, admiring his control.

"Legal rep?" he asked. The question was directed at Freya, but it was Fraser who answered.

"Indisposed," he said, his voice tired from shouting and bitter from the force's finest levels of hospitality.

"Indisposed?" said Ben. "That's a new one."

A sideways glance from Freya cut the quip short, and then it dawned on him who Fraser's solicitor clearly was.

"We can get you a duty solicitor," he offered. "That way we can avoid a conflict of interest too."

"We've been through the options," Freya said, as she placed her hands flat on the table, taking control of the room. "Mr Fraser is aware of his rights, and as of now, we have Mr Fraser's undivided attention for the next twenty-two hours, during which time

I intend to ask pertinent questions to the investigation, and I expect full and pertinent answers in reply. Your responses to my questions, Mr Fraser, will help us decide if you get to go home to your family, or if we apply for a custody extension. Is that understood?"

"Clear as daylight," Fraser said.

"For the purpose of the recording, I am now presenting Mr Fraser with four photographs found in an envelope tucked beneath a pile of gambling related reading material inside his bedside table. The photos and the books were found during a search of his home address, for which a warrant was produced, authorised by Detective Chief Inspector Will Granger. The photographs are evidenced as JH003, JH004, JH005, and JH006. Mr Fraser, do you recognise these photographs?"

At the top of the pile of photos was the image of Jack Fraser and Jessica Hudson inside the caravan. She was wearing her favourite yellow sweater, and a bag of weed was clearly identifiable on the table.

"Do you recognise the people in this image, Mr Fraser?" she asked again, and his response was one of impatience.

"Of course I do."

"Would you care to tell us who you believe them to be?"

"That's me, and that's Jessica," he said, stabbing at the image with his index finger.

"And do you recognise the location? Where was the photo taken?"

The timing of the question was clever. Fraser would not yet have known that they had discovered the caravan or its contents. His response would be indicative of either his ability to lie or his desire to conceal the truth.

He stared at her, as if Ben wasn't there, and he licked his lips.

"I'm waiting, Mr Fraser."

There's a moment, Freya thought, that occurs when a troubled man breaks, and the light in the eyes fades as if the will to delay the inevitable has expired.

And Jack Fraser's eyes faded along with every taut muscle in his face, so that he was expressionless, lost, and was preparing for his fate.

"Brightwater," he said, his voice barely audible.

"For the recording, if you please," said Freya, offering him little compassion in what clearly was the beginning of a difficult confession.

"Chapel Brightwater Holiday Park," he said, articulating the words with a defiance, as if he was daring them to ask for more.

And ask they might, had there not been a knock at the door offering Jack Fraser the chance for a brief reprise.

"Ma'am," said Jackie, leaning into the room. "Apologies. You need to see this."

"Now?" Freya snapped.

For a moment, Jackie Gold hesitated, as if she was questioning how important her news actually was, and if it was indeed worthy of interrupting an interview with a murder suspect. But she drew her own conclusion, and nodded. "Yes, ma'am."

Freya's own contemplation was whether or not to include Ben in the discussion. After a moment of deliberation, she concluded that his earlier tardiness was out of character, and that perhaps she should give the guy a break.

"Have a uniform step inside," she said. Then, with her finger poised over the button to pause the recording, she announced the brief intermission and collected the evidence into her folder.

"I'm sorry, ma'am," Jackie began, when Freya and Ben stepped outside. "I did consider waiting but..."

She paused.

"But?" said Freya, surprising herself at how soft her tone had become with the detective constable, who, in Freya's opinion, just needed a little confidence boost. Giving the girl a hard time would be of little benefit to anybody.

"We just received the lab results," she said, glancing between Freya and Ben, as if she was unsure of who to deliver the news to.

Visually straightening at the news, Ben stepped closer.

"They found traces of DNA beneath Jessica Hudson's fingernails."

"So she fought back?" said Ben, then silenced for Jackie to continue.

"They ran it against the database," said Jackie. "It's a partial profile to that of Derek Barnes."

CHAPTER THIRTY-NINE

Inside Will's office, Ben stood uneasily beside Freya, waiting for the inevitable row to commence.

"You want to charter a helicopter to bring Derek Barnes back onshore?" said Will, and he stared at both Freya and Ben in turn, his face a picture of incredulity. "Do you know what that would cost?"

Despite Ben being the lowest ranking officer in the room, he had known Will the longest, and knew how to calm his temper before the storm set in.

"It's either that or we wait for him to get back, guv," Ben said. "That's another eight days. We can't wait that long."

Sucking in a long and deep breath, Will pondered the position they were in. It wasn't the cost that was the problem. Any fool could see that. It was the conversation he would need to have with Arthur that would create the problem.

"We found skin under Jessica Hudson's fingernails," Freya added. "It's a partial profile to his. The man has a history of grievances with Timothy Hudson, and he lied about his whereabouts on the night of the twelfth. From what I understand, he doesn't exactly enjoy playing by the rules. It's a strong case. I think CPS will be on board."

"It's not definitive," Will replied.

"We can wait the eight days. That doesn't bother me one little bit," Freya explained, using a tone that was far too pleasant to be anything other than her indignant tongue warming up. "In fact, now that the test results are back, we can arrange for Jessica's parents to see the body. Why don't *you* make that call? And while you're at it, why don't you tell them that we're sitting on our backsides waiting for a suspect to get home, because we haven't got the budget—"

"Freya, leave it," Ben interjected, but the damage had been done. Usually calm and composed, it took a lot of friction to rub Will up the wrong way. The few times Ben had witnessed it were embedded in his brain, like a bad tattoo.

"Have you finished?" Will said, his tone relaxed and his breathing slow and steady. It was the calm before the storm, and either Freya sensed it, or she was experienced enough to keep her mouth shut from then on. "I have accommodated you as best I can, DI Bloom. I have disrupted my team. I have even gone head to head with my superior with regards to your position here."

"Shall I leave, guv?" said Ben, sensing the conversation was no longer about Derek Barnes, and more about Freya Bloom.

"No, stay," Will replied. "There's nothing you shouldn't hear. The fact is, Bloom, that whilst you're here, you act under my command. You're not in London now. You're not up against five other DIs in a race to the top. You're in a small team where everyone pulls their weight, everyone looks out for each other, and everyone respects the chain of command. And for you, that's me. So the next time you feel yourself about to give me an instruction, the next time you feel yourself obliged to voice your opinion, just remember this. You're here because Detective Superintendent Harper wants you here. But one more false move, and you're out. Harper or no Harper. Do I make myself clear?"

Silently willing her to agree so they could move on, Ben stood uncomfortably between them. He wanted to tell Will to go easy on her, but he had more sense than that.

"Understood, guv," Freya said, and the room seemed to relax a little, as if somebody had opened a window.

"Good. I'm not an angry man, Freya. I hope DS Savage will vouch for that. I'm fair, and I play by the rules. You'll learn that for yourself in good time if you're here long enough."

"That's good to hear," said Freya, and Ben winced at her persistent desire to have the last word.

"You have Barnes' DNA. He's lied about his whereabouts. That's a good start," Will said, nodding appreciatively. "But it's not infallible. It's not watertight. A good lawyer will find a hole in there if, and I mean if, CPS approve the charges. Get me something else. Get me a rock-solid case and I'll have Barnes flown back here quicker than you can say jack rabbit."

From the corner of his eye, Ben caught Freya opening her mouth. What she was about to say was anybody's guess.

"Understood, guv," said Ben, closing the conversation off.

"Good. You have Jack Fraser in custody, I hear. What's the plan with him? Release without charge?"

"No," said Freya, before Ben could get in there. "No way. I have a hell of a lot more questions for Mr Fraser."

CHAPTER FORTY

They walked in silence to the stairwell. With every step, Freya felt Ben brooding like a child. Away from the heated offices, the stairwell, with its painted block walls, exposed conduits, and emergency lighting, was as cold as the motor home Freya now called home.

"What was that?" said Ben, and Freya remembered how the stairwell was deemed, rather ironically, equal ground. "Of all the people not to upset, he's at the top of the list."

"Where are you on that list?" said Freya, and she leaned against the handrail, folded her arms, and admired the way his chest seemed to swell when he got angry.

"I'm not on the list," he said. "You can piss me off as many times as you like. But if you want to stay here, and if you want an easy life, you need to keep that man on your side. Is this place a joke to you? You act like we're insignificant."

"We're all insignificant," she said. "And no, this place is not a joke to me. In fact, I rather like it. It's quaint."

"Quaint?"

"I'd even go as far as to say it's charming," Freya said, keeping her voice low and her tone as friendly as she could muster. "I think I'd like to stay."

Staring down at her, the beginnings of a smile curled the corners of his mouth. "You've got a funny way of showing it, Freya Bloom."

It was as if he had been enticed into an argument with her one too many times and could now recognise her manipulative ways. She'd have to change tack with him if she was to keep him on the leash.

"So," she said, moving the topic of conversation on, "DNA under Jessica's nails. She fought back. I was right."

He said nothing but studied her eyes and her expression, as a cat might watch an expecting bird forage for worms, hopping closer and closer to where he sat.

"Well?" she said.

"You win," he replied. "Fair and square."

She didn't believe him. His expression hadn't changed. In fact, not a single muscle in his face had altered.

"What would make you truly happy, Ben?" she said, and she pushed off the handrail, stopping just a short distance in front of him. "What can I do?"

"I was late to the interview—"

"I did notice."

"I was late because Arthur collared me. He wants me to report on your mental health."

"Oh, that's a tough one. Even the shrinks couldn't do that, and they all had PhDs."

"I lied," he said, and the strength in his voice faded to what Freya could only describe as a whine. "I lied to him to stop him from giving you a hard time."

"You didn't have to do that."

"If I didn't do it, you'd be in there now, or you'd be seeing some kind of therapist. Either way, you wouldn't be working this case."

"What did you tell him?"

"I didn't throw you under a bus if that's what you're asking. He wants to know more."

"I've told you both everything I know."

"I'm just telling you what he said. I want you to know that I have your back. And so does Will. Just bear that in mind. Given time, so will Arthur."

His candid approach to the lay of the land was appreciated, slightly awkward, but above all, touching. There were a number of responses she could have given. She could have toyed with that masculine weakness of his that she adored, to tame the lion and have him purr at her feet.

"Fraser still has more to say," she said, tiring of the previous topic. Enough had been said on the subject of her behaviour and mental health already. "I'm going to push him. Why don't we split up for the rest of the day? I'll take Fraser. You see what you can find on Barnes."

"We could do," he said, clearly suspicious of leaving her alone.

"Do you think you could get in touch with Jessica's parents? Arrange for them to see her?"

"I was planning to."

"Good," she replied. "Don't mention anything about Jack just yet. I want to see what he has to say. How about we meet at mine later?"

"At yours?"

"I might not have much, Ben, but I do have a stove. Be creative."

"I do a mean beans on toast."

"Beans on toast?"

"The best you ever had," he replied confidently.

"Nine p.m.," she said. As she turned to descend the stairs, she called out, "You can bring another bottle of that little sailing boat if you like."

"Baked beans and a sailing boat?" he called, but she was

already through the doors. He muttered to himself, alone in the stairwell while his mind was elsewhere, "You'll be putty in my hands."

CHAPTER FORTY-ONE

Offering no apologies for her delay, Freya resumed her position in the interview room. Thirty minutes had passed, during which time Jack Fraser appeared either considerably older or more tired. It was hard to tell which.

Resuming the recording, Freya announced the time and remarked that only Fraser and herself remained.

"It's just us now," she began. "Where were we?"

In addition to his dishevelled appearance, Fraser was somehow smaller. Deflated. He shrugged.

"You were just telling me about Brightwater Holiday Park. Why don't we pick up where we left off?"

"It's just a caravan."

"No. Not really. To you, it might just be a caravan, but I doubt it. To me, it's a quandary. A dilemma. It could open up all sorts of doors. Doors that nobody was expecting to open. It's more than just a caravan, isn't it? Tell me about it," she said, wondering which of the doors he would open.

But he said nothing.

"Shall I help you? Let's talk about your gambling problem."

"I don't have a problem. I have the odd flutter, but I don't have a problem."

From the folder, Freya withdrew a sheet of paper prepared by Chapman. She lay it on the table between them, then turned it so that Fraser could read it.

"For the benefit of the recording, I'm showing Mr Fraser evidence JH007. His bank statement for the past month."

"You can't do that," he cried, showing anger for the first time since he'd been escorted from his house.

"I think you'll find I can. You see, each of these lines that have been highlighted are payments to an online gambling website. Yet the only payments coming in are from your employer. I spoke to them by the way. They spoke very highly of you. You're a reliable pair of hands is what they said."

"Is that right?" he said. "So what? I gamble. What does that mean?"

"It means you're prepared to lie, Mr Fraser. Nothing more. You see, if this case goes to court, there will be character witnesses and evidence to show what type of person you are. And now, despite what anybody has to say, we all know you're happy to lie to a police officer, despite being under caution. You see, we found a 4G router in the caravan too, but no laptop, which I'm assuming you take with you and keep hidden from your wife. We did find a newspaper. It was open on the horse racing pages and marked with a pencil. I'll ask you again, Mr Fraser, do you or do you not have a gambling problem?"

Cornered, Fraser offered a sigh.

"My wife doesn't know."

"Are you in trouble?"

"I'm working my way out of it. I lost a big bet. I lost our savings. I'm trying to get it back."

"By gambling?"

He shrugged.

"So if I were to ask you why you rent the caravan, what would you tell me?"

He offered no response.

"Is it somewhere you can go to gamble?"

He nodded.

"For the recording please?"

"I gamble there. That's what I do. I drink there. I smoke there." He stared across the table at her, and for the first time in a while, he appeared carefree as to what she thought of him. "I go there to be myself."

"And what about Jessica Hudson?" she asked. "Why did she go there? To see her Uncle Jack?"

"That's not fair."

"Did she have a gambling habit too, Jack?"

"You bitch."

"Or maybe she went there to smoke weed with her loving uncle?" She flipped his attention to the photo. "You two look awfully close. Is that why we found her sleeping bag in your caravan?"

"No comment."

"I wonder what Tim and Patricia would say if they saw you together like that."

"You wouldn't."

"If this was a photo of Tim and your daughter Beth, what would you have to say?"

"I'd say there are some things you should keep your nose out of."

"Perhaps you can tell me why we found Jessica's sweater in a bush not far from your secret caravan?"

The anger in his face dropped to genuine surprise.

"What?"

"In the forest. We found Jessica's yellow sweater stuffed into a hedge."

"I don't know what you're talking about."

Freya flipped to the next photo.

"For the benefit of the recording, I'm showing Mr Fraser evidence number JH005. Can you please describe what's shown in the photo?"

Refusing to look at the image, he stared at the recorder that was built into the wall.

"Come on, Jack. We found the photo in your bedside table. Surely you can describe what you see?"

He said nothing. Only a single tear worked itself loose from his eye and formed a shiny path along the side of his nose.

"Do you understand how this looks, Mr Fraser? You and two young girls alone in a caravan. Did you buy them the weed, Jack?"

"Of course not—"

"Did you get them stoned and make them perform for you?"

"What? You're sick—"

"So tell me what's happening here."

"It isn't what it looks like."

"Really? Perhaps you would care to explain."

Brazen, he leaned on the table, arms folded, and stared at her with nothing but pure hatred in his eyes, his chest rising and falling.

"Or perhaps you could tell me who the other girl is?" Freya said. "It looks like they're having a damn good time."

"They were old enough to make their own decisions. There's no laws broken there."

"Tell me what happened that night. The night of the twelfth. We tracked your phone. We know you went to the caravan."

Freya sighed as she fingered the photographs, a silent threat that she might pursue a line of questioning he couldn't bear.

"I went to the caravan to see her."

"But she was going to London. Didn't you know about the trip?"

"She was never going to London. She told Tim that so she could have the weekend..." He paused.

"The weekend with you?"

"To herself," he corrected her. "So she could do what she wanted to do. To experience some kind of freedom. Away from the oppression, the rules, and the limitations."

"You don't agree with the way Timothy Hudson raises his children. Is that right?"

"I just gave her somewhere to get away. She's not a child," he said, then corrected himself. "Wasn't a child."

"What did you do when you discovered she wasn't there?"

"I went to the house. Their house. I needed to know she was okay."

"Why wouldn't she have been okay?"

"There had been arguments. Her and Tim. Vicious arguments."

"But you couldn't just knock on the door and ask if Jessica was okay, could you?"

The very mention of her name invoked a choking sound from Fraser, and he composed himself as best he could.

"I went to call Patricia, but I'd left my phone in the caravan. So I threw a stone at the bedroom window. Just a little pebble. She came downstairs. I think Tim was in his office out the back. She told me she'd dropped Jessica at the beach to meet Charlie earlier that day. I knew the spot. I knew where she'd be. So I went back to the caravan to get my phone, it's just a few minutes from their house, and then onto the beach."

"So Jessica's mother knew about the caravan?"

Nodding, he reached for the photograph of Jessica and himself, and a sad smile formed as he studied her.

"She was so pretty. So harmless. Tim didn't deserve her. I told Jessica she could use the caravan for the weekend. Patricia agreed to it."

His tale was growing more twisted with every detail he revealed. It was times like these that Freya had to remind herself to be impassive. She was just a conduit of the law, not a lawmaker.

But even so, it was hard not to imagine him grooming the poor girl.

"Tell me what happened at the beach, Jack," Freya said, noting his trembling lower lip.

"That was when I found her," he whined, and the emotions of the last few days burst through whatever mental barrier he had formed. He wailed, sniffed, and finally, he cried the cry of a broken man.

It wasn't the first time Freya had witnessed such outbursts from suspects in custody. A police cell could be imposing to those not used to the environment, but it was the interview room where the truth really hit home. Maybe it was the way the rooms were portrayed in movies and TV shows? Or maybe it was the relentless questions and inability to escape the truth? Or the claustrophobia those four walls created?

A minute passed, and still, Fraser bawled. Covering his face with his hands, his body seemed to convulse with the memories of the events, of what he had lost, and perhaps, what he had done.

Sitting quietly, Freya waited for the first wave to ease. It always did. Without a doubt, the second wave would follow, but there would be a window of opportunity in which to finish the conversation. Then he could be taken back to his cell to have a long, hard think about his actions.

Taking deep breaths to control himself, Fraser hung his head, cuffed his running nose, and then peered up at Freya, a shamed and broken man.

"I moved her. I know I shouldn't have, but I had to. She looked so uncomfortable. We often went there. To that spot. We'd sit on the dune looking out to sea, and I'd listen to all her troubles, all her dreams. I imagine you saw it. There's a place in the tall grass. A hollow from where you can stare out to sea, sheltered from the wind."

"I saw it," she said.

"Well, that was her spot. She liked it there."

"Why didn't you report what you'd seen?" Freya asked. "If you were innocent then you could have called the police."

"And tell them what? What was I doing there? Why was I out looking for her? Why did I go to her house? The dirty uncle."

"We found her sweater—"

"I took the sweater," he snapped. "I wanted it. It..." He stumbled on his words, perhaps hearing how they would sound before he even spoke them. But the damage had already been done, and he came to the same conclusion. "It smelled of her."

The second wave was imminent. Seizing the chance, Freya sought one final piece of information.

"Was Jessica alone, Jack? Who is the other girl?"

Shaking his head, he flicked through the photographs, lost in whatever sick memories they invoked.

"She was alone," he said finally. "And I made her comfortable. Like she was just sleeping."

The uniform who guarded the door stepped inside when she called out. He waited for Freya's command.

"Take Mr Fraser back to the cells," she said, replacing the evidence into the folder. "He needs some time to reflect on his actions."

CHAPTER FORTY-TWO

"What's wrong?" Jackie asked, before Ben had even sat down at his desk. She hit the enter key harder than she needed to, as if to add finality to whatever it was she had been typing, then swivelled in her chair to face him.

"Nothing really," he replied. "Just a little bemused."

"Anything I can help with?"

Leaning forward, so that Chapman and the uniforms she was talking to wouldn't overhear, Ben spoke his mind. His friendship with Jackie not only outlasted every one of his colleagues, but every one of his friends too. Speaking his mind was allowed, encouraged, but he had to be mindful of her inane ability to seek out the details in any conversation that caught her eye. When it came to facts that were none of her business, she was a magpie.

"I genuinely think there's something wrong with that woman."

"Lover's tiff?" Jackie joked, and braced for a response she may not want to hear. It was true that he and Jackie had been lifelong friends, but like a weight that clung to that friendship was the lifelong crush she had carried. Her infatuation with Ben was so long-lasting, it had bypassed the stage of being secret. It had become such common knowledge throughout the station, it wasn't even mentioned anymore.

"No, Jackie. Definitely not," he said, watching her cheeks redden but choosing not to venture down that route. "One minute she's at my throat. The next she's inviting me to dinner to discuss the case. One minute she wants to investigate Arthur. The next minute she's over it, and is taking my advice. It's a bloody roller coaster, Jackie."

"Was the mention of dinner aimed at me?"

"What? No, of course not. It's not like that. But do you see what I mean? I never know what mood I'm going to walk into, and she's pissed both Will and Arthur off already. She's like a hurricane," he said, and in a flash he remembered the Neil Young song. Maybe it was his mind seeking some kind of light-hearted humour after spending so much time with somebody as intense as Freya. "Sometimes she even makes a joke and it's totally inappropriate, ill-timed, and out of the blue, I don't know if I should laugh or ignore her, or what. She even had me bet with her if Jessica Hudson fought back or not."

"Sounds like some kind of neurotic condition. It's common enough," Jackie said.

"I don't know, Jackie. Something happened to her in London and it has truly left its mark. That's why she's here."

"Like a trauma?"

He nodded. "The only positive thing is, and keep this to yourself, but she doesn't remember a thing about it."

"Amnesia?"

"Yeah, disruptive amnesia or something. Promise you won't tell anyone, Jackie. I'm breaking all kinds of trust here."

"I won't. You know me."

Nodding at her sincerity, he continued, "She keeps disappearing."

"So follow her," Jackie said, not picking up on what Ben was saying.

"I mean mentally. She blacks out. Goes somewhere else. I don't know how to explain it."

"What?" said Jackie, loud enough for Chapman's conversation to stall, and for the uniforms to stare in Ben's direction. "What?" she whispered.

"That's all I know. I said I'd do dinner with her. You know? To see if she opens up."

"I had no idea," Jackie said, her voice compassionate, and it reminded him why at times like this she could be the gentlest of people.

"No, and nobody else does."

"So what's she doing here? Why the hell did Arthur agree to her coming?"

"Because she's good at what she does, I guess."

"Are you going?" she asked.

"Going where?"

"To dinner? With Bloom?"

"Ah, I don't know. I have to call the Hudsons to arrange the viewing. I hate this bit of the job."

"If that's your way of asking me to do it, you can–"

"It's okay. I should do it. I'll get a time from them and you can make the arrangements with the mortuary."

"That's okay. I can do that bit just fine," she said, offering him a smile, which lingered for longer than necessary. "Anything else I can do?"

Sitting back in his chair, Ben stretched out his legs. He'd been on the move all day, and if he was honest with himself, he should have just gone home to bed and slept.

But there were balls in motion that needed guiding. A gentle touch here and there.

"Will wants more on Barnes before we bring him back to shore."

"More?"

"The DNA isn't enough. It's not a perfect match. Let's face it.

Jessica was lying out in the rain all night with seagulls all over her. A decent lawyer will find a hole in that."

"Thanks for reminding me," she said, and pulled a face at the memory of how Jessica's body had been found.

"Have you been in touch with the Airbnb place?" he asked, seeing an angle that he knew damn well he should have seen before, had he not been so distracted with Jack Fraser and Freya's personal issues.

"Not since I told you I had."

"Call them," said Ben, finding life in his weary bones. "Tell them not to take any more bookings, and then get hold of CSI. Talk to Michaela. She's good."

"What are we looking for?"

"I don't know to be honest. But it's all we've got right now. Barnes stayed there on the twelfth. You told me that he and his mistress arrived separately."

"Yes, but—"

"Who's to say he didn't go there after he'd been to the beach?"

Trapping the phone handset between her cheek and shoulder, Jackie flicked through her notes for the number she had jotted down.

"Meet Michaela there. Black light the room, and..." His mind was working overtime. He stared at the whiteboard a few metres away, and his eyes fell to the spot on the floor beneath it. "Sand," he said. "Check for sand."

"Sand?"

"Trust me," he said, revitalised. "If there's sand there, on the carpet or the floor or whatever, then we can bring Barnes back, and if that happens, Jackie, then I'll be giving you the pleasure of nicking him."

"What if they've already cleaned or let the room?"

"Then it needs to be evacuated. Tell them we'll cover the cost of lost business, but under no circumstance is anyone to enter that room. Do you want him, Jackie?"

Nodding, she clearly remembered the taunts he gave when he was released.

"Yes," she said. "Yes, I want him."

"Call me when you're there," he said. "This could be what we need."

CHAPTER FORTY-THREE

Retrieving his phone from his pocket, Ben opened his file and found the number for the Hudson house. But before he dialled it, he paused. With Jack Fraser downstairs in an interview room with Freya and their daughter on a slab in Lincoln mortuary, the family were likely in turmoil. A phone call seemed such a cold way to arrange a viewing. It seemed so impersonal.

Glancing at his watch, he judged he could be at the house before five p.m., and considered a trip to the crime scene on his way back. It would be dark by then. Exactly how it had been for Jessica.

Pulling his coat from the back of the chair, he called out to nobody in particular, "I'm heading out. I'll see you all tomorrow."

"What about the viewing?" Jackie asked.

"I'll call you when I've spoken to the Hudsons," he replied. "I'll see what time suits them."

Irritatingly, the incident room door slammed closed behind him, the noise of which must have alerted Arthur, as he called out when Ben passed his open office door.

"Don't forget, Ben," he said. "On the surface, the statement was harmless, friendly, and non-intrusive, but there were undertones.

"I'm working on it," Ben replied. Then, before Arthur could detain him any longer, he made his excuses. "I'm just planning my conversation with the Hudsons. Sad times. I'll see you tomorrow, Sir," Ben said, and was on his way.

The bite of the cold air in the stairwell marked an unwelcome transition into what the outside held in store for him. The cold front that had blown in from Russia was making its mark, like a silent invasion, incapacitating the people of Lincolnshire and the surrounding counties, and forcing people inside.

When he reached his car, he wasn't surprised to see a light dusting of snow on the bonnet. A blast of the window wipers cleared his windscreen, but when his headlights came on and he saw the flurry in the two beams of light, it was clear there was a lot more of the dreaded white stuff to come. Thankful that the declining weather had been kept at bay for a day or two, so that Jessica's body hadn't been buried beneath a snowfall only to be found a week later, and so that her sweater had been easily visible in the brambles, he considered what challenges the snow might bring to the investigation. Access to the caravan for the forensics team should be fine. Barney maintained the park and the access roads well. With little further access required to the beach, he saw no reason why it should prove a hindrance.

And then it dawned on him. The teams, in their various factions, were doing everything they could to bring Barnes back to shore. Should the search of the Airbnb prove fruitful, poor weather conditions might cause flight delays.

Still stationary, he found Jackie's number and hit dial.

"Ben?"

"What's the news?"

"Well, I'm still holding for Michaela—"

Searching the car park, Ben saw the familiar headlights of Will's Jaguar parked in his usual spot.

"DCI Granger is still in the station. Find him if you need to, get him to escalate it, quote me if need be."

"What's the urgency?"

"Look outside."

A brief pause ensued as Ben imagined Jackie leaning over Chapman's desk to see out of the window.

"Oh, it's snowing," she said.

But, unsure whether she'd made the connection Ben had made, he gave her a prompt. "How would you feel about flying in a helicopter in this weather?"

The silence said it all. She had made the connection, albeit assisted.

"They'll ground the choppers, Ben. Barnes will be stuck there until they resume flights."

"Not unless you can get forensics to hurry the bloody hell up," he said. "I'll be in the area, so call if you need me."

"I'll call you on the way," she said, and the call disconnected. In an investigation where so much relied on the integrity of evidence, urgency was not a detective's friend. Urgency caused mistakes, oversights, and created holes for lawyers to stick their big noses inside, to sniff out an exit for the suspect.

The wheels were in motion on his side of the investigation. Finding Freya's number, he hit dial once more while the engine warmed.

CHAPTER FORTY-FOUR

A straight-faced uniform escorted a sombre looking Jack Fraser along the ground floor corridor to the custody desk. Not once did Fraser raise his head, look back, or offer any kind of resistance. Looking on from the interview room, Freya gave his future a bleak appraisal, and forced herself not to look at the photos. Although not sexual of nature or indecent in material, it was the implied nature of the circumstances under which they had been taken that Freya battled with.

No man of Fraser's age should behave that way with a girl of Jessica's age, and the voyeuristic images of Jessica and the other girl raised the bar another twisted notch.

A vibration in her pocket provided a welcome distraction, and she stepped back into the interview room when she saw Ben's name on the screen. Placing her folder down, she perched on the table and answered the call.

"Give me some good news," she said with a sigh, by way of both greeting him and conveying the result of the interview.

"The good news is that it's snowing," Ben replied, but hidden in that throwaway comment was a potential disaster that wasn't lost on Freya for a single second.

There was a moment's pause.

"Is it likely that Barnes will be stuck out on a rig in the North Sea?"

"If we don't get a move on and nail him for certain, yes."

"How likely is Granger to budge if we pushed him?"

"Zero chance," Ben replied. "He's a good man, fair, but he's a brick wall."

"And this is the good news, you say?"

"Not really. Just my attempt at cheap humour. I've got Jackie and CSI heading to the bed and breakfast now. I've been through Barnes' phone records. There's no link to the Hudson house there. I'm running out of options if I'm honest. How did it go with Jack Fraser?"

"It doesn't get any easier, Ben," she said, and she found herself relaxing just listening to the calming tones of his voice, that subtle Lincolnshire accent once again acting as some kind of aphrodisiac to her nervous system. "He's not the first man I've met like that, and he won't be the last. They can't help themselves, you know? He's adamant he's done nothing wrong. It's a perspective thing. His differs from society's by just enough to alienate him."

"Chapman checked his records though. He has no record of anything untoward. Whereas Barnes does."

"Fraser has no record as such. But that doesn't mean he isn't afflicted. It just means he hasn't been caught doing anything he ought not to be."

"Where are you now?"

"The interview room. Pondering," she added. "You?"

"The car park. Freezing my balls off."

"Thanks for that," she said, wondering if she spent too long working with Ben that she might lose the sense of refinement her father had paid handsomely for.

"Fancy a ride? I'm kind of stuck until I hear from Jackie."

"What do you have in mind?"

"I thought we could pay the Hudsons a visit and arrange the viewing."

"Jesus, Ben. That has to be number two on my list of least favourite parts of my job."

"I'll throw in a big mac meal and a trip to the beach if you're good."

The laugh she issued came so suddenly and between breaths that she coughed into the phone and had to stand to take deep breaths.

"Something tickling you there, Freya?" he asked.

"Is this your way of asking me for help?" she asked, when she had recovered enough to speak.

"You're so eloquent. Maybe you could teach me a thing or two?"

The thought of returning to her cold and empty motor home was far from appealing, more so now that Ben had announced the onset of snow. But to accept his rather lacklustre proposition would be to give in too early.

"I'm Patricia Hudson. I open the door, stuff a tissue into my sleeve, but I don't say hello," she said, hoping he would catch on to her role play. She paced the room slowly, imagining the scene.

"Good evening, Mrs Hudson," he began, then cleared his throat. "I erm... I'm sorry to bother—"

"Sorry, who are you?" said Freya. "I've just lost my child, so much has happened in the past two days."

"Oh, sorry. Don't you remember me? It's DS Savage, and DI Bloom. We came to see you about Jessica the other day."

"How many doors have you had slammed in your face?"

"It's not that bad."

"It's not that bad if you're in a school play and Mrs Hudson is Mary and you're one of the three wise men."

"Harsh."

"Try again. This time with a little more conviction."

"I don't need schooling on how to talk to victims of crime—"

"I open the door with a face like thunder from a raging row with my husband. Oh, it's you again. What do *you* want?"

There was a silence where Ben should have been commanding the situation.

"You need help," said Freya.

"I do not need help. I'm just not used to play-acting a scene where I'm talking to a grieving mother about seeing her murdered daughter's body. It's different in real life. I can handle it."

"Okay, so go alone. I'll get the beans on."

"Oh, come on. Alright, alright. I could have handled it better."

"You do the talking," she said, tracing the line of rivets in the tabletop with a finger that was in dire need of a manicure.

Audibly, he exhaled with reluctance, raising a silent smile on her own face. It was coming.

"That's fine. I'll do the talking."

"I'll grab my coat and I'll be out in two ticks. Get the heater on."

———

The Hudson house seemed smaller than before. It was as if it had slunk back into the trees like a wounded beast. Of the eight windows on the front elevation, a single light shone, and only one vehicle was parked on the drive.

Parking the car, Ben applied the handbrake but kept the engine running while he contemplated Freya's account of Jack Fraser. The light dusting had indeed been the precursor to a heavier fall. The cul-de-sac wore a blanket of white, but it was yet unclear if it would settle. That's always the question, Ben thought, when it snows, people always ask if it will settle. The temperature had dropped enough. If it stayed that way, then Ben guessed it would settle.

A sideways glance at Freya told him she was thinking no such thing. Of course she wasn't. She'd only been in the county for a few days. She wouldn't know how bad the roads could be.

"I think it'll settle," he said, then hated himself for doing so.

"What is it about Tim Hudson that made Patricia and Jack lie?"

"What are you talking about?"

"They lied to him. They told him Jessica was going to London. Yet they both knew she would be staying at Jack's caravan."

"You saw Tim. He's a control freak. His wife even said it the last time we were here."

A silence from Freya Bloom, Ben was quickly learning, spoke a thousand words. He was beginning to understand why she had risen through the ranks and developed such a reputation. At those moments in an investigation when the mind needed a break, she didn't falter. When the brain needed to look at something else – a blank wall, the sea, or the sky – she was imagining the crime. For her, there was no reprise, and she wouldn't rest until she had cracked the case. Which, by proxy, meant that neither would Ben.

He spoke his mind, relaying his latest thoughts.

"It might not be what we want to hear," he said. "But Jack's account matches what Barney said. He said that Jack was to and fro all evening. And like it or not, there's no evidence that Jack did anything he wasn't supposed to do. We'll have to release him tomorrow."

"He's a creep. If he didn't actually do anything, he was leading up to it. The cool uncle gig only gives him so much credibility."

"The cool but creepy uncle isn't a crime."

"He took her sweater for crying out loud. He was at the crime scene. He moved the bloody body. Perverting the course of justice at a minimum."

"You're not going to let him go, are you?"

"No. No, he has a story to tell. What he told me tonight was chapter two. I want to hear chapter one."

"Do we mention this to Patricia Hudson?"

"No, not yet. Let's get the viewing done and dusted," Freya said, as she opened her door and let a draft of cold air blast through. "Come on, Ben. Let's do this. I'm hungry."

The car indicators flashed once as Ben locked it and followed Freya up the drive. She rang the bell and stepped back. But as Ben joined her, she slipped away to peer down the side of the house. Behind the frosted glass, Ben saw a figure approaching.

"Freya," he said, warning her that one of the Hudsons was coming. But she disappeared around the corner, out of sight.

"Detective..." Trying to recall his name, Patricia's expression was not hostile, as Freya's role play suggested. His name eluded her, and she apologised.

"It's Ben, Patricia," he said. "Ben Savage."

"Of course. Why don't you come in?" she said, offering a weak smile, which in the face of what she was going through was admirable, yet clearly a veneer. "You'll have to excuse me. I just need to finish getting Lauren's room ready. She's coming back for a few days. Tim's gone to get her. He should be back soon."

"Lauren?" he said.

"Our other daughter," she replied, then realised the mistake, but saw no reason to correct herself.

"That's fine, Mrs Hudson. You take your time."

Waiting for her to disappear up the stairs with a bundle of fresh bed sheets, Ben moved through to the kitchen at the back of the house. Peering through the window, he saw Freya snooping around the little patio outside of Tim Hudson's home office. He went through and opened the little back door, very aware of the cold air he was letting in.

"What are you doing?" he hissed.

"You said you could manage it," she replied. "So manage it."

"But you can't go snooping around in their garden. What will it look like?"

"I'm afraid we're in a bit of a tizzy," Patricia called out from the distant hallway.

Ben glared at Freya, closed the back door as quietly as he could, then pulled the office door to, before stepping back into the kitchen to make a show of admiring a picture on the wall. It was just a print of nothing in particular, just one of those frames people hang on their walls because the colours match the palette of the room, rather than for the quality of the artwork or its capturing of a memory.

"Ah, there you are," she said, when she found him, and her eyes darted at once to the closed office door.

"I'm sorry, I thought we could talk in here," he said, trying to keep her wandering gaze from the windows. "Did she catch the train?"

"Lauren? Yes. She doesn't drive. There's no point in London, is there? You can get everywhere faster by train. Besides, it's so expensive."

Talking of Lauren seemed to offer Mrs Hudson a distraction from the conversation Ben figured she knew was coming. It had been David who had given Ben his first demonstration on how to handle a moment such as this. Ben remembered it well. There was very little point in asking how the bereaved family are. The answer is always the same, and they don't appreciate being reminded of their misery. Better to get it over and done with. It was time to rip the plaster off.

"I'm sorry for the intrusion. I was hoping you'd both be here."

"Have you found him?" she said, her eyes widening, although her tone suggested she didn't really want to hear it. Not without her husband anyway.

"Would you like to see her?" he said. "I can arrange it now."

Following Freya's earlier foray into amateur dramatics, Ben had spent the drive giving great consideration as to how he might pose the question. In his mind, both Tim and Patricia Hudson would have been sitting at the kitchen table. By his side, Freya would have offered a pillar of experience should he falter.

But Freya wasn't there; she was lurking outside, no doubt

lipreading and judging his body language. And Tim Hudson was out collecting their other daughter while Patricia prepared for the family to grieve together. Keeping his hands in his pockets, he waited, feeling Freya's stare through the glass, though he couldn't look to see where she was.

"Can I?" she said. "I'd like that, I think. I'd like to say goodbye to my baby."

"You can see her tomorrow if you want. You just tell me a time. Or if you'd prefer to talk to your husband first, you can call."

A cold air touched him, and he lost his trail of thought.

"Is she..." She stopped mid-question, but it was enough for Ben to draw a conclusion. The last time he had seen Jessica, she had been lying on a slab, and he knew the injuries were to her neck. But an experienced professional like Doctor Bell would accommodate this fact, and take care when the time came.

"She looks peaceful," Ben said. He wanted to tell her that Jessica would look exactly as she remembered. That she was beautiful and would look as if she was just sleeping. But another of David's pearls of wisdom came to mind. *Least said, soonest mended.* "How about midday tomorrow?" he suggested. "Perhaps you can all go together?"

She nodded, and showed her appreciation via a tight-lipped half-smile.

"I'll make the arrangements. My colleague DC Gold will call in on you in the morning. We can arrange a car for you all—"

"It'll just be me," she said, cutting him off. "Please don't call the house. Is she in Lincoln Hospital?"

"She is."

"I know it. Thank you. I'll make my own way there. I'll call if I have any difficulties."

"If you're sure—"

"Quite," she said, and there was a newfound strength to her tone. "I have a lot to prepare."

"I'll get out of your way, then," said Ben. "I'll see myself out."

CHAPTER FORTY-FIVE

The path along the side of the Hudson house appeared to be used mainly for wheeling the bins out every week, or for access to the garden. Yet still, it had been given the same care and attention to detail as the main entrance. Expensive looking pots containing large and well-manicured plants were dotted along the pathway and decorative lights cast an amber wash over the space. It was beside one of these where something caught Freya's eye, partially buried in the thin blanket of snow. Crouching, she retrieved her pen from her pocket, and cleared the snow around it.

It was nothing more than a cigarette butt that had been spent and crushed underfoot. To many, the detail would have been overlooked, but in Freya's experience, a secret smoker usually had other secrets.

The sound of the front door opening around the corner distracted her, and she stood to move against the wall. The door closed again and the sound of Ben's footsteps was clear, the long spaces between each step a clear identifier of a man with long legs and a lazy gait.

She was about to find her way along the edge of the property to meet him at the car when the front door opened again. The little brass knocker tapped once with the effort.

"Detective?" a voice called, and it could only have been Patricia. Moving to the corner of the building, Freya watched Ben stop, turn, and take a few steps back toward the house.

"Is something wrong?" he said, stopping at the halfway point of the drive.

"I'm sorry. I told myself not to ask," she said, her voice sounding weak and pleading. "Do you know yet? Do you have anybody in mind?"

"I can't really discuss—"

"I need to know. When you do, I need to know, please." That was the voice of a woman in mourning. Somehow, maybe the way the tall evergreens formed a barrier on the driveway and channelled the sound, the acoustics in the alley were startlingly clear. It was as if Freya was standing right beside them.

"Is there something you need to tell me?" Ben asked. "Something you haven't mentioned before perhaps?"

"No," she said, far too quickly, then, "well, yes, actually."

Intrigued, Ben edged closer, giving her time to think about what she would say.

"I feel bad for not telling you sooner. But I couldn't. Not in front of Tim. He would have hit the roof."

Pausing, maybe waiting for Ben to show a reaction or say something, Patricia took a deep and audible breath. Ben said nothing, and his face remained impassive as Freya peered at him from within the alleyway.

"She wasn't going to London," she said. "Jessica, that is. It was a lie, and I feel ashamed."

"That's okay. The main thing is you're telling me now," Ben said, encouraging her to continue.

"My brother-in-law has a caravan. It's not far from here. Chapel Brightwater Holiday Park, it's called. Tim and Jessica have been going through a rough patch recently. Jessica was at her wits' end. I'm sorry to put this on you. I feel like I'm airing our dirty laundry."

"Dirty laundry is my business, Patricia. I learnt not to judge a long time ago."

"Everything Jessica did or said would start a row. Tim isn't a bad man. He loves his children, and before I say too much, he would never do anything to harm them. But the long and short of it is that he's under a lot of pressure at work. Ever since we moved here, I think he's been taking too much on. He's gone from being a small town solicitor to dealing with nationwide cases, growing his team. All because we now have a huge mortgage. Add to that the time he spends investigating Derek Barnes, and well... I'm sorry, I'm waffling..."

"No, let it flow. The more you can tell us, the better."

"Jessica threatened to leave. She said she would move away and try to find work in an orchestra. Tim didn't like that. He wanted her to go to university, get a degree and a good job. I suggested she go on holiday, you know? To think about her options. I wanted her to do what she felt was right for her. If she left, then she would have lost the money for her education. She can't make that sort of decision on the spur of a moment. I suggested a few days away to give her the time she needed to think about what's important to her, without the constant bickering swaying her one way or another."

"So you lied to Tim about where she was going?"

"She needed the space, and Tim doesn't know about the caravan. Nobody knows. Just Jack and I."

"She called yesterday to say she'd made a decision but would stay at the caravan for one more night. I gave her a ride to the beach, and she seemed happier. She said she was meeting Charlie and that she'd be okay." Patricia's voice trailed away, leaving room for her to savour the memory of that final conversation with her daughter. "I guess I'll never know what she decided to do."

———

"I heard every word she said," said Freya as she pulled on her seat belt and sought the warmth from the heater on her hands.

Ben took a breath and let his hand rest on the cold glass, if anything to slow his mind down.

"Good, that saves me repeating it," he said. "I did try to look surprised when she mentioned the caravan."

"Are you listening?" Freya interjected, in that irritating way she did. As if what she had to say was far more important than anybody else. "I said, I heard every word from the side of the house."

"Right?"

"I also found a cigarette butt."

"Okay."

Adjusting the heater controls to his feet, Ben tried to find some cohesion in her two statements but couldn't see what she was getting at.

"Christ, Ben. Tim was in his office that night. What if he sneaked out to the side of the house via the door in his office to have a quick cigarette? Maybe he thought Patricia would still be in bed. But then he heard voices. Then he started to listen to what Patricia and Jack were saying."

"Then he would know about the caravan, but that doesn't give him a motivation to..." He paused mid-thought. "Where are you going with this, Freya? Are you suggesting that Tim Hudson is now a suspect, just because he might have overheard a conversation?"

"No, not at all. I don't really know what I'm saying. I'm just trying to build a picture of what happened that night. Clearly Patricia is being selective about what information comes our way."

"It was interesting to learn that Jessica and her dad argued."

"Yes. Something doesn't sit right. Why would Patricia Hudson let her daughter stay at her brother-in-law's caravan on her own? Doesn't that seem weird? I'm living in a motor home, and if I'm honest, it can get pretty creepy at night."

"Maybe she wasn't alone? Red anorak seems to be familiar with the place."

"She's the missing link here. We really need to find her."

Ben's phone vibrated in his pocket. When he fished it out, the screen displayed Jackie Gold. Answering the call on loudspeaker, he set it on the dashboard and let his head fall back onto the head rest.

"What's the news, Jackie?" he said.

"Sand, Ben," she said with urgency in her voice. "We've got sand. Not much, mind you, but enough. I've sent one of the forensics team back to the lab to see if it matches the sand found in Jessica's hair."

"Good thinking," said Freya, announcing her presence. "Do we think this is enough for Granger to sign off on the helicopter?"

"Without a doubt," Ben said. "Jackie, brilliant work. Thanks for sorting that out. See what else you can find and keep me updated. I'm going to hit Will with the news."

"Will do, Ben," Jackie said, and the call disconnected.

"We've got Barnes," Freya summarised, then left a pause for silence before voicing her thoughts. "Are we sure it's him? What exactly do we have?"

"He's a known criminal who was in an ongoing grievance with Timothy Hudson, who, by the way, is still investigating Derek Barnes. He lied about his whereabouts and we have a partial profile of his DNA found beneath Jessica's fingernails. I'd say it was pretty well wrapped up."

"Again, we don't have the motivation, apart from the grievance. Would Barnes really kill Tim Hudson's daughter over a row with him? Motivation seems to be the missing piece. We have Jack Fraser, the creepy uncle who is obviously in love with her. We have Tim—"

"We don't have Tim–"

"Hear me out. We have Tim, who argued with his daughter, but again, not really enough to give us a motivation. And sure, we have Barnes, who clearly has the means, but I can't make it work in my head. I have a niggle."

"A niggle?"

"A niggle. A doubt. You remember we spoke about that feeling you get when you know somebody is hiding something, but you can't prove it?"

"I do."

"It's the same as that, but flipped on its head."

"You have a feeling that, despite Derek Barnes' DNA being found on Jessica's body, despite him lying about where he was, and despite sand being found in the Airbnb, that he is innocent? Even if he didn't kill her, he's still guilty of something."

"Will Chapman still be in the station?" Freya asked, ignoring the question.

"Probably," Ben said, checking the dashboard clock. "She'll be tying up loose ends and straightening the papers on her desk."

"We need to make this happen tonight. What else can we get on Barnes? If he's cleared of a murder charge, he'll claim for loss of earnings, especially if the contracting firm ditch him as a result of us taking him away from his duties."

"What are you saying? We should pin something on him? That's not really my style."

"No. He's a bloody criminal. There must be something else we can get him on."

"A back-up charge, you mean?" Ben said, with a laugh. "You can't be serious."

"If Barnes comes back clean, Granger and Harper will be looking at me. Not you. Me."

"You really do like it here, don't you?" said Ben, and he glanced through the windscreen at the snowfall. "You're worried they'll get rid of you."

"Not worried, Ben. That's the wrong word. I'm officially homeless and living in a motor home. I don't really want to add being jobless to that."

Reaching for the phone on the dashboard, Ben found Chapman's number and hit the green button. She answered after just two rings.

"Ben?"

"Chapman, are you at your desk?"

"I was just closing a few things off."

"Fancy some overtime?"

"What do you need?"

"Get yourself a takeaway. DI Bloom is paying. It might be a long night."

————

Unlike Chapman, Granger was not in the office when Ben called, and judging by the look on Ben's face, partially lit by the dashboard lights, it came as no surprise when he answered his home phone.

"We've got it," Ben said, and gave a sideways glance at Freya. "You asked for something else on Barnes before we bring Barnes back to shore. We found sand in the Airbnb he stayed in."

"Sand? Is that it?" Granger replied.

"The lab are matching it to the sand found on Jessica Hudson's body, but we're in a good place to put Barnes at the scene of the crime, which, along with the DNA found on Jessica, should be enough to convince CPS."

"How sure are you, Ben?" Granger said, and in the background Freya heard the sound of his shoes clicking on a hard, wooden floor. She imagined him living in an old cottage with roses out the front and a pretty little spot to sit with his wife. She wasn't sure why she thought that would be his style; it was just a judgement, which was made more convincing by the creaking of an old door.

"You know he'll come after us for loss of earnings if you're wrong."

"I've got Chapman interrogating his history right now. We know he's a thief and we know he has form for dealing. Worst case is that we find something at his home address."

"Such as?"

"Drugs. We know his wife is a user. Half the street can smell it."

"He works on the rigs. He'll have to undergo periodic drug testing."

"I'm not suggesting he smokes it, guv."

"You're not filling me with confidence, Ben."

"You asked for something else on him. The sand and DNA give us a pretty strong case. We need to get him back, Will. The weather is getting worse."

A silence ensued. The windscreen was covered in a thin blanket of snow, encapsulating Ben and Freya in a cocoon.

"Do it," Will said. "But I want results, Ben. I don't want to see a letter from Barnes' lawyer on my desk, or it'll be you that deals with it."

"Understood, guv," Ben said, and he reached forward to end the call.

"Ben?" Granger said. "Are you still there?"

"I'm here, guv."

"Good job. Just make it work."

"I'll do my best."

The call ended, and the two of them sat back to think.

"Are you ready for this, Ben?"

"I'll have Chapman charter the flight. That's if they're still flying, I'll have two uniforms there to pick him up. We'll need to contact the contracting firm he works for too to let them know."

"Then what?" Freya said.

"Then we eat. I have a strange hankering for baked beans."

He flicked the wiper blades on to clear the windscreen, and the two headlights revealed the grim night around them.

"I'll be honest, the motor home isn't very appealing," she said, just as Ben's phone began to ring once more.

"Ben Savage," he said, sounding tired.

"Ben, it's Sergeant Priest." The man's thick Yorkshire tones grumbled through the phone's speaker.

"I was about to call you. I need two men to collect someone from Humberside."

"Won't be a problem. We can discuss that in a moment. In the meantime, we have a slightly more pressing matter. How soon can you get to Anderby?"

"Five minutes. Why?"

"There's been a shooting. I've got two units and an ambulance on the way, and armed response are coming in from Lincoln."

"Anybody hurt?"

"One man. Timothy Hudson."

A silence ensued during which time a hundred thoughts raced through Ben's mind, none of them comprehensible.

"Is he alive?"

"It was him that dialled nine nine nine. Said he didn't see the shooter, just an old dog. I don't fancy his chances out there in this snow though, Ben, and Chapman said you were nearby."

"We're on our way, Michael. Do me a favour, will you? Tell Chapman we're clear to bring Barnes back. Ask her to set it up, then to call his employer, and then to let you know the details so you can have him picked up. She'll know what you mean. Call me if either of you have any issues."

Pocketing the phone, Ben found first gear and belted up as he drove.

"We might have to take a rain check on those beans," he said, and the fact that he could find humour in the moment raised a wicked smile on Freya's face. In fact, the more she worked with the man, the more she enjoyed his funny ways.

CHAPTER FORTY-SIX

The weather from Russia was worsening. The incessant winds had yet to cease and the gentle flurry was now a thick, swirling mass, causing Ben to drive slow and unsettling Freya's nerves. A few icy patches on the lanes caused a few breathless moments, but the worst was yet to come and she knew it.

"Get Chapman on the line," he told Freya, while he focused on the road. The call, as the previous calls had, routed through the car's inbuilt Bluetooth system, and due to the conditions, the road speed was slow. So when Chapman answered, he heard her loud and clear. She was in her element at the station, organising the helicopter, arranging Barnes' pick up, and liaising with Jackie and the forensics team at the Airbnb.

"Ben?"

"I'm putting a lot on your plate tonight, Chapman," Freya said by way of a greeting. "How are you coping?"

"I'm fine. I heard the news from Sergeant Priest. What else can I do?"

"We need you to do some digging. Albert Stow," said Ben, then spelt the man's surname.

"Isn't that the old man who discovered Jessica's body?" Chapman asked.

"That's him. See if he has any records for me, and I want to know if he has a gun licence."

"What are you doing?" said Freya.

"Hold on, Chapman," Ben said, slowing for a tight bend in the road. "Priest said the victim saw an old dog. When we paid Stow a visit, he said he walked that dog three times a day, no matter the weather."

"But why would he shoot Timothy Hudson?"

"He said something when we left him. Something that stuck with me. He said he'd be keeping an eye out on that beach, and that we shouldn't worry because old Albert's on guard or something."

"He doesn't have a firearms licence," said Chapman, her fingers tapping away on the keyboard.

"Can you call Jackie? Tell her to leave forensics to it. We have what we need for now, but tell them to keep searching. I want Jackie down at the beach."

"Will do, boss," she said, and the call disconnected.

"I hope you're right, Ben," said Freya, and Ben turned into the beach access road. Dropping to second gear, Ben was scanning the sides of the road and surrounding fields. But the weather made identifying anything further than a car's length away almost impossible. Eventually, the road raised in elevation as it passed through the dune, then dropped down to the right, leading to the small car park for beachgoers.

"There," said Freya, pointing at a dark shape in the snow about thirty feet in front of them.

Opening the door before Ben had even stopped the car, Freya ran ahead. Lying in the snow, propped against a post designed to stop people driving onto the sand, was Timothy Hudson. He had his arms wrapped around himself, and judging by the pool of dark blood he was sitting in, he was bleeding profusely.

"Tim?" she said, as she crouched by his side. "Tim, it's DI Bloom. Do you remember me?"

A weak groan was all he could manage.

Whipping off her coat, she wrapped it around him. "An ambulance is coming, just hang in there. You're doing great. Can you tell me where it hurts?"

He barely had the strength to remove his arms from around him and was visibly shaking. Behind her, Freya heard Ben on the phone giving accurate directions to the emergency services. Then she heard the car boot slam, and he arrived by her side with an old blanket.

"Where are you hit?" he asked, as he removed Freya's coat, and wrapped the much larger blanket around his shoulders.

"Leg," Tim replied, as if just saying the word was painful.

Easing Tim's arms away, Ben began an initial check of his legs using the car headlights to see what he was doing. He applied gentle pressure from his ankles to his waist. His right leg was fine, but when Ben reached Tim's left thigh, he pulled his hands away and held them up. They were dark, and glistened in the bright lights.

"There's a torch and a first aid kit in the glove box, and a bag of clothes on the back seat," he told Freya, and she rose to his needs. It wasn't a time for questioning rank. By the time she had grabbed the bag and the kit and the torch, Ben had ripped Tim's trouser leg off. Using the torch to survey the wound, he gave Freya a serious look.

"Wrap his leg in something from the bag," he said, and he pulled a roll of bandage and a dressing from the kit.

"How bad is it?" Tim asked, doing his best to control his breathing.

"You've been shot in the leg, Tim. I'm not going to paint a pretty picture. There's no exit wound. The bullet is still in there."

Letting his head fall back onto the post, Tim whimpered as the onslaught of shock set in. He began to shiver.

"Shall we get him to the car?" Freya suggested.

"No, we can't move him. Tim, who did this?"

"I don't know. He came out of the dark. A dog. There was a dog."

"Give me a clue, Tim. Was it a male or female? Did they speak at all? What type of dog was it?"

"He spoke. He called me a bastard, then fired."

"This is going to hurt," said Ben, as he prepared the bandage and dressing to go on. "Freya, I need help. I'm going to apply the dressing, I want you to press down as hard as you can. Are you ready, Tim? On three. One, two, three."

His scream was carried on the wind. Freya guessed that if it was Albert Stow who had fired the gun, he would have still been close enough to hear Tim's agony. Neither the old man nor the dog were capable of hurrying.

A pair of headlights came through the pass in the dune then came to a sudden stop beside Ben's car, leaving enough room for an ambulance.

"Jackie, over here," Freya called out, and the familiar figure jogged to the scene.

"What can I do?" she asked.

"Ambulance is on its way," Ben said. "I've given them clear directions, but touch base with control to tell them you're here and in charge. Keep him warm, keep pressure on the wound, and above all else, keep him talking. Don't let him sleep."

"Where are you going?" Jackie asked, alarmed to be left alone.

But Ben ignored her. He roused Tim from his agony-induced daze.

"Tim? Tim, I'm going to find the man who did this. This is Jackie Gold. She'll take care of you. You just hang in there, okay?"

His head rolled from side to side, and he slurred something unintelligible.

Leaning closer, Ben spoke into Jackie's ear, "If he talks, find out what he was doing here. He's supposed to be collecting Jessica's sister from Lincoln station."

"I've got it," Jackie said, and she crouched where Ben had been. "Go."

Climbing into the passenger seat, Freya slammed the door and pulled on her seat belt as Ben reversed in a tight arc, found first gear, and pulled away as fast as the icy concrete would allow.

"Still think it's Albert Stow?" Freya asked, as Ben's phone began to ring.

"Chapman?" he said, raising his voice to be heard above the revving engine.

"Ben, are you there? Did you find him?"

"Yes, I've left him with Jackie. He's comfortable and I've dressed the wound. But there's no exit hole. He's lost a lot of blood, and he's going to need surgery."

"As if he hasn't been through enough already," Chapman said. "I've been doing some digging on Albert Stow. There's something you need to know."

"Go on," said Ben, and he glanced at once at Freya.

"He has a history of mental health problems. He suffers with Alzheimer's disease. In your report, you mentioned that his wife was out when you visited."

"Right?" he said.

"She wasn't out, Ben."

"She's dead," Freya finished, seeing where Chapman was heading. "Damn it."

"She was attacked on that same beach over a decade ago while she walked their dog. They took her purse, wedding ring, and other jewellery, and left her to die."

"Oh Jesus," Ben said. "And now he sees himself as a vigilante."

"He's refused help from the local health service, and there is no family for him to call on. If it was him, he's in a bad way and you need to approach with extreme caution."

"Understood. You're going to have to act as a central point for us. Do me a favour, get hold of DCI Granger. He's at home. Tell him what's happening. I don't want him finding this out from someone else. Give armed response Albert Stow's address. Hopefully we'll beat them there."

"I'm on it," she said, and disconnected the call.

Sighing as they neared the end of the access road, Ben prepared to cross into the opposite lane. But he took a few moments to look at Freya, and answer her earlier question.

"Never been surer of anything in my life," he said. Then he added, "I just hope we can find him before armed response do. If they see him walking about waving a gun, we could have an even bigger tragedy on our hands."

CHAPTER FORTY-SEVEN

Barely thirty seconds after crossing the road into the adjacent lane, a lone figure could be seen ahead of them in the snow. An old dog ambled beside Albert Stow, clearly unhappy at being out in the cold, and Ben shuddered at the sight of the old man.

Driving past him as slow as he dare, Ben glanced at Freya, who looked over her shoulder and confirmed his identity with a nod.

"That's him alright," she said. "How do you want to do this?"

Pulling into the side of the road, Ben applied the handbrake, keeping the engine running, and he rested his hand on the door while he considered the options. He turned to her, his teeth bearing down on his lower lip.

"I honestly don't know. But we have to do something."

A blast of cold air found the sweat on Ben's back when he climbed out of the car. Fastening his coat around him did little to ease his nerves. The passenger door opened, and Freya climbed out, eyeing Ben as she did. The old man was perhaps forty feet away when Ben called out.

"Hi Albert," he said, like a long-lost friend. "What are you doing out in this weather?"

Stepping closer, Albert Stow peered between them with distrust.

"Albert, it's us. Detective Sergeant Savage and–"

"Bloom," Albert said. "I remember now. You're the pretty one that smells nice."

"Thank you, Albert. Isn't a bit too cold to be out with the dog?"

"When you have to go, you have to go, right, Bramble?" he replied, and he yanked on the dog lead to get a reaction. But Bramble wasn't interested, seeming content enough just to be stationary.

"Albert, we've just come from the beach. Have you been down there at all?" Ben asked, and he took a few steps closer.

"The beach?" he asked. "Why?"

"Albert, is there something you want to tell us?"

"Why? What do you want to go hassling me for?" he replied, backing off as far as the dog lead would stretch. "Bramble, come."

With their home just metres away, and the tantalising warmth of his bed nearly in reach, the old dog was not interested in backtracking.

"Bramble, come. Damn dog."

Behind him, toward the beach, the landscape was lit with flashing lights. So many emergency services had been called that there was no way of knowing if the flashing blues belonged to an ambulance, the two units Priest had sent, or if it was armed response.

"Albert, we know you've been to the beach. We want to help you."

"Help me? You don't want to help me. I don't need–"

"We know you have a gun."

He stared back at Ben.

"So what if I do?" he growled. "I fixed it, didn't I? I told you to leave it to old Albert. I told you I'd be on guard."

Whipping his jacket back, Albert revealed a beaten, old

revolver tucked into his belt like a child might stow a toy gun in a game of cowboys and Indians.

Another flash of blue coasted along the main road, just four hundred yards away. But where the first set had turned toward the beach, this set turned into the lane.

"I want you to remove the gun, Albert, and throw it to the ground," Ben said, and from the corner of his eye, he saw Freya duck into the road behind him, preparing to stop armed response from getting too close. "Can you do that for me, please? That's it. Just pull it out and throw it to the ground."

The van door slid open, and men's voices murmured.

"Who are they?" Albert said, suddenly trapped on both sides. He held the gun in the air. "I took care of it, Ben. Didn't I?"

"Yep, you took care of it, okay. There's a man on the beach who is badly injured. You did a fine job of that, Albert. Now I need you to throw the gun to the ground."

From behind the old man, two armed policemen approached, emerging from the blizzard, ghost-like. Two red dots flickered over the back of Albert's jacket.

"Armed police. Put the weapon down and step away," one of the men called.

"What's going on?" Albert said, confused at the lights and the shouting. "You said you wanted to help me."

Holding out his hand to signal to the armed officers that he had it under control, Ben called out, "Please, Albert. Listen to me. Throw the weapon to the ground. Nobody is going to hurt you."

"*Nobody* can hurt old Albert," he said. "I took care of it, didn't I? Did I do well?"

"Yes, that's right. You took care of it. Please, Albert, listen to me."

"Armed police. This is your final warning," the officer called out again.

"Albert, I know about your wife. I'm sorry."

"My wife? She's inside keeping the fire going."

"No, Albert. No, she's not."

"But I saw her," he said, his voice rising with worry. "I left her there. We'll get home and have something to eat. Then we'll sit by the fire. Just like we always do."

Ben was about to convince him otherwise when Freya stepped into view. She held her hands high to show she meant no harm.

"That's right, Albert. She's waiting inside for you."

"There," he said to Ben. "See? She's waiting for me."

"Shall we go inside?" Freya asked, and Ben glimpsed a side of Freya that he knew she rarely revealed. "How about a cup of tea?"

"A tea," he said. "That would be nice. My wife will be waiting, you know?"

"That's right," she replied, as she took him by the arm. "What's this? Oh, Albert. You can't go carrying this round."

"That was my father's. Carried it through the war, he did. Never let him down once."

"I think you should give that to me, and then we'll go and make a nice cup of tea."

"Oh, tea. That sounds nice," he said, as he relinquished his grip on the pistol and Bramble's lead.

Signalling to the ARV driver for him to come forward, Ben admired the way Freya had lied to the man with such ease. The van driver edged alongside him, and the door slid open again.

"Let's just have a little sit down here, eh?" Freya said, ushering him into the van's side door. "Mind your step."

"Oh," said Albert, the way only elderly gentleman do after a long walk. "It's good to get the weight off."

"That's right, Albert. I'll be back in a moment. These gentlemen will look after you. Nobody is going to hurt you."

"You look just like my wife did when she was your age," Albert said. "She was a cracker back then, she was."

The two armed officers approached, their weapons made safe and aimed at the ground.

"Who's handling this?" the first asked, as if the question needed answering, but keeping his voice low.

"If you wanted to take care of the paperwork, I have a feeling you wouldn't have asked," Ben replied.

Joining them, Freya offered the second officer the weapon, who took it, cleared the ammunition, and then placed it into a clear plastic bag.

"All safe," he said confidently. "How's the victim?"

It was a stark reminder that the event had been a brief distraction from what was to be a long and tiresome night.

"Which one?" Ben asked.

CHAPTER FORTY-EIGHT

For Freya, it was a sad moment when Albert Stow was driven away, convinced he was off to have a nice cup of tea with his wife. But she shed an even greater tear when she handed Bramble over to the handler, who would home him until the process governed that he either be re-homed or euthanized.

"I don't think either of them will ever be back," she said to Ben, and couldn't even try to hide the guilt on her face.

"He's not your responsibility, Freya," Ben replied. "Neither of them are."

She had to admire the man who peered at her compassionately over the car roof. It was his polite way of urging her back into the car, and she took the hint.

It was when she climbed into the car, belted up, and felt the warmth on her freezing cold feet that she sighed out loud, much like Albert Stow had.

Waiting for her to compose herself, Ben's finger was poised over the button to answer a call. She nodded, and readied herself for another round.

"Jackie?" he said. "What's the news?"

"He's stable, but in a lot of pain. The ambulance has just left. Should I follow?"

"Did you talk to him?"

"As much as I could," she said. "He said he was down there to see where it happened. He said he was supposed to pick Lauren up from the station, but he came here on the way."

"So who's picking Lauren up?"

"Patricia has gone. I called her from Timothy's phone. He asked me to."

"How did she take it? The poor woman's had a rough few days."

"Oddly, she wasn't surprised. She sounded..." Jackie sought the right word, then chose, "Numb."

"Do you blame her?" Freya added.

"Not really. She said she'd pick Lauren up and go straight on to the hospital with her."

"Good work, Jackie," said Freya.

"He said something. When I was calling his wife. He said to say he was sorry, and that he knows. I don't know what he was talking about."

"He knows?" said Ben, and he turned to Freya, cupping his ear to mime him listening in on Patricia's conversation with Jack Fraser.

"What did he mean?" asked Jackie.

"Did you search him, Jackie?" Freya asked, without directly answering her question.

"I had to get his phone from his pocket. But I didn't give him a pat-down. Should I have?"

"What did you find?"

"Nothing, really. His car keys, his phone, of course. Some loose change."

"Anything else?"

"Nothing really of any interest."

"No cigarettes or a lighter perhaps?"

"Not that I found," Jackie said, and Ben offered Freya a disappointed look.

"We think he overheard a conversation between his wife and Jack Fraser. There's some kind of secret between Jack, Patricia, and Jessica, and he knows it now. Find that secret, and we'll be one step closer to finding out why she died."

There was a silence while Jackie digested what Ben had said, then Freya gave a deeper explanation.

"If you think back to the phone records and the map we made of the 4G masts, Jack Fraser went to his caravan, left his phone there, then went on to the Hudson house, where he had the conversation and a secret was aired."

"Tim overheard it, and went to the beach to find his daughter?" suggested Jackie.

"That's the bit that doesn't add up," said Freya. "Right now, that's where Tim Hudson's story comes to a halt, and Barnes' story takes over. The sand, the DNA, the feud with Tim. We need to make that link."

"So Jack Fraser is innocent? Is that what you're saying?"

"Not entirely innocent, Jackie," said Freya. "Guilty of something altogether different. That's something that, if I'm right, will come out in the wash. I don't particularly want any of us to be the ones that bring his crimes to light just yet. It'll muddy the waters. Right now, we're focusing on Barnes, and thanks to you, he's on his way back to shore. Chapman has lined up an escort, so by the time you get to the station in the morning, he'll be a few hours into his custody."

"What do you need from me? What can I do to help?" she said, eager but audibly tired.

"Get some sleep," said Freya. "I'll be lining up some warrants for the morning. I want you to lead a raid on the Barnes house. Obviously we're looking for a link to Jessica's murder, but we also have reason to believe he's back at his old habits."

"Drug dealing? Surely not?"

"If we can't link him to the murder, then he'll have grounds to come back at us for loss of earnings. Given that he's on ten-day, off-shore shift work, we're effectively making him unemployed for three weeks, and that's if his employer even keeps him on. He's still out on licence following his sentence, and still working through a probationary period at work."

"Bloody hell. So basically, anything we can get on him to make his trip back to shore worthwhile?"

"Anything you can get on him that will prevent grounds for a comeback would be a good start."

"A start?" she said, sounding unclear.

"We still need Charlie Barnes. He's conveniently been missing since all this began. We need to bring him in. It might be that his dad has stashed him away somewhere, in which case he'll be perverting the course of justice. When you're done at the Barnes house, can you meet Patricia Hudson at the mortuary? I need someone like you. She's fragile right now."

"Okay," Jackie said, sounding a little unsure.

"It's a big ask, Jackie. Are you up to this? I know you have other commitments. You have a little boy, don't you?"

"Yes, Charlie," she said, without hesitation. "I'll ask my mum to come early. She looks after him in the mornings before nursery. I'll be in an hour early to go through the warrants and I'll brief the team."

"Your mum helps you? Are you... I mean, do you have a partner?"

"He's not around, ma'am," Jackie said, clearly unwilling to go into detail. "But it doesn't stop me. I mean, I won't let it get in the way of work."

"That's what I like to hear, Jackie. You've been brilliant tonight. Tomorrow is going to be even harder, so get some rest."

"Will do, ma'am."

The call disconnected, and Freya imagined the detective constable's bright, smiling face during her drive home.

"She's going to be a good detective one day," she told Ben.

"She already is a good detective," he replied. "She just doesn't have the confidence to admit it to herself. Where to next?"

"Home. It's late."

"Too late for beans?" Ben asked, and again, his smile could be heard in his words.

"Ben Savage, how long have you known me?"

"A few days. Long enough," he quipped.

"Well, over time, I hope you get to know me enough to know when I'm being serious, and when I'm not." She stared at him, as the bleak winter snowfall entombed them in Ben's car. "I will never, and never have, eaten baked beans. Now take me home."

CHAPTER FORTY-NINE

The alarm Ben had set to wake him at four a.m. sounded distant in his dream, like some faraway church, over the hills and faraway. But within an instant of opening his eyes, his active mind replayed the previous day. Jack Fraser's interview, Timothy Hudson's shooting, and Albert Stow's arrest. It was only when his mind reached Derek Barnes that he remembered the chartered flight. Four a.m. He would be at the station by now, he thought. Perhaps he was sitting in a cell, or at the custody desk being processed.

The thirty-six-hour window was now ticking away.

The water wasn't yet hot, as the boiler in Ben's kitchen was set to kick in at five a.m. But he suffered through the lukewarm shower and by the time he was dressed and warm had forgotten about the discomfort.

An insulated mug accompanied him on the drive to the station. The aroma of coffee filled the inside of his car yet left room for Freya's lingering perfume, which a small part of him hoped would never leave.

The drive to the station was usually a ten-minute run, three of which were spent getting off his father's land by way of the long access road. But the deluge from the previous night had yet to ease, reminding him of the Beast from the East, a huge snowstorm that hit the UK just two years previously. Much like the rest of Lincolnshire's roads, deep dykes lined the farm track to drain the county's flat terrain of water. They had the Wolds, of course, a series of stunning, rolling hills that ran parallel to the coast a few miles inland. But other than that, the land was flat, large, and fertile enough to make a huge contribution to the nation's vegetable supply.

The dykes, however necessary, were a menacing threat to lone drivers in poor conditions. Deep enough to engulf an entire car, Ben had witnessed many a driver fall foul of them; remote icy roads and speeding were a significant contribution to the cause.

The sun wouldn't rise for another three to four hours, and with Barnes in an interview room, there was a strong possibility that Ben wouldn't be seeing the sun at all. A sombre thought, broken only by an incoming call.

"I thought I'd give you a wake-up call," she said, and somehow the sleep in her voice was even more alluring.

"Beat you to it. I'm halfway to the station. Do you need picking up?"

"Is it out of your way?"

"Yes, it's completely the opposite direction. In fact, I'd have to drive past the station to get to you."

"In that case, yes please. I've been walking to the main road and calling a local taxi, if you can even call it a taxi. It's a retired man making a few extra quid to supplement his pension. But somehow I don't think he'll be awake this early."

"I'll be with you in twenty minutes," Ben said.

"In that case I'll consider getting dressed. That's if I can summon the willpower. I lit the stove to take the chill off, but by God it's cold in here. I'll shower at the station, so I'll be ready in ten minutes."

Imagining the motor home under a blanket of snow and ice,

Ben could see her wrapped in her duvet, wearing pyjamas, and waiting for her kettle to boil.

"Ben?"

"I'm here," he said, roused from his thoughts.

"It finishes today. Be ready."

"I've been ready to put Barnes away since I first heard his name on the case. He's gone too far this time."

"Goodo," she said wearily, and hung up the call.

Her voice, her language, and mannerisms were part of her appeal, he thought. She was a breath of fresh air. A taste of what he shouldn't ought to, his old dad would have said. A diamond in the rough.

He wondered how polished that diamond would be with just twenty minutes to buff it.

CHAPTER FIFTY

It was four forty-five when Freya saw Ben's headlights creep into the car park. It reminded her of two nights before, when she had had her little panic and accused him of peeping through her window. She cringed inwardly.

Locking her motor home, she dropped the keys into her bag and stepped down into a couple of inches of snow. The deluge had eased slightly, but showed no signs of stopping any time soon, and its wintry bite found and explored her exposed skin.

"Thank you," she said, as she closed the door and drew the seat belt across her. Ben said nothing, only stared at her admiringly. "How did you sleep?"

"Like the dead," he replied, which Freya considered an awful turn of phrase, especially in their line of work.

Opening the window a few inches, Freya let the cold air rouse her from the sleep the car heater and the motion were inducing. She felt Ben glance across at her while he was driving, and thought he might question the window being opened. But he didn't, of course; his mild manners wouldn't allow an early morning argument.

"We need a plan," she said, reinvigorated by the rush of cold air, and Ben was visibly startled by her sudden outburst. "Jack Fraser goes home today unless we have something on him. What do we think?"

"I think we can agree he's guilty of something altogether different."

"We can," she said. "Barnes will be opting for a no-comment strategy, and he won't talk until his solicitor is present."

"At least we can be sure his solicitor won't be Tim Hudson. What makes you so sure he'll go down the no-comment route?"

"He's seasoned. This is the most serious crime he's been involved in, and with a history of convictions, he knows the courts will go hard on him. We need to draw out his story. Get him riled enough that he opens up about that night."

"And how do you plan on doing that?"

"I'd like to know a bit more about his children," she said flatly. "Specifically Charlie. The man already has one son in prison. Does he really want two?"

"You wouldn't?"

"It's the only card up our sleeve. We need him to talk. Sure, we have the questionable DNA, the sand, and yes, you could say he was motivated to hurt Tim Hudson's daughter. But the only way we can guarantee a conviction is by getting a confession. And with a man like Derek Barnes, confessions don't come easy. We're going to have to play him at his own game. We're going to have to play dirty, and for that, we need to use Charlie Barnes, wherever he may be."

CHAPTER FIFTY-ONE

Getting into work early was rarely a pleasure. But on that particular morning, Ben felt the positive energy in the building. By the time Freya had showered and dressed, polishing the diamond to what Ben considered showroom standards, she was wide awake and at the whiteboard.

Taking the opportunity to grab a coffee, Ben descended to the ground floor and walked the corridor to the custody desk.

"You're in early," Ben said to his old friend Michael Priest.

"Big day today, Ben. I want this place shipshape for when Barnes is escorted through those doors for the last time," he said, then added, "in my lifetime, anyhow."

"We need to nail him yet. Freya says we need a confession, so don't be surprised if you hear screaming from the interview room today. I reckon old Derek Barnes may have met his match with her."

"I think you might be right," concurred Michael, his concentration unfaltering.

"Which suite did you put him in?"

"He's in four, furthest one from the door. Last time he was here, he cried blue murder all bloody night, so we wanted to put some distance between him and our other guests." He looked up from his paperwork. "The shouters get the others going, see. Won't get any bloody peace and quiet if he starts that up again."

"It's your hotel, Michael," Ben muttered, as he peered through the window in the door to the corridor of cells.

"How's Timothy Hudson doing?" Michael asked, changing the subject.

"Stable, from what I can hear. But it wasn't pretty. It was an old service revolver. A Webley. It's a miracle the old boy even hit him. Must have been some distance away too. The bullet didn't come out the other side."

"That's going to sting," Michael said with a wince, as he finished what he was writing, pocketed his pen in his breast pocket, and leaned on the custody desk. "And the old man?"

"Haven't heard. He was taken to Lincoln HQ. They tried to push him our way, but we're busy enough. Besides, he'll need care. You can't put an old man like that in a cell, no matter what he's done."

"They will, you know."

"I know," Ben said. "It's just sad. Hopefully they can keep an eye on him. Listen, do you mind if I...?"

He gestured at the cell corridor. It was enough for Michael to understand.

"Are you going to poke the beast?"

"Not poke him. I don't believe in cruelty to animals," Ben replied, as Michael placed his ID to the door access panel.

The magnetic lock released, and the big man held it open for Ben.

In all his years at the station, Ben wondered if he'd ever been alone in that corridor before. The door closed and the magnet engaged with a loud click, amplifying the peace. His shoes clicked on the concrete floor, made smooth from decades of prisoners and officers alike.

He listened at the door of the first cell. The soft grumblings of a sleeping Jack Fraser greeted him. But Jack wasn't who Ben was there to see.

At the door of cell four, Ben listened again. Expecting to hear snoring, he was surprised to hear nothing at all, not even the squeak of a sweaty body rolling over on the blue mattress the force provided.

Taking care not to make a sound, he unfastened the viewing hatch, and peered inside.

"Detective Constable Benjamin Savage. I thought I could smell something," Barnes said, from where he was perched on the edge of the bench, as if he'd been waiting for Ben. His grin showed a row of white teeth, and his eyes revealed a long and sleepless night.

Only the guilty prisoners sleep, David had once told him when Ben had been wet behind the ears. Yet Barnes, ever the picture of a guilty man, defied that rule with a practised and blatant arrogance.

"It's Detective Sergeant now, Derek," he said. "How did you sleep?"

"Like I was lying next to your old lady," came the obscene reply. "Except this mattress tastes nicer, and is more comfortable."

Engaging with the man's insults would be a pointless waste of time and only serve to make the interview harder. Ben didn't have the heart to tell him he had no 'old lady'.

The first time he had peered through the door at Derek Barnes, Ben had been much younger. It was so long ago that smoking was still permitted in the cells and the interview rooms. These days, smoking was banished to the corner of the car park. Remembering that first encounter, Ben pictured him sitting exactly as he was now, lighting a cigarette with a Zippo lighter, which during the ensuing interview, Ben had noticed was embossed with the words 'Born 2B bad'.

How true the sentiment, Ben thought, reflecting on the moment.

"Have you called your solicitor yet?" he asked.

"The big man has taken care of that," he replied, gesturing toward the custody desk. "Getting me a free one. On the house, as they say."

"Whatever it takes, Derek. I just wanted to make sure you didn't miss your appointment. It's the big one this time."

He knew he was provoking Barnes, but there was something about his smug grin that Ben just wanted to wipe off, preferably with a wire brush, or at the very least, a murder charge.

"I'll be seeing you," he said, and began to raise the flap.

"Not if I see you first," Barnes called back, but there was something in his voice that told Ben he wasn't as confident as he had been making out. He was worried. And just as Ben had thought only ten minutes before, getting into work early was rarely a pleasure. Today, however, the pleasure was all his.

CHAPTER FIFTY-TWO

"How's our customer this morning?" Freya asked, when she heard Ben enter the room. It wasn't that he spoke or made a noise; it was the irritating door that squealed and slammed, and at that time of the morning, only Ben was around to join her.

"Bitter, twisted, and as foul as ever I remember him," replied Ben. "You're going to love him."

"My favourite flavour," she replied, without looking up from the whiteboard.

In the short time she had been in the room, she had flipped the whiteboard and begun clearing her head of all thoughts regarding the two lead suspects, each of whom were assigned a side of the space. Jack Fraser on the left-hand side and Derek Barnes on the right. Below each of their names, she had listed thoughts, notes, evidence, and key gaps in knowledge, which the interview needed to fill.

"This is what I call a whitespace analysis," she said, stopping to take a sip of the terrible coffee. "The whitespace needs to be filled. Therefore, our questions need to be designed to extract the relevant responses, provoke the right emotions, and shine some light on anything we might have missed."

He seemed impressed, but said nothing while he studied the details.

"We need to deliver this interview in a particular order. We give him only what we want to give him, when we want him to have it."

"In that case, I'll let you lead," Ben said. "This is your investigation and it looks like you have the entire station backing you."

"Everyone except Granger and Harper," she said.

"Put Barnes away and you'll have Granger's vote."

"And Harper?"

"He'll turn with time."

"Like a fine wine?"

"No. More like a little sailing boat, and you're the breeze."

"That's poetic. I'm enjoying the deeper side to you, I have to say."

"I wouldn't say I'm deep, Freya. I'm just a simple farm boy, remember?" he said with a smile.

"You're in a good mood?" she said, noticing his square shoulders and a glint in his eye that hadn't been there before.

"Who's in a good mood?" said a familiar voice from behind them, and Ben grinned that boyish charm.

"Ben is," she said, and she turned to face the door as it squealed and slammed closed. "With any luck, by the end of the day, we'll all be sharing Ben's high spirits."

"We'll see," Granger replied, non-committal. He gave Freya a brief visual appraisal, then turned his attention to Ben. "So this is what five-thirty looks like, is it? Here's me thinking there was only one per day."

Smiling at the bad joke that Freya read as a reminder of his rank, and therefore him not being required to undertake shift work, Ben teased the conversation back on track with far less judgement.

"Have you come for the warrants?" he asked.

"I have. It's worth an early start to get that bastard behind bars."

Clearly the sentiment regarding Barnes ran consistent throughout the station.

"Have you had much dealing with him?" Freya asked, which as a newbie to the team was a fair question.

"He was a boy when I was nicking his old man," Granger said, catching Freya by surprise.

"So it really is a family business then?" she said, coaxing him for more information. "What was his father like?"

"Light fingered," Granger replied without any hesitation, then followed with a more detailed explanation. "Clive Barnes was born of the foulest swamp known to man. I swear if you had cut him open, it would have been mud that bled from the wound."

"Was he just a thief?" Freya asked, pushing to see if anybody else in the family had ventured into crimes beyond that of the everyday crook.

"He was not just a thief, Freya. He was *the* thief. If something was stolen, you could bet your left arse cheek it was him at the bottom of it. Cars, drugs, and jewellery, wallets, bags, and purses. You name it, he stole it. Couldn't help himself. Like it was an illness."

"Kleptomania?"

"Something like that," he said.

"Where is he now?"

"Rotting," Granger said. "Bit off more than he could chew."

"Murder?"

"He set light to a caravan with a family inside," Granger muttered, his tone serious.

"Provoked?"

"Drunk," Granger replied, then added the sickening punchline with a shake of his head. "It was his son's family – Derek's brother, his wife, and little boy. Only his little girl escaped."

There was nothing Freya could say that would serve any real value. She absorbed the information objectively, and pushed on.

"I'll bear that mind," she said, closing the conversation off.

Granger nodded, eyeing her reaction with interest. "Right, tell me the plan."

"Well," Freya began, snapping the lid back on the pen. She checked her watch. "DC Gold is leading a raid on the Barnes household."

"Alone? Can she handle that?"

"I've called in a favour from DI Standing," Ben said. "He's sending DS Gillespie to give her some support. Although she can probably handle it."

"Was Standing okay with that?"

"He made his opinion known, but at the end of the day, it'll help his team stats."

"Don't talk to me about his stats," Granger mumbled.

"Gillespie is good. He'll have her back," Ben added.

"They're on their way now," Freya said, regaining control of the discussion. "DS Savage and I are about to interview Derek Barnes."

"Legal rep?" Granger asked.

"Duty solicitor."

Nodding, Granger eyed the board with the two names.

"And Fraser?"

"Once we've extracted the truth from Barnes, we should be in a position to deal with Fraser's..." She searched for the right word. "Tertiary crimes."

"Tertiary crimes?"

"His relationship with his niece was highly inappropriate. I can't release him until we have Jessica's killer. There's too much at stake."

"Understood," Granger said. "And how's the father holding up?"

"He'll live. The family have been through a lot. When DC

Gold has finished at the Barnes house, she'll be meeting Mrs Hudson to see the body."

"Gold is ideal for that. Very compassionate girl, that one."

"My thoughts exactly, guv," Freya replied. "Our sole focus right now is Derek Barnes. I can't let him get away."

"That's all that matters. The sooner you put him behind bars, the quicker we can all forget the Barnes family ever existed."

He stared at them both as if he was giving thought to Harper's decision to bring her into the team, and if Ben would have handled this investigation on his own. He could have, in Freya's opinion, but it would have been a very different approach. Granger nodded slowly, as if choosing to play the cards he'd been dealt.

"I want to know every little detail as soon as it happens. Nothing happens without my say-so. I've put my neck on the line here. Barnes is a risk," he grumbled. Then, by way of having the last word, the way that senior officers like to do, he added, "Get to it."

The door opened and closed with its usual percussion, and Ben pulled his phone from his pocket, gesturing to Freya that she should stay where she was.

"Jackie?" he said, and then changed the phone settings to route the call through the loudspeaker. "How's it going?"

"We're ten minutes out," she replied. "You're on loudspeaker."

"Did Gillespie show?"

"Aye, he showed alright," Gillespie said, his thick Glaswegian accent seeming to be accentuated over the phone. "Do me a favour though, eh? The next time you need help in the middle of the night, call somebody else."

"Ah come on, Jim. The early bird and all that."

"Aye, yeah, I'd tell you what you and the early bird can do, but I haven't had a coffee yet. In fact, when we break the door down, Jackie, I'll search the kitchen. I can make myself a cuppa while I'm there."

"Think what this'll do for your stats, Jim," Ben said. "You'll be leagues ahead of the rest of Standing's team. We're doing you a favour."

"Right. Next time you've got a favour for me, keep it to yourself, eh?"

"Listen up," Freya said. "Joking aside, this is important. We need something on Barnes. Call a dog team in if you need to. There must be something in that house that we can use against him. Tim Hudson has been building a case for months. He's no slouch, by all accounts. There has to be something in it."

"We'll find something, ma'am," Gold said.

"Good. The moment you have it, I want you to call DS Savage. We're heading down to interview Derek Barnes now. We need to be in sync."

"Aye, got it," Gillespie said. "Coffee's on you when we get back though, eh, boss?"

Freya smiled at his nerve. Or maybe it was his charm?

"If we nail Derek Barnes, DS Gillespie, I'll be buying you more than a bloody coffee."

CHAPTER FIFTY-THREE

"Derek Barnes," Freya began, setting out her folder and her notes before her. "I need to remind you that you are suspected of murdering Jessica Hudson on the twelfth of November twenty twenty-one, and you have been cautioned. You don't have to say anything but it may harm your defence if you don't mention when questioned something you later rely on in court. Anything you do say may be given in evidence."

She spoke the words as fluently and as naturally as Ben could recite the words on his mother's gravestone. He wondered how many times she had said those words, and if, like himself, the true meaning of the statement still bore any true meaning, or if it was just a process to follow. A box to tick, as it were, to fulfil the requirements of the law.

But very little seemed to elude her, especially the silent kisses Barnes blew her while she spoke.

She announced the date, time, and her name and rank, in that order, then invited the rest of the room to follow suit.

"Detective Sergeant Ben Savage," said Ben, to the amusement of Barnes.

"Duty Solicitor Kate Winslow," the young female who was

unlucky enough to be sitting beside Barnes announced.

All eyes fell on Barnes, while they waited for the interview to commence.

"Derek Barnes," he eventually grumbled, pulling his sleeves up to his elbows, and sitting forward. "Bloom, was it?"

"Detective Inspector Bloom," she replied.

"Pretty name for a pretty girl."

The compliment fell foul of Freya's innate ability to brush off anything that stood in her way.

"Is there anything you wish to say before we begin?"

"I'll start as I mean to go," he said, and his solicitor rolled her eyes. "No comment."

"Where were you on the evening of the twelfth of November, Derek?"

"No comment."

"Did you go to the beach at Anderby, or indeed any other beach?"

"No comment."

"Did you see, talk to, or interact with Jessica Hudson in any way?"

"No comment."

"Have you had any altercations with Jessica Hudson's father, Timothy Hudson, in the past twelve months?"

"No comment."

"Are you aware that Timothy Hudson is building a case against you to investigate an offence for which you were previously detained?"

"No comment."

"I can do this all day, Derek."

"So can I, sweetheart," he replied with that smug, charmless smile.

"Did you rent a property via the Airbnb app for a room in Anderby on the night of the twelfth?"

"No comment."

"Did you tell your wife that you would be flying out to your place of employment on the twelfth?"

"What I tell my wife is my business."

"I must warn you that a search of your house is being undertaken as we speak. I'll repeat my earlier question. Is there anything you wish to tell us about now that might help you later in court?"

He stared at her, then at Ben.

"You can't search my house," he snarled. "You haven't got anything on me. This is your doing, you lanky prick."

"The warrant is signed, Derek. All we have to do is wait," said Freya, gaining control of the room with relative ease. Ben had heard worse, and from far more intimidating men. But there was something in his stare. An imbalance, Ben thought. He was reminded of the fate of the last imbalanced man he had met the previous night.

"On what grounds?"

"On the night of the twelfth of November, Jessica Hudson was murdered at Anderby beach, or, as I believe it's called, Moggs Eye. DNA with a partial profile to yours was found beneath her fingernails, suggesting a struggle."

"I didn't bloody kill her—"

"We later found that you had rented an Airbnb located at fifty-two Chester Place, Anderby, for that evening. The host saw you leave to catch your flight at four a.m. the next morning."

"Can you tell me why you rented the room when it's just a mile from your house?" Ben asked.

"Have you met my wife?" he said, and for a moment, Ben thought it was another of his warped jokes, until he saw the deadpan expression on Derek's face.

"So you did, in fact, rent the Airbnb?" said Ben, seeing the hole Derek had created with his off-hand comment.

"No comment."

"That's funny, Derek," Freya began, "because our forensics

team discovered sand in that same room yesterday. Sand that matches the sand found in Jessica Hudson's hair. That room was cleaned before you arrived, and nobody else has been in there since. Can you please explain how that sand came to be there?"

The flippant comments were over. Barnes' face was a picture of guilt.

"No comment," he said, but with far less conviction than his previous recitals.

"It's a pretty strong case," Freya explained. "DNA, sand, the lies, and then we have the dispute with Jessica's father. The motive. You're looking at life, Derek."

"You're looking at the wrong person."

"You've been inside before. You know what they do to people like you inside, don't you?"

"They stay clear of me is what they do," he snapped.

"I wonder if your father would be proud," she said, and even Ben was alarmed at the words. Though not as alarmed as Barnes, who sprang to his feet and lunged at Freya, who was sitting opposite. Holding Barnes by his shoulders, Ben restrained him long enough for the guard who had burst into the room at the sound of the struggle to restrain him.

Freya hadn't moved a muscle. She hadn't even flinched at his outburst. She just nodded for the guard to reseat Barnes, then waited a few moments for his temper to ease.

"Tell me about Charlie," she said finally, just as Ben's phone began to vibrate in his pocket. He waved the phone to Freya and indicated that he was stepping outside to take the call.

"Ben," Jackie said, when he was out of the interview room and had answered the call. "Are you questioning him yet?"

"We started ten minutes ago. How's it going your end?"

"Have you asked him about his son Charlie yet?"

"We're getting to that now. Freya is still in there."

"Stop her, Ben. I know who she is. The girl in the red jacket. You have to get in and stop Freya."

CHAPTER FIFTY-FOUR

"Charlie could be in a lot of trouble," said Freya, drawing his attention back from the door that Ben had left through. "You understand that, don't you?"

"No comment."

"We've been looking for Charlie for three days. We even paid your wife a visit. It's a criminal offence to hinder our investigation. Did you know that?"

"No comment," was all he replied.

"I'm sure you do, Derek. Not a lot gets past you, does it? You see, I wonder if you're thinking what I'm thinking," said Freya, as the door opened again, and Ben re-entered a little more urgently than he had left. "I'm wondering if you know anything about DNA. You see, beneath Jessica Hudson's fingernails, we found traces of skin. Somebody else's skin. And you know, from those tiny particles of skin that survived the storm, we extracted DNA. That DNA is very close to your DNA, which, of course, we have on file."

Regardless of how adept the man was at being a criminal, his facial expressions and body language needed serious discipline.

He stared at Freya with little else but malice in his eyes, his top lip curled to finish the look.

"Talk to us about Charlie, Derek," Freya said quietly. "Tell us why we can't find–"

"We know she's involved," said Ben, and Freya had to keep her own expression and body language in check at Ben's words. Or, more specifically, word. Singular.

She.

He glanced at Freya as if to say, *I've worked it out.*

"Her footprints were found at the crime scene. She was seen later at the very spot where Jessica Hudson's body was found. Yesterday we saw her at a holiday park, quite near to your home. She was hiding the yellow sweater that Jessica Hudson had been wearing. It's very possible that the DNA we found beneath Jessica's fingernails belongs to Charlotte," Ben finished. "Your dead brother's daughter. The one you were supposed to be protecting."

Picking up on the pieces that Ben had pulled together, Freya jumped in.

"That's a conundrum, isn't it, Derek? Do you confess to the murder of Jessica Hudson, or do you lead us to believe it was, in fact, your niece, and you were just covering for her? What would your brother want you to do, I wonder? Or your dad?"

"You leave my family alone," he growled.

"Then you tell us exactly what you did that night," Ben said, slamming his hand down on the table. He raised his voice to match Barnes'. "I want to know what you did and when, from the moment you left your house on the twelfth to the moment you walked through Humberside Airport. Every last detail."

Nodding, the young duty solicitor leaned in to speak into Barnes' ear, and a period of silence passed while Barnes contemplated his options.

"And if I don't speak?" he asked, laying his cards on the table.

"Then we proceed with the murder charges. You lose," Freya said, notably calmer than Ben.

"And if I tell you what I did that night?"

"That depends on what you say. If you can demonstrate an alibi, we can drop the charges," Freya said. "In which case, we'll pursue the only other feasible line of enquiry, namely your niece, Charlotte."

"You've got me over a rail here," he said, and for a moment Freya considered she'd heard a hint of admiration in his voice.

"You put yourself over the rail, Derek."

There comes a time during an interview when a suspect weighs his options, and whilst those options are being considered, the suspect very often stares at the door. Perhaps because the door represents freedom. At least, that was Freya's experience, which she thought rather pertinent.

"What would your father do, Derek?" she asked.

"I told you to leave my old man out of this," he said, then sniffed, not from tears or emotion of any sort, but through ill-manners and ignorance of decent common behaviour. "I took the Airbnb for the night, and yeah, I told Christine I'd be flying out on the twelfth. It's not a crime to tell your wife a little white lie, is it?"

"Your marriage is your concern, as you made abundantly clear earlier, Derek. What time was this?" Freya said, marvelling at the man who was about to condemn his own flesh and blood, an act of sheer spinelessness.

"Eight o'clock. Give or take. I stopped at the corner shop, you know? To get some supplies. You can get stuff on the rig, but it's all crap. I've got a bit of a sweet tooth. I bought some of those little bear sweets. You know? The ones where the adverts have that annoying little song."

"Haribo," Ben suggested, falling into Barnes' trap. Freya flashed him a glance, hoping to convey a warning.

"I also like the ones that are so sour they make your face twist," Barnes continued, but Ben said nothing.

"Where did you go from there?" Freya asked, moving the

subject along. She knew he was playing her at her own game. She had asked for detail, and detail was what he was providing. Procrastinating at what he would consider Freya's request.

"I went to the place, didn't I? What was it, fifty-two Chester Place? That's where I went, and that's where I stayed. I had no reason to leave. In fact, you might say I had every reason to stay. My alarm went off at stupid o'clock and I drove to Humberside Airport for ten days of lovely peace and quiet on a little island out in the North Sea. That's what I did. No deviation. No lies. So if you found sand in that room, I suggest you look a little harder. The place was filthy, probably hadn't been cleaned for months. And as for a motive, my little ongoing saga with the high and mighty Timothy Hudson might be a thorn in my side, but I'm not going to kill his bloody daughter over it. What do you think I am?"

There were several answers to the question that Freya could think of, but she kept them to herself, choosing instead to focus on maintaining eye contact and keeping her expressions in check.

"I presume whoever you met at the Airbnb can testify to that statement?" she asked.

"If pushed. It's probably best we don't go down that route," he said, and offered her a wink that told her extracting that information from him would be just as challenging. Freya was up for the challenge.

"Let's say your statement is confirmed. You do realise that we now have little option other than to pursue the investigation into Charlotte," said Freya. "You just sentenced your own niece, Derek."

He smiled, and Freya's control over her emotion waned. The desire to reach across the desk and slap some morals into the man was overwhelming. But what he said next changed things entirely.

"Charlotte wouldn't kill Jessica Hudson."

"People do all sorts, Derek. What makes you so sure?"

"Because, my pretty little Bloom, Charlotte, or Charlie as she's now known in her new guise, is as gay as they come."

"She's gay?" Freya said, and a connection was made. "So? Is that a problem for you?"

"She thinks I don't know. Thinks I'd hit the roof or something. I don't know. The truth is that she is who she is. I'm proud of her for being brave enough to be herself, and I reckon my brother would be too."

"That's big of you," she said.

"If I'm honest, I find it hilarious. Jessica Hudson is all she ever talks about." He leaned across the desk, and Freya felt Ben's body twitch in preparation for another outburst. But there was no such outburst. "Can you imagine how Timothy Hudson must have taken the news? A Barnes, sleeping with his daughter?" He smacked his lips together, making a pucking noise, and sat back with a smile, shaking his head at the image of Tim Hudson's rage, no doubt. "Priceless."

CHAPTER FIFTY-FIVE

Calling a break in the interview, Ben watched as Freya, with full composure, paused the recording, stood, and made her way towards the door, clearly angered, and all to Barnes' amusement.

"I'll be finding myself a proper lawyer," Barnes called out after her, just as Ben was leaving the room. "You lot probably just cost me my job, and through no fault of my own, you understand? Nice little pay-out should see me through for a bit."

From the corridor, Freya motioned for Ben not to engage with the man. But he couldn't help himself. He leaned back into the room, met the man eye to eye, and let him savour that smile for a few more moments.

"I wouldn't be so sure of that, Derek," he said. "A significant quantity of class B drugs has been found at your home address. And with the evidence Timothy Hudson has been building against you, I'd say you're still due a little holiday at Her Majesty's pleasure. I'll leave you to ponder that one, and I'll have somebody bring you a nice cup of warm water."

He closed the door and a rush of satisfaction struck all the right chords as, from inside the room, Barnes let fly a torrent of abuse and profanities.

"True?" Freya asked.

"Never a truer word spoken," he replied. "Jackie found a kilo of weed stashed in the lining of the dog basket."

"So Timothy Hudson was right."

"That's not all," Ben said. "Guess what the dog's name was?"

"Oh God, no. Piper?"

Ben nodded.

"So it was Christine Barnes that Albert Stow met on the beach on the morning of the thirteenth?"

"The one and only. Not that it matters now. What matters is that we have Barnes."

"A kilo of cannabis? That's not going to be for personal use."

"No, I imagine Derek will, right now, be having a difficult conversation with himself. Will he hold his hands up? Or will he blame his wife?"

"After that last conversation, it wouldn't surprise me whatever he chooses."

"I expect that if his wife goes away for dealing, he'll be left jobless and in charge of a tearaway kid. He'll have an easier time inside."

"Sad but true," Freya said. "What do you want to do about Charlotte? I can't believe I didn't get that, and I can't believe that with all the research the team have done, nobody picked up on it."

"Don't blame Chapman. We've put a lot on her these past few days. Besides, we only get to hear about the bad ones when they come of age, as it were, and start to join the family traditions. It looks like Charlotte entered the family business in style. Straight in at the top."

"I knew families like that in London. You'll never rehabilitate them. It's in their blood."

Nodding, Ben leaned against the wall and stuffed his hands into his pockets. "What's next?"

"We check his story out, then we recharge him for a whole

new offence. The tricky part will be finding Charlotte Barnes and bringing her in."

"Are we going back inside?" Ben asked, as Freya mused on their position.

"No. No, let's leave him to stew. Have Priest send him back to the cell, but keep the solicitor local. In fact, have Priest arrange four uniforms and have Jack Fraser prepared for an outing. We might just see some daylight today after all."

CHAPTER FIFTY-SIX

Leaving one of two liveried cars on the main road with two of Priest's men, the convoy of two vehicles rolled into Chapel Brightwater Holiday Park purposefully slowly to reduce the attention they would draw.

But still, the ever-watchful Barney emerged from the single-storey building into the snow and raised a hand to bring them to a halt. Catching his attention, Freya waved him over to her, and he came to the passenger side of Ben's car where she lowered the window.

"Morning, Barney," she said, and waited to hear his remark about the car behind them.

"You brought the cavalry, I see," he said, which told Freya he clearly hadn't seen Fraser in the back seat of the police car. "Should I be asking for some kind of warrant?"

"That all depends on how helpful you want to be."

"I don't want any bad press. Times are hard enough."

"I find the press can often misinterpret situations. But I think it all depends on how they learn about a particular event."

For a simple man of simple means, Barney was astute enough to read between the lines.

"Keep to the tracks. Keep the noise down. There are families in the next field."

"We'll be discreet. Thank you, Barney," she said.

He nodded a stern approval, then stood back.

"Stop the car here," she told Ben, when they were about to round the last bend, leaving them three hundred yards to Fraser's caravan. As instructed, Ben pulled the car to a stop. "I'll brief Fraser, you turn the car around."

"Are you sure she's going to be in there?"

"She's not at home. Jackie would have found her. And in this weather, she'll need someplace warm."

Climbing from the car, she closed the door quietly and approached the liveried car. She opened the back door and gestured for Fraser to get out.

The uniforms followed suit, so that three men stood before her.

"Do you understand why we're here, Jack?" she said.

He nodded, but his face remained saddened by the thought. "If I said Charlie was innocent, would it count for anything?"

"Not really," she replied. Then she addressed the two uniforms, "Charlotte Barnes is a suspect of murder. She's in the caravan at the end of this road. Plot two three three. You won't miss it."

"How will we know? They all look the same," the first uniform asked, a man Freya knew to be Griffiths.

"Because it'll be the only unit without snow on the roof. She's inside, and she'll be keeping warm. I want one of you to approach from the right, and the other to approach from the left. Hang back. Keep your distance. But make sure you have a view of the door. If she runs, then you get to stretch your legs. There's a path into the forest a hundred feet away. If she runs that way, she'll meet the two cars we left on the road, and we'll have her trapped. I'd prefer for her to come quietly, but we can't afford for her to get away. Understood?"

Both men nodded and went their separate ways, leaving Freya to address Fraser.

"A chance to redeem yourself, Jack. You know what you need to do."

"Keep her talking until you come along."

"I'll make sure it's noted in your file."

"I know you think I'm a bad man—"

"Right now, this is about finding Jessica's killer. Whatever you did with her when she was alive can wait for another day. And Jack," she said, closing the gap between them, "don't even think about running. I'll make damn sure that everybody sees those photos. Your family, your friends, the media. Everyone. Clear?"

"You've got me all wrong."

"Let's move," she said, stepping back and inviting him to make his way toward his caravan. "And don't look back. Make her think you're alone."

Watching him walk from behind an empty caravan, she thought him a broken man. His shoulders were hunched and his gait was lazy, so that his feet dragged across the snow-covered road.

Flanking his path between the first row of homes, Freya manoeuvred around gas bottles and darted across the open spaces. Each time waiting for him to walk into view. She reached the last caravan and peered around the corner in time to see him ascend the few steps to the door, where, oddly, he knocked.

Glancing to her right, she saw Griffiths in place. He nodded once, and she returned the gesture.

The caravan door opened, but the angle was too acute to see who had opened it, and Jack Fraser stepped inside.

Thirty seconds passed, enough time, Freya thought, for Fraser to have greeted the girl but not long enough that he might warn her.

She made her move, walking cautiously to the caravan. At the foot of the steps, she glanced to her side and found the other uniform. He was peering out from between two caravans in the next row.

She pulled the door open and stepped inside, hoping to catch Charlotte by surprise. But the surprise was on her. At the far end of the corridor, standing outside the bedrooms, Jack Fraser stared back at her, his face panicked.

"I'm sorry," he said, his hands held up in defence. "She just ran."

In disbelief, Freya paced to the bedroom, barging Fraser out of the way, only to find the bedroom window, which, just as inside her own motor home, opened out fully to serve as a fire escape.

"She's running," Freya screamed through the open window.

"She saw you coming," Fraser said, entering the room behind her, his body language defying the lie he had told.

"I'll deal with you later," she said, and she tore past him towards the door.

CHAPTER FIFTY-SEVEN

A woman's voice echoed through the holiday park. It was Freya. Unmistakably Freya, Ben thought, as he sat waiting in his car. He checked every mirror for signs of movement, then climbed from the car and ventured around the corner to see what the racket was about.

Men shouted, and a uniform darted from behind one caravan to the next, visible for a second but no more. He was running toward the forest.

Instinctively, Ben ran. His path to the forest was obstructed by four rows of caravans, forcing him to crisscross between them, slipping on the snow-covered ground. By the time he reached the stile and peered into the trees, all was still. Glancing back at the caravan, he saw the end window blowing open and closed with the breeze. But there was no sign of Charlie, and no sign of Freya.

Hopping over the stile, he gave chase. Though the trees had kept most of the snow at bay, his smooth-soled brogues slipped in the muddy corners, forcing him to slow. When the path opened up into the broad forest, he glanced left at where Jessica's yellow sweater had been hidden, but seeing nobody there, he continued on at a jog, half running and half-listening for signs of life.

And then he heard it.

A scream as wild as that of any beast, followed by the shouts of men.

"No. No. No," the girl screamed, and he rounded a corner to find the girl in the red anorak face down on the ground being handcuffed. While two of the uniforms dealt with her, the other two were checking the forest path, presumably to make sure she hadn't tossed anything of any use.

Feet planted, legs astride, Freya looked down at Charlie Barnes, appraising her for the very first time and receiving an earful of abuse in return for her efforts. Two uniforms hauled her to her feet. Sensing movement, Freya glanced up at Ben.

"What are you doing here?" Freya asked, as Charlie was led towards the road, where the waiting police car would take her to the station, and the forest had once more returned to its natural silence.

"I heard the commotion," he said. "Thought I might be of some use."

"You fool," she said, her eyes wide with panic. She turned to the officers beating the bushes to the side of the path, and she called out, waving at them to head east. "Block the exit road."

"Bloody hell," said Ben, realising his mistake.

"Bloody hell indeed, Ben," she replied, and together they ran.

Guilty of his mistake, Ben led. His long strides made small work of the distance and, having run the route only minutes before, he knew which parts were the muddiest.

Reaching the stile, he hopped over, and was surprised at Freya's agility as she too scaled the obstruction with little effort. Each of them taking a side of Fraser's caravan, they approached the steps to the door. Ben was the first to enter, and to his horror, he found the living room empty.

"You bloody idiot," Freya scathed, and for the first time, she showed signs of an outburst. She swiped the newspaper from the table, still open on the sports pages, and let them settle on the old carpet.

More to be out of her way than out of curiosity, Ben stepped into the corridor, routinely checking each room as he passed.

"I gave you a bloody job, Ben," she spat. Not that there was any need for her to make him feel bad. His palms were sweating and he was already beating himself up over the stupid mistake.

Then he peered into the master bedroom, if that is what it was called in a caravan, and sitting on the edge of the bed with a photo in his hand, Jack Fraser stared up at him.

A wave of relief washed over Ben, and he felt his chest loosen as if a valve had let the pressure escape through his audible sigh.

"In here," he called out, and nodded to Freya as she appeared at the end of the corridor then ran the few steps toward him, squeezing beside him to stand in the doorway and see for herself.

"I miss her," Jack said, his voice thick with genuine sorrow.

Freya's face curled with disgust, and she turned away, unable to look at the disgusting images and all they stood for.

"Show me," Ben said, gesturing at the photo Jack was holding.

Reluctant to give it up, he held the picture to his chest, and as Ben leaned forward to take it, something broke inside the man. For the second time in under twenty minutes, Ben witnessed a sound akin to that of an injured animal.

Dropping to his knees, Jack Fraser buried his head, sobbing uncontrollably. The limited space in the room restricted Ben from getting close. Awkwardly, he stepped over the sobbing man, and placed a hand on his back, much to the disapproval of Freya.

"You can't bring her back, Jack," Ben said, ignoring Freya's bitter expression. "I'm sorry."

"I want her," he said. "I never got my chance to be with her."

"Cuff him," Freya snapped. "I've heard enough. I can't stomach any more of this."

Whipping his head up from where he knelt on the floor, Jack glared at her.

"I'm not sick. I'm not what you think I am," he said.

"I saw the photos, Jack. I know why you rent this place."

"You know nothing," he snapped, and his voice faltered as the bitterness in his tone faded to what Ben could only describe as suffering. Genuine suffering. "I didn't get to love her. I didn't get my chance to be with her. I didn't get the chance that a father should have."

Stunned, Freya's mouth hung open at the words. She turned on the spot and peered down at him aghast.

"I hoped nobody would ever find out. I tried to keep it from my wife, from Tim, and from Beth. This place is for Jessica. I got it so we can be together. She's my daughter."

———

Ben accelerated from the holiday park toward the main road. He came to a stop beside the parked police car, where two of the officers were waiting beside it; the other two were inside, along with Charlotte Barnes.

Noting the looks that Fraser and Barnes exchanged, one of gratitude, the other of solidarity, Freya opened her door and approached the car. Opening the rear door, she stared down at the girl.

"Out," she said, and stepped back to demonstrate she meant no harm. Instinctively, Ben climbed from the car, but a polite gesture from Freya set him at ease.

Climbing from the car, Charlotte Barnes waited tentatively for an instruction.

"If you try to run, I'll presume you're guilty and I'll act accordingly. Is that clear?"

The girl nodded.

"Walk with me," Freya said, and led her along the lane.

She followed one step away from Freya's side, and one step behind, her wide eyes fearful of Freya's confidence.

"I understand you were close to Jessica, Charlotte," Freya began, and she turned in time to see the girl nod. "You miss her?"

"She was kind," Charlotte said, and somehow, coming from a Barnes, the words were alien. "She was good to me."

"I keep hearing how nice she was. But I'm afraid it's a serious situation we find ourselves in. Somebody hurt her, and it's my job to find out who did it."

"It wasn't me. I would never—"

"I believe you," Freya said. "But you understand there are procedures I need to follow?"

"Like what?"

"We found DNA beneath Jessica's fingernails that could belong to you, or they could belong to your uncle."

"Uncle Del?"

"He's been arguing with Timothy Hudson for a while now, hasn't he?"

"That's got nothing to do with Jessica and me."

"It's okay. I just need to understand something. I just need you to tell me what happened that night. The night Jessica was killed."

Charlotte stopped and glanced behind her at the waiting police car.

"We're alone, Charlotte," Freya said. "You can tell me anything."

But she said nothing.

"Were you and Jessica lovers?" Freya asked, hoping that the question wasn't too bold as an opener.

But she nodded shyly.

"I'm told that Jack rented the caravan so he could see Jessica. Is that right?"

"Jack wouldn't hurt her—"

"I know. Jack was Jessica's father, wasn't he?"

"Nobody is supposed to know."

"So you kept his secret and he kept yours. Is that right?"

She nodded again.

"He let you both use the place to be together. An arrangement, as such."

"Yes," she said.

"Where did you get the mark on your face, Charlotte? Is it recent?"

Charlotte, turned away, hiding the scratch across her brow.

"Did Christine do that?"

"Yes," she said.

"I'm going to tell you what I think happened, and I want you to tell me if I'm right or wrong. Is that okay?"

She nodded, and Freya cast her mind back to the very beginning of the investigation, when Ben was leading the case and Freya was just an interfering member of the public.

"I think you and Jessica were planning on running away together. I think you waited for your uncle to go to work for a ten-day shift and then you told your Aunt Christine you were leaving. An argument took place, and she hit you. So you left to find Jessica at the beach. How am I doing so far?"

"Close enough," Charlotte mumbled, and Freya sought to complete the picture.

"You met Jessica at the beach, and you lay in her favourite place."

"Our favourite place," Charlotte interrupted. "It was both of our favourites. That's why we went there."

"And you made love?" Freya said, imagining her and Jessica and the freedom of youth. "You lay beneath the storm, protected from the wind, and you made love."

"Yes," Charlotte said, unabashed.

"It must have been beautiful," Freya remarked, stopping and turning to face the girl.

"I'll never forget it," Charlotte said, and there was a fire in the girl's eyes.

"This is where my understanding falls down. Perhaps you can

help me? You see, I don't believe somebody could have hurt Jessica while you were there. I believe you would have helped her. You would have defended her."

"I would have killed for her."

Ignoring the choice of words, Freya pushed for her to embellish the statement, growing ever more convinced at the girl's innocence.

"What happened?" she asked.

"We slept," she said, and smiled at the memory. But her smile faded as she recalled in her mind the events of that night. "A car woke me up, and a man began shouting Jessica's name. Her dad, I think."

"Timothy Hudson went to the beach?"

Nodding, a sneer formed on Charlotte's pixie-like face. "I knew he'd hit her if he found us. He would have taken her away. Jessica told me what he was like. I didn't know what to do. I could never stop him. He's a fully-grown man."

"So what did you do?"

"I ran."

"You ran?" Freya said, a little bemused at the image she was forming in her mind.

"Towards him," Charlotte said. "I grabbed Jessica's sweater, pulled it over me, and I ran. Close enough for him to see the sweater, but far enough away that he might think I was her."

"And did it work?"

She nodded. "I ran all the way to the main road, then I hid in a dyke until he drove past. Then I ran all the way back to the caravan. Jack was supposed to meet us there. I knew he'd help us."

Marvelling at the young girl's courage, Freya smiled as the pieces began to fall into place.

"But he wasn't there, was he?"

"I missed him, I think. I know he'd been there because the key had moved, and his phone was there on the table."

"So you returned to Jessica."

"That's when I found her," she said, and for the first time, the steely girl Freya had been hunting down, and who carried with her the shame of the Barnes family, broke. "She was dead."

CHAPTER FIFTY-EIGHT

"Get her to the station," she called out the window, then considered Derek Barnes who was already in custody. She eyed the girl as a uniform helped her into the back of the car. With her short, messy hair, pointy ears, and boyish face, she reminded Freya of a sprite. "Take her straight to the interview room. Make her comfortable. She won't be any bother."

"Ma'am," came the reply, and the car moved off slowly.

Turning to the two uniforms who were standing beside the car, Freya assigned them a new role.

"Get the car out of the park and meet us at Skegness Hospital. We're going to pay a visit to Timothy Hudson."

"Will do," Griffiths replied, and without waiting for a direct order, Ben pulled out onto the main road.

"What about me?" Fraser asked from the back seat.

"If you are who you say you are, you have nothing to worry about," Freya replied, then turned to look at him over her shoulder. "I hope for your sake you are."

"I am."

"Why didn't you just tell us in the first place? You could have saved yourself so much trouble, and us a lot of time."

"Nobody was supposed to know," Fraser mumbled. "I wasn't even supposed to know. Patricia managed to hold onto the secret for all these years. I guess it finally all got too much for her. What with Tim never being around, they've been arguing a lot. If you ask me, he's taken on too much, and worse, he's been trying to change the family."

"Change them?"

"To be more respectable. To show off. It's all about his image. They can't let the family down. They can't let the neighbours know about their dirty business."

Processing what Jack was saying, Freya searched for the catalyst amongst the information they had gathered over the course of the last few days.

"Jack, did Jessica come out recently? Did she announce that she was gay?"

He pondered his response for a moment, then nodded slowly.

"I don't see the problem with it," he said. "If that's who she is, then that's who she is."

"Not everybody thinks like that."

"No. No, they don't," he replied sadly.

"Tell me about Charlotte Barnes," she said, opening a new dialogue that Freya hoped would be further from Jack's heart and therefore be more fruitful.

"Well, if it wasn't bad enough that Jessica announced she was gay, announcing that she was in love with a Barnes would have been the straw that broke the camel's back."

"Patricia kept it from her husband? Is he really that bad?"

"Timothy doesn't know anything. He doesn't know who Jessica's real father is. He doesn't know about Jessica's sexual preferences. And he certainly doesn't know about Charlie," Fraser explained, then a look of panic washed briefly over his face. "He can't know. He mustn't find out."

Freya watched him in the mirror as he gazed out at the snow-covered fields.

"Well, I don't suppose it matters now," he continued. "She told Patricia everything, and she told her about Charlie. That was when Patricia brought her to me at the yard. Seemed an odd place to be told I have another daughter, but we couldn't go to my house, and we couldn't go to Pat's house."

"That was when you paid Barney a visit," Freya said, joining the dots, and he nodded once more.

"I went direct. Told him I needed a place fast. I told him it had to be near the forest. I knew Charlie would go there, and if anybody saw her coming and going it would raise eyebrows. Everyone knows everyone around here, see? We couldn't even let Tim know Jessica was spending time with a Barnes, let alone that she was in love with one of them. The man is obsessed with Derek Barnes and his family. He's made it his mission to build what he calls an infallible case against him, and don't think for a minute that the obsession is all one way. There's no love lost between Derek and Tim."

"So Charlie wasn't allowed to see Jessica either?" Freya muttered, and a cog clicked into place.

"Hell would have opened up," Fraser said, his voice dry and tired.

"So you harboured Jessica and Charlie in your caravan? You gave them a place to be together and a place you could go to see Jessica?"

"It was like a shared secret," Fraser explained, his tone almost childlike. "Charlie knew about me and Jessica, and I knew about Charlie and Jessica."

"And Patricia knew everything."

"Her little girl was safe and happy. All we had to do was plan how to get Jessica out of there. We spoke to Lauren, Jessica's sister. Well, Pat did anyway. The plan was for them both to move down to London. Start afresh under Lauren's watchful eye."

"But the escape didn't go to plan, did it?" Freya said.

Shaking his head, he looked up guiltily. "I was supposed to

meet them at the caravan on the twelfth. Charlie's dad was supposed to be away that night, and Jessica had made her escape the day before."

"Why did Jessica leave a day earlier?"

"So we could spend some time together," he replied, and his eyes filled as he remembered those moments. "I went to the caravan as planned, but they weren't there. So I went to Pat's house. I knew she'd be in bed, but like I told you before, I tossed a stone up and she came down."

"Tell me exactly what was said, Jack," Freya said.

He shrugged. "Not much really. I was only there a few minutes. I told her the girls weren't at the caravan. I might have been a bit hard on her. But it mattered. It really mattered. She hissed at me. She's a hisser. A real spiteful cow when she wants to be. I guess that's a result of being married to a control freak. She said that I'd only been her father for a few weeks and I'd already lost her. Said I didn't deserve her and that she wished she hadn't told me."

Freya winced at the comment. "That hurt," she said.

"She told me to check the beach."

"Why the beach?"

"It was Jessica's favourite place. Even as a kid, she loved the beach. When they lived close by us, we'd all go down together for the day. Strange to think that I was her uncle for all those years. And now..." His voice trailed off as they pulled into Skegness General Hospital car park.

The liveried car pulled in behind them a few moments later and parked at the entrance, out of the way of emergency vehicles.

"What now?" Fraser asked.

Ben glanced across at her as he turned off the engine, and both men waited with bated breath.

"Now we finish this," she said.

CHAPTER FIFTY-NINE

Scarborough ward was a busy place at eleven a.m. on a weekday. Laughter came from a nurses' station as two nurses shared a joke then resumed work. They looked up when Ben leaned over the desk offering a tired smile.

"Morning, ladies," he said. "Looking for Timothy Hudson."

They pointed into the ward as soon as he flashed his ID.

"First room on the right," one called out. "Just past the orange wall."

If Timothy Hudson hadn't smelled Freya's perfume coming, he would have heard her heels on the hard floor. A few other heads turned to see the unlikely threesome as they moved through the corridor, then Ben spied the uniform that had been stationed at the door who nodded a greeting and moved to one side as Ben approached.

Inside, the room was exactly as Ben had imagined it to be. Several machines had been placed on either side and behind Tim's bed, one of which beeped every two to three seconds, although Ben was unsure which machine was the culprit. Tim stared up at them, then his eyes widened when he saw Fraser enter behind Freya.

"Morning, Timothy," Ben said. "How's the patient?"

"Jack? What are you doing here?"

In lieu of a timely response from Fraser, Freya spoke, "He's been helping us with our enquiries. How's the leg?"

"I'll live," he replied after a pause.

"No visitors?" Freya said, and she looked about the room for a sign that somebody had been and gone, but there was nothing. No flowers, no card, and no grapes.

"Patricia is at Lincoln," Ben reminded her. "With DC Gold, remember?"

"Of course. Perhaps that's for the best," Freya said. "Mind if I sit, Timothy?"

"I'm in no position to stop you," he replied, his eyes resting on Jack.

Taking the guest chair, Freya brushed it free of dust, then sat.

"Timothy, I know this is an extremely difficult time, but I was hoping you could help us. You see, we seem to be missing a few key pieces of information."

"I've just been shot, detective, and I've just lost my daughter. In case you hadn't noticed–"

"I did notice, Tim. I was there, remember?"

"Vaguely."

"Can you tell me why you went to the beach last night?" Freya asked. "Why then?"

"I wanted to see..." he said, and shrugged. "I wanted to be there. Where she went. Where it happened."

"I understand. It must be hard for you. Especially after such an argument with Jessica. I can't imagine."

His eyes rolled to one side so that he peered at her through narrow slits. But he said nothing.

"Do you think it was partly guilt that drove you there?" she asked.

"Guilt for what? For giving her a home? For working hard so she could have the best of everything?"

"Tell me about the night of the twelfth, Tim. Tell me exactly what happened from, say, the moment Patricia went to bed, leaving you alone."

"I've been through this with you."

"I'd like to hear it again."

"I'm the bloody victim here. Why do I feel like I'm being questioned?"

"Because you *are* being questioned. Because I believe you haven't told us the truth about that night. I believe there's something we need to know, but you're afraid to admit it."

"I don't know what you're talking about."

"You know exactly what I'm talking about. I'm talking about you in your office while Patricia was in bed. I'm talking about the unexpected visitor."

The unexpected visitor Freya was referring to was standing beside the door near Ben. The unexpected visitor carried with him his own shame and guilt, and his own loss hidden deep in his heart.

Yet at the mention of the visitor, Tim Hudson's eyes never strayed towards him once. Instead, he studied Freya's eyes for a hint of the truth.

"I found the cigarette butt," Freya said, urging him on.

When a man is trapped and beaten, he'll find the most mundane of items interesting. A place to stare and think. A thing to focus his regret into. Tim Hudson stared at the water jug which rested on his table.

"It was late," he began. "Patricia was in bed, but I don't know what time it was. There was a knock on my door. The back door."

"A knock?" said Freya, and Tim nodded, then finally stared at Jack.

"He was there. The bastard had walked down the side of my house and was watching me through the window. I don't know how long for. All I know is that he knocked, and he was there. Bold as brass."

Turning in her seat, Freya gave Jack a questioning look, to which he responded with a shrug and a shake of his head.

"He seemed to know more about Jessica than I did. It's funny, isn't it? You raise a child. You're there for them when they need you. You hope to be their world, their everything. But in a heart-beat, they're older. You don't matter anymore and everything you do upsets them. I didn't mean to drive her away. I would have loved her no matter who she was. But there he was, telling me about my child. Things that no other man should know. Things that she should have been able to come to me about. I would have helped her. But no. I had to find out from him. Of all the people, it had to be him."

"Tim, who was it that came to your door that night? Just to be clear, please."

Shaking his head in irritation, as if he made it abundantly clear, Tim growled the name with every ounce of hatred in his heart.

"Derek Barnes," he said.

"What was he doing there?"

"He came to tell me about Jessica and Charlotte. At least that's what he said. He said he had a job. That he'd would be working away, so I could call the surveillance off for the next ten days."

"He just came to antagonise you?"

"But that wasn't all he told me," Tim said softly, his eyes still boring holes into his brother-in-law. "See, I told him I was going to call the police on him. I had my phone in my hand. But he stopped me, not violently. He put his hand on mine, and I let him. I'll never forget what he said. Not as long as I live."

"You don't have to say it here, Tim," Freya said, her voice suddenly soft.

But Tim was lost in thought, the memories playing over and over in his mind, as they do when your world comes tumbling down.

"He told me he was about to knock on our front door when a car pulled up outside. So, Derek Barnes being Derek Barnes hid down the side of my house. He saw a man arrive. He heard things. Things that matter. Things he knew would break me apart. Do you want to know what he said to me that night?"

"You don't have to—"

"He told me my girls aren't mine," he said, and he gave a wet, phlegm-filled cough, a sign that his spell in the snow had caused more damage than Albert Stow's World War Two bullet. "He may as well have ripped me open with a blade," Tim said, his voice melancholy and monotone, and his eyes closing with fatigue. But then a smile crept onto his face. It was the smile of a man who had lost a fortune, only to find a shiny penny in the most unexpected of places.

"What is it, Tim?" Freya asked, giving Ben a worried glance. "What's amused you?"

"Every cloud," he replied, lacking the energy to articulate, and he closed his eyes.

"Come on now," a voice said, and the nurse from reception briskly entered the room and began to fuss over the machines. "You can come back tomorrow."

"Just one more minute, nurse," Ben said. "Tim, what do you mean, every cloud? Is there something you need to tell us?"

But while the nurse offered her second warning, shooing them from the room, there was just enough time for Tim Hudson to give a weak and tired laugh, and to offer Jack Fraser a malice-filled stare.

Seeing his opportunity for a quiet word in Tim Hudson's ear dwindling, Ben watched Freya and Jack leave the room. He held a hand up to the nurse, quietening her for just a moment, and as Tim's eyes closed and sleep took him, Ben whispered something in his ear that he hoped might change the course of one man's life, and create some good from the disaster that had unfolded.

CHAPTER SIXTY

"That's enough now," the nurse said, ushering Ben toward the door. "He needs to rest."

"I don't know how I should feel," Jack said, as Ben closed the door behind him. "But I feel terrible."

Usually, Freya would have replied with some kind of intelligent response. But she said nothing, walking away, then turned on her heel.

"Jack, how long were you and Pat having an affair?"

Of all the questions she could have asked, she chose one that struck like a dagger to a man who was already on his knees under the weight of his guilt.

He shrugged.

"It wasn't just the once, was it?" she said.

Again, he said nothing.

"A year?" she asked, almost incredulous at his lack of response. "Two years?"

"Three or four," he said finally, and peered through the window into Tim Hudson's room to make sure he was asleep. He bit his lower lip, embarrassed.

"Ben, call Jackie," Freya instructed.

"What? Why?"

"Just call her," she replied, and then began to pace the room, watching Ben dial as fast as he could.

He put the phone on loudspeaker, and she stopped to listen in.

"Ben?" Jackie said, her voice a whisper. "I can't talk right now. I'm in the waiting room–"

"Jackie, this is Freya. Are you at Lincoln Hospital with Patricia Hudson?"

"Yes, ma'am," she replied. "She's in there now. Poor thing, I can hear her wailing from out here."

Fraser closed his eyes at hearing her words, and Ben considered making the call in his presence insensitive, to say the least.

"Jackie, is she alone? Is Lauren with her?"

At this, Fraser's head cocked to one side and his eyes narrowed.

"No," Jackie said. "Mrs Hudson said Lauren's aunt is looking after her. She couldn't face seeing her sister like that."

"Her Aunt Hetty?" Freya asked.

"Yes, I think so. They're at Patricia's house."

"Thank you, Jackie," Freya said, and she ran from the ward, leaving Ben and Jack staring after her.

Following close behind, the two men emerged into the car park to find Freya leaning on the parked police car, and by the time they reached her, she had climbed into the back seat and was closing the door.

"Freya, what the bloody hell–"

"Hold on," she said to the driver, holding onto the door. "There's no time to lose. I need blues and twos. Lauren is in danger. Follow us."

"What? Lauren? Why?"

"Because the one person we've overlooked in all of this is your wife, Jack. I'm sorry," she said. "You're not going to want to hear this. Her phone was on the move that night. We saw her moving from mast to mast. We found sand on the carpet of an Airbnb Derek Barnes had rented. It was from Hetty's shoes. They were having an affair. I'm sorry."

"What? How can..." Then it struck Ben. Tim had said something about a silver lining, knowing damn well Jack's world was about to come tumbling down.

Where there should have been surprise, there was only an impassive sigh. Where there should have been anger, there was acceptance.

"I know," he said, his voice more of a despondent breath than a word. "I've known for years."

"She killed your daughter, Jack," Freya said with certainty as she slammed the door and lowered the window. "Derek Barnes overheard you and Patricia talking. It was him down the side of the house. It was him that told Hetty everything he'd heard. He knew full well it would drive her insane to know that her own sister bore her husband's children."

"He would even have known where she could find her," Ben said. "He overheard everything."

Nodding, Freya looked glum. "Did you hear what Tim said in there? He said *his girls aren't his*. Plural."

"Lauren?" Jack muttered in disbelief.

With two taps on the driver's shoulder, Freya slammed the door and the car sped away, turning out of the car park and screaming into the distance with the lights flashing.

CHAPTER SIXTY-ONE

"My wife?" Fraser said, as he pulled the passenger door closed.

"Seat belt," Ben said, and flicked the windscreen wipers on, hoping they had the power to brush the loose snow from his windscreen.

Before pulling away, Ben looked Fraser in the eye. "Keep it together, Jack. This is about Lauren now. This is about making everything right again, because no matter what happens, you'll be the one that has to pick up the pieces."

Nodding, Fraser fumbled with his hands, tensing them and then letting them relax, as if he needed to lash out. Ben knew the feeling well. Frustration, helplessness, and anger all rolled into a single useless emotion.

The journey to the Hudson house was mostly silent. It was only as they were approaching the small town that Jack, who was clearly musing on what might have been, what should have been, and what should never have happened, voiced his thoughts.

"The sad thing is, Ben, that it was never meant to happen. Pat and I. All those years ago. It was a rough time for me and Hetty. We weren't really communicating. I always assumed she was sleeping with somebody else, and if I'm honest, at the time I thought it was Tim. Everything was Tim this and Tim that. They all knocked about together when they were kids. Did you know that?"

"I did, yes," said Ben, not wanting to say too much for two reasons. The first was because he didn't want to disrupt Jack's flow. The second was because the snowfall had become a thick, treacherous deluge.

"I was the outsider. It was a novelty at first, being the different one. But I wasn't aware of what my wife had done when she was a teenager. I wasn't aware of how close she had been to shacking up with Derek Barnes."

"With Derek?"

"He was quite the ladies' man," he assured Ben. "Gift of the gab, they call it. But I never saw him as Hetty's type. I always found her to be frigid and boring. You know? Sex was just a thing you did to make babies. It wasn't something you did for fun."

While Jack delved into the realms of awkwardness, discussing his wife's sexual tendencies, Ben focused on the road. Every so often, the front end of the car would slide on the ice and he would have to correct the steering, ease off the accelerator, and at times, he had to just hope they wouldn't slide off the road entirely. But there was too much at stake for him to ease off completely.

"I think that was why when Pat made a move on me, I went for it. You know? I had to let it all out. All that pent-up energy and tension. I thought it was all over when Lauren was born. I thought her and Tim had finally got a handle on their marriage. We had a break, Pat and I. Things even started to get better between Hetty and me, and well, Beth is a result of that. But as soon as Hetty was pregnant, it was like I had done my job and wasn't needed anymore."

"So you went back to Patricia?"

"None of this was planned. I'm not a bad man–"

"I'm not here to judge, Jack," said Ben, as he turned the car into the Hudsons' road.

The police car was parked at an angle outside the house, and there were two lines in the snow where the car had slewed to a stop. One of the uniforms was positioned outside, which Ben guessed was on Freya's request. Footsteps in the snow from the passenger door to the house marked Freya and the other uniform's routes, but the silence was eerie. It was as if the blanket of snow that covered the street muted the noises from within.

Climbing from the car, Ben stopped and leaned inside, meeting Jack eye to eye. Man to man.

"You should probably stay here for a moment," he said.

"It's my wife," Jack said, his hand on the door handle.

"It might not be suitable for you to see, Jack. I'll take care of it for you. Trust me."

He waited for Jack to relent and give him the nod. Ben closed the door and gestured to the uniform standing beside the car to keep an eye on him, then followed the footsteps.

The front door was open, and on closer inspection, he found it to be forced. But there was no shouting, no screams. Just a terrible silence. Perhaps it was the adrenaline that coursed through Ben's body, but although he tried, he couldn't seem to identify Freya's perfume.

Then he heard it. A low grumbling voice coming from the kitchen.

Stepping through the lounge toward the kitchen with as much caution as he could, he found them. In the kitchen, the uniform was standing with his hands raised, like a bandit from a wild west movie. Freya filled the doorway, her body tense.

"You don't have to do this, Hetty," she said, and Ben wondered if she had heard Ben enter and was communicating to him surreptitiously. "Look at her. She's just a girl."

"She's his girl," Hetty spat. "And *hers*. Not mine."

Stepping back as quietly as he could, Ben left by the front door, darted across the front, and went down into the side alley where the whole episode had begun. Then, cautiously, he peered around the corner, edging toward the giant glass doors until he caught sight of Hetty.

As he had hoped, Hetty had her back to the rear garden, and he approached the bi-folding doors, praying that neither the uniform nor Freya would give his position away.

They were talking, but from outside, he heard nothing. He inched closer, until his hand rested on the handle. Lying motionless on the kitchen table between Freya and Hetty, like a funeral pyre, was an eerily similar, older looking version of Jessica. For a moment, Ben saw the girl in the sand. The peaceful resting face. But where Jessica's face had been dew-covered, Lauren's was shiny, as though she had been doused in water.

Then Hetty moved. It was sudden, as if she had been angered by something Freya had said. Ben froze. She raised her trembling hand and the glint of something shiny caught his eye. It was a cigarette lighter, the refillable type, and as it snapped open, Ben's mind imagined the metallic click. Without even studying the embossed design, he knew it was the infamous Zippo that bore the slogan 'Born 2B Bad'.

It was the lighter Barnes had used throughout his previous time in custody in the days when smoking was permitted in the interview rooms and cells. It was the lighter he had used to light a cigarette when Ben had opened the doors and set him free, likely given to Hetty for safe-keeping during his stay out on the rig where no lighters or matches were allowed.

The lighter itself was insignificant. But on closer inspection, Ben noted the kitchen table on which Lauren was lying had a sheen far greater than any polish could bring out. Freya's reflection stared back at him, her eyes serious and her face steeled as she prepared for the worst, and she glanced across to a spent fuel can that had been tossed across the room.

The pieces all came together in Ben's mind. The fuel can, the liquid, the heated argument, and the look of desperation on Hetty's face.

And the lighter.

'Born 2B Bad'.

Hetty struck it alight with a single flick of the striker.

Fearing the doors may be locked, Ben reached down and collected the two-foot-tall, cherub-style bird bath that was in the centre of the patio. The flame was visible through the double glazed doors, and both Freya and the uniform were pleading with Hetty to put the lighter down. Without hearing their voices, their animated actions and expressions appeared to Ben as an old silent movie.

Hurling the garden ornament with such force that the glass shattered in an instant, their voices came alive, like the sound of the movie had just been turned on. He hurled himself at Hetty Fraser as the glass continued to fall, reaching for her wrist to secure the naked flame. Intuitively, Freya darted for Lauren, covering her with her own body.

The Zippo fell from Hetty's oily hands, and though he tried to catch it, Hetty's struggles hindered his efforts. It was like time slowed for those few terrifying moments as he waited for the pool of petrol to catch.

But it didn't. Not at first. While Ben wrestled Hetty towards the back doors, Lauren was dragged into the garden by Freya and the uniform. But somehow, Hetty managed to wrap her legs around the heavy kitchen table. The movement sent a small wave through the pool of petrol spilling over the table edge, where it hit the floor with a gentle splash.

Just enough for the vibrant fumes to seek the warmth of the flame.

With his arms around the desperate woman, Ben gave one last hard yank and he tumbled backwards with her into the garden as the audible rush of flames raged. Instinctively, Ben rolled on top of Hetty to protect her, pulling his jacket over their heads, waiting for the initial flames to settle. Only once the heat on

Ben's back had subsided did he uncover her and push himself up to his knees.

He glanced behind him to find the entire kitchen ablaze, and to his left, Freya and the uniform were kneeling beside Lauren, protecting her from the heat and naked flames with their jackets.

They met, Ben and Freya, eye to eye, and nodded in silence to indicate they were unhurt.

Finally, Ben looked down at the woman on the ground before him. She unfurled her hands, took two big handfuls of her own hair and for the third time that day, Ben witnessed a scream so visceral that the tiny hairs on the back of his neck stood on end.

CHAPTER SIXTY-TWO

"Hetty Fraser," Freya began, helping Ben to his feet, "you are under arrest on suspicion of the murder of Jessica Hudson, and the attempted murder of Lauren Hudson. You do not have to say anything, but it may harm your defence if you do not mention when questioned something which you later rely on in court. Anything you do say may be given in evidence."

Behind them, the fire roared, its flames reaching out of the kitchen and licking the exterior walls. With the heat becoming more unbearable, Freya gave the uniform a nod.

"Take her away," she said, and he bent to cuff her.

"At least allow me the dignity of walking out of here unaided," she said, to which Freya reluctantly nodded, seeing the woman spent and defenceless.

Holding his hand up against the heat, Ben covered Freya. A gesture of a true gentleman.

They exchanged no words, only tired expressions. There was nothing to be said.

Flakes of white ash fell with the snow and tiny hisses could be heard as the snowflakes met a fiery end.

"Hetty?" a voice said, and Freya looked up to find Jack Fraser standing in the alleyway.

"Get away, Jack," Ben said. "Make room, we're coming out."

But Jack, his face a picture of confusion, sorrow, and bitter hatred merged, was resolute.

"How could you?" he said, shaking his head, and holding his hand out toward Lauren, who was by now stirring. "How could you? Look at her."

"How could I go on?" she snapped. "How could I go on knowing that..." She paused, retched, and spat, then stared at him through the long, lank, petrol-soaked hair that hung over her face. "Knowing that they were *your* children. With my sister. My *sister*, Jack? How could I?"

"There were other ways," he said, and he stepped forward, placing himself between her and the fire. "All this. For what? You killed her, Hetty. You killed my flesh and blood, your sister's flesh and blood, and..." He shook his head, appraising her with a sneer set deep into his upper lip. "You're evil, and I hope you rot."

Her face blackened by the smoke, soot, and carnage, Hetty stared up at her estranged husband, but words failed her. The tracks of bitter tears carved two rivers of pink across her grimy skin, and her grimace revealed teeth that were ivory against shades of ebony.

And then she sprang.

Like a coiled viper leaping from the ornamental palms, she tore herself free from the uniform's grip. She met Jack with full force, sending him reeling back towards the fire. For a moment, Freya thought he might stop her. Restrain her, maybe. But he stumbled and fell, then rolled to one side. Instinctively, Ben shoved Freya away out of harm's way, then dived at Hetty's feet, where she too fell to the hard patio with a thud. Scrambling with every ounce of energy she had remaining, her fingernails scraping on the flagstone slabs, Hetty dragged herself along, inch by inch, closer to the fire, reaching out for the flames to take her, and screaming for Ben to let her go, to let her die, to let her end it all.

But it was Jack, the man that despite both their wrongdoings had stood by her, who recovered from his fall and joined Ben in pulling her away from the blaze. Together they dragged her across the patio, her arms outstretched before her.

Climbing on top of her, Jack leaned in and spoke into her ear, and every morsel of malice came flooding out of him in a single, staccato sentence.

"I hope you suffer."

Seeing the man's anger raging but his adrenaline waning, Ben pulled Jack off his wife, leaving her sobbing on the cold, wet ground.

"It's over," he spoke in Jack's ear, eyeing Freya with wild eyes. "It's all over now."

Giving the uniform a nod, Freya instructed him to place the cuffs on the woman, just as a spray of freezing water fell from the sky.

Two firemen ran from the alleyway, unrolling a hose as they came. The first, at Freya's command, carried the still unconscious Lauren to safety. The second escorted the party to the front of the house and out to the road, where the emergency services were setting up camp.

"Are you okay, Jack?" Freya asked him, as he stood beside Lauren on the ambulance gurney. He touched her sleeping face, wiping away a snowflake that had settled in her hair. Then he nodded once.

"Yes," he said finally, his voice tired and cracked.

"If you need anything at all..."

"We have a long way to go. But we'll be okay." He stroked her hair once more, then looked up at Freya. "Beth, Lauren, and I."

CHAPTER SIXTY-THREE

Gesturing to Ben that they should leave Jack to be with his daughter, Freya walked away, finding refuge from the chaos beside Ben's car. As much as he wanted to stay with them, Ben agreed, they needed time. Inside Freya's boots, her feet were frozen, aching and in need of attention. But there was so much to be done.

Awake now, Lauren was being tended by paramedics. The raised bump on her brow looked tender, and she winced at the man's touch.

"It's okay, Lauren. He's just cleaning it," Jack said, and his tone was how it should have been – gentle, caring, and fatherly.

Moving away, Ben meandered through the ensemble, making his way toward Freya.

"When did you know it was her?" he asked, leaning on the car with an audible sigh and savouring the cool touches of snow on his forehead.

"Honestly?" she said. "I didn't. But Hetty Fraser was the only one we hadn't really investigated. It's funny, isn't it? How appearances distract our judgement? She should have been at the top of our list. The signs were all there. We saw her mobile phone signal move from mast to mast, and her performance when we delivered the bad news wasn't exactly worthy of an Oscar. If we had dug a little deeper into her sooner, all this may not have happened."

"We did what we could, Freya, and if I'm honest, I think we got some pretty good results. Derek Barnes will go away for a few years at the very least. Jack has his family. They'll need some time to recover, and maybe they never will, but they have each other."

"And Tim Hudson?" she asked.

"I think deep down, he got what he wanted. It strikes me he wants the high life, you know? To be the big cheese. His family were just holding him back. Or, who knows, there's a chance he and Patricia will stay together, for Lauren's sake, at least."

"There's a chance," she said. "There's always a chance."

"What about Charlotte?"

"Charlie? I think in light of what's happened, one might say she aided us. She did lead us to the sweater. I think she truly loved Jessica. I also think that had we scraped Charlie's nails that evening, we would have found Jessica's DNA. They were in love. Exactly as I said. They were not the scratches of a struggle, a fight for survival. They were loving caresses, the sordid pain of passion."

Ben was silent, but Freya figured she could read his thoughts clearly. A theory that she promptly tested.

"You're not embarrassed are you, Ben? About two young girls in love?"

Offering her a sideways glance, he shook his head, but said nothing.

"There was no struggle, Ben."

"Don't, Freya," he said, and her theory was proved.

"We agreed that if you were right, we do things your way. The proof is there, Ben. There was no struggle."

"Just..." He stopped himself, then sighed, rubbing his forehead with a dirty hand, so that a dark mark ran across his face.

Of the dirt, Freya said nothing. But of what Ben was thinking, she pressed further.

"Still want to be my friend?" she said, in a playful reference to his speech at her motor home. "I can't help it if I'm inquisitive."

He turned suddenly and stood before her. Bracing herself, Freya widened her stance, ready to accept him should he come forward. An inch more, perhaps? She could smell him, warm and masculine. A man who baulked at the idea of using an aftershave or scent. For whom fine wines were drunk from bottles with little sailing boats on the printed labels, and for whom a sense of loyalty was held in higher regard than right and wrong.

An inch closer, she thought, and wetted her lips with a slow sweep of her tongue.

But the inch never came. Stoic and commanding, he stood tall above her. His chest swelled, and all around him the snowflakes filled the sky like he was a prince of his world.

"I'll be here," he said, and Freya was expecting one of his authoritative, moral-driven speeches.

"But?" she said, and tilted her head back to meet him eye to eye.

"I need to know what happened."

"You do? Or Harper does?"

Ben said nothing.

"He spoke to me, you know? That time you found me outside his office."

"One of your episodes?"

"It wasn't an episode. I was thinking."

"So one of your episodes then?"

"No, genuinely. I was thinking about what he had said to me."

"And what was it he said?"

"About my future," she said. "Here. Whether I stay or not, it's his decision. But for him to make that call, he needs to know what happened to me."

"That's why he asked me," Ben said. "That's why he wanted me to tell him if I thought you were a risk."

"He's protecting his team. Can't really blame him for it."

"So what? You have to tell him what happened?"

"That's just it. Something happened to me, Ben. Something terrible. It's a long story, and one day, who knows, I might remember it all."

"It's not permanent though, right?" said Ben, clearly not understanding what she meant. "This amnesia thing, it'll pass, surely?"

"I don't know what happened to me, Ben. I've lost three days of my life, and every shrink in London has tried to get them back. I've lost my husband, his child, my house, my everything. The truth is, I don't know if I'll ever be the same. I don't know if my episodes will ever stop and I don't know if I'll ever be the person in that report on Harper's desk."

"So what now? I can talk to him if you like. I can explain."

"I'm thinking that it's his decision. If I'm to stay, then it should be for the right reasons. I am who I am. I'm thinking that whatever happens, whatever he decides, it's good to have a friend in you."

"If he says you can stay?"

"Then I'll stay. The team are good, and I think I'm slowly falling for this place."

"You'd have to find somewhere to live. You can't live in that motor home. We have some old cottages on the farm. I could convince my dad to let one to—"

"It's all hypothetical, Ben."

"You think he'll send you away, don't you? What will you do?"

"Then I'll take my little motor home, and my funny little ways, and I'll go find somewhere quiet to be. Somewhere my episodes aren't a risk to anyone but myself. I envy Hetty Fraser a little," she said, and felt her face tighten with the humour. "At least her future has some certainty."

CHAPTER SIXTY-FOUR

Ben wasn't expecting anything when they returned to the station, other than a list of reports to generate, an hour-long call with CPS, and a hundred questions from Will to ensure protocols had been followed.

To open the screeching door to an applause was overwhelming. Granted, the applause from Priest, Chapman, Will, and Jackie wasn't exactly deafening, but it was the thought that counted. Graciously, Ben smiled, and nodded as the team each shook his hand, feeling hot beneath his soiled collar.

Freya, on the other hand, rode the wave to the whiteboard with practised elegance. She spat on the rag and wiped the board clean. It was perhaps the most unladylike thing he had ever seen her do.

He watched her from the far side of the room, cleansing the names from existence, from her life, so that maybe she could have clarity and closure.

"We've got young Charlotte Barnes downstairs," Priest said, distracting him from Freya. "What do you want me to do with her?"

Pondering the young girl for a moment, and what she would

be facing over the coming years, he gave thought to what Freya had said.

"Caution her for wasting police time," he said. "She's been through enough."

"And her uncle?" he asked, and Jackie looked on, her breath held.

"He's DC Gold's," he said, louder than his previous response, so that everybody heard him say it. "I imagine she'll charge him. She knows what to do."

Responding with that charming, girlish smile, Jackie nodded while in mid-conversation with Will.

It felt good to hand Barnes back to Jackie. Her previous efforts to prosecute him had failed, and for her hard work and loyalty, she deserved the chance to sign her name on his charge sheet.

"Have we heard anything about Albert Stow?" Ben asked, and the murmuring in the room quietened.

"He's being held in a secure home. Tim Hudson had a change of heart. He's dropped the charges, but it's doubtful he'll be allowed to return home."

"And his dog?"

Priest sighed, but then smiled. "He's where he belongs. By Albert's side."

"That's good news, Michael."

"Sounds to me like somebody convinced him it wasn't such a good idea," Priest suggested.

"I might have had a little word. I suggested that all the research he did on Barnes could be put to good use after all. Or it might just be lost. The decision was all his."

"You're a kind man, Ben Savage."

"And your boys did good today. Griffiths especially. I want him on my team again."

"I'll pass on the sentiment," said Priest, and Ben's wandering gaze found Freya on the far side of the room staring at the blank whiteboard. A few seconds passed and she hadn't moved.

"Excuse me, Michael," he said, and shoved off the desk he was perched on, avoiding eye contact with Jackie who was waiting to talk to him.

"Freya?" he said, and he waved a hand in front of her eyes. He glanced around the room, to check that nobody was paying attention, then touched her shoulder. "Freya, it's me."

———

Warm breath licked at the fine down on Freya's nape and an icy chill ran the length of her spine in the space of a single timeless heartbeat.

He exhaled with the pleasure of success, like an orgasm of the mind.

The sound of his saliva as he licked his lips was loud, and although he stood behind Freya, she could see him clearly in her mind's eye. Her body tensed in anticipation of his touch, yet her eyes never once wavered from the old house in the forest just two hundred feet away, and the lake that shimmered in the night.

How long they stayed that way, Freya could not recall. In previous memories, regressions, and the endless nightmares, that had been the point at which all recollection ended. But, just as a new dream unfolds, so too did her ordeal, desaturated, as if it was being played back on old thirty-five-mil film.

"You found me," he whispered, and his voice carried with reverberation amongst the trees. "I hoped you would."

"It's over, James," she said, hating the fear in her voice, but too tenacious to give in. "Where is she?"

"Turn around," Marley hissed, and even without seeing, Freya heard him speak through gritted teeth. "I want to see you."

With no weapons to hand, and no chance of backup, Freya shuffled her heavy feet in the dry leaves, just enough that she could peer over her shoulder at him.

"All the way, now," he said, and he gave another little pleasure-filled sigh.

Her jittery breath flared her nostrils, and fearful of the impending blow, Freya held her head back, not wishing to see what he might be doing to cause the apparent delight in his breathing and sighs.

"Oh, my dear," he muttered. "It is you. Just like I saw on the TV."

A warm sensation formed in the pit of Freya's bladder, and she forced herself to hold onto its contents. She couldn't give him the pleasure.

"Give it up, James. You're surrounded."

"I think not," he replied, and a single row of white teeth shone in the dim light. "You want me for yourself. You're alone, aren't you?"

"Come quietly and I'll see that the jury knows you cooperated," she breathed, fearful of voicing her command out loud in case her voice gave away her true fears. "It's over for you."

Reaching out of the darkness, James Marley raised his hand to her face, caressing her cheek with the back of his index finger, then curling her hair behind her ear.

"No," he said, and for a second his eyes softened, revealing the man within. "For you, dear, it's only just beginning."

———

The cork of a champagne bottle popped to the cheers of the remaining team, and Ben turned to acknowledge the merriment, before returning his attention to Freya.

With a sharp intake of breath, her eyes widened, and she blinked away the stare, before she settled her gaze on Ben briefly, then reddened for the second time that day.

"Deep in thought?" he asked, alluding to her excuse the first time he had seen her zone out.

Checking around her, she sought control of her breathing.

"Nobody saw," Ben reassured her, and he reached for a glass of water from the table and handed it to her. She drank, licked her lips once more, then placed the glass down with an unsteady hand.

"It's time," she said.

She averted her gaze, but Ben had already noted how moist and red her eyes had become. Her mouth opened slightly, and she licked her lips as if she might talk. He was sure she was about to offer a clue as to where she had been, or what she felt or saw when she was gone. But the incident door squealed open slowly then slammed shut, and once more, the room fell quiet.

All eyes fell on Harper, who ignored the team, ignored Ben, and stared directly at Freya. He had seen her. He'd been watching her from the corridor. He'd seen her go and he'd seen Ben bring her back.

And she knew.

"I hear congratulations are in order," Harper said, as he approached with a casual stride, with all the time in the world. Ben nodded his thanks. Then, like the rush of a falling guillotine blade, Harper began his sentencing with just three sentences, each as cold and callous as the last. "Detective Inspector Bloom. My office. Now."

CHAPTER SIXTY-FIVE

The drive home for Ben usually took less than ten minutes. But the steady snowfall had carpeted the town so that the parked cars and footpaths were vague undulations and the breath of passers-by formed clouds. But in town, passing cars turned the roadside snow into black, mushy ice, tainting the otherwise picturesque scene with the stain of humanity.

Once out of the town, however, the untouched blanket rose and fell with dykes and fields, so that patches of trees appeared to have broken through from beneath, a testament to life on these beautiful yet wild fens, where nature hunts and preys from the sky to the land, and the Savage family had survived winter after winter for decades.

The sun, distant and bright, had given all it had to give that day, and was on its journey to cast light and warmth to some other place, as if it had failed to stop the deluge, and was woefully retreating to warm new lands.

The farm track from the main road featured a crossroads. To turn left would lead him home to the threesome of Savage houses, while turning right would take him deep into his father's land, to the old farm worker's cottages, and further still to the grain stores.

He stopped there at that crossroads. Dark against the sunset, Ben's house waited, uninviting, a deterrent almost. And Ben drove on, straight forward. He drove through the cut in the fields to the end of that arrow-straight track the Romans had hewn from the golden soil, where a small copse of trees remained untouched, and the fertile land around it had borne crops since man first settled there.

He stopped the car, rather than parking it, as no other vehicle ventured this far, save for the tractors that tilled the land and those combines that harvested the crops each year.

Peering from the window, Ben appraised the falling snow in the beams of his headlights, then prepared for the cold and climbed from the car. Tall grass grew around that tiny copse of fruit trees, and from the ground rose a dozen or so stones, each marked with the name of a Savage, a celebration of their time on this land.

Visits to the family graves were fewer than he'd like. But each time he came, he felt the warmth of his kin, like he was meant to be there, and he was grateful they chose this place. The newest of all the stones was his mother's. No flowers had been laid upon her spot, or any others for that matter. But a bed of wildflowers – orchids, marsh hellebore, vetchling, mallow, and more – all lay beneath the snow, waiting for their chance, like the kestrels and kites in the sky, ready to take their share of all the glorious sun could offer.

Melancholy and still, Ben stood before his mother's grave. He said nothing. But somehow, even in death, his mother's presence soothed his mind.

"There, there," she would have said, and everything would have been better.

The spread of fields offered few places to hide from prying eyes, and the sounds of life travelled far, unbound by objects. The call of a crow, arrogant and unseen, the boom of a distant bird-scarer, timely yet sudden, and the crunch of gravel under tyres, trespassing yet welcome.

Headlights bounced along the track, and there was light enough for Ben to see the lumbering vehicle that followed, laden with everything his new friend owned. Like a pack horse, tired even before the journey had begun.

She stopped the motor home behind Ben's car, and the great beast seemed to sigh with relief. Springs settled, the engine quietened, and snowflakes hissed on the hot bonnet.

It was ironic, Ben thought, that in that place of life and survival, things thrived that should never have thrived; nature overcomes, regardless. It finds a way. It was a place of hope, and the ground on which Ben stood, the lives that place remembered, was testament to that hope, to that promise.

Yet as she peered through the windscreen, holding his gaze for what felt like an eternity, there was no hope, and no promise.

CHAPTER SIXTY-SIX

"I feel like I'm intruding," she called out, as she pulled her coat around her and raised the over-sized collar.

"No," was all he said in reply, and made no move to greet her.

Stepping forward, cautious of what lay beneath the snow, Freya approached him and offered a weak smile, which he returned with sobriety.

The spot, in Freya's opinion, was wonderful. Though the open fields offered little protection from the never-ending barrage of wind, the little patch of trees gave shelter enough for a pocket of silence to exist.

There were a number of stones of various sizes. All similar in colour. She guessed them to be from the same bedrock, and only time and weather had provided the variety in tone. Ben had chosen to stand before a single stone. It was significant to him, she thought, and she read the words on the stone aloud.

"So the Phoenix signifies, fresh in the fold, the might of the God-child, when he rises once more from the ashes into the life of lives, equipped with his limbs."

The line from the poem had been hard-carved with love, not

paid for with sweat. The work of his father, Freya guessed, though it was a question she would never ask.

"You miss her," she said, a statement rather than a question.

"Every day."

The words hung in the air, though the cold air and snow muted them.

"My mother died too. A long time ago now. I should go to her grave, but it's been so long, she'd probably question why I was there."

He gave a little laugh. Not much. Enough to show he listened and he understood.

"I come here when I close a big investigation. I think it's my way of showing her I'm grateful, and that I survived. It's become a habit, I guess."

"My habit is to clean the whiteboard," she said. "I think it gives me closure."

"I know. I saw," Ben replied. "Who was she?"

"My mum?" she asked, surprised at the question, and he ventured off into his imagination.

"I see her as a grand lady. A marquis. Wining and dining, and with powerful eyes."

"You'd be very surprised then," Freya said. "For a detective, your imagination is way off."

"How so?"

Aware that she was shuffling her feet, embarrassed, and if she was honest with herself, ashamed, she said, "My father was a wealthy man. Not too far from what you just described, although he wasn't a lord or a sir, or anything other than Mr Bloom whose bank account and address book was healthy enough for society to sit up and listen."

"And your mother?"

"A traveller's daughter," she said, and it felt good to say it.

"A gypsy?"

"My father fell for her. It doesn't matter who you are when infatuation casts its spell."

Wide-eyed, a crude smile formed on Ben's pale face. It was a beautiful thing to see, and Freya selfishly savoured it quietly.

He glanced once at the motor home, then back at her, to see if she had made the connection. And she had, of course. A long time before.

"She set down her roots with my father. She became a stationary thing. I often think about her, and wonder where she would be had she not met my father. She was a seed blowing in the wind, but one which should have never been allowed to settle. I was the fruit and my father the wind. Together, we burdened her boughs until one day she fell."

Ben was silent, contemplating the analogy with apparent wonder.

"Those were the words that formed my eulogy."

"It's beautiful," he said, and he inhaled long and deep. "So, you're now the seed. Which way will the wind carry you?"

It was his way of asking what Harper had said, afraid of hearing the answer.

"Oh, not far, I hope," she said, and he cocked his head, trying to read her impassive expression. "I was looking for a little farm worker's cottage to rent."

"You're staying?" he said, breathless from anticipation.

And she smiled up at him, confident in her decision.

"For a while," she said. "If you'll have me."

The End

ONE FOR SORROW - PROLOGUE

There was a finality to the door slamming behind her. The closing of a dark chapter. It was as if the house itself mirrored her husband's sentiment with the clear message – *and don't come back*.

The whites of Daniel's eyes had been red with rage and his pupils had been dark and wide enough for her to see the furious corners of his mind, or so she had thought during those moments when his words seemed distant, overridden by the uneasy sense of abandonment.

She loitered for a moment. At least the neighbours couldn't see her. Even if they had heard the argument and the front door slam, the house was tucked way back from the road and tall Leylandii lined the front garden. They wouldn't have seen.

It had been her pocket of paradise. A south-facing haven in which she had whiled away many a week. The garden had been her pride and joy. It made her smile every time she came home and each time she ventured out.

At the end of the driveway, perched on the brick wall, was a single magpie, its glossy feathers lit by the moonlight. It stared at her, head cocked, inquisitive. Taunting her.

A sign, maybe?

"One for sorrow," she whispered to herself, and then skipped a few lines to the last line of the poem. "A secret never to be told."

A small part of her thought to search for a second magpie so that she might announce, "Two for joy," if only to find some comfort in the fabled rhyme.

But she didn't look. She knew the magpie would be alone.

Bright as the moon was that night, a shadow swept its cloak over the fruits of her labour so that only the front door could be seen. The door to hell. It was as if nothing else existed. The light from inside shone through the square pane of glass. A portal into another world. Her world. The world she would be leaving behind. As desperately cruel as that lonely world was, leaving it wasn't something she was quite ready to do. She could accept her marriage had suffered and was likely over. But leaving the home they had built together was a different story.

The square of light showed him approaching, a lean shape moving fast toward her. The door snatched open and, for a moment, she saw his features – his square jaw, his deep-set eyes and broad forehead. She had always loved how trim he kept. His cheekbones were pronounced and his eyes glistened, not with sadness but with that rage she had cowered from time and time again.

A small suitcase, the type that fit into overhead lockers on planes, landed at her feet and bumped her shin. But she didn't feel it. Not really. He tossed her heavy coat after it.

He paused, one hand on the door handle, and for a fleeting moment, their eyes met. He was going to say something. He was going to make everything alright. He was going to say he was sorry for all the times he had hurt her.

But the door began to close and his face slipped from view, until it was obscured by the frosted glass, featureless.

"I'll tell everyone," she said, yet she didn't know why.

The closing door slowed to a stop. Seconds passed like

minutes as her words permeated his arrogant mind. Then, slowly, he pushed it open.

Another chance.

"If you throw me out, that's it. I'll tell everyone what you do. I'll tell the world who you really are."

He said nothing. Instead, he stared at her, a silhouette in the door frame lit from behind.

"It's not just me that loses, Daniel. We both lose."

Considering her words with evident scorn, the shape of his face altered as he smiled. He stepped forward from the doorway and she stepped back, eyeing the case on the ground. With a light kick, he moved the case to one side and took a step closer.

There was no use in running. He would catch her. There was no use in shouting. The neighbours had heard it all before.

But there was something about the way he was standing.

"No, Jane," he grumbled, tired of it all as much as she was. "No, you won't tell anybody. You have nobody to tell."

He paused, offering her the chance to argue his words, but he was right. She had nobody to tell and nowhere to go. For a moment, she thought he might say something else, but instead, he seemed to look up at the sky, then at the trees, and then, finally, he gave her a contemptuous look before closing the door on her.

The square of light seemed to shimmer in Jane's watery eyes. Then that portal of hers to a world she had loathed closed as he switched off the hallway light.

She stopped a horrified gasp from escaping her lips with her hand clamped over her mouth.

It was happening. It had happened. It had really happened this time. Dragging her small case behind her to the road and pulling on her coat as she walked, she gave a cursory glance back over her shoulder. Not at the house, and not at the door in the hope that he might have changed his mind, but at her garden, hoping to catch a glimpse of the roses she had nurtured. It was the dead of winter, and they had all been deadheaded, but in her mind, their flowerless skeletons remained noble and majestic. The king of the flowers.

But the kings remained in shadow, their lifeless limbs bowed as she passed.

With her options amounting to a single phone number that she dared not call, she walked. The wheels of her carry-on were loud in the night, loud enough that the neighbours would hear. She imagined them in the dark confines of their bedrooms, tugging at curtains to see who was making such a row, then letting the drapes fall back and saying to their partners, "It's okay. It's just the weak girl from up the road."

Turning from Acacia Drive onto the main road brought with it a sense of relief. A confidence grew in her. She would be okay. She wasn't the only guilty party here. A shadow beneath a tree seemed a suitable place to stop and tug her phone from her pocket. The messaging app on her phone contained a number with no name, a number she had never once called but had messaged frequently. Her hands trembled as she typed a text blurred by tears, and twice she thought she had heard Daniel following her, his footsteps approaching from Acacia Drive.

Then she heard it. The angry growl of his diesel van. Stepping into the shadow of a tree, she took a final glance at her message, and with her teeth biting down on her lower lip and Daniel's headlights approaching, she hit send and watched the message go.

I need to see you. You know where. Please.

ALSO BY JACK CARTWRIGHT

Secrets In Blood

One For Sorrow

In Cold Blood

Suffer In Silence

Dying To Tell

Never To Return

Lie Beside Me

Dance With Death

Join my VIP reader group to be among the first to hear about new release dates, discounts, and get a free Wild Fens Novella.

Visit www.jackcartwrightbooks.com for details.

VIP READER CLUB

Your FREE ebooks are waiting for you now.

Get your FREE copy of the prequel story to the Wild Fens Murder Mystery series, and learn how DI Freya Bloom came to give up everything she had, to start a new life in Lincolnshire.

Visit www.jackcartwrightbooks.com to join the VIP Reader Club.

I'll see you there.

Jack Cartwright

AFTERWORD

Because reviews are critical to an author's career, if you have enjoyed this novel, you could do me a huge favour by leaving review on Amazon.

Reviews allow other readers to find my books. Your help in leaving one would make a big difference to this author.

Thank you for taking the time to read my work.

COPYRIGHT